PENGUIN BOOKS
The Catalpa Tree

Denyse Devlin was born in Boston in 1958 and is the daughter of
an Irish diplomat. She studied Arabic and English at University
college, Dublin and subsequently worked as a translator in Iraq.
She travelled extensively in the Middle East, and also lived in
the USA, Belgium, Australia, Italy and the UK, before settling in
Co. Cork with her English husband in 1987. She has two teenage
daughters.

denyse devlin

the catalpa tree

PENGUIN
IRELAND

PENGUIN IRELAND

Published by the Penguin Group
Penguin Books Ltd, 80 Strand, London WC2R 0RL, England
Penguin Group (USA) Inc., 375 Hudson Street, New York, New York 10014, USA
Penguin Group (Canada), 10 Alcorn Avenue, Toronto, Ontario, Canada M4V 3B2
(a division of Pearson Penguin Canada Inc.)
Penguin Ireland, 25 St Stephen's Green, Dublin 2, Ireland
(a division of Penguin Books Ltd)
Penguin Group (Australia), 250 Camberwell Road, Camberwell, Victoria 3124, Australia
(a division of Pearson Australia Group Pty Ltd)
Penguin Books India Pvt Ltd, 11 Community Centre, Panchsheel Park, New Delhi – 110 017, India
Penguin Group (NZ), cnr Airborne and Rosedale Roads, Albany, Auckland 1310, New Zealand
(a division of Pearson New Zealand Ltd)
Penguin Books (South Africa) (Pty) Ltd, 24 Sturdee Avenue, Rosebank 2196, South Africa

Penguin Books Ltd, Registered Offices: 80 Strand, London WC2R 0RL, England

www.penguin.com

First published 2004
1

Copyright © Denyse Woods, 2004

The moral right of the author has been asserted

Set in 11.5/14.75 pt PostScript Monotype Sabon
Typeset by Rowland Phototypesetting Ltd, Bury St Edmunds, Suffolk
Printed in Great Britain by Clays Ltd, St Ives plc

A CIP catalogue record for this book is available from the British Library

ISBN 1–844–8029–X

For Susan,
and her daughter Eva,
in loving memory

acknowledgements

With warmest thanks to: Christian, Gisèle, Eva and Rolf, for their hospitality and generosity; Finola, Tamzin and William; Lynn Crowley and Pernilla Vizard; Patricia Deevy, Michael McLoughlin, Gráinne Killeen and Brendan Barrington at Penguin Ireland; and with particular thanks to Jonathan Williams.

part one

1

The tall thin nun held a tissue to her nose and sniffed; the small round one made for the door with a brisk step and left the room. Her footsteps could be heard retreating along the corridor and across the hall, until absorbed by distance. Oliver needed to smoke but was too intimidated to do so; instead, he sat and tried not to fidget. Sr Aloysius was fidgeting enough for both of them, pulling at her tissue until there were shreds all over her desk. She was young for a principal, Oliver thought, but there was an undeniable air of authority about her.

She stood up, crossed her arms, and walked over to the bookshelves behind her desk. 'How did it happen exactly?'

'A couple of young lads lost control of a speedboat when Michael was rowing across the harbour. They split the tender in two.'

'He drowned?'

'No. He also was split in two.'

'Don't tell her that. Don't let her see him.'

Oliver nodded without commitment. He was sweating, the cold sticky sweat of sleeplessness and dread, and still there was no sound from the corridor. The classrooms, the girls, must be some distance from this office at the front of the school, where the crisp stillness of the surrounding Connemara hills seemed to have infused the building.

Sr Aloysius paced, her stomach churning. This was ghastly, ghastly, but she had to be cautious. However distressed, she had to remember that she was responsible for the girl. She couldn't simply hand her over to the first man who came in out of the wilderness and asked to take her away. She trawled through her brain, searching for clues. Had Michael Feehan ever spoken about sailing? Had he or his daughter ever mentioned Mr Sayle? And could one pupil, one child, be so unlucky, so stricken, before her fifteenth birthday? She glanced sideways at the unexpected caller. He was leaning forward in the seat by her desk, looking at the floor, running his thumb along his lower lip. A young man, mid-thirties probably, he was certainly agitated and his countenance weary, and when he looked up she caught a glimpse of grief in his eyes. She had never heard about a Mr Sayle, she was certain of that, and yet who else was there?

'What about her aunt?' she asked. 'Jude has an aunt, hasn't she?'

'Yes. Lee. We're trying to find her. She's in India.'

'And is there really no one else?'

'Just her grandmother, Mrs Dempsey.'

'Ah. I understand she's quite infirm.'

'She's in a nursing home in Dublin.'

'And no grandfathers, of course.'

'No. One dead, one absconded.'

After a moment Sr Aloysius said, 'Perhaps your wife should have come with you?'

It was in his favour that he seemed more confused than unsettled by her questions. His mind was concentrating on what would happen when Jude came through the door – he

4

had thought of nothing else all night – and he had no idea what the nun was getting at. 'We have a young child,' he said, by way of explanation. 'And we live in London.'

'I see. I'm simply concerned that perhaps . . . that it might have been better for Jude if a woman had come to take her to Dublin. This is going to be very difficult and a friend of her father's is perhaps not the best person—'

Oliver looked at her directly. 'I am also a friend of Jude's,' he said. 'And, as of yesterday, her legal guardian as well.'

'Oh, you're one of her guardians?'

'The only one.'

'But what about Mr Feehan's sister?'

'Lee didn't care to be involved. And because Jude's mother was an only child, her grandmother is her only other living relative. Unfortunately, she's unable to look after herself, let alone a teenager. That leaves me.'

'I see.'

Oliver nodded, and along the rim of his eyelids, Sr Aloysius saw the raw residue of distress. This man wasn't scheming. He seemed, more than anything, to be terrified, and she could hardly blame him. 'So young,' she said, thinking about Jude.

Oliver's eyes had glazed over. 'Thirty-six,' he said, thinking about Michael.

The sound of footsteps in the corridor drew their eyes to the door. Sr Aloysius swept into her seat. Oliver's heart pounded against his rib-cage. There was a whisper outside, then Jude came in, curious and bright, and then amazed.

'Oliver!' She bounded across the room and hugged him as he stood up. Her blue uniform and navy socks made her look younger, more vulnerable, than she did in the jeans and sweaters she wore at home. Her long hair, which usually fell around her face, was tied back in a neat ponytail, exposing a healthy complexion and mildly freckled cheeks. Oliver shivered to see Michael's hazel eyes beaming at him. 'What *on earth* are you doing here?'

He looked at the nun, which helped. 'I was passing through. Thought I'd look you up.'

'Excellent!'

Oliver's thoughts raced but led him nowhere.

'Jude,' Sr Aloysius came around her desk, 'Mr Sayle has—'

Oliver suddenly realized he couldn't do it in this breathless office, with Sr Aloysius looking on. He had to get out. Get Jude out. 'Actually, Sister, if it's OK with you, I'll take Jude for a spin.'

'Oh, well, yes. All right.'

'Thanks, Sister! I'll get my coat.' Jude ran out of the room.

'A good idea,' said the nun. 'She might otherwise associate the school with this dreadful news and be reluctant to return. I'll be here when you get back. We'll pack some of her things.'

'Let's have lunch in Clifden.' Jude leapt into the car, threw her coat over the seat and released her hair from the constraints of a hair-band.

'Later. I fancy a walk first.'

'But I'm starving!'

'And I need a blast of air. Why don't you show me the way to a beach, to one of Connemara's famous bays?'

'Oh, all right. But a nice lunch in a hotel afterwards. Or else I'll make you have supper at school.'

'That's some threat, I suppose?'

Jude chattered, firing a string of questions at Oliver which apparently needed no replies. What did he think of St Malachy's? And Sr Al? How were Patti and Tim? Had he ever seen her in her school uniform before? Didn't it make her look childish? 'Turn right,' she said when they reached Letterfrack. 'And you still haven't told me what you're doing here.'

'I met with some friends in Galway last night. I promised Michael I'd call in on you.' The lies came so easily.

'I can't *believe* Sister let me out. How's the book going? Dad says you're behind with it.'

'He always says that.'

'Where is he anyway? I tried to call him on Friday.'

'You did? . . . Oh, we went to Spain for a few days.'

'Spain? He never said anything about Spain.'

'It was a last-minute thing.'

'But why didn't he tell me?'

'It was all a bit rushed. A friend of mine hired a yacht in Majorca, but he was called back to London on business, so he asked me to take it for the second week. Patti couldn't get off work, so I rang Michael and we agreed to go.'

'But neither of you knows anything about sailing.'

He glanced at her. 'We didn't go for the sport, did we? We kept the yacht in port and lay around on deck. We fancied a bit of a break.'

'A booze-up, more like. No wonder he didn't tell me.' She turned to him. 'Do you like dying?'

Oliver swung around. She was looking at his cigarette.

'You really do have a death wish, don't you?'

He stubbed it out. 'No, Jude, I do not have a death wish. I just needed a smoke.'

She shrank back in her seat. Oliver was clearly in a bad mood and he looked awful. This was unusual. Unlike her father, who looked permanently unkempt, Oliver went for a smart, casual style – well-cut jackets with jeans and baggy shirts – and usually looked great. Usually. She glanced at him. The blue shirt was all wrong with the brown cords and his straight black hair was greasy and curling over his collar. His beard looked as if it had had a bad night. Jude tried to read his eyes. Oliver had weird, pale blue eyes; large and unevenly slanted, they crinkled at the sides when he smiled and looked unbelievably doleful when he didn't. Either way, you couldn't dodge the effect, but he was concentrating on the road now, and wouldn't look at her.

Oliver longed for Jude's banter to resume. Her silence was like an open gateway inviting him in, urging him on, pressing him to flail at her like a man with a dagger and inflict the one horrible wound that was his purpose. He tried to speak, but his tongue was thick with grief. He remembered the feeling. It was the same after Catherine died, when he and Michael had sat around, wordless and gutted and useless to each other, their mouths dry, their stomachs churning. He remembered too their desperation when Jude screamed without reprieve every night and refused to do anything for either of them until her mummy came back, and when at last she slept, Michael lay beside her sobbing so thoroughly that Oliver felt sure he would never live through it. But he had, until now, and this time Oliver had to deal with Jude on his own.

'Is everything OK?' she asked suddenly.

'Yeah, fine.'

He smiled, but doubts were creeping all around her. 'Nothing to do with Dad?'

'God, no.'

He said it with such conviction that she relaxed. At Tullycross, she directed him down another road and it seemed to Oliver that they were driving along endlessly winding

8

tracks, as in a nightmare, going nowhere. He wanted to say, 'Look, this isn't some happy excursion we're taking,' but it seemed kinder to allow her this snippet of delusion, for these were the last minutes she would know of the security of parental love. He glanced up at the brown granite hills; he hadn't been to Connemara for years and on any other day would have been moved by such magnificence.

'Over there.' Jude pointed towards a thin cream line of beach.

The grey March day was brightening. Slivers of sunlight slipped through the dwindling cloud cover, allowing shadows to move across the hills. They drove down to the beach and drew to a halt.

'That's Little Killary,' said Jude, pointing towards an inlet to their right. 'And out there – you see that tower? Those are the Carrickglass Rocks.'

'You really like it here, don't you?' Oliver asked, suddenly aware that it was now entirely in his hands whether she stayed in this place or not.

'Course. I wouldn't be here if I didn't.'

'Isn't it lonely?'

'Lonely? Living with a hundred people?'

The moment had come. They could go no further. His cowardice had reached its boundary. He had to speak, get his parched mouth around the words, and yet doubt prevailed. Had this been a mistake? Would it have been better at the convent? The desolation of the beach was piercing – or was it his own desolation that had spread out across the strand and thrown itself at the elements in such a way that even the seagulls screamed in protest?

'Right,' said Jude. 'Let's walk. Then I want lunch.' She jumped out before he could stop her, pulled off her shoes and socks, and walked across the marram grass.

9

'Jude!' Oliver got out of the car. 'Put on your shoes. You'll catch your death.'

She turned, smiling, a child on the brink of absolute desertion. 'Don't be such a ninny!' she called, running over the dunes and down to the sea.

Oliver followed her across the hard, moist sand. The tide was out. The sea was remarkably still, and lazy waves broke low, and with monotonous regularity, as if theirs was as tedious a job as working on a production line. The only other sound was the cry of the gulls and curlews.

Jude ran into the water and ran out again even more quickly. 'Agh! That's so cold it hurts!'

'I warned you.'

She skipped ahead, delirious with unexpected freedom, but the more she enjoyed it, the harder Oliver's task became. He thought he might retch, so stubbornly were the words jammed in his throat, and he tried to gather strength from their surroundings. Behind them, low clouds topped a huge benevolent mountain which seemed to cradle them in their isolation.

Jude had flitted off again. It was like trying to catch a butterfly in order to pull off its wings. 'Come on! I want to show you the pink rocks.'

He followed the prints of her bare feet along the strand. At the end of the beach, a gathering of low rocks put their heads above the sand and, as Oliver approached, he saw they were indeed a smoky pink colour. Jude climbed around, her feet white with cold.

He had cornered her at last. She must have been speaking, because he registered the end of a sentence: '. . . but this is my favourite one.' She hopped on to a long low rock. 'It's completely pink!'

He walked over to the rock and put one foot on it. She

stood above him, looking down with a weak grin, her long brown hair tossing about her face, her uniform billowing in the breeze. 'Jude,' he said.

'It's like a beached whale.'

'Jude,' he said again, and his heart heaved itself into his mouth.

2

Through the smudged, wet window-pane, they watched the plane's slow slide out of the dull sky. It hit the ground and taxied in, more gradually than usual, Jude fancied, in deference to its cargo, perhaps, and to her. The pilot surely knew she was there, somewhere, waiting for him to bring her father home. Without taking her eyes from the Aer Lingus jet, she said, 'Can we go out to it?'

Oliver looked over his shoulder. 'I don't know if—'

'Of course,' said a voice behind them. 'This way.'

They remained by the door of the building until the plane had stopped right in front of them. When they moved towards it, a hearse slid in from the left, like a jackal approaching the kill. With a great sigh, the aircraft's engines died. Oliver's grip on Jude's elbow tightened. Two stewardesses stood behind them. The fixers. The door of the aircraft opened and the stairs came out, like a limb stretching, and settled on the ground. A luggage trolley positioned itself near the hold as the procession of mourners came down the steps. Anthony Murray, Michael's old classmate, emerged first. He had gone to Spain to bring his friend home; they had come on scheduled flights, through London, which seemed more appropriate than a chartered flight full of happy, tanned holiday-makers. Stephen Sayle followed, his eyes shooting straight to his brother's; then Patti, who rushed to Jude and smothered her in an embrace which only a mother could give. Others too, whom Jude didn't recognize, disembarked quietly and gathered behind her, like a wedding party behind the bride. There was a whirring in the hold. Patti, weeping, grasped her by one arm; Oliver, trembling, by the other. The coffin appeared. In silence, the baggage handlers-turned-undertakers lowered Michael on to his home turf, where his daughter stood waiting.

3

Oliver turned the key, stepped into the hallway and kicked the door shut. Michael's jacket and cap were hanging against the wall; Oliver eyed them as he would someone who was about to strike him. At the time of the funeral, seven weeks before, he had been forced to ignore Michael's 'personal effects' because he would not have survived those terrible days otherwise. Now he stood alone in the hallway, dreading the despair that would come with sorting Michael's possessions. He braced himself. He had to get on. Certain things had to be dealt with before Jude came back from school the next day.

He started with Michael's bedroom. The bed was made now, but it hadn't been when he had come back from the convent in March and put Jude into it. She had wept for hours up there, while he sat downstairs, drinking gin and making calls, saying, 'Michael's dead,' 'Michael's been killed,' 'I've got Jude,' 'Jude's here.'

Michael's suitcase lay beside the bed. Oliver pushed up the lid with the toe of his shoe. Daily necessities – sunglasses, razor, wallet, clothes – had all been chucked in, reduced to a redundant heap. He stared at the shorts and

T-shirts, challenging them to suck him in, to allow him to wallow in self-pity, but nothing happened until he opened the closets and found Michael standing there, waiting to get out . . . Or so it seemed. It was only his jackets. They hung there, still smelling of him, still holding his shape, and the force of familiarity made him present and absent all at once with such violence that it shook Oliver. He put his hand on one of the empty shoulders. 'Come back, you rotten bastard.'

He left the room, found some whisky, poured a glass, and sat on the stairs waiting for Michael to haunt him, spook him, to come and claim his daughter back even, but the house remained still. Michael was everywhere, and nowhere.

By the end of the day, the house had been cleared of most of his belongings. Plastic bags full of clothes were piled in the hallway waiting to be delivered to charities; toiletries had been chucked, magazines dumped, electrical appliances set aside for sale. Finally, Oliver came to the study. He was afraid to go in, to step into Michael's lair, into his chaos and his mind. He put his hand on the door and, after a moment, pushed it open.

Nothing had been touched. There were papers all over his desk, a scarf thrown over the chair, legal tomes rising from the floor in stacks, and, leaning against some books on a shelf, a photograph of Michael and Catherine leaving the church on their wedding day: Michael looking even younger than he was, and slightly nerdish, and Catherine smiling and reaching towards a hand, in the corner of the frame, holding out a set of keys. The best man's hand. Oliver's hand. He picked up the photo and looked at his friends, and found himself wondering if loving them had really been worth the pain of losing them.

*

His friendship with Michael went back twenty years. They had met at a bus stop, when Oliver was thirteen and Michael sixteen, shortly after Oliver's family moved to Ireland because his father had taken a job with a Dublin newspaper. Since they shared the same bus route, they were thrown together often and, in spite of the age gap, became good friends. By the time Michael left school, they were spending every free hour together. Both talkers and thinkers, they liked to lie around chatting, listening to heavy rock and smoking dope, but there was a determination in Michael which Oliver couldn't match. By his mid-teens, Michael had decided he wanted to become a barrister and, upon leaving school, went straight to University College, Dublin to study Law. By the time Oliver got there, Michael was already at King's Inns. Few of his friends were surprised when he married at only twenty-one, because Michael had been working so hard since his teens that he was bursting with unspent love. And Catherine was exceptional – twenty-four, already a practising solicitor, and gorgeous, she was the great passion he had been waiting for, and he wasn't prepared to lose her to an older man.

Oliver's career had been more a case of cat and mouse. He had always been a scribbler, but the lonely life of a writer, as he perceived it, held no appeal, so he continually ducked it – and it continually pursued him. He was a regular contributor to the school magazine, but insisted he would not be a journalist like his father, and when he had short stories published in journals while studying English and History at UCD, he still claimed writing was a hobby. After graduating, he went to America with his mates and worked in bars for six months while considering his options. He was still considering his options – and wiping up beer slops – when an idea for a novel germinated in his mind of its own accord. Oliver continued to resist. Writing for a living seemed such an uncertain road to take when all he had to do was join his parents, who had returned to London by then, and find a job in some kind of business there.

He never got to London. Instead, shortly after leaving America, he found himself in a bedsit in Dublin typing up his first novel.

The phone rang, and yanked him back to Michael's study. 'Hello?'

'Oliver?' It was a long-distance call, but he knew the voice too well.

'Lee.'

Part hippie, part schoolgirl, Lee Feehan belonged in some other time and place, where very few people had ever been. For fifteen years she had been bumming around Asia, landing at regular intervals on her brother's doorstep in search of recuperation and funds. He always conceded. Their father had walked out on them when Michael was ten and Lee seven, and although Michael had tried hard to make it up to his sister, he got little in return and Jude even less. Lee had no time for kids.

'I got your letter,' she said now. 'What's this about selling the house?'

'I'm very well, thank you. How are you?'

'You should have consulted me.'

'You weren't here to consult.'

'But it's the family home.'

'*Was* the family home. Michael bought you out, remember? It belongs to Jude now, and she needs the money.'

'Isn't there life assurance?'

'Yes, but . . . Look, I'm not prepared to go into it, Lee. As executor of Michael's estate, I'm the sod who has to sort everything out and the house has to go. That's all you need to know.'

'But I was going to go home and live there!'

Oliver went cold. He should have seen it coming: he had come *this* close to having a sitting tenant on his hands. 'It isn't yours to live in.'

'He left the whole thing to Jude?'

'Of course he did.'

'But what about me? What did he leave me?'

It gave Oliver inordinate pleasure to reply, 'His Bob Dylan LPs.'

'And?'

'And nothing. That's it.'

'What? Just some records?'

'Yup.'

'But I thought—'

'What did you think? That Michael would bail you out for the rest of your life? Barristers don't make much in the early years, Lee. Anything he gave you in the past cost him, you know, and all he left behind was the house and the policy.'

'And no one can touch either except you? Good one, Sayle.'

Oliver could imagine Lee biting her lip. How would she get around the fact that he now held the key to the coffers?

'Well,' she said, eventually, 'I might as well stay here then.'

'Don't you think you should come back to see Jude?'

'What for?'

'You're her aunt, remember? You're family.'

'Ach, I don't buy that family shit. Besides, Michael has seen to it that she has an in-built family with you guys.'

'You're really something else, Lee, you know that?'
'And you're as charming as ever, Mr Sayle.'

Oliver sat for a long time at his friend's desk, writing cheques, closing accounts and cancelling subscriptions. Finally he switched on the answering machine and Michael's voice came into the room, bodiless, person-less, and horribly alone. The recording sounded grainy, unnatural, as if he was calling from the next stop, having failed to get off where he should have.

The following afternoon, Oliver collected Jude from the Galway train. He was nervous bringing her back to the house, but she seemed resigned, as children so often are when there isn't much they can do about things, and since rather a lot had happened to her that she couldn't do anything about, she was possibly getting used to it. Losing her home so soon after losing her father seemed like a blow too many to Oliver, but perhaps she didn't understand the significance of what they had come to do: clear out her house, take what they needed, chuck the rest. She certainly seemed less stranded than she had been in London at Easter, when she had wandered about as though she were looking for someone.

She hesitated when they came in, then ran up to her room. Her radio went on. As Oliver busied himself with dinner, he felt easier. He had dreaded this weekend. Convinced that he had no idea how to look after a fourteen-year-old girl who had lost everything that was rightfully hers, he had lain awake at the prospect of these few days, but now that she was here, it was all coming back to him. He had looked after Jude often; this was simply one more extended child-minding job. The first time Michael and

Catherine had dumped her on him, she had been a year old and he only twenty, but he took it in his stride. He had always been easy around kids – having a brother eleven years his junior probably helped – and that first assignment had worked so well that the Feehans dumped on him again, lots of times. He allowed it only because it got him out of his bedsit and into their comfortable home, but minding Jude wasn't exactly his idea of a fun weekend. 'Just you wait,' he had warned her parents. 'One day you can return the favour – and I'm planning on having a very large family!'

That day had never come. Instead, his Jude-minding skills became invaluable when Catherine first found the lump in her breast and then struggled with the treatment. After that there was a lull, a short remission, but she was dead by the time her daughter turned five.

Oliver ran the potatoes under cold water as he peeled them. This would work out. It had to. He knew Jude, knew her well, and he would cope with whatever she threw at him as she grew up. She was polite, sensible, solid. Like her dad. Michael had done all the hard work, she was basically reared; all Oliver had to do was guide her gently when she came to make . . . *all the most crucial decisions of her life!*

'Christ.' He stopped peeling. What would he do if she wanted to marry a numbskull? If she became some kind of dope-head? What if she wanted to give up her studies and live in a hut on the side of a mountain? Where, when, how would his responsibility end? Would it ever end? What if they didn't get on when she grew up? Jude's radio was loud enough to drown out these thoughts. Good, he thought. That's what teenagers should do. Play loud music. That's healthy. *Even if the music is crap.*

As his panic lifted, he became proprietorial. He was the right person for her. The only person. He'd known her longer than anyone else and possibly knew her better than anyone else. Sometimes irritatingly giddy, Jude could be prone to extroversion that knew no bounds; she could also be impenetrably moody and single-minded, but she was basically a nice kid. Besides, Oliver missed her father almost as much as she did; the two greatest traumas he had suffered were the same tragedies that had befallen Jude. This alone would surely hold them together.

Over dinner, he explained why her home had to be sold. 'When your mother died, the mortgage on this place was paid off by the insurance policy – that's the way the system works, to protect the building society's investment – and Catherine's life was insured, but not for much. They had taken out the only policy they could afford, so Michael got about twenty thousand pounds. He invested a couple of grand for you, the rest went on child-care and school fees. He could never have afforded St Malachy's if it hadn't been for your mother's policy. Anyway, now we're dealing with his life policy, which again is modest, but it will cover your needs – school fees, clothes, etcetera – until you're eighteen. Beyond that, we have to make provision for when you finish school. You'll need an income if you go to college, and that's why we're selling this place. The proceeds will go into a trust fund which should cover your third-level education and might even help you get a place of your own one day. The nest-egg your dad put aside for you after your mum died is quietly gathering interest, so we should leave that alone. It could be a nice cash bonus for you when you want something special. Am I making sense?'

'Sort of.'

'Never forget that it's *your* money, Jude. I'm only

minding it for you, and if ever there's something you really want, we'll talk, OK?'

She nodded. 'What about Nan?'

'Her needs are covered by her own policies, and the nursing home has my number in case of emergencies.'

'What about all our stuff?'

'We'll put the good furniture into long-term storage with Michael's books and papers, but we'll sell the rest. As for the smaller things – his wedding ring and . . .' Oliver faltered, experiencing again the piercing shock of finding Michael's smudged spectacles in a jacket pocket. 'Well. We'll take those to London. Tea?'

'I'll make it.' She got up.

Oliver lit a cigarette. 'Jude, there's something else we need to clear up.'

'What?'

'It's about your dad's accident.'

She put her hands on her hips. 'What now?'

'Come here.'

She edged into her seat, her eyes wide.

'I wasn't with him when he died.'

Jude's facial muscles all dropped at once, as though her face was about to fall off. 'But you said—'

'I know. I said I was there, that I saw it happen, but I didn't.'

'You mean he was all alone?'

'No. He was with his girlfriend.'

'He didn't have a girlfriend.'

'Yes, he did. I wasn't even in Spain, Jude. I was at home when Sinéad phoned from the hospital. I'd never have got to you so quickly if I'd come from Spain, but I came from London. It seemed best at the time to say I was the one who was with him.'

22

'Who's Sinéad?'

'She's a jeweller he met just after Christmas. She has a shop in Rathgar.'

'So why didn't he tell me about her?'

'Look, he wasn't trying to hide anything and he wasn't sneaking off behind your back—'

'But he did! He *did* sneak off. I didn't even know where he was. What if something had happened? He always said where he'd be in case I got sick or fell off a mountain or—'

'Calm down.' Oliver squeezed her wrist. 'Calm. Down.'

Jude heaved with indignation.

'Now look, none of this bothered you when you thought he was with me, so be fair. Michael always put you first. He never made any decision without considering its implications for you. Never. Until Spain.'

'But if he hadn't gone to Spain – if he hadn't been there with *her* – the accident would never have happened!' Her eyes filled.

Oliver stood up and paced. He looked at the ceiling, he looked at the floor. When Michael had asked him to be his only child's legal guardian, in the unlikely event of her suffering a double calamity, he had considered it a great privilege. What an honour, he had thought, to have his best friend's daughter living in his house and eating at his table with his own children! His ego had blotted out the reality – this reality, where he was left to deal with the child's despair, with the ramifications of her father's decisions, the complications of his love-life and much else besides. Seeing Jude struggle beneath the shock of Michael's deception, the enormity of Oliver's responsibilities bore down on him with such weight, he thought his knees would buckle.

He sat down. The kettle came to the boil and switched itself off. 'He was in love, Jude, and he hadn't been in love for years. He wasn't very good at it. Then Majorca came up. It was a friend of Sinéad's who had rented the yacht and was forced to come home early, and she and Michael had to go immediately or not at all. But he was going to tell you about her when they got back. He promised me he'd sort it out with you as soon as he'd sorted it out for himself.'

'But if he hadn't been away with her, he wouldn't have died!'

'Listen, I know this is hard and I know everyone keeps asking a lot of you – asking you to cope without him, to put up with me as an alternative – but I'm going to ask you one more thing. Nobody knows what Michael went through when your mother died, but I have a better idea than anyone because I was living with him. I stayed here for six weeks after she died and they were the worst six weeks of my life, bar none. I used to hear him howling during the night. The way you used to howl, except you didn't try to muffle it in your pillow.' Oliver fiddled with his cigarette. Jude waited. 'The point is,' he went on, 'that Sinéad was the start of something new. When I first saw them together, it took a weight from my shoulders that I didn't even know was there, and the relief of having it lifted, suddenly like that, well . . . The feeling that he was walking around with no trousers on vanished. You know, for a long time, whenever Michael came into a room, we'd all be waiting for the rest of him to follow, to come along behind him, but she never did. She never did, Jude.'

Jude watched him with unshifting eyes, as though she were looking into him, and beyond. 'Sometimes I think you were in love with my mother.'

'Don't be silly. I miss her a lot, that's all.' He glanced at her. 'I'm sorry, I shouldn't be dragging this stuff up.'

'Why not?'

'Because all this maudlin talk isn't good for you. I have to preserve your childhood, somehow.'

'But every one else is afraid I'll burst into tears if they mention Dad, so if we don't talk about him, nobody will.'

Oliver nodded. 'See – you're wise before your time.' He sighed. 'About Sinéad. I know it wasn't right of Michael to go off without telling you, but you'll have to let it go. Forgive him and be done with it. He was in love and he was out of practice. He was afraid you wouldn't like her, and nervous that she might not want to take on a widowed man and his teenager, so he played the carefree lover.'

'That's stupid. And what if I hadn't liked her?'

'Then I hope you would have made an effort for his sake. You wouldn't really have wanted him to turn away happiness when it took him so long to find it, would you?'

'*I* made him happy.'

'Of course you did, sweetheart, but it's hardly the same thing.'

'It isn't fair you knew about her and I didn't. And the accident would never have happened if she—'

'You can't blame her for that and I won't let you. This has been tough for Sinéad. She's been gutted by his death.'

'Well, I can't do anything about that, can I?'

'You could meet her. She very much wants to meet you.'

'Why? What's the point?'

'The point is that she's out in the cold, Jude. Do it for Michael, would you? Do it for me.'

4

As soon as they walked into the tea rooms at the hotel in Killiney the following afternoon, Jude spotted her. Graceful and poised, Sinéad was sitting by a window in an olive-green suit with her ankles crossed, and she clearly recognized Jude as easily as Jude had known her.

She stood up. 'Oliver,' she said, embracing him. 'Lovely to see you.'

Jude stood awkwardly, praying that her father's girlfriend wouldn't start crying. Oliver patted Sinéad's back as they drew apart and Jude suddenly understood why he was wearing a suit. He had dressed up because they were meeting a smart businesswoman, not because he was taking her, a stroppy teenager, out to tea.

'Sinéad,' he said, 'this is Jude. Jude, Sinéad Mannion.'

'Hello, Jude.'

'Hi.' Jude plonked herself into the deep couch. Oliver sat beside her.

'I've ordered the full afternoon tea,' Sinéad said a little breathlessly.

'Great,' said Oliver.

He and Sinéad began chatting, and all Jude could think

about was that this was the last person who had been with her dad. Oliver was leaning forward, attentive to Sinéad's every word, and she, in turn, was clearly at ease with him. Maybe she even fancied him. Most women did. It was his charm, apparently. Oliver made people feel good, Michael used to say, because he was interested, he listened. *The way he's listening to her*, Jude thought.

'It must be nice to get out of school,' Sinéad said to her. 'Did Oliver get you a few days off?'

'No.' *Why? Want him to yourself, do you?*

'She's going back tomorrow,' said Oliver, overriding Jude's rudeness.

'Is it a long journey, Jude?'

'Yes.'

'About four hours,' said Oliver.

A strand of auburn hair fell across Sinéad's face. She pushed it aside, her green eyes holding fast to Jude's. 'I gather you've decided to stay on there?'

Jude shrugged.

Oliver stepped in again. 'Yeah. We'd love to have Jude with us full-time, but it would be hard to move to an English school at this point, so she's opted to stay where she is.' He added pointedly, 'Haven't you, *Jude?*'

She didn't reply, as determined to win the point as he was, but when she saw Sinéad raise her eyebrows at him, a curious panic surged inside her. *You can't have him as well*, she thought angrily. *He's busy with me!* She and Oliver were together somehow, partners in exceptional circumstances, and she couldn't let this Sinéad person come between them; but just as she began to fear she would be cast out on her own, forgotten even by Oliver, he placed his arm across her lap with unconscious affection. Everything he had told her began repeating itself, travelling through his arm into hers and echoing along her veins. She didn't have to imagine what it was he had heard through the walls when her father had cried for her mother; she had heard it herself. Unable to believe her own father could make such an awful noise, she had begged God to make him stop. Eventually, he did.

'Ah. Here's the tea.'

And here was Sinéad. Sinéad, who made him happy again.

'Tea, Jude?'

She took the cup. The tray that had been delivered was piled high with food – the best way to any boarder's heart.

'So, how's the packing coming along? Are you all set for London?'

She made it sound as if they were going on some kind of holiday.

'There's a lot to do,' said Oliver. 'We've been working flat out all morning.'

Sinéad handed sandwiches around. Having failed to entice Jude into the conversation, she had obviously decided to ignore her for a while. 'How's the book going, Oliver?'

'So-so. I'm trying to get my head back into it.'

'Michael liked it, you know.'

'No, he didn't. He thought I was selling myself short again. He always believed I had a great book in me some-where. Deluded sod.'

Jude was working her way through the sandwiches. *This is fine*, she thought. *Let them chat away for a bit and then we can all go home.*

'How did you get started exactly?'

'With difficulty,' said Oliver. 'Nobody wanted my first novel – a thriller with a convoluted plot – so I wrote another one, and nobody wanted that either. But for some inex-plicable reason, I carried on. There's arrogance for you.'

'But what did you live on?'

'Very little. I had a grotty bedsit in Terenure, and in return for rather a lot of babysitting, Michael and Catherine allowed me to stay on really cold nights. They kept me alive probably. Dad helped a bit, while my mother kept hoping that poverty would drive me into a "proper" job.'

'But it didn't?'

'Oh, it did. Eventually I succumbed to bare financial need and began working for a magazine in London.'

'They fired him after two months,' Jude mumbled.

'Did they?' Sinéad was delighted by this grumpy contribution.

'Yeah, but that's another story. From there, I went to Egypt to teach English. See,' Oliver nudged Jude, 'that's *two* proper jobs. And while there, I wrote the one that got me across the threshold. I haven't done an honest day's work since.'

'Patti supports him now,' said Jude.

'None of your cheek, Madam.'

'But you do make a living from it, don't you?'

'Of sorts. My sales in England and Ireland are fairly steady, but I'll never be in the big money – not unless I write that elusive best-seller.'

'Some chance,' said Jude.

'I'm ashamed to say I haven't read any of your books,' Sinéad admitted. 'I can't get into thrillers.'

'You're not missing much.'

Oliver poked Jude in the ribs for that one. She squirmed away and even giggled, and Sinéad could see a dynamic at work between them which was dissipating Jude's persistent scowl and throwing some light on Michael's extraordinary decision to leave his daughter entirely in the care of his best friend.

The ice had been broken. 'Right,' said Oliver, 'would you ladies excuse me?'

'Where are you going?' Jude snapped.

'For a smoke.'

She glowered at him, too furious to speak; her eyes followed his back as he headed for the door. He seemed to be smaller than usual. His shoulders sagged and ran shapelessly into his arms. Jude bit her lip. By being sulky and difficult, was she being unduly hard on Oliver? After all, the person she wanted to get at wasn't even there, and that was hardly Oliver's fault.

'Your father made a good choice of guardian for you,' said Sinéad.

Jude munched on a scone. 'Yeah. Patti's great, too.'

'So I believe.' Sinéad fidgeted, picking bits of invisible dust from her skirt and dropping them into the air. 'I'm sorry we didn't come to see you before the accident, Jude. Your dad was longing for us to meet, but we didn't . . . well, we didn't know time . . . would be, you know, cut short. Quite the opposite, in fact.'

Jude helped herself to a slice of cake. 'You really ordered the works, didn't you?'

'I went to boarding school myself. I know what it's like to get out. More tea?' She poured Jude another cup. 'I really appreciate your coming today. It means a lot, because as long as I didn't know you, I couldn't really know Michael, could I?'

Jude looked about. She wasn't interested in hearing a load of romantic twaddle. At a nearby table, a granny was having tea with The Family – mother, father, daughter, son, and something about a year old which held itself up by gripping its father's sweater with one hand, while poking the cakes with the other. Granny didn't seem much diverted by this cuteness and looked beyond her family for entertainment.

'What happened?' Jude had spoken without meaning to.

'Are you sure you want to know?'

'Yes.'

'We ran out of milk.'

'What?'

Sinéad put down her cup. 'That's what happened. We ran out of milk one evening and I like milk in my tea. Michael said he'd row in and get some. He said his life wouldn't be worth living if I didn't have my tea.'

The baby at the next table lost its balance and landed roundly on its nappied bum.

'While he was gone I lay on deck, and then . . .' Sinéad's attempt to speak dispassionately failed her. She put her hand over her mouth. 'It happened so quickly.'

Jude looked around for Oliver.

'I heard the boat before he did. I heard something happen, like it was de-clutching or something, and there was shouting, and when I looked up, I saw Michael right in its path. I roared at him, God, I screamed, but it was the sound of the speedboat that made him turn.' Sinéad searched her bag for a tissue. Her tears so embarrassed Jude that she scarcely heard what was being said. She looked frantically towards the door. 'I yelled at him to jump, but he tried to get out of its way instead. That's why he was hit from the side. If he'd been hit from behind, he might have been propelled into the water.'

Oliver appeared as from nowhere. He stubbed out his cigarette, pulled Sinéad into the couch, mouthed 'I'm sorry' at Jude, and turned his attention to the woman with perfect hair crying all over his good jacket.

The granny looked over; her face brightened. Jude glared

back. *Not in a blue moon, Granny, will you work this one out!* She stood up. 'I'm going for a walk.'

Killiney Beach was more crowded than she would have liked, with families walking, couples talking, and hang-gliders dropping out of the sky, but at least it had got her away from Sinéad. She didn't know what she felt towards Sinéad – anger or sympathy. She didn't know anything, except that whenever she left the cosy perimeters of the convent, she couldn't escape reminders of her father's death. At least at school she could behave as if it had never happened, because that was the way her friends behaved. They never mentioned her dad, or the accident, so Jude didn't say anything either, and in some ways that helped. Besides, the only time she was truly alone was at night in the dormitory and she couldn't possibly think about her dad then, in the bleak darkness of her box cubicle, because there would be no knowing what might take hold if she did. She felt as if something horrible was always behind her, just over her shoulder, waiting to be acknowledged, but thought that if she ignored it, it would eventually go away.

Ignoring it was much more difficult away from school, however, where it seemed no one could forget Michael's death because she was the walking reminder of his loss. Oliver, who watched her constantly as though waiting for a main to burst, was both a comfort and a pain. They tried to make things easy for each other, but they were like two wounded fledglings sitting in a broken shell, the recovery of one being dependent on the recovery of the other, and they hadn't made much progress. Jude wasn't sure what to do about Oliver. He was always tired and stressed, and he took his responsibilities as her guardian far too seriously. Patti, by contrast, was like a light breeze. She was the one who told Jude it was all right to have fun, that it was even all right to feel angry with her father for dying, but Jude hadn't felt angry at all – not until she heard about Sinéad.

The stones on the beach wobbled under her feet. Hang-gliders who had taken off from the top of Killiney Hill dallied overhead in the warm spring air before lurching into a spin and lining up for a smooth landing. Jude watched as they tripped down on to firm ground and skidded to a stand-still. It was satisfying to watch – so distracting, so neutral, so removed from Sinéad and cartons of milk.

Knowing her father had been in love before he'd died made it harder, not easier. It was so unfair. If it hadn't been for Sinéad, people would have said, 'At least he's with Catherine now,' but Jude hadn't heard anyone say that at the funeral. For all these weeks, she had found consolation in imagining that her parents were together at last, but now she had to wonder – was her dad happy to be with her mother or was he wishing he could be with Sinéad instead? Wouldn't it all be much easier to accept if his death had returned him to his beloved wife?

As for the rest, these were details Oliver had spared her. He had told her Michael hadn't even heard the boat; stupidly, she had believed him. Now, instead, she saw her father frightened and trying to escape. Her heart began to palpitate, but she stilled it, cancelling immediately the image of him panicking in a small boat. She was good at dispensing with such visions. She had to be.

A hang-glider swept on to the beach and botched his land-ing, running waist-high into the sea. Companions ran out to help. As she watched, Jude became more agitated. The knot in her stomach tightened. *He was hit from the side. Not drowned. Hit. Smashed.* The great wave moved in on her, but she was confident she could keep it behind her, even though the May evening seemed to be falling into shade. *Paddling his oars to get out of the way.*

She headed back towards the hotel. The big black tidal wave, for that was what it felt like now, had loomed behind her for weeks and was suddenly gathering pace. Thus far she had kept ahead of it by moving swiftly, by ducking into a crowded room perhaps, or into a conversation, but every now and then it gained on her, bigger and blacker than before. He would have said, 'Holy shit!' He would certainly have said, 'Holy shit,' when he saw the speedboat. She could hear him saying it.

The irregularity of her heartbeat wouldn't be stilled this time, but she couldn't allow herself to be overtaken here, in public, and panic spread through her as she realized she might lose control. Her legs and arms were shaking, and she feared she would curl into a ball and howl if she didn't get back to Oliver. By the time she reached the tunnel that led under the railway, she was hyperventilating, but she ran up to the hotel, thinking, *Was I eating? Studying? Laughing? Was I laughing when Daddy was hit by a boat in Spain?* Breathless, she reached the hotel car park and stumbled up to the entrance. *When did he stop living? When they hit him or when he hit the water? Was he very, very frightened when he tried to get out of the way? And did he think about me?* She ran up the stairs. *When did he last think about me?*

She stopped in the doorway of the lounge. Oliver was sitting on the couch with Sinéad. Jude wiped the palms of her hands on her jeans and glanced over her shoulder. There was nothing there. No thundering mass bearing down on her. She caught her breath. Granny and family had left;

waiters were clearing tables. Jude's heart steadied; she stopped panting. She would not, after all, have to throw herself on Oliver.

They were in Dalkey before Oliver noticed that Jude had scarcely spoken since she'd come back from the beach. It was to be expected. It had been a hell of a weekend, and if it was hard for him to drive Michael's car, then it had to be harder for her to see him doing so. She was entitled to her silence. It was a bright Saturday evening, with a sharp sniff of summer in the air, and half the population seemed to be out walking their dogs, their babies or themselves. As they came into Dun Laoghaire, Jude suddenly said, 'Take me to the Coal Harbour.'

Oliver obliged, driving to the hooked pier and landing slip located near the West Pier, but before he'd switched off the engine, Jude was out of the car and had zipped through the gate that led down to the slipway. He caught up with her as she was walking past the looming wooden hulls of unseaworthy fishing boats.

'Are you all right?' he asked, worried now that the meeting with Sinéad had been a mistake. 'Maybe my timing was a bit off, Jude, but I wanted you to know what happened. Hey. Would you please slow down?'

She strode ahead, stepping over ropes with her head in the air as if she had eyes in her toes. Oliver tried to saunter beside her, looking casual and dignified, but she was moving too fast. 'Jude! People will think I'm harassing you!' She didn't even glance at him. Her eyes were set, and dark, and with every step, Oliver knew she was moving further away from him than was advisable. 'Stop this,' he said, grabbing her arm. 'Talk to me.' She pulled away, stepping around a girl with her leg in a calliper who was lying with her boyfriend in the sun. 'Did Sinéad upset you? Look, I thought it would be good if you talked.'

A strong smell of diesel and rotting fish, as acrid as Jude's mood, soured the evening air. At the end of the pier, she walked around the ice plant, an ugly squat building, and sat down on the cast-iron capstan facing out to sea. Oliver looked nervously over the edge, two feet from where she was sitting, at the deep water below.

He paced the short end of the pier. The Coal Harbour. No wonder. Michael and Jude often came there. It had been one of their favourite haunts. He kicked a bollard. His plan had been an evening of light entertainment, dinner and a film perhaps, but no heavy stuff, no heart-rending, no empty-ing out of drawers; just the two of them, relaxing. That obviously wasn't to be. Jude was going down, faster than the pebble he now kicked into the sea, and would soon be out of reach. No warning, no signs. Only silence. He stood beside her. She sat on her hands, her eyes set on the opening between the piers. Oliver looked down at the green water, where an empty crab shell was floating about with an old bucket. The sun made the water glitter with sharp flashes of reflected light. 'We were here, once,' he said to Jude's back, 'with Michael. You must have been about six. The water was reflecting the sunlight like this and you said, "Look at all the sparklies! The fish must be taking photos."'

She didn't turn, or even move.

Right, he thought. *This is all part of it.* She was either begging for attention because of Sinéad or punishing him for lying about Spain. She might even be taking her anger with her father out on him. Well, that was OK, that's what he was there for . . . Except it wasn't OK. He desperately wanted Jude to speak to him, and yet the more he implored her to do so, the more she recoiled. He came alongside her. 'Jude, talk to me.'

Nothing.

He sighed. She was entitled to this. Everyone agreed that she was dealing with her loss really rather well and she had made things relatively easy for him and Patti. She had even got over her first fatherless birthday, a week before, without crumbling, so Oliver could hardly begrudge her a fit of speechlessness. And yet he did. As the self-appointed guardian of her grief, he felt betrayed because she had taken it from him and directed it against him, and no amount of reasoning could compensate for a curious sense of abandonment. This child on the capstan was his soul-mate, the only one who knew exactly where he was, but she had withdrawn and left him standing alone and he couldn't bear it. He walked around her. Her shoulders were shivering. He crouched down. 'Jude, stop. Please.'

With a look of disdain, she got up and brushed past him and he heard himself ask, 'Why are you doing this to me?'

She walked back along the pier, behind the wall, her arms crossed around her. When Oliver put his arm tentatively on her shoulders, she swung around and attacked.

She kicked his shins and thumped her fists against his chest. It was so unexpected that he stood for a moment, giving her free rein to beat him, but when he registered what was happening and tried to restrain her, her strength was overwhelming. Her teeth clenched, she pummelled him. In the shade behind the wall, they couldn't be seen by the other strollers who kept to the sunny side of the pier. Oliver caught Jude's wrists, only to lose them again; then he grabbed her elbows and pushed her arms against her, but her knee smashed into his thigh. She began to cry and as they struggled, they came dangerously near the edge of the pier. He begged her to stop. He didn't say, 'Go on, let it all out. Let it go.' He just kept saying, 'Stop, Jude, please. Stop. Stop it,' and he heard his own voice breaking.

She went on thumping him until he held her so tightly against him that she couldn't move any longer.

5

Oliver was laughing. Sitting at the kitchen table with one arm over the back of a chair, a glass of wine in his hand, he was laughing at Stephen's hilarious account of yet another botched job interview. Jude's friend Fiona, who had just arrived from Dublin, also seemed to be rapt. Jude fiddled with her cheese. They had finished dinner and were sitting around the table, a low light illuminating their faces and the rest of the room in shadow. Patti twisted her streaked blonde hair into a bun, which immediately fell out, and glanced at Oliver, then smiled at Jude. *At last,* she seemed to be saying, *he's lightening up.*

Patti Sayle was one of the best things that had ever happened to Jude. She had burst into her life when Jude was seven years old and they had been buddies ever since. Patti was kind, zany, always on for a laugh, and she had brought a new dimension to Jude's life, for which Michael had been immeasurably grateful. No one was more delighted than he when Oliver and Patti got married, except Jude perhaps, who thought the day was all about her, because so many people cooed as she trundled around in her voluminous flower-girl's dress. And later came an added bonus: Tim.

From the moment Jude first held him, she had doted on him – and he was a great excuse for more frequent visits to London.

She had always enjoyed staying with the Sayles. She liked the activity, the noise, the evenings the four of them squashed onto the couch and watched cartoons over supper. When Patti was out teaching during the day, Oliver took Tim and Jude to the shops or the park, or on fun summer outings, and in the evenings, while Oliver worked, Patti and Jude went to the cinema or sat in the kitchen nattering. Jude talked about friends and school; Patti gossiped about her colleagues and the handsome foreign students she taught. Jude loved it. She loved their life, their home. It smelt nice. Her own had seemed dull in comparison: her father so often preoccupied with work, his head buried in his cases. In fact, the Sayles' house had often seemed more like a home than her own house in Dublin – until it actually became her home.

Everything looked quite different from within. When she had first arrived in June, it had been like any other visit, except this one never came to an end. The first week was great – out of school, chat with Patti, games with Tim. The second week was good too, but by the end of the third, Jude was ready to go back to where she had come from and it was then she realized, with a jolt, that she could never again do so. Her house was gone, her garden, her father, their car. She missed Dublin and the great expanse of blue that hugged its shores, and she missed her friends. At night, she cried herself to sleep, set off each time by something else, like remembering their neighbour Mrs Twomey who, until Jude was eleven, had always insisted on taking her across the main road whenever she went to the shops and who watched from the window until she saw her coming back again. Mrs Twomey was gone, gone from her life like so much else, and it seemed so unfair, and sometimes unbearable, whenever she turned out her light.

Then one night Oliver came to her room – alerted, Jude reckoned, by the puffy eyes she had failed to conceal at breakfast – and sat on the end of her bed. He didn't try to jolly her along. In fact, he didn't say anything at all. He just sat it out with her, two nights in a row, and it was hard to feel quite so miserably alone when there was another person in the room. The following evening he brought her cocoa. She hated cocoa – drinking chocolate was much sweeter – but she turned on the light and drank it, and asked him about the family who had bought her house. After a few night-time chats like this, spent talking about Dublin or Tim or Oliver's novel-in-progress, Jude found it easier to get to sleep.

But she still wondered if she would ever get used to the different pace of this household and its different ways. Every family, she discovered, had its own timing, and she was out of synch with the Sayles. She had to learn to cope, long-term, with Oliver's moods, Patti's foibles and Tim's relentless demands. She had to suppress the urge to do things her own way, and although the Sayles' house was as familiar to her as her own – she knew where everything went and how exactly Patti liked to set and clear and put away – cancelling her own inclinations, during the holidays as well as during term, proved a tough task for the only child of a single parent. Odd things annoyed her, like their accents. Oliver's accent had been diluted by his years in Dublin, but it was unreasonable to expect Patti and Tim to speak any differently, and yet Jude often wanted to throttle Tim for the way he said 'Mummay', dragging the word out to its very last syllable. It also infuriated her that he kept bursting into her room without knocking, as if she was there for his entertainment alone. But Patti and Oliver were fair. They gave her space and yet never made her feel she lived on the periphery, even though she did and always would.

Fiona's arrival, when she came to spend two weeks in late July, was timely. The very sight of her eased the homesickness and gave Jude something else to think about, because the diminutive brunette came with a blast of teenage enthusiasm, planning to shop till she dropped and to check out all the sights. She thought Jude was pretty lucky to be living in London, but when she set eyes on Stephen, that first night at dinner, Fiona decided that Jude was 'absolutely steeped'.

Stephen Sayle – or 'that nasty little afterthought' as Oliver liked to call him – was one of those likeable irritants whom everybody pretended to tolerate, but whom they secretly loved to see. In spite of, or perhaps because of, the eleven-year age gap and a verbally abusive relationship, the two brothers were unusually close, and Stephen spent so much time with the Sayles that the house always seemed emptier when he wasn't around. He had recently completed a degree in Economics and was looking for a job, none too successfully.

When he had finished telling them about the interview he had kyboshed, Fiona nudged Jude. 'So what's the talent like around here?' she asked.

'Well, if you're desperate, there's Thierry the Belgian. He's staying with a family around the corner. He's blond, which is in his favour, but he's kind of pasty-looking and thin, which puts serious dents in his sex appeal.'

Fiona wrinkled her nose. 'Ick.'

'He's lovely,' said Patti. 'A nice, courteous type. The kind of boy your mother would like.'

'If you had a mother,' said Jude. 'And then there's Paul. Now Paul, by contrast, is positively chunky. He's tall and dark, wears a leather jacket and rides a motorbike. Basically: gorgeous.'

'Now you're talking!' said Fiona. 'When do we meet?'

'Tomorrow.'

'You know this guy?' asked Oliver. 'Two houses down?'

'Yeah. He's always in the front garden,' Jude said to Fiona, 'fiddling with his motorbike. All we have to do is walk by and—'

'Ask him to check out your undercarriage,' said Stephen.

Jude and Fiona snorted.

'*Stephen,*' said Patti, getting up. 'Go on, you two. You're off duty tonight.'

The girls raced up to Jude's room.

'You forgot one major hunk around here, Jude,' Fiona whispered.

'Who?'

'Stephen.'

'Stephen? You can't be serious? All that long, straggly hair and that sad excuse for a beard?'

'Gorgeous!' Fiona fell on to her camp bed. 'Does he come around often?'

'*Yes.* He doesn't have a decent kitchen, so he's forever coming over here to cook. It seems I've inherited a whole family. Stephen's like this awful older brother who never lets up about the dreadful music I listen to and the woeful clothes I wear.'

'At least he notices you.'

'Fiona, you *can't* fancy him! He's a total womanizer.'

'Excellent!' They hooted with laughter.

Much later, Oliver and Patti lay awake, listening to the rumpus next door, to the thuds of limbs against walls, to the squeals and muffled hysteria. 'She's just what Jude needed,' said Patti. 'Even if we don't get any sleep.'

43

Oliver sidled over to her. 'No point lying here idle.'

It was after two when the girls settled down.

'Listen to the rain,' said Jude. 'It always reminds me of that rain pipe at home – remember the one near my window that used to go drip, drip, drip whenever it rained?'

'Do you miss it?'

'The drain?'

'No. Home.'

'Yeah. I try not to think about it, but . . . I don't know. It's hard to ignore the fact that nearly everything I own, you know, everything that belongs to me, is in this little room. The rest of the house has nothing to do with me; it's full of other people's stuff. There aren't any photos of me as a baby or books Dad read to me when I was small, and I try not to leave my clothes and shoes hanging around because it's not, like, my territory, you know? All I have is this room. My life has shrunk, Fiona.'

'But you said earlier your family's got bigger.'

'Except it isn't my family, is it? I'm just a tenant here. Oliver's the landlord and Patti's like a room-mate.'

'I wouldn't let Oliver hear you say that.'

'I mean, it's mostly fine. But sometimes I can't stop think-ing about home, about the house, because it's like Dad's still there and I want to go back to him, but I can't, you know?'

But Fiona couldn't know.

The following morning was fine and warm. Fiona slept late, so Jude got up, spread a rug on the back lawn and sat munching her cereal in the sunshine while Tim ran about, playing in the sandpit with buckets and dumper trucks. He was like his mother, fair in looks and cheeky in character, and even though his needs always came first, Jude still adored the little imp. She put her cereal aside and started making sandcastles with him. 'I'm Rapunzel in the tower,' she said, 'and you're the prince and you've got to come and save me.'

'But I don't want to.'

'Thanks a lot!'

'Dadday!'

'Oh, look,' said Oliver, coming out with a coffee. 'Her ladyship is risen.'

'Oh, look,' said Jude. 'We're playing sandcastles in a box. He wants a proper beach, that's what he wants, and so do I.' She went back to the rug and lay down.

'All in good time.' Oliver sat cross-legged on the grass. 'Where's Fiona?'

'Asleep.'

'Have you got sunscreen on?'

'Don't nag, Oliver.'

'Why not? That's what I'm paid for.'

Jude frowned. 'Do you get paid for being my guardian?'

He laughed. 'Of course not, nitwit!'

'Anyway, I'll need a good tan if I want Paul to notice me.'

'You're not serious about that useless heap of junk, are you?'

'He isn't a heap, he's lovely.'

'He's a walking cliché – leather jacket, bikes and chicks – and I won't have you and Fiona hanging around his garden wall trying to fish a date out of him.'

'Why not?'

'Let's just say there's an element of expertise about him that you're not quite ready for.'

Jude leaned on her elbows. 'Excuse me, but being my guardian does not give you the right to tell me whom I can and cannot fancy.'

'Maybe not, but I *can* tell you that you're not equipped to deal with someone like Paul.'

'I have to learn sometime.'

'Not now, you don't, and you don't need to learn what he has to teach. Besides, what about Thierry? He strikes me as a nice lad. A nice *safe* lad.'

'He's a weed.'

'Weeds become the nicest men. I was a weed.'

'You were not. You were a heart-breaker, Dad said. Anyway, you can't stop me going out with whoever I want.'

'I can, and I will too.'

Jude sat up. 'You . . . !'

'You're a bright girl, Jude, but if you start throwing yourself at wasters like Paul, I'll be there to stop you.'

'That's not fair. Dad would never have stopped me dating people of my own choice!'

'You wanna bet?'

Jude did not want to bet. She lay down again and put her arm over her face.

'Hey, we're not going to start having rows over boys, are we?'

No reply.

'You know, this lark isn't easy, Jude. Trying to exert some sort of parental control when we've always been good pals doesn't come easily.'

'You could have fooled me.'

He sighed. 'You can be a real toad sometimes.'

'So can you.'

'Look, I'm not planning to put all your prospective boy-friends through a suitability test, I'm only saying we need to know where we stand about relationships and . . . and things.'

Jude sat up again. 'What things? I don't need a pep talk

about being careful with boys, you know. They've done all that at school. And I'm not about to start sleeping around.'

'I'm delighted to hear it.'

'I'm only fifteen.'

'That's right. You *are* only fifteen.'

'And I know all about contraception and AIDS awareness, if that's what you mean.'

'That's not what I mean.' Oliver looked away. 'Christ. Trust Michael to leave me with the difficult bits.' He turned back to her. 'It isn't about contraception, Jude, it's about sussing people out and knowing who'd be good for you. You only have to look at Paul to know what he's after.'

Tim poured a bucket of sand over Jude's feet.

'Not on the grass, Tim,' said Oliver.

'Not on my feet!'

Tim chortled and ran away.

'Look, I don't mean to come across like an overbearing, jumped-up father-figure, but the fact is you're growing up without the day-to-day guidance of your father and your mother, and I just want you to know that I'm in there somewhere, trying to be a bit of both of them.'

'Some chance.' Jude lay down again. This whole conversation was mortifying and it gave her an overwhelming longing for her father's awkward, bumbling ways. He had never been straightforward like this, which had made him easy to manipulate, but Oliver was a tougher nut to crack.

She hated the way he had manoeuvred himself into a position of subtle authority in her life. He often pulled rank on her now, which she bitterly resented. Consequently, she was often tetchy with him and they bickered a lot, and at such times he was no more than an irritant whose constant presence reminded her of what had happened to her dad.

Besides, if he thought she needed a Big Talk about boys, why couldn't he get Patti to do it?

But Jude knew, at heart, why he didn't. Patti had not taken her on the way Oliver had. He handled everything from her dental appointments to her bad moods, and perhaps that was deliberate, because her friendship with Patti had remained intact, while her relationship with Oliver had changed. Jude wished it hadn't. For as long as she could remember, he had been coming and going, like a benevolent tide, bringing presents for her and company to her father, brightening their house with his visits. He had been a playmate then, an ally against her father's occasional decrees, but now she had to obey him, answer to him, and it didn't seem fair.

She glanced at him from under her arm. He didn't look very happy. 'Sorry,' she mumbled.

'Never mind, love. We'll get this right with time,' he said, standing up. 'I hope.' As he went inside, he called over his shoulder, 'Put on sunscreen, Jude.'

'Nag!'

She spent the afternoon sitting on Paul's wall with Fiona, trying to fish a date out of him.

Fiona's visit had one unexpected result. Instead of making Jude yearn even more for her Dublin life, she began to see her London life through Fiona's eyes. 'You'll get used to hanging your towels up in the bathroom,' Fiona assured her, 'and at least Patti doesn't yell at you when you forget, like Mum yells at me, *and* she doesn't hassle you about your room, a*nd* they let you watch films I'd never be allowed a sniff at. They're not a bit strict.'

'I know,' said Jude. 'It's as if they think I'm older than I actually am, because I'm so much older than Tim.'

'You're lucky. They could have done the opposite – treated you like a kid – *or* been really over-protective.'

All this was true and it gave Jude a new perspective. One evening when they were sitting in the kitchen before dinner, she glanced around her. Patti and Fiona were deciding which shoes Patti should wear with a particular dress. Tim was sitting tight against the table, eating his bedtime bowl of cereal, his little hand gripping the big spoon and his wide, tired eyes following his uncle, who was flapping around the lower part of the kitchen, cursing the food he was preparing. No matter how delicious, no meal ever turned out as Stephen intended. Oliver, absentmindedly brushing Tim's fringe off his forehead, told his brother to 'stop fucking swearing in front of the girls'. Jude felt a warm swell inside her. She could do worse, she supposed, than have this lot as her family.

Her new outlook was about to be threatened, however. A few days later, after a hard slog on Oxford Street, she and Fiona let themselves into the house and followed the sound of Tim's chatter to the living-room, where he was sitting on the floor talking to some Lego people.

'Hello, gorgeous,' said Jude, leaning over him.

'Jude, look!' Fiona whispered.

Jude's aunt was stretched out on the couch, fast asleep. Her long knotty hair fell towards the floor, her boots were perched over the armrest, and her fingers were entwined in multiple strings of beads. Jude turned on her heel and made for the kitchen. Patti was at the sink; Oliver having a coffee over a newspaper.

'What's *she* doing here?'

'Excellent question,' said Oliver.

'She's on her way back from India,' said Patti.

'What does she want?'

Oliver smirked. 'Why, to spend time with her niece, of course.'

'Yeah, *right*. And when Fiona's here, too. Why does she have to turn up just when I'm enjoying myself?'

'Lee always turns up at the wrong moment – or maybe,' Oliver frowned, 'there *is* no right time for her to show up?'

'Oliver,' said Patti, 'give it a rest.'

'Well, she won't be staying long,' said Jude. 'I'll freeze her out of here.'

'Now listen,' said Patti. 'I don't want her here any more than you two do, but she's our guest and she deserves some common courtesy.'

'I'm all out of common courtesy,' said Oliver. 'You got any, Jude?'

'Even if I did, she wouldn't recognize it.'

'She can't be that bad,' said Fiona.

'She's awful,' said Oliver.

'She never even came to Dad's funeral!'

Patti dried her fingers on a teacloth. 'She's a bit eccentric,' she explained to Fiona. 'But her own dad walked out on her when she was seven.'

'At least he didn't die on her,' said Jude.

'Your dad loved you, Jude. Her father didn't even want her. So give her a chance.'

'She's had loads of chances.'

'Hear, hear,' said Oliver. 'Why should Jude make allowances for someone who has never made allowances for her?'

'Bit of a nerve turning up now,' Fiona muttered. 'Four months late.'

'She had her own farewell ceremony on top of a rock in Uttar Pradesh apparently,' said Patti.

'Screw that,' said Oliver.

50

Fiona cleared her throat. Lee was heading their way. She came in, stretched like a cat unfurling, and said, 'God, I'm starving. Hi, Jude. How long have I been asleep?'

'A couple of hours,' said Patti.

'Great. I was beginning to think I'd never sleep again.'

'God forbid,' muttered Oliver.

'Come on, Fiona, let's go.'

Lee was relieved by the curt greeting she received from her niece. Gone, at last, were the days when Jude hankered like a puppy for her attention. 'Any food about?' she asked, sitting down. 'A bowl of cornflakes would hit the spot.' She reached over to take Oliver's cigarette from his hand and slowly took a drag.

'How long are you over for?' Patti asked, putting out cereal.

'For good. I'm done with India.'

'Oh?'

'Yup. Time to go home and settle down.'

'Lee, that's great,' said Patti. 'It'll be so good for Jude!'

'How'd you mean?'

Oliver leaned forward. 'What she means, Lee, is that you have never given Jude as much as five minutes of your time and now would be a good opportunity to reverse that pattern.'

Chomping on cornflakes, Lee shook her head. 'Don't get any ideas on that score. I've no experience with kids. I don't know how they work.'

'This is your chance to find out,' Oliver snapped.

'I don't want to find out. If I'd wanted kids, I'd have had them myself.'

'Heaven forbid.'

Lee scowled at him. 'Don't you ever tire of being foul to me?'

51

'Don't you ever tire of leeching off people?'

'Stop it, both of you,' said Patti. 'This bickering won't do Jude any good. The thing is, Lee, Jude needs all of us in different ways.'

'Sorry, lads, but Michael chose you, not me. I have no responsibility towards her, or anyone else, and that's exactly the way I want it.'

'Want?' Oliver hissed. 'I don't particularly *want* this responsibility either! You have a niece who has no parents. That's a responsibility whether you like it or not!'

'Not as long as *you* are the one responsible for that niece,' said Lee. 'Mind if I take a shower, Patti?'

When she left the room, Oliver folded his newspaper. 'That went rather well, don't you think?'

'Honestly,' said Patti, 'you'd think you'd have learnt to handle her by now.'

'There *is* no way to handle that woman.'

'Look here, Oliver, you have to be firm. She's not coming scrounging off us now Michael's gone. We've got his daughter; I'm not getting stuck with his sister as well.'

'We already are stuck with her. She's more in need of a bleeding guardian than Jude is.'

Patti sat down and said quietly, 'It's freaky having her here. I feel as if I'm looking at Michael but I can't quite see him, you know? She's so like him.'

'She isn't like him at all.'

Lee quickly settled into their living-room, which soon looked like a field in the aftermath of a rock festival, and she wasted no time, either, in telling Oliver why she had come. The day after she arrived, she sidled up to him in the kitchen when he was loading the dishwasher. 'Can I have a word?'

'What is it?'

'I'm broke.'

He carried on loading.

'Fact is, I don't even have enough to get to Dublin.'

Oliver slammed the dishwasher closed.

Lee looked at him with her big grey eyes, fiddled with her sleeve and said, 'If you could help me out just this once—'

'Bloody hell. Is that why you came here? Money?'

'Where else am I to get it? Jude's my only relative.'

'Oh, suddenly you're related! That's handy!'

'I just need something to get started, and Jude must have plenty to spare, what with the house and the policies. It must add up to something.'

'Tell me, Lee, where *did* you get this idea that everyone owes you a living?'

'From Michael. Remember?'

Oliver did remember. Michael had adored his little sister, but in his attempts to compensate for their father's disappearance, he had over-indulged her to a point where she had become intolerable. 'Yes,' he said, 'and how well you repaid him. Not even coming to his funeral.'

'Oh, that old chestnut. Look, I have nowhere to live and Jude won't need that money for years. If you could give me enough to get my own place—'

'Ever heard of work?'

'I'll try to get a job, but—'

Oliver pointed into her face. 'You're not getting a penny of Jude's money. Do you understand me? Not one penny.' He stormed out of the kitchen.

Lee went after him. 'What about yours then? If you could—'

The door to his study slammed. Jude was standing at the foot of the stairs. 'Gee,' said her aunt, 'he's cute when he's mad, isn't he?'

Jude let herself into Oliver's study. He was balancing on the back legs of his chair, staring at the wall. 'Are you going to give her money?'

'Did you hear the entire conversation?'

'Most of it.'

'Well, next time, don't listen.'

'But she'll never go away if you don't fix her up. What are we going to do about her?'

Oliver sighed. 'Poison is always clean.'

Two days later, Stephen arrived, announced it was barbecue weather and set to in the garden. Lee stood beside him, nibbling the peppers he was about to grill, while Jude and Fiona sat with the Sayles in the evening sun. A motorbike roared in the distance.

'There goes Paul,' said Fiona, 'out for the evening without us.'

Jude sighed. 'Why do I always want the ones I can't have?'

'This is one of life's greatest mysteries,' said Patti.

'I always have the ones I can't have,' said Stephen.

Oliver smirked. 'That doesn't surprise me.'

'I suppose I could try my luck with the scarecrow,' said Jude.

'Oh, Jude,' said Patti. 'You mustn't be so awful about Thierry. He's terribly sweet.'

'I don't want sweet, I want rugged!'

'Ah, well, that's a shame because I've, er, invited him for supper.'

'Patti!'

'Stop eating my peppers.' Stephen took a slice of pepper from Lee and ate it himself. 'If you want to help, set the table.'

'Sorry, I have to pack.'

Jude, Oliver and Patti turned.

'Pack?' said Patti.

'Yeah, I'm heading home tomorrow. Call me when supper's ready.'

As she disappeared inside, Stephen said, 'But I haven't asked her out yet.'

'Asked her out?' Jude hissed. 'You don't fancy her, do you?'

'She's gorgeous. A bit grubby maybe, but—'

'She's much older than you!'

Stephen beamed. 'What is she? Late twenties?'

'She's thirty-three – ten years older than you.'

'Ah, the lure of the older woman, Judy. You can't beat it.'

Patti watched her husband. 'You're taking this in your stride. Why aren't you jumping with glee?'

'I'm delighted she's leaving certainly, but I'm not surprised. She's sorted out her finances, you see.'

'Good God, Oliver. You haven't given her money?'

'It was either that or have her live here indefinitely.'

'You never even consulted me!'

He blew smoke through his teeth.

'How dare you throw money at her without discussing it. And whose money did you give her? Not Jude's?'

Oliver glanced at Jude.

She was rigid. She didn't care about the money, but she had no experience of domestic rows and found them mortifying.

Stephen whistled as he turned the steaks.

'Oliver?'

'Oh, as if I'd touch Jude's stash!'

'Well, at least you got that right. God, I cannot believe you'd pay her off without asking me. You do know we'll never see it again?'

'Look, she's Michael's sister and she's broke. What else could I do? I'm open to suggestions.'

None were forthcoming. The doorbell rang.

'Ah,' said Stephen, 'that must be the Belgian nerd.'

'He is not a Belgian *nerd*!' said Jude.

'What is he then? French?'

6

Early autumn sunlight raced across the landscape, up and
over the hills, evading the grey-blue clouds that pursued it.
They caught up with it occasionally, shading the sandy
screes and darkening the slopes, but the sunlight kept ahead,
covering more ground and giving Connemara an air of
slumbering satisfaction. Jude looked up at the Twelve Pins
and waited for the warmth of homecoming to flow through
her. It didn't. Usually the mere anticipation of returning to
this place excited her; now it made her tearful.

Oliver was chewing on a piece of carrot and speeding. He
loved driving these winding, empty roads. He waved a
carrot at Jude. 'Want one?'

'No.'

' "No, thank you, Oliver." '

'I wish you'd give it a break. It's like travelling with a
rabbit.'

'Hey, you wanted me to give up smoking, so I gave up.
You can't complain if I eat carrots instead.'

'I couldn't care less if you smoke or not.'

'So why were you always badgering me about the fags?'

'That was ages ago. If you want to kill yourself, that's your business.'

'Well, that's all right then. You needn't worry about me choking to death on a carrot.'

Jude had been in a deeply sultry mood since Athlone and the closer they got to the school, the quieter she became. This was unusual. Oliver had driven her back to school several times in the fifteen months she had been living with them and she generally became giddier, not quieter, as they drew closer. *It must be rough for her, stuck out in the wilds of Connemara during the dark winter months,* he thought, but this was not the time for her to start getting homesick.

Jude looked out. If she said too much, Oliver would guess what the problem was, and she didn't want him to know what was wrong, because he was part of the problem. She had never before had any trouble waving him off when he took her back to school, but this time she was dreading it.

Her second summer in London had been very different from the first. It was a lot of fun. Fiona and Emer, another school pal, came over for a week, and Thierry had come back, but the real difference was that Jude had settled. According to Fiona, she had blended into the Sayle land-scape. She picked up her towels and left her shoes in the hall; she had spread out from her room into the rest of the house. Her photograph was on the mantelpiece. Tim was easier too; he had become used to having her around and was less demanding of her time. The only disappointment had been Patti's extended working hours. She had taken on additional evening classes, and the days she didn't come home for supper were sometimes long, but Oliver had done his best to keep Tim and Jude entertained. They had gone to Wimbledon and eaten strawberries under an umbrella in a downpour; they had chased one another around the maze at

Hampton Court, and had spent a few days with family friends in Somerset. At night, Jude and Oliver had watched videos and waited for Patti to come home, and that was probably why she now felt bereft. All summer, Oliver had been the wallpaper on her day – there when she got up, there when she went to bed, and there when she needed a lift anywhere – and the prospect of leaving him was upsetting her. His family, his house, his life had become her home, and she hated being deposited outside the front door like a stray cat just because the summer had come to an end.

He took the car around a particularly satisfying bend. He knew he should press Jude, ask what was wrong, but he feared the answer. He persuaded himself it must be Thierry.

When the young Belgian had returned to Chiswick that summer to spend another month learning English, his friend-ship with Jude had taken a major step forward. The year before, she had spent time with him to satisfy the Sayles, but had found to her surprise that he was witty and good com-pany. He rose further in her estimation when he wrote to her at school, which gave her enormous kudos, and when they met again, a year later, he had grown into his gangly frame and become furiously attractive to her. Within days, she was in love.

The Sayles were delighted. They not only trusted Thierry, they were indebted to him. No longer was the burden of Jude's happiness solely on their shoulders. She had someone all of her own and the grey aura that had surrounded her vanished, but now she had to face the school year far away from Thierry, and Oliver felt for her.

He drove up the school drive, swung the car around in front of the building and parked facing the lake. There were cars, parents, small siblings, suitcases and sports gear strewn across the tarmac. Oliver switched off the engine. His worst fears were confirmed: Jude didn't budge.

'Welcome to Mallory Towers,' she sneered.

'I thought you loved this place.'

'I do. I mean, I did, but it's just, well, I've been wondering –'

Oh God, thought Oliver, *here it comes*.

'– if I should take you up on that offer to go to school in London.'

He stared at her. 'You can't be serious?'

'Why not?'

'Jude, you can't dump this on me now. *Here*. This is neither the time nor place to start discussing that, and even if we had, I'd be against it.'

'You wanted me to do it when Dad died.'

'That was then. Now you've only got two years left. It's vital you settle down and concentrate on your Leaving Cert. A-levels are a whole different kettle of fish. Switching systems at this point would be detrimental.'

'I'd catch up.'

Oliver sighed. Jude looked miserably across the black lake. He squeezed her wrist. 'You'll be fine once you've settled in.' Her eyes filled. 'And before you know it, it'll be Christmas and . . .' *And what?*

She covered her face with her hands.

'Oh dear.' Oliver took out his handkerchief, retrieved a slice of carrot that had become entangled in it, and gave the hanky to Jude. 'Is it Thierry?'

'No. I just don't see why I can't live with you all the time.'

'You'd swap this,' he waved around the lake and mountains, 'for London?'

'Not for London. For Patti and Tim, and even you. I'll miss you.'

60

'I'll miss you too, but—'

'No you won't. You only do it for Dad!'

'That's absolute rot. Jesus, the crap I take from you sometimes.'

'Why don't you get rid of me then?'

He leaned towards her. 'That's a very attractive prospect at the moment.'

'Fine.'

'You know very well I don't do it for Michael. You're like my own daughter, for Pete's sake.'

'Well, you're not like my dad. Not one bit!'

'I don't want to be and I'm not trying to be! Christ, you do pick your moments, don't you?'

Jude stuck her nose in the air.

Oliver needed a cigarette and had some carrot. 'Come on, nitwit, cheer up. I can't leave you like this. Of course I'll miss you. After all, who's going to peel my carrots for me?'

'I'd just love to stay home for a while.'

Oliver inhaled sharply. This was her sixth sense speaking. 'It wouldn't be worth it, Jude. The next two years are too important.'

There was commotion all around them: girls screeching, nuns flitting, parents shoving cash into envelopes.

'So that's it, is it? I have to go off to a miserable boarding school in the back of beyond, even though I don't want to?'

'Yes,' said Oliver quietly, 'that's it.'

Jude got out of the car; Oliver felt like a complete heel.

'You've got a room, you lucky brat!' Fiona came running along the corridor as Oliver and Jude carried her luggage to the dormitories. 'You're sharing with Emer.'

'Ah, Mr Sayle.' Sr Aloysius breezed out of nowhere.

'Lovely to see you. Do stop for tea in the parlour before you go.'

Jude's new room was empty. Oliver put down her bags. 'What do you want me to do? Will I stay for tea, or go?'

'Go.'

She led him back through the labyrinthine corridors, her arms crossed and shoulders hunched, scarcely acknowledging the girls who spoke to her. Oliver felt guilty about ducking her distress, but there was nothing he could do about it. At the car, Jude reached in for her tennis racket and another bag.

Oliver fiddled with his keys. 'Right. I'll phone tonight.'

'Don't.'

Cars were pulling out, pulling in; parents were hugging their daughters; girls were crying over their dogs; arguments were going on about money and camogie sticks. Oliver pecked Jude on the cheek. 'Be good.'

She nodded, apparently riveted by a pebble that she was grinding into the ground with her toe. Oliver got into the car. As he reversed, he winked before pulling away.

Hugging her tennis racquet, Jude watched him go. She had been absolutely horrible, and all she wanted now was to rush inside, throw herself on her bed and cry for at least an hour. She watched as the car made its way down the avenue and around the lake – and stopped. Jude stepped forward. The evening sun escaped the confines of a cloud and shone down on the car as it came tearing backwards along the driveway and stopped again, twenty metres from where she was standing. She dropped her things and ran.

Oliver got out. 'Come here, you.'

It was exactly what she needed. A hug, a real hug, just as mothers were hugging their daughters behind them; just as her own father had hugged her there, a long time before.

Oliver pulled back. 'You've had to wait too long for that.'

She smiled.

'Better?'

'Much.'

When he got back into the car, Jude said something she hadn't said to him since she was six years old. 'I love you.'

He winked. 'Me too.'

7

It was a dull February morning and it had been a bitter February night. Jude finally got to the phone in the office at ten and dialled the Sayles' number.

'Hello?'

'Patti? It's me.'

'Jude, hi. What's up?'

'What are you doing home?'

'I'm sick. What are *you* doing out of class?'

'You won't believe it, but I have to come home – today.'

'Goodness, are you ill too?'

'No, but there's been a fire in the kitchen and they have to close down the boarding section because they've nowhere to cook for us or feed us.'

'A fire? My God, are you OK? Was anyone hurt?'

'Everyone's fine, apart from a few cases of hypothermia. They rushed us outside in the middle of the night. It was bloody freezing!'

'Poor things.'

'Yeah, but listen, I have to be quick because everyone's queuing up to phone home. I thought I'd get a lift to

Dublin with Fiona and try to get a flight tonight, OK? . . . Patti?'

'Yes?'

'Is that OK?'

'Wait a minute, Jude. Wait a minute. God, I don't believe this. Listen, I'll have to get Oliver to ring you back.'

'He can't ring me back. There are forty people waiting for the phone.'

'Oh, right. You'll have to call him on his mobile then.'

'Why don't I just ring when I get to Fiona's?'

'Because I want you to speak to him first,' said Patti tersely. 'Call him on his mobile now.'

'But couldn't you ——'

Before she knew it, Jude was left standing with the phone beeping in her hand. Oliver took care of most of her affairs, but this was ridiculous!

He answered immediately. 'Jude? What's wrong?'

'Nothing much, apart from the school burning down and the fact that we're homeless for the next couple of weeks.'

'What *are* you on about?'

'There's been a fire. The school is wrecked. But Patti insisted I phone you myself to tell you I'm coming home.'

Oliver said nothing.

'Oliver?'

'Yes?'

'Can you get me on to a flight tonight?'

'A fire? Christ. Did everyone get out safely?'

'Yeah, it didn't spread beyond the kitchen and the ref, but they have to close down until it's fixed up. Two weeks, they reckon.'

'Two weeks . . . So you'll have to come over.'

'*Obviously*. If that's not too much trouble?'

'Of course it isn't. It's fine. Fine.'

He sounded less than thrilled. Jude had never felt so unwanted. All the other parents had rushed out the door when they got the call. She went on irritably, 'I'm sorry to put you out, but if you wouldn't mind *terribly* getting me on a flight tonight, unless you're too *tied up* to have me right now?'

'Of course I'll get you a flight, but not tonight. You'd better stay with Fiona and come over tomorrow.'

'But I'm dying to get home.'

'I'd never get you a seat at such short notice.'

'But Oliver—'

'Yes, Jude?'

Now *he* was sounding terse. *Who's the one who's just been through the bloody disaster?*

'I'll call you later with your flight details,' he said.

Jude had never been so irritated with both Oliver and Patti at the same time. When she emerged in the Arrivals hall at Heathrow the next day, the wicked stepfather, wearing jeans and a leather jacket, threw her such a fleeting smile that she almost missed it. Outside the terminal, he lit a cigarette.

'What happened to the carrots?'

'What happened to "So how are you, Oliver?"?'

Jude scowled.

He led her to the car park. 'So how did the fire get started?'

'Something sparked in the kitchen and the whole place went up, and now there's water damage too. The place is a mess.'

'Was there panic?'

'Course there was. The juniors went *ape* when the alarm went off and then the lights went out. Everyone screamed and . . .'

If you want to improve Jude's mood, Oliver thought wryly, *get her talking*.

She was still chattering when they reached their car in the multi-storey car park. Oliver squeezed the back of her neck. 'Thank God you got out,' he said simply.

Jude sat back in the car, beaming. Two days earlier, she had been in class. Now, in a blink of an eye, she was in London, driving home with Oliver for cups of tea and chat with Patti.

'I'm sorry Patti was snappy on the phone,' he said, when they pulled away from the airport. 'So's she.'

'It doesn't suit her, me coming now, does it?'

'She's just tired.'

'She isn't pregnant, is she?'

Startled, Oliver laughed. 'Pregnant? That's quite a leap.'

'Well, if she's tired *and* sick . . .'

'She isn't pregnant,' said Oliver. 'One little Sayle is quite enough at the moment.'

'But I thought you wanted more kids?'

'I do.' He pulled himself up in his seat.

'And Tim is nearly six already.'

'Jude, people's reproductive lives are usually their own business.'

She blushed. 'Sorry.' As they came into London, Oliver drove past their turn-off. 'Where are we going?'

'Stephen's.'

'But I want to get home. Can't you go over later?'

He shook his head and took exaggerated interest in the traffic.

'How long will we be?'

'I've a few things to do there.'

Jude crossed her arms and huffed.

*

Stephen was at work. Oliver let them in and went straight to the kitchen. It was a small flat, with bedroom, bathroom, living-room and, behind a counter, a narrow kitchen.

'Tea?'

'Suppose so.' Jude wandered around the living-room.

'It's amazing the whole school didn't burn down,' Oliver said. 'It's so isolated. How long did it take the fire brigade to get there?'

'About twenty minutes. They came from Clifden. God, is all this stuff Stephen's? The video and sound system?'

Oliver nodded.

'He must be doing all right.'

'He certainly is doing all right. He's moving on and up in the busy world of export.'

Jude leaned over a stack of compact discs on the floor. 'Since when has he been a Cranberries fan?'

'It must have been wild, all those schoolgirls running about in a panic?'

'Wait a minute . . .'

'Here, take the mugs, will you?'

'These are *my* CDs. What are they doing here? You didn't lend them to Stephen, did you? He'll wreck them.'

Oliver put his palms on the counter, pursed his lips and said, 'All right, enough.' He came out of the kitchen and led Jude to the couch. They sat down. Something turned in her stomach. Oliver ran his thumb along his lower lip. *What now?* she thought. *What is it this time?*

'First of all, there's no need to worry,' he began. 'This doesn't affect you. Or rather,' he waved his hand between them, 'it doesn't affect us. Right?'

Jude wanted to say, 'What doesn't?' but nothing happened when she tried to speak. *Worry about what?*

'The thing is . . .' Her eyes were wide with dread. Patti

68

and Stephen had tried to reassure him that Jude would take this in her stride, but he knew exactly how it would go down: badly. 'The thing is, this is where I'm living at the moment. Patti and I have split.'

She gaped at him.

'I moved out two weeks ago.'

'No.'

'Sorry, love.'

'You've split up? Why?'

'Because it wasn't working.'

'What wasn't?'

'Our marriage.'

'But you're mad about each other.'

'Not any more.'

'And everything was fine at Christmas!'

'Nothing was fine at Christmas. Christmas was a nightmare.'

'It *wasn't*.'

'Look, we were making a truly heroic effort and for the most part, we pulled it off.'

'But there wasn't any—'

'Fighting?'

She nodded furiously.

'We were beyond fighting. Believe me, you know you're in deep trouble when you can't be bothered to have a good row.'

'I don't understand. You were really happy together.'

'We weren't happy, Jude. We haven't been for some time. I thought you'd pick up the signs, but you just didn't seem to see it. Maybe you didn't want to.'

She still gaped as if he were speaking a foreign language, and behind her eyes he saw Michael's ire glare back at him. 'Why didn't you tell me?'

'Because nothing had been decided, so there was no point alarming you.'

'But you can't break up. What about Tim? What about me?'

'This is hard on both of you, of course it is, but we can't stay together any longer.'

'Why not?'

'Because . . . Because . . .'

Jude pulled away. 'You've been with someone else!'

Oliver shook his head. 'This affects you, Jude, I'll grant you that, but that kind of detail simply doesn't concern you.'

'That means yes. You've gone off with someone else!'

He looked at her. 'I'll make that tea now,' he said, getting up.

Jude hid her face in her hands. *Oh God, Oh God, Oh God! How could they be so stupid? How could they give up so easily? It has to be Oliver. Women are always fawning over him – he must have had an affair. Or maybe several?*

It was hard to think straight, to know what to do, but it came to her, in a foggy sort of way, that her loyalty lay with Patti, that she should be with her, giving her support when she needed it so badly. She stood up. 'Take me home right now,' she said, reaching for her bag.

Oliver looked up, perplexed. 'What?'

'I want to go home.'

He stood for a moment, then came to her again. He pushed her gently back onto the couch. 'Jude,' he began, and that was as far as he got, because this hadn't occurred to him. In all the times he had anticipated this meeting, Jude had never asked to go back to Thornton Avenue. He sat down. 'Jude, you can't go back there.'

'Why not?'

'You . . . Because you're with me now.'

'No. I want to be with Patti.'

He was taken aback by her determination to be with his wife when he'd invested so much time in her himself, and even Patti hadn't imagined that Jude's natural inclination would be to stay with her. While they both appreciated that losing her new home would be tough on Jude, they nevertheless believed that as long as Oliver remained in her life, she would get over it. But if Patti was the one she wanted . . .

'Take me over there,' she insisted.

'I can't.'

'Why not? Where am I supposed to go? Where am I going to live?'

'You'll live with me.'

'But I want to be with them!'

'That just isn't possible.'

'I'm going to ring Patti.' She lunged towards the phone on the table. 'I'm going to tell her you won't take me over!'

'No, you're not!' Oliver grabbed the receiver from her hand and slammed it back on to the table. 'Now listen, Jude. I know this is difficult, but the fact remains that in the eyes of the law I am your guardian, and in a situation like this, you have to stay with me. That's just the way it is. You're like my toothbrush – wherever I go, you come too. You have never been Patti's responsibility and you certainly aren't her responsibility now.'

Her eyebrows dipped the way they always did when she was confounded.

Oliver lit a cigarette. He mustn't take this out on Jude. 'Patti's just not up to taking you on at the moment,' he said more gently.

'Why not? What have you done to her?'

His eyes narrowed. 'She needs time to adjust.'

71

'I'll help her.'

'She'd rather you stayed with me.'

'You mean she doesn't want me?'

'It isn't quite like that, Jude. Be fair.'

'Why should I be fair? No one's being fair to me! You just don't want me to hear her side of the story, do you?' As Oliver made his way to the kitchen, she grabbed the phone again. 'Well, I'll find out anyway.'

'Bloody hell!' Oliver swung around; they wrestled over the phone. 'She doesn't want you there, Jude. Get that into your thick head. She doesn't want either of us!'

Jude recoiled, and finally fell apart. 'But where am I to go?'

Oliver put two mugs on the table and pushed Jude's legs out of the way to sit down. 'Hey, you. Tea.' She emerged from the cushions, snivelling. 'It isn't as bad as you think,' he said. 'We're moving house, that's all.'

'Why won't she see me?'

'Because she's trying to get things on to an even keel for Tim. If you go charging in like a headless chicken, it'll only upset him.'

'But what about my things?'

'Your clothes are in suitcases at a friend's. I'll fetch them later. All your other stuff will stay in storage with mine until we have a place of our own. I kept your CDs out for you.'

'You mean, I've moved out already?'

Her face was stained with the hot uneven smear of tears. Oliver couldn't bear it. Bad enough that he should do this to his own child, but to do it to somebody else's as well . . . He squeezed the back of her neck, which prompted her to throw herself against him. 'You never got a hint of it?'

'A hint of what? I don't understand what happened.'

'It's what didn't happen that matters.'

'You have a lover, haven't you?'

'No,' he sighed. 'I don't have a lover.'

'So why don't you have a trial separation and then—'

'That isn't an option.'

'Why not?'

'Because I say so.'

'Poor Patti. Is she very upset?'

'She'll manage.'

Jude sat up and sipped some tea. 'What about Tim? Is he all right?'

Oliver flinched. 'Of course not. Look at you, and you're not even our own daughter.'

It was Jude's turn to flinch. 'So we have to stay here?'

'Yeah. Stephen has moved in with Karen, his girlfriend. You can have the bedroom. I'll kip here on the sofa bed. I had planned to have something organized by the time you came for Easter, but you caught me on the hop. Seems we'll have to be nomads for a while.'

'I can't believe this.'

'Me neither.'

Jude sat for a long time in a daze.

'Why don't I make you a sandwich?'

'I'd rather lie down.'

'Of course. You must be worn out.' He led her into Stephen's bedroom, pulled off her shoes and covered her up. 'I'm sorry, Jude. I'm so sorry we've let you down like this.'

She woke two hours later with a headache and looked around the room. It was a proper man's room, cluttered and untidy, with a faint smell of socks and stale air. There was an open suitcase against the wall, with clothes piled into it. Jude put her hand on her forehead. What was she to do? She was nearly seventeen. It was time to make some decisions for herself perhaps, and Oliver's open suitcase said it all. They were effectively sharing a room and that didn't make much sense. It certainly wasn't what her father had in mind when he had asked Oliver to be her guardian, and yet, as long as he remained so, what say did she have in her own life? She tried to think of an alternative to living with him and couldn't find one, unless she wanted to live in the convent until her eighteenth birthday.

She sat up suddenly. Who had packed her things? Not Oliver? Surely Patti would have done it? Surely Patti would have realized that there would be underwear and Tampax and love letters and . . . She pulled the pillow against her face and groaned. If Oliver had packed her bags, then this was only the beginning of the long list of embarrassments which living with him was bound to entail.

When she went out to the living-room, her suitcases were standing in the hallway. They gave her a jolt. This was no bad dream, no mix-up. Here was the reality: two suitcases in a hall. A new life had begun, without warning. From here on, she would have to follow Oliver, go wherever he went, like his toothbrush, as he said, dragging her belongings behind her. She was homeless now, as well as orphaned. Her fellow vagrant was sitting on the couch, working at his lap-top computer. His glasses were perched on the end of his nose and Jude felt a mixture of sympathy and fury. If only he had tried harder, if he had worked at his marriage, they wouldn't be sitting in this wretched flat with nowhere else to go.

He looked over his glasses. 'Feeling better?'

'A bit.'

'I bought some cakes for tea. Put the kettle on, would you?'

'You can't butter me up with cakes.'

He peered over his rims, his large eyes still.

'You got my cases.'

'Yeah.'

'Oliver, who cleared out my room?'

'I did.'

'Did Patti help?'

'Nope.' He took a final drag on his cigarette and stubbed it out.

'Why not?'

'I don't know why not. She saw it as my responsibility, I suppose.'

'But there were things. Personal things.'

'Nothing I haven't seen before.'

'Oliver, *please*.'

He took off his glasses. 'Look, Stephen and I cleared your room from top to bottom, but I didn't exactly have my mind on the job, all right?'

'*Stephen?* Oh God.' She skulked into the kitchen.

Oliver put his laptop aside and rolled his head around to ease the tension in his neck. Jude made him coffee and tea for herself, and brought a tray back into the living-room. 'What's going to happen about Tim?' she asked.

Oliver rested his head against the couch, his eyes closed.

'Can he stay with us whenever we want him to?'

'Yes, but . . .'

Jude bit into a chocolate muffin. 'But what?'

'We might as well discuss it now as later, I suppose.'

'Discuss what? God, what else is there?'

'There's plenty more, Jude, so I wish you'd stop biting my face off.' He spoke as concisely as the subject allowed. 'Patti and I will share custody, but in practical terms, well, these situations are stacked against dads. I've had to move out. I've nowhere to put Tim. So while I have an equal claim to him, the reality is that he'll effectively be living with Patti. During the holidays, he'll mostly be with me, wherever I happen to be . . . and, in the immediate future, that's probably going to be in France.'

'France!' Jude choked on a crumb of muffin.

Oliver slapped her back. 'Remember Anthony and Sal's place in the Jura?'

'Vaguely,' she said, coughing. 'Dad talked about going there on holiday.'

'Well, it's empty. They don't get over as often as they'd hoped – it's too far away for long weekends – so they try to fill it with whoever they can whenever they can. They've been at me for ages to go there to write and now I'm free to do so. Truth is, Jude, I don't have much option, because as long as my finances are tied up with Patti, I don't really have any.'

'Any what?'

'Finances. Being offered a place rent-free, even in France, is a gift I can't afford to refuse.'

Jude gasped. 'We've no money?'

'I've got enough to live on, just not enough to buy a place. Even renting would be a stretch. Besides, I need to get away. I have a book to finish and it has to be good. My last one didn't do very well – possibly because I didn't have the heart for it after your dad died – and I can't let that happen again. I have to come up with something better, something with a bit of zest, and I feel about as zesty as a banana at the moment. What has happened stinks, Jude, but I have to take it for what it's worth because if I don't get out of this rut, we'll end up squashed into a place like this,' he waved around the flat, 'and you and Tim deserve better.' He held up his palm. 'Push.'

She pushed against it with her fist.

'I can do one of two things. I can push back or,' he let his arm drop, 'I can fall down.'

'You wouldn't have to do either if you'd stayed married.'

'Jude—'

'You can't go away! What about me? What about Tim?'

'It isn't ideal for Tim, granted, but he'll be with me all summer, and you can come over as soon as school's out. It'll be great – a fantastic opportunity to improve your French.'

'I don't care about French. I want to be near my friends during the holidays. It's been bad enough living in London. I'm not going to bury myself in some remote village in France!'

'And what if Michael had moved away? You'd have refused to go, would you?'

'He was my father. I wouldn't have had the choice.'

'Well, guess what, honey? You don't have the choice with me either.'

'This isn't fair! Why have I absolutely no say in what happens to me?'

'You're screaming at me again.'

'What do you expect? First you tell me that you and Patti have separated, then that I have to live with *you*, now that we're going to France – and I'm supposed to go along with it all. Dad wouldn't like this one little bit. In fact, he'd be dead sorry he ever asked you to be my guardian. I'd be better off with Lee!'

That was the last straw. Oliver stood up and grabbed his jacket. 'Since I picked you up,' he said, with a thin grasp on his temper, 'you've accused me of every damned sin in the book. You'd think I'd committed bloody treason!'

'Well, maybe you have!' Jude shouted.

'Maybe fuck. You'd do well to get a few things straight, young lady. I know this affects you, but your needs won't be overlooked now or at any time in the future, and what really concerns me at the moment is that my family has been torn into shreds. That's the issue here – not whether you want to go to France or not!'

He stormed out of the flat.

Jude curled up on the couch. She wanted her cosy bedroom; she wanted Patti and Tim; she wanted her own home, not someone's abandoned French villa! Then, as she lay there, the stillness in the room drew her attention. She was alone at last. She grabbed the phone and dialled too quickly. A man answered. 'Oh, I'm sorry, I've got the wrong number.'

'Who were you looking for?'

'Patti Sayle.'

'Yes, that's right. I'll get her for you.'

A moment later, Patti came to the phone. 'Hello?'

'Patti?'

'Oh, Jude. You got here all right?'

'Yes, but listen, Oliver won't even let me go over to you, but he's gone out in a huff, so I'm going to call a taxi and—'

'No, don't do that.'

'Why not?'

Patti sighed. 'It would only make things harder. On both of us.'

The phone slipped through Jude's hand. 'You don't really expect me to live with Oliver? Not long-term?'

'Why not? Jude, he's your guardian.'

'You don't want me to come home?'

'It's not that I don't want you, it's that—'

Jude hung up. This was too bewildering. She had believed she meant as much to Patti as she did to Oliver; she'd been living in a fool's paradise. It was time to let it all go. She cried and cried, and when she heard Oliver come back, she didn't stir, even though he'd be irritated to find her still slumped on the couch feeling sorry for herself.

'Hi!'

She looked up. It was Stephen, not Oliver. She hardly recognized him: he'd cut his hair, shaved off his so-called beard, and he looked quite smart. 'Hello.'

'Oh dear. You've heard the news then?'

'It's *awful*.'

'Yeah, he's been through the mill all right.'

'But what about me? What am I supposed to do?'

'You'll be fine. You still have Ol. Where is he, anyway?'

'He's gone out. We had a fight.'

'Ah. Er, well.' Stephen retreated to his kitchen.

Oliver came in not long afterwards. 'Steve. What are you doing here?'

'Karen's having the girls in. I'm one too many.'

'You always have been.'

Jude didn't look up when Oliver sat beside her. He had clearly calmed down, and she was going to blow it. She blurted it right out. 'I phoned Patti.'

'I told you not to,' he said wearily. .

'Who is he?'

'Who?'

'The guy who answered the phone.'

'That would be Jeremy. Her new live-in, to all intents and purposes.'

'Live-in?'

'You shouldn't have phoned.'

'I wanted to speak to her.'

'So. Now you know.'

'Know what?'

'That I've been well and truly cuckolded.'

'What does that mean?'

'It means my wife took a lover.'

Jude nearly swallowed her own tongue. Everything she had said all afternoon had been hateful. 'What? *When?*'

'It got off the ground last summer, I think.'

'While I was there?'

'The extra evening classes, remember? And the yoga?'

'She *was* doing yoga.'

'Hmm.'

'But that means . . . at Christmas? You must have been dying.'

'More or less.'

'The bitch! She's wrecked it for all of us!'

'Hey. I won't have that kind of talk. If we hadn't been on the rocks already, it wouldn't have happened. There are no affairs in happy marriages, you know.'

'But why didn't you tell me?'

'Because it's Patti's business and I knew you'd hold it against her. You two are good friends. Don't let this ruin that.'

'She's already ruined it.'

Stephen handed Oliver a can of beer.

'So that's why I can't live there any more.'

'Yeah. He'll be moving in as soon as . . . Tim can deal with it.'

'God, I've been so stupid.'

Oliver squeezed her knee. 'Can't you turn off the taps, love? I haven't seen you cry so much since your dad died.'

'This is like another death. To me, anyway.'

'Yeah. Me too.'

8

Stephen's bachelor flat had not been designed to accommodate two individuals for whom any degree of personal intimacy would be considered not only unacceptable but even criminal. Like a man stepping through a minefield, Oliver had to weave around Jude so as not to trespass upon her privacy; he wore pyjamas for the first time in years and dressed every morning in the bathroom before she got up. She, meanwhile, was hiding all her dirty clothes in her suitcase, dreading the prospect of having to hang her underwear around the flat to dry, but that eventuality was avoided when they made a trip to the laundrette with their respective bags of washing. In such limited space Oliver found Jude's untidiness more intolerable than ever, while she found his need for order infuriating, but by the end of the week they had settled into each other's company and both had some idea of what the future would be like.

As to the break-up of the marriage, Jude could not be dissuaded from holding Patti entirely responsible and insisted that she never wanted to see her again. Other than that, she said very little about it. Instead of pounding Oliver with intrusive curiosity about Patti's affair, she faced its consequences, and her capacity to move forward every time fate knocked her back was impressive. Over the years, Oliver had watched her build an inner structure, a fortified frame which held her upright when all else collapsed around her, and it gave him hope that she would ultimately emerge from the detritus of her blighted childhood as strong an individual as her mother had been. There was always the possibility that some insignificant event would one day pull the bottom brick from her foundations, causing her to crumple into a heap, but should that happen, he hoped to be there to pick up the pieces. For now, he could only be relieved that, upon losing so much, she had found it in herself to get up and go on without much help from him, because he had nothing for her.

He was entirely preoccupied with Tim. Every day his stomach churned when he walked up his own garden path and rang his own doorbell, but he refused to take Tim out, to McDonald's or the park, like a Sunday father. He insisted on seeing him at home, on cooking for him, reading to him, and bathing him as usual, and although Patti went out whenever Oliver arrived, signs of her life with Jeremy were so manifest about the house that he wondered that he had ever lived there himself.

He had tried not to leave. Through many dark nights, he had yelled at Patti that she should be the one to go, but her solicitor had advised her that if she left the family home, she might jeopardize her claim to live with Tim. And so she stood firm, but that had been easy for her – she was in love and had the support of her new partner. Oliver's only advantage was that he worked from home and cared for Tim during the day, although that served only to expose him to their child's increasing confusion. They couldn't go on as they were: one crushed, the other waiting like a bride for her honeymoon to begin, and a child in between, looking up. In his heart, Oliver didn't want to separate Tim and his mother. They were too close, and it was a bitter fact that she already had another life to offer their son. If she moved out, Tim would be left with the broken parent, the one who must recover from the blows, rebuild himself, and then – but when? – find happiness.

In the end, Oliver's departure was not one of dignified acceptance. He left in a rage of jealousy when pride had eaten right through his resolve, but returned three days later with the intention of telling Patti to go. When he got there, he met with a scene of such peaceful domesticity that he knew it was over. Tim looked well. For three days there had been no tension, no territorial games played over his head, and he looked better for it. He was full of chat about Jeremy, that was the worst of it. How Oliver wished Patti's lover would be so distasteful to their son that he would insist on living with his dad! But no. Jeremy was a good man and Tim's recovery was already under way. These three, Oliver knew, could make a family without even thinking about it.

He settled for damage limitation. To keep Tim in his own home, he agreed to let Patti and Jeremy buy him out of the house; to give Tim stability, he agreed not to move him around during the school term, but to take him for holidays and alternate weekends. Then all he had to do was learn to live with his decision to leave. He had to get used to being a part-time father, a single man, and still, somehow, have something left over for Jude.

For her part, Jude made some slight effort to work out what was going through Oliver's mind, but not much. She had enough hurt of her own to absorb without dealing with his as well. She silently raged at Patti. She wanted to yell at her; she *so* badly wanted to yell at her and ask how she could take Tim and their home from under their noses, just because she fancied some guy, and then leave them here like this. It was like being punished for something they hadn't done. They had been discarded. Thrown out. Expelled. For no good reason at all.

It would have been better, Jude reasoned, if Oliver had left Patti two years earlier and gone to live with her in Ireland, in *her* house. Then she would never have had to leave home or go through all that other stuff, like standing around awkwardly at Patti's parents' place, wondering where she should sit or how much to say, and never having the luxury of leaving the kitchen in a mess after baking a cake. Jude didn't get it. What had all that effort been about? What had been the point of building a new home for her, if it was going to be yanked from under her like a carpet?

As for Oliver, she was not unmoved by her new connection to him. In spite of an initial sense of abandonment, she soon realized that she still had some link to someone who cared and sometimes, when Oliver was sitting at his laptop, she found herself thinking, *this is it. He is all I have now.* And since he was all that was left to her, he would have to do. Besides, he had always been there and she believed he always would. She could not entertain the idea that he might one day vanish from her life, as so much else had. Oliver had to be constant; nothing else was, apparently.

A few days into their new arrangement, Jude was in the bath one evening when Stephen turned up shortly before Oliver was due to go out with friends. He took a couple of beers from the fridge and gave one to his brother. 'Have this before you go.'

'Thanks.'

Stephen sat down. 'I've been wondering,' he said. 'This business with Jude. Is it, you know . . . is there any chance she could be taken off you?'

'I've been trying not to think about that.'

'Well, you ought to think about it. Seems to me the nuns aren't going to like the idea of her living with a born-again bachelor.'

'Why not? It's legal. If I'd never married, I'd still be her guardian.'

'Maybe, and maybe not. The point is: what'll you do if the nuns think she should be fostered out to a proper family?'

'They'd have to make her a ward of court first, and they couldn't do that without proving I can't offer what she needs.'

'And you can't.'

'Sorry?'

'For crying out loud, Ol, you don't even have anywhere to live.'

'I soon will have.'

'Yeah, *where* is the question.'

'She's sixteen, Stephen. That gives her some rights. She'll have a say in where she goes – if it comes up, which it won't.'

'Are you sure she wants to stay with you?'

'Why, thank you for that vote of confidence!'

'Are you?'

'Pretty much.'

'Oliver, listen. You've no place to live, you want to go to France, and Jude's coming along with all her teenage angst . . . Are you sure,' he lowered his voice, 'it wouldn't suit you if she were to live with friends in Dublin?'

'I can't believe you said that.'

'Yeah, well, I'm not the only one who's saying it. Mum thinks it's inappropriate for Jude to live with you now, and if Mother thinks it, the school probably will too.'

Oliver sat forward. 'What do you expect me to do? Turf her out? Has anyone thought about what it would do to Jude if I told her it was "inappropriate" for her to stay with the only person she's got? Has anyone considered that while she's homeless in literal terms, she certainly isn't homeless in any other sense? Nor will she be as long as I have anything to do with it.'

'Very admirable, I'm sure, but you've got to get your own life together and that won't be easy with Jude hanging on to your shirt-tails.'

Oliver ran his thumb along his lip. 'Are the parents really going to come down on me about this?'

'They just want what's best. They reckon you've done your bit for Jude.'

'Christ. I've "done my bit", have I?'

'And certain realities have to be faced.'

'Absolutely. Certain realities *do* have to be faced. In case you haven't noticed, I haven't had such a good run lately. I've lost my best friend, my wife and my home in just under two years, and I now have limited access to my son, so why on earth would I want to ditch Jude?

'I know you're fond of her, but—'

'Not *fond*. She's been around since I was nineteen and she's been a part of my family for the past two years – that amounts to a little more than "fond", for Chrissakes.' He got up and paced. Stephen's eyes followed him.

The bathroom door opened; Jude skipped into the bedroom wrapped in a towel. 'I'm not going to fuck this up or let anyone else do it for me, Stephen. I know what Michael wanted for her and I'm going to make sure she gets it.'

'All right, all right. Keep your hair on.'

'She'll be seventeen soon. Who's going to bother causing trouble now?'

'Our mother for one.'

'Christ. Talk to her, would you?'

'I'll try to get her on side, yeah, because if you're going to be living with a female teenager, you're going to need your mummy!'

Oliver dropped into the couch. 'I thought you knew how I felt.'

'Not sure I did, frankly. She's a nice kid 'n' all, don't get me wrong, but you have to get your own house sorted.'

'I would if I had one!'

'Instead of worrying about Jude, you should be out there finding yourself a woman.'

'Strange as it may seem to you, mate, a woman is the last thing I need.'

'Oh,' said Jude, emerging from the bedroom. 'You're still here.'

Stephen looked comically around the flat. 'Isn't this my home?'

'He's had a fight with Karen,' said Oliver, getting up, 'so be nice to him.' He kissed her goodnight and headed for the door.

'You mean he's staying?'

'Ol?' called Stephen.

'Ya?'

'Cool it.'

'Yeah, yeah, yeah,' he muttered, slamming the door behind him.

Jude crossed her arms. 'So what were you and Karen fighting about?'

87

'Oh, er, sex. She wants it all the time and I don't want it at all.'

'Very funny. You haven't really had a fight. Oliver set this up, I'll bet.'

' 'Fraid so.'

'For God's sake! What does he think I am? Five years old?'

'He didn't want you to be alone is all. Not at the moment.'

'Jesus! Having a babysitter when I'm sixteen! How humiliating.'

'I'm not here to babysit. Oliver simply thought you'd like some company, and if you don't mind my saying so, you could do a lot worse.'

He was right. Jude had a wonderful evening and thoroughly enjoyed Stephen's company. In fact, she more than enjoyed it, which was rather inconsistent with her situation and deeply worrying.

It started when he leaned across her to get the remote control for the television. A barely perceptible flutter ran across her chest, so fleeting she might have imagined it, but later, when a friend of Stephen's rang and he stretched out, with one leg on the table, to chat, Jude became unintentionally preoccupied with everything about him. His dark brown hair was shiny and thick and . . . She swept these thoughts away. She was in love with Thierry. *His* lovely blond hair was, well, rather wavy and indecisive, but his eyes were like a lake in the French countryside. She glanced sideways. Brown. Not any brown either, but deep, *deep* chocolate brown, and he had prominent lower lashes. Stephen glanced at her then and yes, his eyes were quite piercing, especially at certain angles when a thin white rim cupped the iris. This line was unusual. It made him look obstinate. Stubborn.

How had she never noticed it before? He shoved his hand into his hip pocket. Jude swallowed.

She stared blindly at the television, unmoved by the sweeping vistas in *Out of Africa*. Stephen tapped her arm and pointed towards his wine. Her insides tightened as she handed him the glass; his fingers brushed over hers. The effect was startling. She felt such a surge inside her that she was sure he would turn to see her glowing. Disgusted with this mental infidelity, she switched on her love for Thierry and tried to make it shine like a beacon in a corner of the ceiling. If she looked at it long enough, she believed, these purely physical responses would be burnt out by sheer will-power . . . Except she didn't want to burn them out, because she hadn't felt so gloriously inebriated for quite some time.

As Stephen's call ended, Jude resolved that she could not fancy him. He was eight years older than her and Oliver would have a fit if he guessed she was attracted to his brother. Besides, what would he see in her, a silly teenager with a medium-sized chest? Stephen liked real women: grown-up ones with fantastic figures and pouty lips. His own lips were narrow: straight mouth, thin lips, good teeth. Thierry's mouth was, was, oh, she couldn't remember. On screen, Meryl Streep gasped at Robert Redford as they heaved about under the mosquito netting. 'Don't move,' he said to her. 'Don't move.'

Jude sighed.

Oliver brought her breakfast in bed the next morning.

'What's this?' she snapped. 'A peace offering?'

He put the tray across her lap. 'What have I done now?'

'Getting Stephen to babysit. Honestly!'

'Oh *gawd*. He just couldn't stick to the sodding script.'

'I've never been so embarrassed in my entire life!'

'Look here, you. I don't expect you to understand where I'm coming from, but don't ever question what I do, or don't do, in looking out for you, right?' He sat on the bed beside her. 'Now, I've just been on to the school – they're reopening on Wednesday, so we'll fly over on Tuesday, OK?'

'You don't have to come.'

'I do. I need to speak to Sr Al about our changed circumstances.'

Jude shrugged. 'I wasn't going to bother telling her.'

'That would back-fire, love.'

'Maybe, but she's not going to be dead pleased.'

'I know. That's why I want to talk to her, but before I do, I need to be sure that this is what you want. If you'd rather live with friends instead of dragging around after me, I won't mind. If that's what's right for you, we should arrange it.'

Jude frowned. She had become completely reconciled to the idea of living with Oliver – indeed, she clung to the concept as to a life-jacket – and now he was saying what? 'What?'

'Fact is, Jude, some people might have a problem with this arrangement. So if you'd be more comfortable—'

'What do you mean?'

'They might . . . suspect my motives.'

'They'd never think . . . ?'

'They could, and some probably will. We have to be prepared for every eventuality.'

'But you're my guardian. They can't change that, can they?'

'Not if it's what you want.'

'Of course it is.'

90

'Are you absolutely sure?'

'*Yes.*'

Pleased by the warmth of her assertion, Oliver winked. 'That's decided, then. I'll tell Sr Al what's what.'

'But what are we going to do about Easter? Where'll we go?'

'Scotland.'

'To your parents? Oh God. Your mother terrifies me.'

'Ah, she's fine. She's like a bright, frosty morning – icy at first, but sure to thaw.'

'If you ask me, she's more like the Ice Age.'

'All the same, be nice to her. You need a woman in your life.'

'I need *your mother*? Jesus, things are worse than I thought.'

Oliver laughed. 'Anyway, Stephen'll be there. He'll keep her sweet.' He bit into a piece of her toast. 'And look, you mustn't worry about all this when you get back to school. As soon as I can organize it, you'll have your own bedroom in our own place, all right? Nothing will stop me from giving you the home you deserve. Nothing.'

'I know. I know that now.'

St Malachy's looked unchanged when they drew up, apart from the pile of debris at the side of the building and lorries blocking the drive, and when Jude opened the car door, Fiona and Emer appeared from nowhere, squealing in delight. The three girls made their way into the building, exchanging news with every step, and as Oliver came in behind them, Sr Aloysius swept past.

'Mr Sayle. Lovely to see you.'

'Actually, Sister, I need to speak to you.'

It took several steps before she drew herself to a halt. 'Yes?'

'Er, could we . . . ?'

She led him to her office where he took a seat in front of her desk. Sitting in the same chair in front of the same nun was eerily reminiscent of the day he had come to tell Jude about Michael. He wondered if the nun had a similar feeling.

'What can I do for you?' she asked, hands clasped, cheeks red.

Oliver pulled at his jacket. 'I thought you should know that there have been some changes in my domestic arrangements, and therefore in Jude's.'

The principal's good humour at having her school reopened wasn't in the least bit splintered; she expected him to say they had moved house. 'Yes?'

He wiped his palms along his jeans. 'The thing is, my wife and I have separated.'

Her face dropped. 'Separated?'

'I'm afraid so.'

'Gracious. And is this a . . . temporary arrangement?'

'No. We plan to divorce.'

'But where does this leave Jude?'

'With me.'

'I see.' Sr Aloysius didn't see. Why should Jude stay with him? Surely the obvious course of action would be for her to stay with his wife and child – a family environment of sorts? She cleared her throat. 'But Jude is very close to Mrs Sayle, is she not?'

'They got on very well, yes.'

'Oh dear. How dreadful for her. How is the poor child coping?'

'She's upset of course, but against the wider picture, she's got herself through worse than this.'

'Indeed. All the same, she is quite devoted to you both and —'

'As I am devoted to her.'

She looked at him. 'I don't doubt it, Mr Sayle, but in the circumstances would it not be better for Jude to live with your wife?'

Bugger, thought Oliver. *This is going to be a bitch.* 'My appointment as Jude's guardian predates my marriage by several years. Patti has no legal responsibility towards her.'

'Legal? Perhaps not, but don't you think, all things considered and in view of everything Jude has been through, that—'

'Yes, I do. I have no doubt that Jude would be better off with my family, but I'm afraid it isn't an option.'

'Why ever not?'

'Patti isn't in a position, I mean, she doesn't feel able, at the moment, to remain involved in Jude's welfare.'

'You mean she is washing her hands of a young girl who—'

'The break-up of a marriage is never simple, Sister. Patti has been very good to Jude, but she has our son to take care of now.' *And her lover to attend to.*

'Of course,' the nun said quickly. 'This can't be easy for any of you, but it could be deeply . . .' *damaging,* she thought, but she said instead, 'disturbing for Jude to lose two families in such a short space of time.'

'I know that. She's torn between me and Patti, and yet she doesn't actually come into the bargaining. In fact, she's the most uncontroversial part of the carve-up. Legally, she comes with me and that's all there is to it – which is ironic in view of the fact that I don't have such a straightforward claim to my own son.'

Sr Aloysius shook her head. You could only wonder at such a mess. 'What about her aunt?'

'Last we heard she was living in a cottage in West Cork with a lad of twenty. I think you'll agree that Jude will be better off with me.'

'Frankly, Mr Sayle—'

'Oliver, please.'

'I'm not at all sure I do agree. You must appreciate that this is most unorthodox. I do understand that legally Jude is your responsibility, but you must consider the broader picture. Has it occurred to you, for instance, that her friends might not be allowed to visit her because she lives with a man in your situation? Have you considered the implications, the simple day to-day logistics, of living with a young woman? You must see that it is hardly appropriate for a girl of sixteen to live with a single man?'

'I would say it depends on who that man is. And bear in mind that my son will be with me for much of the time that Jude is.'

'But not all of it?'

'No. She gets longer school holidays than he does.' As the nun considered every negative aspect of his claim to Jude, Oliver couldn't bring himself to tell her that this devoted guardian would actually be living hundreds of miles from his charge.

Sr Aloysius tapped her hand on her desk. Mr Sayle sat there, in his jeans and blue jacket, with his vivid blue eyes and low grainy voice, looking like charm personified. With his quirky good looks and status as a mildly known author, he would probably have a string of women floating through his home at the earliest opportunity. 'I'm sorry, Mr Sayle, but in my view, this proposal is not at all conducive to the stability we should wish for Jude.'

'Stability? I'm the only stability she has. She sees me as a link to her father. Cut me out of the picture and she'll be rootless.'

'I'm not suggesting you should be cut out of her life, simply that her living arrangements should be more . . . wholesome.'

'She insists she wants to live with me.'

'But she's only sixteen! She doesn't necessarily know what's good for her.'

'I believe she does. She's more mature than other girls of her age.'

'That's what worries me.'

'And if she doesn't know what's good for her, I certainly do.'

'Then you must see she would be far better off with your wife!'

Oliver was stung, but impressed by her spirit. 'My wife will soon be living with someone else. For that reason alone, it is inadvisable for Jude to stay there. My son, at least, is with his own mother.'

The nun sighed. 'Oh dear. This just gets worse.' It alarmed her that she was speaking to this man not as a parent, but as if he were an old friend. It went back, she knew, to those awful minutes, two years before, when they had waited together for Jude to come into the room. She went to the window. Since she acted *in loco parentis* for Jude for most of the year, this was a development she didn't like to ignore, but she was moving beyond her brief. Michael Feehan had made a decision about his daughter – she had no right, and no grounds, to interfere with it now. On the other hand, Mr Feehan could hardly have imagined that Jude would find herself, at sixteen years of age, with no other option but to live with a thirty-something divorced man.

'My parents and brother are fully behind me, Sister,' said Oliver, 'and my mother will be happy to take care of any personal matters that might arise vis-à-vis Jude.'

She turned. 'Oh, but I had no idea your parents would be involved. Do they live in London?'

'They have recently retired to Scotland, but if Jude ever feels the need of female company, my mother would be happy to take her,' he lied.

Sr Aloysius scratched her forehead. 'None the less, this is far from ideal. Perhaps we could approach the parents of some of Jude's friends and ask if they could take her for a few weeks at a time during the holidays?'

'You mean pass her around like a parcel? I don't think so.'

'But you must appreciate my position? We both know I can't stand in your way, but after you, I am the person who is most concerned with Jude's welfare, and if this situation isn't right for her, you can understand why I feel I must speak up.'

'Of course, but I had hoped to have your support.' Oliver was running out of steam. If he was to win this battle of wits, he'd better get to it. He put his elbows on her desk and said, 'Look, here's the deal. Either Jude stays with me or she's sent off to some family she doesn't want to be with simply because it's deemed more "wholesome". Even worse, you and I fall out about it and start haggling over her. Now, which of those is likely to be most traumatic? I mean, let's get things clear here. My marriage is finished, my child is confused, my work is neglected, and it would be very easy for me to say, "Here, you deal with Jude. I've got enough on my plate." That would be dead easy, Sister, but it isn't going to happen. Do you think I sat here two years ago and went through all that just to give her up now because my wife has left me? Do you have any concept of what I've been through with the child?'

The nun shook her head.

'Sister, I need your wholehearted and unconditional support for one reason and one reason only. There is nobody left – and I mean nobody – who loves Jude as much as I do.'

Some time later, from the window of her office, Sr Aloysius watched Oliver and Jude leaning against the wall, looking out over the lake. *Talk about the odd couple*, she thought. She could have tried to persuade him that Jude should live with friends, but what would that be like for her? Always a visitor, never at home, she would become the perpetual guest, never free to make a cup of tea in someone else's kitchen. No. The only person who could give her a home, of sorts, was this wandering writer of no fixed address (as she had just discovered), who stood now with his elbow on the shoulder of his dead friend's daughter. *Circumstance is a curious manipulator*, thought the nun, and she wondered what Jude would make of the accidents of her adolescence. Would they destroy her potential, or fire it?

9

No major fanfare heralded the seismic shift in Jude's affections. Stephen simply walked into his parents' sitting-room two days before Easter and she knew that any lingering sentiment for Thierry had been squashed. Obliterated. She wasn't surprised. It had probably been inevitable that she would eventually fall in love with Stephen, and now that she had, he overwhelmed her thoughts by day, her dreams by night. And such was the euphoria that came with loving him, she didn't even care that she was far too young for him. All that mattered was that she should be in his company at every opportunity. That, for a while, would be enough.

It was imperative, however, that nobody should know that her romantic perspective had changed, and that was going to be difficult, because Oliver had an uncanny habit of reading her moods with pinpoint accuracy.

They were reading by the fire when Stephen arrived. Mrs Sayle greeted him with delight, then went off to the kitchen. 'Come along, Timmy, let's make tea for Uncle Stephen.'

Stephen moved to the fire and stood warming the backs of his legs. 'And how's Judy?'

'My name is Jude.'

'Still giving Ol a hard time?'

'Feck off.'

'Ah. "Feck." The great Irish cop-out. Why don't you just say "fuck" like the rest of us?'

Oliver looked over his newspaper. 'Don't encourage her, Stephen.'

'Sorry. So how's Mother behaving herself?'

'OK,' said Oliver, 'but we only got here last night. Give her time.'

'Are you on the carrots again?'

Mrs Sayle returned with a large tray. She was a stocky woman who, in Jude's limited experience, always wore tweed skirts and sensible shoes. Her silver hair gave her round face a square frame, and her brown eyes twinkled in any light. 'So, darling,' she said to Stephen. 'Karen couldn't come?'

'He's with someone called Liz now,' said Oliver.

'No I'm not. I'm with Meredith.'

'What happened to Liz?' asked Oliver.

'What happened to Karen?' asked Jude.

Oliver chuckled. 'You're fairly racing through the alphabet, aren't you, Steve?'

'Well,' said their mother, 'I'm glad she didn't come, whatever her name is. It's been too long since you both came home together. It'll be a lovely family Easter, just the five of us – oh, and Jude, of course.'

Jude glanced at Oliver. He winked. Reassured, she feasted her eyes on Stephen. It astonished her that she had managed to block him out for so long. He was good-looking, carefree and funny, and under all that repartee, there was an exceptionally kind person who was unashamedly loyal to his brother. Indeed, such were his many attributes that Jude felt weak. She was so focused on Stephen that when he drank his tea, she thought she was the one who was swallowing it.

She had little experience of being discreet in matters of the heart, but she had to learn, and learn quickly. She had to feed like a whale, taking in the whole room and everyone in it, nourishing herself only on the minutiae of Stephen's every move before spewing out the rest. Bit by bit, she swallowed his personal details. His waist kept drawing her in; it was neat, slim, and the point at which his shirt met his jeans was erotic in a way that was new to her. As the Sayles chatted, Jude sat quietly, imagining the pleasures of walking over to Stephen and ingesting him whole.

The Sayles' converted farmhouse, outside the village of Cleigh near Oban, was so enchanting that Jude longed to feel welcome there, but to do so she would have to earn Mrs Sayle's affection. Any rapprochement of that nature, however, was likely to be an uphill battle because the break-up of Oliver's marriage had made his mother more than usually tetchy. It was one of the reasons he had come to see her and although nobody knew it, Stephen had come home for the same reason. He suspected his brother was in for something of a pummelling.

He was right. The following day, as they finished lunch, when Tim went outside to cycle, Mr Sayle lit his pipe and said, 'So, Patti and her friend have agreed to buy you out of the house, Oliver?'

'Yeah, but it could take a while, because they can't re-mortgage until Jeremy sells his flat, so it's a good thing I've been offered this place in France. The sooner I get out from under Stephen's feet, the better.'

'Alleluia,' said Stephen.

'France, indeed,' said their mother.

A jaded look passed between the brothers.

'I don't know how you sleep at night, Oliver,' she said. 'How can you so easily surrender your son to a man we know nothing about?'

'I haven't surrendered him to anyone. When he's not with me, he's with his mother. And I know her pretty well – I lived with her for nine years.'

'Very funny, I'm sure, but it isn't good enough. You should be staying here and making sure Timmy is properly cared for. The last thing he needs is his father running off to France.'

Mr Sayle, a broad man who looked too big for the table he was sitting at, fiddled with his long white moustache and puffed on his pipe (rather selfishly, Jude thought, in view of the fact that Oliver had recently given up smoking). 'It will do Oliver good to get away for a bit, Anna,' he said.

'I don't doubt it, but I am more interested in what is good for Timmy.'

'Mum, I don't actually have anywhere else to go.'

'You could stay here.'

'We'd kill each other.'

'Stay with Stephen then.'

'I'd kill myself,' said Stephen.

'And where am I supposed to put Tim and Jude? Tim's welfare is largely dependent on my income, you know, and my income is somewhat static at the moment. I need to come up with something fresh and I can't do that cramped into a flat in London. If I can turn out one good book, Tim will be the first to benefit.'

'And doesn't that make it so easy for Patti? Why should she have Timmy more than you do? She's the one who took a lover!'

Jude concentrated on her stewed fruit.

101

'Patti can offer him much more stability than I can at the moment.'

'Oh, poppycock. You just won't stand up to her.'

'I stood up to her for as long as Tim could cope with it!'

'This should wait until later,' said Stephen.

Oliver's father chewed his pipe, his eyes moving from one side of the table to the other, as though he were watching his wife and son playing tennis. Their voices were rising with every shot.

'That man took your wife, and you let him,' said Mrs Sayle. 'He's virtually moved into your house, and you've let him. And now he'll have your son for most of the year, and you're letting him!'

Stephen flashed an encouraging smile at Jude. She almost poured off her seat and on to the floor.

'Mother, please,' said Oliver.

'I will not please! How can you back out so easily?'

'Whoever said it was easy? There's been enough belligerence in the last year to last Tim a lifetime! It was far better for him that I went quietly.'

'Went quietly, indeed! You'll explode one of these days, the way you go on. You've allowed yourself to be scorned,' she slammed her palm on to the table, 'and you've allowed your family to break up without so much as a whimper!'

'Mum, for God's sake,' said Stephen. 'You don't know any better than the rest of us what Ol's been through these last months.'

'Of course I don't. He's like an automaton. You'd wonder he has any feelings!'

'Steady on, Anna,' said Mr Sayle.

His wife leaned across the table. 'When are you going to give this up, Oliver? This restraint? This fairness? Patti's done wrong by you and your son, and yet she wins the main prize!'

'Drop it, Mother.'

'I simply don't understand. You've no problem looking after someone else's child, but you've walked out on your own!'

'Jesus, Mum,' Stephen hissed.

Jude felt as if she'd been slapped; Oliver looked as if he had been. He stood up. 'That's it. Enough.'

When he left the room, Jude followed, as though pulled by an invisible string, for her only place in this family was by Oliver's side.

'Mum,' said Stephen. 'You're missing the point.'

'What point?'

'He's still in love with Patti,' said her husband.

Jude expected Oliver to drive over her toes and swerve down the driveway, but he spared her toes and allowed her to get in beside him. They drove for a long time without speaking, apart from Oliver saying, 'Damn, I've no carrots.'

He drove at speed towards Benderloch, playing B. B. King on the car stereo. Oliver loved the blues. He always worked in silence, but whenever he left his study he had to have a blast of the blues. Jude didn't much like it but, by force of exposure, was growing used to it. Her own musical tastes were equally clear-cut. Anything Irish won her devotion, and since this included U2, Aslan, Emotional Fish, and Jude's particular favourite, the Cranberries, Oliver found her tastes tolerable, except when she listened to the radio.

He pulled off the main road beside a stony shore. It was a sunny afternoon, but there was a cool breeze and Jude had no sweater; Oliver threw her his leather jacket and stomped down to the water. From a sheltered spot beside some boulders, she looked across Ardmucknish Bay. The landscape was akin to Connemara and yet so different that it was like having no bearings in a familiar place. The water chopped about in the breeze, but Oliver tried to skim stones across the giddy waves.

'Sorry about the onslaught,' he said when he wandered back to her.

'I don't know how you keep your cool with her.'

'I didn't keep my cool. That's why we're here.'

'Yeah, but you mostly do. How do you put up with it?'

'I have no feelings, remember? I'm an automaton.'

'Except you aren't, are you?'

He met her gaze. They both knew what she was talking about.

It was curious, Jude thought, that she could remember dispassionately the details of the funeral – the grey faces, the grim procession of cars, the grave where they lowered her father's coffin on to her mother's – she could see all this, as through frosted glass, without crumbling. And yet thoughts of that one night in Dublin still harrowed her, because she couldn't seem to control her memories of Oliver's grief as easily as she could blunt reminders of her own. Then, as now, she relied on his composure to distance her misfortune, but his momentary collapse had dissolved that breach, leaving her pressed against a polished mirror, the reflection brutally clear.

Unable to sleep one night, days after the funeral, she had come downstairs to watch television and found Oliver hunched over a glass of whisky. The shake in his hand when he smoked, the shudder in his shoulders and the tears sliding down the bridge of his nose were all her own, and she hated him for exhibiting the coarseness of their mutual despair.

Transfixed, she had stood in her nightdress in the doorway until, sensing her there, Oliver had looked round.

She had always found the memory of those eyes turning to her raw and unpalatable, as well as deeply embarrassing, but now it acquired new life. It gave her something, a part of Oliver no one else had, and it demonstrated that she knew him better than even his own mother.

'Yes, well,' he said now, 'sorry about that,' and this was the first time they had mentioned that night. He sat down on the stones. 'Don't worry about Mum, Jude. She was getting at *me*, not you.'

'She was horrible.'

'Horrible, but right. I *have* let Jeremy stomp all over my family.'

'Why did you?'

He sighed. 'Because I couldn't hold on to Patti any longer.'

Jude considered the man next to her. All her life, she had known him on her terms, as a moon circling her little world, but this situation was drawing her into his orbit and it was a much harder place to be.

'I was too laid back for her,' he said, unprompted. 'Patti takes life in great hungry bites. She wants everything, goes for everything, never stops. It could be pretty exhausting living with her. There was always something else happening.'

'That's what I loved about her.'

'Yeah, me too. It's good to be around someone like that. It'll certainly keep Tim on his toes. But you have to know when to stop, and I stopped far too often for her. I appreciate things at a much slower speed. I like to reflect, think about things. My idea of a nice evening is a meal with some friends, good wine and good conversation, but Patti would rather be out partying.'

'Is that why you broke up? Because you're too quiet?'

'There were other factors. Our child-minding arrangement wasn't ideal – what with me minding Tim during the day, then disappearing into the study as soon as Patti got home.'

'Do you think she'll stay with Jeremy?'

'She'd better. I'll kill her if she does this to Tim again.'

'You worry too much. Tim's fine.'

'He isn't fine. He's sore all over. Do you know what it's like for a kid of six never to have his mum and dad in the same room at the same time?'

'I hardly ever had mine in the same room and I'm all right, amn't I?'

Oliver smiled. 'Yeah, you're all right. You're the best.' He stood up and helped her to her feet. 'And I'll tell you something about my mother. She was very fond of your dad, so once she's over the shock of my marriage packing up, you get her talking about him. It'll give you common ground.'

Stephen stayed for four days. The most thrilling moment came when they were climbing a hill and he took Jude's hand to pull her over a boulder. She got over the boulder, but almost fell down the hill. It became increasingly difficult to keep her eyes off him and whenever he caught her watching him, she tried to switch the hot, hungry expression into the blank stare of someone who had forgotten what they were looking at. Already, being with him was no longer enough; she wanted contact. The ache inside her throbbed without mercy and her mouth became dry. She had trouble eating. It was difficult to be herself, for how could she be light and breezy when she was parched with desire for the lanky individual who teased her like a little girl?

Oliver's suspicions about Jude's mood were confirmed the night Stephen left for London. Thierry had phoned that morning and it was clear she was struggling with the relationship. He decided to broach it the next day and, leaving Tim with his mother, took Jude out for a drive. She welcomed the escape. It was a strain being continually pleasant to his parents when her mind was so driven upon one limited subject.

In a small tea shop in Taynuilt, she regained her appetite and helped herself to a cream bun.

'I'd kill for a ciggie,' said Oliver.

'If you can give up smoking in a crisis, you don't need them.'

He looked towards the counter. 'Maybe they'll give me a carrot if I wiggle my whiskers.'

'I wish you'd get rid of your whiskers.'

'Get rid of my beard? Are you mad?'

'There could be a nice face under there. Stephen has a lovely face.' She winced, but Oliver missed the reference to his brother.

'Listen, nitwit, we need to sort out the summer holidays.'

'I thought we were going to France.'

'We are, but what about Thierry's invitation to Brussels?'

She shrugged and turned her bun around with her fork. Oliver tried to catch her eye. 'It's over, am I right?'

She nodded.

'Have you told him?'

She shook her head.

'I see.'

'Oliver, do you think you could put up with me for the whole ten weeks of the holidays?'

'Course. Why not?'

'I might cramp your style.'

'I can exercise my style – or what's left of it – when you're in school.'

'You know what I mean.'

'Listen, Tim and I would love to have you all summer, but let's get back to Thierry. Why the change of heart?'

'I'm fed up having a boyfriend I hardly ever see.'

'You should tell him then. Don't drag it out.'

'I'll write.'

'Ouf. That's rough. A *Dear John* letter.'

'What's a *Dear John* letter?'

'"*Dear John, I don't love you any more. I've met someone else.*"'

'But I haven't! Where could I possibly meet someone else?'

'You never know. The school caretaker maybe?'

'He's ninety if he's a day and Sr Philomena has her eye on him.'

'Don't write to him,' said Oliver. 'It's a horrible way to be told.'

'How were *you* told?'

He flinched. He was sitting sideways, with one foot on the chair beside him. 'I came home one day and found him sitting at the kitchen table with Tim on his lap. "Oliver," said Patti, "this is Jeremy. Jeremy, Oliver." All very civilized.'

'You hadn't suspected?'

'Oh, I'd suspected all right. I just didn't expect to come home and find him all over my son in my kitchen. Patti didn't exactly expect me to show up just then either.' He turned back to her. 'About Thierry. He's been good for you, Jude. You owe it to him to do this thing nicely.'

'I will.' A rush of sunlight brightened the shop and warmed Jude's back as she swallowed the last of her bun.

'You were right about your mother. She isn't so bad when you get talking to her. And I *love* your dad.'

Oliver smiled.

'But why is she so hard on you and so soft on Stephen?'

'Because she had to wait so long for him. Eleven years, three miscarriages. Besides, he's no trouble, like Dad, whereas I'm like her and she hates being reminded òf what a miserable old bag she can be.'

'You're not a miserable old bag.'

'Patti thinks so.'

Jude looked on to the street. 'Isn't it odd how you're more than twice my age and you still have both your parents while I have none?'

He squeezed her hand. 'Odd, and grossly unfair.'

'Do you believe in God?'

'Christ.'

'Christ. God. Either.'

'I meant, Christ, where did that come from?'

'I was just wondering. I mean, if my parents are floating around me somewhere, why don't I sense it?'

'I feel their presence all the time.'

'You do? So you believe in the afterlife?'

'Not exactly, but there could be some level of existence we don't understand. Or maybe we're the ones who keep them alive?'

'I try. It doesn't work. I mean, if Dad's really with me, he's keeping very quiet about it.'

Oliver sat forward. 'Tell me something, Jude, while we're on the heavy stuff. Why did you beat me up that day in the Coal Harbour?'

She stuck her teaspoon into the sugar bowl and ground it around. 'I wanted to get you away from me.'

'Because I wasn't Michael?'

'No. It was as if I was buried in a very deep hole and everywhere I looked, no matter which way I turned, I could see him trying to get away from that boat. Trying to save himself. It was like being inside my worst nightmare. Or his. And whenever I tried to get out of the hole, you got in the way. You wouldn't let me escape.' She glanced at him. 'It was the fear that was horrible. Seeing him frightened. Like watching a fox being chased by dogs, a beautiful, slick fox being split in two by hounds. I mean, if there is a God, how could He allow it?'

Oliver had no answer to that.

10

The house in Landor was bigger than Oliver had expected.
Colder, and quiet. God, so quiet. No traffic. No bustle. But
it wasn't the hum of city life he missed, it was the sound of
Tim. Tim talking to himself, to imaginary foes; Tim calling,
'Dad?' As Oliver wandered around the empty rooms, his
mother's words made more sense than anything else she had
ever said to him: how was it that his wife took a lover and
got the child? How was it that he was here, in France, in the
holiday home of a generous friend, without his son? Was he
a fool? Soft? If he had fought for custody, would he not have
won?

Not on his income.

The hall was dim and cool. An old timber staircase stood
on the right, and beneath it a doorway led into the large,
bright living-room. It was the only room that had been
recently furnished, with a plush aquamarine suite, glass
tables, and a polished parquet floor. Garden furniture lay
folded against a wall and French windows led straight on to
the lawn. It was also the only bright room on the ground
floor. The kitchen was cavernous, with a flagstone floor,
small windows, vaulted arches, and even an old oven built

111

into the thick stone wall, but in spite of the gloom it had an aura of hot summers, fresh fruit, good wine. Empty bottles stood in the corner, the sink was an old enamel job, and a heavy timber door led through to the dining-room. With no windows at all, this room looked and felt like a chapel. A long oak dining-table took up most of the space, and double doors led outside. Oliver immediately chose this as his work-place. Dark, cool, and no views to divert him.

Upstairs, a bright corridor led to four bedrooms. He claimed the main bedroom for himself. It had a bathroom, and French windows opened on to a stone balcony on the side of the house, which offered a glorious view of the hill-sides, covered in vineyards, sloping up behind the red-tiled roofs of the village. It was Arcadian, idyllic, and yet it made no dint on the desolation he had brought with him. Which would win out, he wondered, his mood or this place? It was an ideal working environment, worlds away from the cramped study where the sounds of family had always distracted him, but could he work in such isolation?

He explored the village that evening. Around the corner from the house, milk could be bought in a plastic bucket from the *laiterie* and there was a well-stocked *boulangerie* across the bridge. Besides these and a small food store, there were no shops; he would have to shop in one of the nearby towns. There was a small hotel on the broad main street, a church, a school, but scarcely any people about, and only the campsite beside the river promised to bring some life in summer. Oliver worried about Jude – this place could be altogether too quiet for her – but as he walked back across the bridge, he stopped to look over. There was a stretch of stony yellow beach on the left side of the river Loue, and houses with blue shutters backed straight on to the bank opposite. On that side also, the remains of an old stone bridge, bombed in the war but now covered in flowers, jutted out into the water. Downstream, the wide green river was flanked by wooded slopes until it swerved out of sight about a mile beyond the village. Its most interesting feature, in Oliver's view, was just below him. Here, water gushed between the flattened uprights of the old bridge, which created a series of rapids that looked safe enough to swim through. Tim, he knew, would love it.

Oliver walked on. He had to endure only one month alone. In four weeks' time, he would return to London to fetch Tim, and Jude was due to arrive a week later. The iron gate of the villa creaked as he pushed it open. A month seemed a long time.

It was. The isolation made him taut. He found it hard to get up in the mornings, but slept on under his pillow, shielding himself from the empty house. Finally risen, he took coffee after coffee in front of a blipping screen. Then a walk, to explore his new surroundings. Siesta time was the worst of all. Everything closed from twelve to four. The whole village slumbered. Nowhere to go. Nothing to do except sleep again, and wake in the late afternoon with a thick head, less than ever able to concentrate. He counted the days until he could go home and escape this *impasse*.

But one morning a loud and persistent downpour woke him early. It was such an invigorating display of energy that it made him get up. He sat down without any coffee in his veins and started writing. At eleven, he had still not eaten, but he rejoiced. It was done. He had broken the back of his own depression and was riding up the other side.

By the time Jude arrived in early June, Oliver was gagging for company. He had settled into a pattern of solitary living, but it was fairly torturous – his surroundings had failed to

113

win the battle against his perspective – and Tim had not come, so he had never been so pleased to see Jude as when she sailed through those airport gates in Geneva. She was in high spirits. During the two-hour drive back to Landor, she scarcely stopped talking and Oliver loved every minute of it.

When they got there, he pushed open the gate and led her into the garden. She gaped at the sandstone house, the garden, the white cotton hammock hanging between two trees, and back at the house.

'Will this do?' asked Oliver.

'What do *you* think?'

He brought her suitcases up to her bedroom and opened the long white shutters. 'Come down when you're ready.'

A threadbare rug covered the broad floorboards of her room and her very own double bed stood on the left, draped in mosquito netting. Jude went over to the window. There was a lemon tree beneath it. The walled garden was long and narrow, with a rough lawn and a few shrubs, and across the street, an old woman was sitting outside her kitchen door, snoozing. As she gazed around in bewilderment, Jude thought about her old house in Dublin and wondered how on earth she had ended up here.

The hammock, she soon discovered, was the place to be. She jumped in and lay staring up at the canopy of broad heart-shaped leaves overhead. There was a buzz in the air, the somnolent drone of warm-weather insects that made lazy days lazy. 'What kind of tree is this?' she asked, when Oliver came out with two tall glasses of iced tea.

'It's a catalpa. An Indian bean tree.'

'I can't believe Anthony gave you this place for nothing.'

'He calls it his contribution to the arts. Actually, he needed a house-sitter. He didn't want it empty all summer.'

'They're not coming over?'

'Nope. This is one investment he regrets – it's too hard to get to – but as long as I'm here, he doesn't have to worry about it.'

Jude struggled out of the hammock and joined Oliver at the marble table by the door. 'What's this?'

'Iced tea, and don't say you don't like it until you've tried it.'

Tim's absence hung over them like a veil. *Just me and him,* Jude was thinking. *No friends or shops or television. Above all, no Tim.* She didn't want to ask, but she had to get it out of the way. 'So. What happened with Tim?'

Oliver stirred his tea, the lemon swirling, the ice tinkling against the glass. 'He just couldn't do it and I couldn't make him. He'd been madly excited about coming, about getting out of school early, but reality dawned when we got to the airport. Patti stood there looking like I was sucking the very blood from her veins, and when Tim realized he had to leave her, he cracked. After all the upheaval he's had this year, leaving his mum to go off to the unknown was beyond him. It was quite a performance – the two of them clinging to each other sobbing, and me not much better. That's when our family really broke apart, right there in the airport.'

'It must have been hard getting that flight.'

'Nigh on impossible.' Oliver frowned at his drink. 'Those two people used to be mine. They belonged to me and I belonged to them, and I'd rather be ten thousand miles away than watch them get along without me. Cowardly, I know.'

'But what are you going to do about Tim?'

'I'll see him when we go back at the end of August.'

'And you can't go any sooner because of me.'

'It isn't that simple.'

'It is. If it weren't for me, you could go home whenever you wanted, sleep on Stephen's floor and see lots of Tim.'

115

'That's as may be, but I have work to do and I can't go flitting about any longer. I've lived out of suitcases for three months. I need stability, same as you do. Besides, Patti's taking Tim to Spain in August.'

'But won't you miss him?'

'Jesus, Jude, don't ask such bloody stupid questions.'

'Sorry.'

'Anyway, enough about me. What happened with Thierry?'

'I did it over the phone.' She sipped her drink. 'It's bitter, isn't it?'

'Not when you get used to it. How'd he take it?'

'Not very well.'

'Regrets?'

She shook her head. 'Oliver, are you all right for money?'

'As long as I don't eat.'

'Seriously.'

'I will be. Jeremy's sale has almost gone through. Meanwhile, I'm living on *your* money.'

'Yeah, sure.'

'I do have an income, you know. Some people actually buy my books.'

'How's the new one going?'

'Good.' Oliver scratched his beard. 'Truth is, I'm working better than I have in years and, much as I hate to admit it, that's because Tim isn't here. I'd forgotten what it's like to be able to write whenever I want to and to be able to concentrate for hours on end. There are no interruptions, no arguments with Patti . . . What a price to pay for a good day's work, eh?'

'It isn't your fault.'

'Actually, it is.'

Jude hated this. How was she supposed to deal with a

childless father/dumped husband all on her own? What was she to do? A lizard scuttled across the flagstones. 'Ooh, lizard!'

Oliver glanced around the garden. 'I looked after Tim every day for six years. Every single day. And now I'm expected to . . .' it seemed an age before he added, 'endure this.'

Instinctively, Jude kissed his cheek. 'It's all right. I'll be such a pest, you won't have time to miss him.'

'Nor will you, I hope. Stephen's landing in on us in July and—'

'With Meredith?'

'Nope; she's going away with the girls. Wise woman.'

Jude's head spun. The dread of having to share a house with Stephen's girlfriend had been preoccupying her for weeks. Now it vanished as swiftly as if Oliver had blown it away. 'How long is he staying?'

'Three weeks, God help us.'

Jude was on the point of wilting with delight when Oliver added, 'And he's going to overlap with Sinéad.'

'Sinéad? Dad's Sinéad?'

'Yeah. She's coming out too.'

'God, you could have asked me – or am I just another visitor here?'

'Of course not, but what's the problem with Sinéad?'

'I just feel odd about her, all right? She'll bring back those awful memories.'

'Listen, Jude. You need someone in Ireland who could help out if something came up when I'm not around. Sinéad's a woman on her own. If you liked her, you could stay with her at half-term, go shopping and stuff.'

'Maybe I could even go sailing with her and get myself killed?'

117

'Come on, love. You have to let that go.' He put down his glass. 'Now, let's go shoot some rapids.'

'It's freezing!' Jude squealed.

Oliver had waded thigh-high into the river. He reached out to her. 'Come on.'

'I'll be swept away.'

'That's the general idea, but you can get out downstream.'

Jude continued to grumble – about the icy water, the stones, the unlikelihood of surviving the rapids – but Oliver cajoled her until she allowed him to lead her to the best spot for catching the current, which flowed between the two heaps of rubble which were once the foundations of the old bridge. The water gushed past, almost knocking her off her feet. She gripped Oliver's fingers.

He tried to shake her off. 'Let go. Let the river take you.'

'No.'

'You'll love it. It's shallow at first, so keep your knees up, then it gets deep.'

'You go first in case I can't get out.'

Oliver shook his head, swam into the current and went bobbing off down the river. Cautiously, Jude lowered herself into the crystal-clear water and swam only two strokes before being dragged into the flow. She was sucked through the chute between the rocks, tossed through sharp, choppy waves that whipped her face, but she giggled out loud as she was swept along. Oliver stood ready to catch her, but she swam into the shallows and got out before reaching him. 'Worth the angst?' he called.

Jude was on her feet, hobbling up the stony shore to do it again.

*

In such a gracious house, living alone with Oliver was not as bad as Jude had feared. There were irritations, of course – his tidiness was tiresome to someone who spent much of her life suppressing an inherent untidiness in a four-by-eight-foot cubicle – and there were embarrassments too. Jude loathed dealing with their amalgamated laundry, but could not allow Oliver to handle her personal items, and she found it impossible to conceal it when she was crippled with period pain. But Oliver was discreet and caring, and he went out of his way to make life pleasant for her.

Every morning when she went downstairs she found warm croissants, apricot jam, chocolate and fresh figs laid out on the table under the catalpa tree. Oliver always joined her for breakfast, then went back into his cavernous study while she skipped off to the beach. His working schedule was very different to what it had been when he was minding Tim. Jude had never seen him go at it so hard. Perhaps he was trying to distract himself, to hide amongst his words from the pains in his life, or maybe he just had a deadline. Either way, he started early every morning and worked even through the hottest, sleepiest part of the day until the late afternoon when he went for a swim. He would have worked all evening as well, Jude suspected, if she had not needed dinner, and his company.

The house was completely still while he worked, and the street too was quiet, apart from the rattle of an occasional tractor humping past, or the *klaxon* of the meat truck come to sell its wares. Jude had been dreading getting stuck out in the sticks with nothing to do and Landor initially lived up to her worst expectations. She thought her brain would implode in such tranquillity, but after a few days, she too became still. Every morning she lay in bed listening for every sound that was not of boarding school – a moped going past, the squeak of the gate as Oliver came back from the *boulangerie* and the clicking of wheels as he pushed his bike across the grass. She found the peacefulness comforting, not isolating, and she was never as bored as she, and Oliver, had feared, although it helped that she was an avid reader and an incurable sun-worshipper.

When the weather was overcast, she wrote e-mails or cycled along the country lanes, exploring. It was very green, this place; the low round hills thick with trees. Green, but not at all like Ireland. When it was hot, she lay on the shore in a heat-induced haze fantasizing about Stephen, until hunger drew her back to the house. After lunch, she read and snoozed for a while before returning to the beach, where Oliver joined her for an evening swim.

They both came to love Landor. He loved the sandstone buildings; the red tiled roofs, pitched high for winter snow-falls; the turrets and towers, the barns and wood stacks, the vineyards creeping up surrounding hills. Jude loved the chickens which ran across the road, their squeaking chicks in hot pursuit, and the great white goose, a dead ringer for Jemima Puddleduck, who occasionally graced the street to honk her displeasure at whomsoever had the temerity to pass. She loved opening her shutters every morning and seeing the old woman sitting outside her door across the road. She enjoyed cycling to the *laiterie* to get milk, shooing the chicks out of her way, and practising her French on the young man who worked there, decked out in his white rubber apron and boots. Above all, she loved the river, the way she became part of it – fluid, fast, cool – when it hurtled her along.

The village was certainly no hub of activity, but the campsite was filling up and there were always families on the shore, canoes on the water and enough going on to dismiss any feeling that she was stuck in a pastoral painting.

And yet hers had become a solitary existence – for almost four weeks her only extended conversations were with a middle-aged man who was mooning over his defunct marriage – but solitude suited her. How could it not, when she *was* solitary, and had no family? Besides, she had the company of her infatuation: Stephen absorbed her thoughts all day long.

Without television, the evenings sometimes dragged, but on those nights that did expand too much, when she and Oliver seemed to shrink and the house throbbed with emptiness, they went out for dinner at the local hotel, or in nearby towns like Arbois and Mouchard. Jude enjoyed being seen with Oliver. Stripped of his family, he had become more clearly defined to her; she was more than ever aware of his presence, his habits. There was an urbanity about him that made her feel terribly grown up. She liked the way he guided her through a crowd, knew what she wanted to eat without asking, and she loved that he listened to her, no matter what she had to say. But he was clearly struggling. He still looked like a man who had been winded, floored, and didn't know why. Sometimes he wore an expression of absolute perplexity; at other times he appeared to be in actual pain.

Every night, after Jude had gone to bed, he went outside with a glass of whisky and sat on a stone bench under a yew tree by the garden wall. It reminded Jude of the loneliness she'd seen in her father but, as with her dad, she kept away, certain that she could make no dint on it.

At the end of the first week of July, Jude looked into the freezer one evening and found they had run out of chocolate ice-cream. Life had been sailing past with such grace and decadence that this struck her as calamitous. She insisted

Oliver drive her to Mouchard before the shops closed.

'I don't even like ice-cream,' he grumbled on their way home.

'So who finished it? There was plenty left when I went to bed last night.'

He parked on the street outside the house. 'Are you suggesting I raided the freezer during the night?'

'Yes. You're a closet ice-cream fiend!'

They pushed open the gate, walked across the grass, and stopped dead. Their jaws dropped. Oliver searched for an appropriate curse, but none equalled the shock.

'Where on earth have you two been?'

They gaped at the figure squatting on their doorstep.

'How the hell did you get here?' said Oliver.

'Boats, trains, lifts.'

'But how did you find us?' asked Jude.

Lee stood up. 'The Reverend Mother – Sr Alfonsus, is it? – very kindly told me where you were. She thought it a splendid idea that I spend time with you.'

Oliver stepped past her to unlock the door. 'And where's the toyboy?'

'At home.' Lee followed him in, dragging her rucksack behind her.

In the kitchen, Oliver took a beer from the fridge and slammed the door. This was going to require careful handling. If there was one person who could undermine Jude, could throw her off balance just when she had achieved some kind of equilibrium, it was her own aunt.

Jude stood by the door, the tub of ice-cream under her arm.

Lee helped herself to a pear. 'Nice place you've got here,' she said, looking into the dining-room, 'but I suppose you two can afford it now.'

122

Oliver eyeballed her as he yanked open his can. Jude's skin registered the cold of the ice-cream. She took spoons from the drawer and went out to the living-room. Oliver followed and sank into the couch beside her. Jude felt sorry for him and sorry for herself and sorry for the lovely time they'd been having. There was nobody for whom Oliver felt greater antipathy, and it was her fault Lee turned up everywhere he went. She offered him a spoon. He shook his head. He needed a cigarette, not ice-cream. He needed his wife.

Lee ambled in, munching on the pear. She hadn't changed. Her hair was stringy, her jeans and top looked as if she'd slept in them for weeks, but in spite of her rough lifestyle, she looked younger than her thirty-five years. Jude could think of only one thing: Stephen had once expressed interest in Lee. What if he fell for her now? She cleared her throat. 'Em, how long are you staying?'

'Dunno.'

'No job to get back to, I suppose,' said Oliver.

'I did have a job – in a pub in Skibbereen – but I threw it in when I had enough money to get here, so I'm a free agent.'

Oliver raised his can to drink. She knew, so well, how to wind him up.

'But Stephen's arriving next week,' said Jude. 'There won't be room.'

Oliver shot her a look. Pleading lack of space was a bit limp.

'Oh goody. The lovely Stephen!'

'And Sinéad's coming too, and there are only four bedrooms.'

'Who's Sinéad?' asked Lee. 'One of your women, Oliver?'

'She was Daddy's fiancée,' Jude lied.

'Michael was engaged?'

123

Jude sucked on her spoon. Oliver drank. They'd thrown her.

'But then I have to meet her! She might have been my sister-in-law!'

'Like you cared for your last sister-in-law,' Oliver muttered.

'Anyway, there's plenty of space. This place is massive. Mind if I look around?' She got up and left the room.

Oliver put a foot on the low table. 'Damn, damn, damn.'

'Cheer up,' Jude pleaded.

'Give me one good reason.'

She couldn't. She was crestfallen; her lovely French holiday had taken on a whole new aspect. What would she do if Stephen fell for her crazy aunt?

'I loathe the way she uses Michael to get around me,' said Oliver. 'She knows I can't say no to her because of him. I always pay her off in the end.'

'But she wouldn't have got here if she needed money.'

'That's what worries me. What the hell is she after this time?'

The following morning, Jude was blearily crossing the landing when Oliver came along and hustled her into the bathroom. 'Get Lee out of my face!'

'What?'

'She's been hanging around the dining-room since nine o'clock this morning, so get her out of here, please.'

'Why should I get stuck with her?'

'Because she's *your* aunt,' he whispered.

'*You've* known her longer!'

'Jude, I have work to do and if you know what's good for us, you'll remove her from this house *pronto*!'

As they stepped out of the bathroom, Lee came along the

corridor. Her eyebrows shot up. 'Goodness,' she said, sweeping past. 'Cosy.'

Jude took her down to the river.

'So,' said Lee, pulling her dress over her head, 'who's the guy?'

Jude was too gobsmacked to answer. Her aunt was wearing a minimalist bikini, and her figure, usually draped in baggy clothes, could carry it. 'What?'

'Who'd Patti run off with?'

'Nobody we know.' Never having perceived Lee as a threat, Jude had never before noticed the long legs, slim waist and impressive breasts. She was as gorgeous as Michael had been good-looking, while Jude's only physical claim to her father was his hazel eyes. She mostly took after her mother, who had been dark and slight, and if there was any family resemblance between herself and Lee, she couldn't see it. All she could see, as she glowered at her aunt from behind sunglasses, was that she didn't stand a chance. Stephen would love it. He'd throw himself into that cleavage as soon as he arrived.

It wasn't only the bikini that bothered Jude; it was the attitude. Over the next few days, Lee flaunted herself as she never had before, wandering around the house in a T-shirt or the smallest available towel. She had always scorned her appearance, but now she was clearly shaving her armpits and legs, and she brushed her hair at length in the garden, swishing it about like a model advertising shampoo. As it grew blonder, her skin grew darker. Jude couldn't understand it. How did Lee manage to remain so taut when she had spent half her life trudging around the world's sweatiest places being infected with parasites and infectious diseases? Shouldn't she look a bit *ravaged*? A bit *old*? Jude fell into despair. All her hopes for Stephen were being sapped only days before his arrival.

There were other marked changes in Lee. She wasn't quite the slob she had been. She tidied up; she cooked; she carried travellers' cheques. Even Oliver was forced to admit that the settled life in Ireland seemed to have improved her.

It had improved her so much that within four days, Jude had fallen comprehensively into her aunt's shadow and saw herself only in the worst possible light. She was flat-chested, spotty and pale, and the more Oliver treated her like a daughter, the more Stephen would see her as a child. She was so quiet at dinner one evening that Oliver and Lee were forced into conversation, which became quite cordial when a second bottle of wine was opened. Doom and gloom of the widest proportions invaded every corner of Jude's psyche. It had been insanity to think Stephen might notice her. At only ten o'clock, she went to bed and fell into a deep, dejected sleep.

She woke the following morning at nine. Oliver wasn't up yet, so she decided to bring him tea; she desperately needed to have a good bitch about Lee, and Oliver would never guess that her increased ire had anything to do with his brother.

With a mug in each hand, she pushed down the handle of his bedroom door with her elbow and nudged it open. When she stepped inside the room, she looked up to see him lying with his back to her, naked. She stopped so suddenly that tea spilt on the rug. Blood rushed to her face, her jaw clamped shut, and when she stepped backwards to get out of the room, Lee popped up behind him and said, 'Do you mind?'

*

Jude ran through the village barefoot. Humiliation, anger and embarrassment raced along with her. The chickens scattered. Two black cats jumped off their usual perch on the stone wall. This was beyond redemption. She could never forgive him this. *Never*.

She crossed the blue steel bridge, turned into the tree-lined avenue that ran alongside the river, and kept on going until she found a spot on the river-bank where, concealed by bushes, she sat down and gathered her arms and knees around her. How could she face either of them again? How could Oliver be such a hypocrite? Such a bloody fool?

It didn't take him long to find her. He had her in sight from the moment he reached the bridge, and when he came alongside her, he stood with his hands on his thighs, catching his breath. 'Jude?'

'Go away.'

'I'm sorry.'

'Go away.'

'Jude, ease up. We had too much to drink last night and things got out of hand. It wasn't a smart move on my part, but I didn't mean to upset you.'

She kept her head buried in her arms, her legs crossed under them. She couldn't look at him. Finding anyone in bed with someone was awkward enough – but Oliver with Lee!

'Sweetheart?'

Jude snapped. 'It makes me sick! You're such a hypocrite! As soon as she came along flaunting herself, you couldn't resist, could you?'

Oliver couldn't argue with that. 'Like I said, things got out of hand.'

'I thought you had some respect for people.'

'I do.'

'Not for her, and certainly not for me!'

'Look, she's been throwing herself at me all week. So I succumbed. It's no great sin, is it? It's been a while, you know.'

Jude blushed. She did not want to know about his sex life, or lack of it. 'That's no excuse.'

'Maybe not, but I don't happen to need an excuse.' He raised his eyebrows at her. She cupped her palms around her eyes to shut him out, but he held out her wrists and made her look at him. 'I'm sorry you walked in this morning and I'm sorry I slept with your aunt. I have indeed been hypocritical and I thank you for pointing this out. What more do you want from me?'

Jude pulled away. She was hungry. She wanted croissants, she wanted everything to be normal again, but how was it to be done?

Oliver sat down. 'Your dad would love this,' he said ruefully. 'I'm in trouble with his daughter because I slept with his sister – and it's his fault I got lumbered with you two in the first place.'

Jude stared at the river.

'Christ,' he muttered. 'I must have been out of my sodding mind. She'll eat me up and spit me out.'

'Serves you right.'

'Oh pity, please.'

'Tell her it was a mistake and make her go away.' But as she spoke, another possibility occurred to Jude: if Lee continued to sleep with Oliver, Stephen would be safe. This thought helped towards her rehabilitation with her wayward guardian. She glanced at him and a small trace of sympathy swept through her. She knew he got lonely late at night.

'Lee isn't that easy to get rid of,' he said.

'You should have thought of that beforehand.'

'All right, all right. Enough righteous condemnation. I thought you were my friend?'

With a little smile, Jude relented. 'I am.'

Over breakfast, Lee was irrepressibly cheerful and made contact with Oliver at every opportunity, which so irritated Jude that she left the table as soon as she had finished. She went into the hall, stopped just inside the door, and listened.

'Let's go out,' Lee was saying. 'We need time alone together.'

Oh no you don't, thought Jude.

'No,' said Oliver. 'We don't. Last night was a once-off, Lee. It can't happen again.' He got up and went into the house – and found Jude standing inside the door. She hadn't heard him coming. They stared at each other, then Jude scampered up the staircase, with Oliver at her heels. He followed her right into her room and came at her in a fury. 'Don't *ever* do that again!' he hissed, shaking his finger in her face, before slamming out of the room.

Jude threw herself on her bed. It wasn't even eleven yet, but she'd been to hell and back already. Family life had to be better than this, she thought, tossing from one side to the other, her thoughts sorely cornered between two dreadful slide shows. On the one hand, Oliver's expression when he caught her eavesdropping kept flashing at her, but any attempt to dislodge that image left her open to something worse – the sight of him lying in bed with Lee bouncing up behind him like a jack-in-the-box. She would never get over the mortification of seeing them like that.

Some time later, Lee let herself into Jude's room. She leaned against the door and said, 'I don't know what you said to Oliver this morning, but I'd rather you kept your nose out of my business.'

'Don't carry out your business right under my nose then.'

'I don't have any choice, do I? Everywhere he goes, you go.'

'Tough.'

Lee took a deep breath. 'Jude, do me a favour. Don't attempt to come between me and Oliver again.'

Like a cat before a fight, Jude's nose puckered.

'I've waited a long time for this,' said her aunt. 'About nineteen years in fact.' She opened the door and added without turning, 'I've been in love with Oliver since I was sixteen, so don't get in the way. Please.'

11

Stephen groaned with pleasure. 'Judy, Judy! This is orgasmic. What is it?'

'Comté – the Jura's most famous cheese. The pâtés are local too.'

'Wonderful! You were right, Ol. This is the place to live.'

'Glutton.' Oliver stood up. 'I'm going back to work.'

'Eh?' said Stephen. 'I've only just arrived!'

'You may be on holiday, but I'm not.'

'Why don't you two go for a swim?' suggested Lee. 'I'll clear up.'

They didn't need persuading; as soon as Stephen had changed, he and Jude headed off to the river. But Lee had no intention of clearing up. Instead, she had a shower, wrapped herself in a towel, and went to the dining-room. Oliver was at his computer, typing. She perched on the edge of the table beside him. Without looking at her, or even at the legs so strategically placed, he shook his head. 'No way. Not a good idea.' She swung her legs on to the table and lay on her side, facing him. 'I told you,' he said. 'It isn't going to happen again.' He typed something. Lee slid along the table, elbowing his keyboard out of the way, and began unbuttoning his shirt. He grabbed her hand. 'I said *no*.' She smiled and leaned forward to kiss him. He might have had some chance if she hadn't discarded the towel at that point, but in the face of such temptation, he capitulated.

Stephen followed Jude across the stones. 'Lee clearing up? Is she ill?'

Jude threw down her towel. 'I have never been so glad to see you in my entire life!'

'Aw, Judy. I never knew you cared.'

'My name is Jude. And that's not what I mean, you oaf. You'll never believe what's been going on around here.'

'What?'

'Lee and Oliver.'

Stephen pulled off his T-shirt. His skin was pale and the line of dark hair which ran from his navel to his waistband made Jude tingle. 'What about them?'

'They slept together.'

Shading his eyes, he squinted at her. 'You've had too much sun, Judy.'

'I'm not kidding.'

His eyes darted about, an increasingly comic expression spreading across his face. 'Oliver and Lee? Are you serious?'

'Yes.'

'Bloody hell. He's that desperate?'

'Desperate? I thought you fancied her?'

'She's gorgeous, but that doesn't mean I'd sleep with her. It'd be like making love to an igloo. Are they still at it?'

'No, but it's really awkward. She keeps trying to get rid of me and he keeps using me as a gooseberry. I thought you'd never get here. She has serious designs on him too. She told me she's in love with him.'

'What? This is getting better!'

132

'It's not funny!'

'It's hysterical. Have you told Ol?'

'No way. I'm not getting any more involved than I already am.'

'Yeah, but. Forewarned is forearmed and all that. If he knew, he wouldn't risk messing around with her again.'

'He's not going to mess around with her again. He's so relieved he got away with it once, he wouldn't take another chance.'

Jude tried everything. She tied her hair up to make her neck long and left it down to swish it around; she exposed as much tanned flesh as was feasible during the day and wore sexy little numbers at night; she held herself well, didn't giggle too often, and tried to sound mature every time she opened her mouth. And even though the age-gap was a stumbling-block, she wouldn't accept that it gave her no chance. She looked good, better than she ever had, and she was determined to make it work for her.

In the end, it wasn't the tan or the skimpy clothes that did it. It was the rapids.

Stephen was like a child every time they went swimming, but so was every other person who allowed themselves to be swept down that river. Old men did it, pregnant women did it, children in arm-bands and multiple inflatable toys did it: alligators, dinosaurs and bananas carried their owners over the gush. Every day, a steady stream of swimmers paddled cautiously into the torrent, then slid through the deep middle channel, where they were tossed about in the turmoil before being carried smoothly along as far as they wanted to go.

Stephen was mad for it. Within days he had acquired a large inner tube which carried him over the rapids in style.

133

Then he noticed, beyond the remaining plinth of one of the old bridge's uprights, a backwater where the river was still and warm. It took him two attempts to swim his way out of the current to reach this eye in the storm, but when he urged Jude to join him, she couldn't escape the pull. She kept sweeping past Stephen until, on another attempt, he caught her hand. He swung her around in a great arc, dragged her into the backwater and almost into his arms. She knew, then, that she would get what she wanted. The next time they did it, she put her arm around his neck when he caught her, but, like a shot-putter, he whirled her around and released her back into the current. So much for romance.

Stephen picked his own moment. The following afternoon, when Jude was reading in the hammock, he leaped in on top of her.

'Ouf! What are you doing? Get off!'

'Judy, I thought you cared?'

'My name is Jude. Get off me, Stephen!' She tried to push him away and couldn't believe she was doing so. He found this hugely amusing and lay over her, grinning. The hammock wobbled. When he tried to kiss her, she turned away. 'Stop! Oliver'll kill us.'

He kissed her neck. 'Oliver's out. He won't know.'

'I'll tell him. Besides, you're far too old for me.'

'Am I? What age are you?'

'Seventeen.'

'That's nothing. I've been out with a girl of sixteen.'

'When?'

'When I was fourteen, but—'

Stephen hadn't stopped smiling since he'd jumped in. He had dimples in each cheek, but at close range the eight years between them were all too obvious. There was nothing soft or adolescent about Stephen's stubble – this was well-

134

established beard – and his skin was different, not tougher exactly, but more worn. In short, he was a man and Jude had only ever been with boys. 'Stephen, get out. We can't.'

He kissed her collarbone. 'But we are.'

'What about Meredith?'

'I'm on holidays from Meredith. Come on, Judy. I know you want to. You're only marginally less obvious than Lee is with Ol.'

She blushed, spat, struggled. 'You conceited—'

'So let's enjoy it. I mean, hey, this is the land of love.'

His face was becoming familiar again.

'I won't push it,' he said, pulling back, 'but—'

Gathering all her courage, Jude kissed him before he retreated any further.

'Ah,' he said. 'That's what I thought.'

Over succeeding days, the two couples waltzed around one another, enjoying furtive sexual encounters where possible. Oliver and Lee took their sex in the mornings when the younger pair were asleep, but Stephen and Jude had to go further afield, and Jude soon discovered that Landor was an ideal place for love. There was nothing more romantic than squeezing on to the inflatable tyre together, all wet and chilly and oily with sunscreen, and pushing off into the current. Beyond the turbulence, they often drifted downstream to a willow hanging over the bank, beneath which they could lie undetected, their kisses deep, their slimy bodies pressed together. Sometimes they went cycling, past orchards and beehives and vast fields full of clicking grasshoppers, and found deserted hideaways along the river. Jude took Stephen to one of her favourite places – a flat rock that jutted out on a bend in the Loue – where they sat and drank in the still afternoon. They saw an otter there, his cheeky bottom curving into the water as he dived.

Oliver never bothered them. He was at home, in the dim dining-room, working. It clearly never occurred to him that Jude might arouse his brother's interest. To him, she was a child. This both annoyed and suited her. As long as he was not even suspicious, they could do more or less as they pleased.

But these stealthy gropings couldn't last. One day, Jude and Stephen cycled a long way out of the village and ended up at a fork in the river, where it branched off behind a small island. They were in the depths of the countryside. The tributary was shallow, golden, its waters gushing over boulders as it went off in its own direction. In contrast, the Loue was green and broad, its high banks covered in oak trees. With only crickets and bees and cows impinging on their seclusion, Stephen wanted to skinny-dip, but Jude demurred. She wasn't ready to see him prancing around in the altogether. 'Canoeists might come down the river,' she said. So they swam in their togs, then sunbathed on the island. Jude was in heaven. She adored Stephen. When he touched her, it was as if her insides were being scorched.

'By the way,' he said sleepily, 'they're at it again.'

'What? Who?'

'Oliver and Lee. They're having it off.'

Jude sat up. 'How do you know?'

'I know our Ol.'

'*Feck!* Why don't they own up to it?'

'Why don't *we*?'

'Good question,' said Jude.

'Because he'd kill me, that's why. Having my way with his protégée? He'd have my balls.'

'It's none of his business.'

'Right. And it's none of our business if they're bonking either.'

'Except that he can't stand her!'

'You sure about that?'

Jude shook her head. 'I don't get it. How can he fancy her and hate her at the same time?'

'Lust.' Stephen pulled her down and lay over her. 'The most unlikely relationships can easily turn to lust,' he said, removing her bikini top. There was intent in his eyes.

'Stephen – I don't want to go all the way.'

'Fine.' He ran his hand up her leg – and stopped. 'What did you say?'

'I'm not going the whole way. I never have.'

He pulled a face. 'So *le Belge* wasn't up to much then?'

'Thierry was a respectable boy who wouldn't put pressure on a girl.'

'Ah. Like myself.' He nuzzled her breast.

'But you can have my virginity when I'm done with it.'

'Great.'

'I'm just not done with it yet.'

'Fine.'

'Although—'

'Jesus, Judy, would you ever stop talking?'

Oliver woke early. Lee was creeping into his bed again. She always took him at his most vulnerable, in the early morning, when he was sleepy and easily turned on. This time, increasingly bothered by the fact that he was allowing this unsavoury affair to continue, he resisted her advances and lay with his back to her. His attempts to find common ground with her had repeatedly failed, yet she continued to overwhelm him; she was an extraordinary lover, and he only wished that he could like her.

She was not easily shrugged off. Leaning over his shoulder, she ran her tongue along his lower lip. It was exquisite; he kissed her and tried to infuse it with affection. He had never been so repeatedly seduced, so well taken, and he had nothing left to fight it with, least of all the will to do so. She kissed his chest, his stomach. Oliver abandoned all remorse. Lee was having her way with him again and he really didn't care.

He didn't care, that is, until later, when they were in the bathroom and he heard Lee mutter, 'Oops,' followed by a little pop. When she went back into the bedroom, he took her packet of contraceptive pills from the cabinet. Beside the one she had just taken, there were three she hadn't.

A chill so cold that he might have swallowed frozen nitrogen ran through Oliver's veins. He followed Lee into his room, held up the packet and said, '"Oops"?'

She was getting back into bed. 'Yeah, I forgot a few.'

'Jesus, Lee!'

'Relax. I'm hardly going to ovulate after missing a couple.'

'Of course you could! Missing one day can throw the whole thing out. For Christ's sake, what the hell are you playing at?'

'I forgot, all right?'

'No, it isn't fucking all right! What are you? Seventeen? You don't know how these things work?'

'I didn't see you using anything.'

He held up the packet. 'I thought we *were* using something!'

'Oh, calm down. So I might get pregnant. Maybe I'd like that.'

Oliver almost choked. 'And maybe *I* wouldn't! There are enough complications in my life without you taking bloody

chances like this!' He went to the window. He couldn't
grasp it. In his entire life, he had never been so unutterably
careless.

'We can use condoms for a bit,' said Lee.

'Not bloody likely.'

'Why not?'

He came back to the bed. 'Look, we have to call a halt.
This whole thing has been a mistake.'

'A mistake? You've made love to me over and over and
now you —'

'We've had *sex*.'

She inhaled sharply. 'It meant nothing to you?'

He sat down beside her. After a moment, he shook his
head.

'So it was all about – what? Your own gratification?'

'Mutual gratification, I thought. You have a lover and I'm
on the rebound, for God's sake. I'm in neutral. I thought
that was bloody obvious.'

'I wanted to give you a kick-start.'

'The kick was very pleasant, thanks, but I don't want to
get started. Besides, sneaking around like this, well, it isn't
very . . . wholesome, is it?'

'Wholesome?' she scoffed.

'I have Jude to think about.'

'She doesn't know.'

'She will do, if we carry on, and she's already been
compromised once.'

The tenderness that had recently crept into Lee's features
vanished. 'I don't understand how she can have anything to
do with this.'

'No, but then you've never understood anything about
Jude, have you? If you had, you'd see this affair is like a
double slap in the face for her. If I'm to do the job *you*

should be doing, I need Jude's trust and respect, and this isn't the way to get either.'

Lee sat forward. 'I won't be tossed aside for some teenager!'

' "Some teenager"?' Oliver stood up, exasperated. 'She's your niece! What *is* your problem with her? She's never done a damn thing to you!'

Lee lay back on the pillows. 'She has the exclusive attention of the one person I love.'

He looked at her askance. '*Love?*'

She turned her cool grey eyes on him. 'Yes. I've only ever loved two people. Just you, and Michael.'

'And yourself, let's not forget.' Oliver pulled on some clothes. 'This is over, Lee, not because of *some teenager*, but because I don't like the way you operate. I never have. I can't even be sure that an "accidental" pregnancy wouldn't suit you – you probably figured it would give you grounds to live off me for the rest of your life!'

He thought he saw her blush slightly. 'Fuck, that's it, isn't it? You've been trying to make a living out of me.'

'Of course not.'

He could not believe her, and it made him spin with rage. He grabbed his keys and pulled open the door.

'Now that you're done, I suppose you want me to leave?' Lee said.

'I suppose I do, but you're not going anywhere until I know whether you're pregnant or not.' He had no means to stop her, but he knew she wouldn't go. He knew now that he was the draw. The compulsion. 'And for the record,' he added, 'if I'd known you fancied yourself in love with me, I would never have touched you.'

He hurtled down the corridor, bumped into Jude, shoved

her out of the way, and stormed out to the car. As he started up, she hopped in beside him. 'Out, Jude.'

'Not until I know why you knocked me over.'

'Skid!' he roared.

'No! Wherever you're going, I'm coming. Otherwise you'll crash the car, you're so het up!'

Oliver hit the accelerator. 'You're a fucking pain in the backside sometimes.'

'And your language is the pits.'

He hurled the car around the quiet country roads, an Eric Clapton tape blaring. It was drizzling. In the fields, the sunflower shoots drooped. Jude held her tongue. She even tolerated her growing hunger for some distance, but could not wilfully control her bladder.

'I need to pee,' she said at last, 'and I haven't had breakfast.'

'Bugger.'

'What is eating you, anyway?'

'Me. I'm eating myself.'

He took her to a *pâtisserie* in the square in Arbois, which served drinks on the pavement under an arcade. Jude had hot chocolate and a *pain au chocolat*, while Oliver fumed over an espresso.

'Patti asked to speak to you again last night,' he said. 'Every single time they phone, she asks for you, and every single time you refuse. How long do you intend to keep this up?'

'Don't start taking your bad mood out on me.'

Next to them, a young mother who looked like Audrey Hepburn leafed through a *Paris Match* while her small daughter sipped Orangina and gazed at the cakes displayed in the window.

'So.' Jude daintily patted the corners of her mouth with a napkin. 'Had a lovers' tiff, have you?'

Oliver sighed. He could thank Stephen, no doubt, for spilling the beans.

'So much for the "once-off,"' she added.

'You can be a sarcastic little madam when it suits you.'

She raised her eyebrows and munched on her *pain*.

'All right,' he said, 'so I've been a complete bloody imbecile, but I'm not proud of it and for what it's worth, I've called the whole thing off.'

Jude put her finger to her chin. 'Now, where have I heard that before?'

'Cut it out.' He looked into his espresso, stirring the thick, sticky brew as if seeking to dissipate it, much as he was trying to dissipate the glutinous whirl in his head. Having a child with Lee was too horrible a prospect to contemplate, yet he had allowed it to become a possibility. He shivered.

'So she's leaving?' said Jude.

'Not yet.'

'Why not? God, how much longer do we have to put up with her?'

Best avoid that one, Oliver thought. 'However long it is, I want you to keep clear of her. Her feelings about you are more warped than I thought, and now that I've ended it, she'll probably blame you, so . . .'

'Of course she will. She thinks I have some kind of hold over you.'

Oliver smiled suddenly. 'You do.'

'Why does she hate me so much, anyway?'

'She doesn't hate you, she bears grudges, big time, and she can't forgive you for coming between her and Michael. She didn't get on with her mother, so he was the absolute centre

142

of her universe and he totally indulged her, as you know. Then Catherine came along and Michael was so smitten he dropped Lee like a hot iron and never even turned to see where she'd landed. While he wallowed in his great love affair, his spoilt little sister was left floundering in its wake.'

'Careful,' said Jude. 'I'm almost feeling sorry for her.'

'Yeah, well, even I felt for her then. Michael had cosseted her to make up for their dad walking out, but then he abandoned her too and he never even saw the correlation. She cut a sad little figure when she went away that first time. She was only trying to get his attention, but it backfired – Michael was delighted she'd finally become independent of him. Trouble is, she became so independent she's almost a degenerate now, and she knows it.'

'That's harsh.'

'Well, I'm feeling harsh. You know, after your mother died, Lee came back – not out of love, not to help him, but because she thought she'd be top dog again. Only she hadn't reckoned on you. Your dad was utterly absorbed with you, and when Lee showed no interest, offered no help, they fell out, badly, so she took off again and only ever came home when she needed something. In short, her life's been generally messed up and she blames everyone except herself: Michael, Catherine, even you. And now she also resents your relationship with me, so I am henceforth going to make sure she keeps right out of your life. I only wish I'd done so sooner.'

'I'm not afraid of her.'

'*I* am. And she's not done with me yet,' he muttered. He knocked back the last of his coffee, looked at Jude and said, 'So, what is it with you and Stephen?'

She couldn't control the rush of blood to her face, but

managed to stop her eyes from propelling themselves out of their sockets. 'Humph?'

'You can't have thought I didn't know? And you can't have imagined I'd be pleased about it either. He's almost nine years older than you and he has a girlfriend. It isn't very attractive, Jude.'

It was cool, it was calm, and it was entirely damning. No amount of rage on his part could have so reduced her.

'I figured you were brighter than this,' he went on. 'You know very well what a shallow bastard he can be.'

Jude's mortification turned to anger. 'Like you, you mean?'

His eyes held hers. Ice blue. 'My behaviour with Lee does not reflect the way I treat women, whereas Stephen—'

'Can be a real shit. Right. So how come I'm the one who's getting stick? Why don't you corner him instead?'

'I intend to. But Stephen can do what he bloody well likes. You, on the other hand, cannot.'

'I can so!'

'Jude, you're having some sort of fling with an older man who happens to be in a relationship. It would be negligent of me not to talk you out of it.'

'That's rich.'

'You've had your say about my mistakes, now I'm having mine about yours. Fortunately, in view of your age and situation, my view carries more weight.'

'I hate when you talk down to me.'

'And I hate when you make me. How far has this gone?'

'As if I'd tell *you* that!'

Oliver leaned towards her. 'Tell me this then: who are you going to run to when he goes back to Meredith? And who'd bail you out if you got pregnant? Somehow, I don't think it'd be Stephen.'

'Pregnant?' she hissed. 'I'm not that stupid!'

The woman at the next table looked up from her *Paris Match*. Understood English, no doubt. If there was one thing Oliver loathed about being the divorced guardian of a teenage girl, it was the incorrect assumptions he so often read in people's eyes. As it was, the people in the village thought he was a cradle-snatcher. He lowered his voice. 'You might not be that stupid, but you could get your heart broken. Messing around with someone else's boyfriend is a risky business. Honestly, Jude, you must have run into this blind.'

'I did not. I've wanted it to happen for ages.'

Oliver closed one eye. 'So that's what happened to Thierry. How did I miss that?'

'I made sure you did.'

'And don't you care about Meredith?'

'I've never met her.'

'Charming.'

'Anyway, why is it one rule for me and another for you? Lee has a boyfriend too.'

His eyes narrowed. 'There's only so much lip I'm going to take from you, young lady. You know very well what the difference is: about nineteen years.' He moved his seat closer to her. 'Listen to me, Jude. You're leaving yourself wide open. You may think the age-gap doesn't make a difference, but I'm here to tell you it does. Stephen's been around. He's experienced, and you're not. Yet. You look bloody marvellous at the moment, I can see that, but I don't think Stephen much cares about what'll happen when he leaves here. And I do. I'd hate to see you get hurt.'

'I won't get hurt. It's just a bit of fun.'

'How much fun?'

She looked out across the grey square. It was raining heavily now.

145

'How much fun has it been, Jude? How far has this gone?'

'Leave me *alone*.'

The woman looked up again.

Oliver sat back. 'I can't do that. Stephen's not right for you, not by the longest possible shot, and I'm going to keep on reminding you of that until you get sense.'

12

Their relationship sank to an all-time low. Oliver tried to be fair, but Jude was like a snake, hissing and spitting at every opportunity. It didn't help either of them that Stephen managed to remain neutral. He refused to endorse Jude's spleen or to heed Oliver's warnings, because as long as Oliver had to work, there was nothing he could do to stop the affair from continuing.

It continued in earnest. By day, Stephen and Jude went out driving. They walked in the Forêt de Chaux, the oldest oak wood in Europe, visited the Cascades du Hérisson, and drove to Besançon, where they toured the canals in a glass-topped *bateau-mouche* and walked hand-in-hand through cobbled streets. Jude felt entirely adult. She had a man and he had a car, his own car, and he earned a salary and had plenty of cash. Like a *bona fide* girlfriend, she helped him choose expensive, continental shirts in a men's shop and was gracious when he bought her a handbag she couldn't put down. They bought *gaufres* smothered in hot chocolate sauce from a salesman in a back street, then sat in a café writing postcards like an old married couple. And since her education had also been extended to the bedroom, Jude believed there was no more growing up for her to do.

The first time Stephen had come to her room at night, she had thought him crazy.

'Don't worry,' he said, lifting her nightshirt over her head. 'Oliver would be a very suspect guardian if he were to come into your room during the night. Anyway, he sleeps like a hibernating mole.' He took off his boxer shorts and got in beside her.

Jude lay rigid. This was a first.

A door opened in the corridor. Stephen ducked under the sheet.

'Like he wouldn't know you were there if he burst in!' Jude giggled. 'Wait till I tell them about this in school.'

Stephen re-emerged. 'School. God, I'm in bed with a schoolgirl.'

'Bet you'd fancy me in my uniform.'

'Bet I would, too.' He stroked her hip. 'You are so unbelievably gorgeous.'

'Stephen . . . why aren't you pressurizing me . . . I mean, how can you put up with less than . . . you know?'

'I'm not in a position to pressurize you. Not when I'm involved with someone else. And you are quite young really. I also value my life.' He kissed her. 'Besides, I won't be left wanting.'

Nor was he. Over succeeding nights he introduced her to intimacies, the pleasures of which she could never have guessed at. With Thierry, heavy petting had always been enough, but with Stephen Jude discovered the hard ache of longing and in its resolution relinquished modesties she no longer cared for. He sensitized her, sensualized her, and although she enjoyed the ease and irreverence of his personality, she didn't actually care what he said or did as long as she could gaze at the almost black irises of his eyes and feel his long fingers running over her. This alone was enough to satisfy her, which is why she never made demands, never whined for promises that Meredith was history. To be wanted was enough.

With nights and days so pleasantly spent, Jude found the evenings tiresome, because Stephen's only interest then was cooking up the best French ingredients while chatting to his brother over a good wine. Jude continued to be crisp with Oliver, who was too preoccupied with his own concerns to sort it out, while Lee was hanging around like a wounded prisoner. The affair over, her old persona re-emerged. Her hair grew stringy, the bikini sank to the bottom of her rucksack, and her characteristic, if mercenary, cheerfulness expired without trace.

Into this strained assembly came the innocent Sinéad, delighted to escape the stresses of running a business and thrilled to find herself in France. But arriving in Landor was like stepping into an overcrowded lift. The atmosphere in the house was taut. Jude was grumpier than ever, Oliver's charm had flagged, and Stephen, although well into his twenties, was evidently up to something with the teenage Jude. It was all rather distasteful, and within two days, Sinéad longed to return to the easy frenzy of her shop. The worst bit was that she had to share a room with a bedraggled woman who scarcely spoke; that this person was her beloved Michael's sister was incomprehensible.

On their way to the river one afternoon, she tackled Oliver. 'I wish you'd tell me what's causing the collective bad mood around here.'

He laughed. 'Let's see. Lee isn't speaking to anyone because I won't sleep with her; Jude won't speak to me because I won't let her sleep with Stephen; and I'm peeved with Stephen because I know he'd sleep with Jude given half the chance. Stephen, however, remains unfazed by all of the above.'

Sinéad couldn't think of a single thing to say.

'I'm no good at this lark, Sinéad. Sr Al was right. I've exposed Jude to all the worst influences. She'd be better off with some nice family in Dublin.'

The street was empty, hot. The cats sat on the wall, like sphinxes, watching them pass. Jemima Puddleduck honked.

'I swear, if I had ever dreamt Stephen would get to Jude,' Oliver went on, 'I'd never have let him come here. I can't afford to fall out with her – she's going into sixth year, she needs all the support she can get – but if she goes off the deep end about Stephen, we're sunk. She's already furious with me for trying to intervene, and if he drops her, she'll never forgive me. I can't win.'

'Can't you explain all this to Stephen?'

'Ach, I've tried, but he sees Jude having a lark and he reckons that's no harm. And maybe he's right. He takes Jude as she is, here and now, whereas I always see where she's been and worry the hell out of where that might take her.'

'Maybe you're going through that fatherly thing too – you know, when dads realize their little girl isn't quite so little any more? That other men —'

'Yeah, yeah, and it isn't made any easier when the other man is your own brother.'

They walked some way across the bridge, then stopped to look over. Stephen and Jude were frolicking in the back-water. He unhooked her bikini top and threw it into the current; with a screech, Jude swam after it. Oliver turned away.

Sinéad watched them. 'You don't think—'

'I hope not.'

'You trust him?'

'Barely. I've had bloody matchsticks in my eyes staying up until they're both asleep, but I feel like a matron in a boarding school. I really hate this guardianship business. You can't give as much leeway as a parent and you don't *get* as much leeway as a parent. It's thankless. It's like being handed a bubble that mustn't burst.'

Sinéad took his arm as they walked on. 'An hour ago, I was wishing I hadn't come, but maybe Michael, way up there or wherever he is, thought you needed some moral support? I'll play gooseberry this evening. You get an early night.'

Stephen and Jude had also planned an early night. Not long after dinner, they both claimed exhaustion and went to their respective rooms.

Sitting at the table under the catalpa, Lee peeled an apricot. 'Got you fooled, haven't they?'

Oliver looked over the candles. 'Sorry?'

'He goes to her room every night.'

Oliver stood up so suddenly that Sinéad jumped. He knocked over a chair as he headed for the door, then stopped, put his hands on the door jamb and stood for a moment. He came back, placed both palms on the table and leaned into Lee's face. 'You have outstayed your welcome in my home and in my life. I want you to leave tomorrow. And if I were you, I'd think twice about ever darkening my threshold again, pregnant or otherwise.'

Sinéad gasped.

'Relax. I'm not pregnant. Thanks be to *Jayzuz*.'

Oliver stared at her. 'Are you sure? Absolutely sure?'

Sucking on the apricot, Lee nodded.

His head dropped between his shoulders. 'Well,' he said,

151

after a moment, 'thanks for keeping me informed.' He strode into the house.

'Coffee?' he asked, when Sinéad followed him into the kitchen. 'I'm all out of champagne.'

She snatched the coffee jar from his hand. 'If you don't have the sense to use contraception, what are the chances your brother will?'

'See, now *you're* losing faith. And with good reason.'

'Look, this is the tough part, Oliver. You have to get it right. She's barely seventeen. What are you going to do about these trysts?'

He took the jar back. 'I'm going to do the only thing I can without alienating Jude in the process. I'm going to do what Patti would have done.'

In a happy blur of desire, Jude listened as Oliver and Sinéad called goodnight to each other. Twenty minutes later, her door quietly opened and she pushed back the sheet, but instead of getting in beside her, Stephen crashed to the ground with a thud and Jude heard a great splash of water.

Oliver's shape appeared in the doorway. 'You need to cool down, young man.'

Another splash and a yelp from Stephen. Jude switched on the light and saw Oliver drop a bucket, pick up a jug by the door and come straight at her. 'No!' But he poured ice cubes all over her. Stephen grabbed Oliver's legs and knocked him over. To Jude's amazement, he went down laughing. Then Sinéad appeared, shaking a bottle of Perrier water which she unleashed in Stephen's face as Oliver tussled with him on the floor.

'You leave my ward alone, you bloody chancer.'

'Jude, quick!' said Sinéad. They ran to the bathroom and refilled the jugs, but when they came back into the room,

Stephen grabbed Sinéad and forced a handful of ice down her cleavage. Oliver pulled him by the belt, flung him on to the bed and turned just as Jude hurled the contents of her bucket. He ducked, giving the water free passage to his brother.

'Oops. Sorry!'

Sinéad picked ice cubes out of her bra.

Stephen shook his head and tackled Oliver again. They rolled off the bed, fighting like puppies. Sinéad emptied another jug on to them and ran to refuel with Jude, but slid across a puddle in the bathroom and crashed to the floor. Creased up with laughter, they refilled the containers and rushed back in to the room, where Jude fully soaked Oliver, thereby discharging some of her anger with him. It was enormously satisfying. Sinéad got Stephen again.

'Ah, sod you!' He hurled himself towards her, but Oliver tripped him up and called a halt.

'Enough! Truce! We'll wreck the place.'

'Screw the place,' screeched Stephen. 'I'm drowning here!'

'Look at this bed,' cried Jude. 'I can't sleep in that.'

Sinéad shook the melting cubes off the sodden sheet. 'Nonsense.'

'I'll sleep in the wet patch,' said Stephen, sitting on the floor.

'Like hell you will,' said Oliver.

All three caught his tone. The fun dissipated.

'Butt out, Ol. She has reached the age of consent, you know.'

'She still needs my consent to sleep with you under my roof and she's not getting it.'

'Who said anything about sleep?'

Oliver stood by the door. 'Come on, Stephen. Out.'

The white rims appeared beneath the irises of Stephen's

eyes. His wet shirt stuck to his skin. Jude longed to peel it off him. He stood up, tossed dripping hair from his face, pinched her waist and left the room. Oliver followed.

Jude stomped her foot. 'Bugger Oliver, anyway!'

Sinéad picked up a bucket. 'Fancy a pancake?'

'What?'

'Let's go make pancakes and chocolate sauce.'

Jude was nonplussed. 'Now? Why?'

'Because there's more to life than men, Jude.'

By the time they went to bed, hours later, Jude had a friend for life.

At dawn, Lee left the house. Nobody gave a moment's thought, later that day, to the broken heart she took with her.

13

Jude lay in the hammock, in the dappled shade of heart-shaped leaves, wondering how she had managed to have her way with the most desirable individual she had ever met. What puzzled her more, however, was that she was not suffering throes of agony, even though he was now back in London with Meredith.

Oliver came out and placed two plates on the table. They were alone again. Sinéad had left that day. 'It's time you improved your culinary skills, nitwit.'

'I offered to make supper.'

'So you did, but I didn't fancy eggs. You need to expand your repertoire.'

She joined him at the table. 'And you're offering to teach me?'

'Someone has to.'

'We'd only argue. Why can't I learn by hit and miss?'

'Because you always miss. Besides, you want me to teach you to drive.'

'Yes, but I *want* to learn to drive,' said Jude, running her hand through a bunch of long beans that was hanging from the branch over her head.

'So I do have my uses,' he said, a little bitterly.

Jude had not yet forgiven him his trespass into her love life. His attempt to persuade Stephen to ditch her had caused a breach, which only Jude could mend. She was not unfriendly, just remote. She simply withheld her thoughts – a punishment keenly felt, for from the age of two, she had been pouring words over Oliver as though he were a receptacle with no other purpose. Now she might have been mute for all she told him.

The night felt oppressive. In June, Jude had enjoyed being alone with Oliver, but now the thought of returning to that quiet existence filled her with dread. Throughout July, she had found romance in rafting, pleasure in Stephen, and happiness in the back of Oliver's car when they went driving at sunset. Now she faced the last stretch of summer with a sense of foreboding. Being left behind with Oliver was like facing three weeks on a desert island without a radio.

But those last weeks weren't as she expected them to be. In the wake of their visitors, they fell into a rhythm of living so smooth that neither could deny its benefits. Oliver missed Tim appallingly, and it got worse, but he concealed this from Jude, and the effort of hiding his despair often soothed it. He regularly phoned Tim for comfort, only to end up more bereft, but he always pulled himself together, because the girl in the next room deserved better than to mop up the tears of his mistakes. It was hard to admit that Jude needed him more than even his own son, but in nurturing her, he eased the nauseating void in his own heart. In fact, her very presence was pulling him through the lowest times. He couldn't run for cover or go back to Tim without dragging Jude with him, and seeing her contented did him good. He might have failed his son, but he had not yet failed Michael's daughter.

And so he bought her croissants every morning and helped her cook dinner every night, with much cursing on his part and sloppiness on hers. Jude knew she was distracting him, and that was enough for her to do, because she couldn't mention Tim. His absence was there again, like another person in the house, and Jude was reluctant to acknowledge it for fear of upsetting the careful balance they had achieved. After dinner, they often walked around the labyrinthine village and along tracks that wound their way into the hills behind the vineyards, or they played Scrabble by candlelight outside, bats whipping like white birds over their heads. But even with Buddy Guy playing his blues in the background, Oliver no longer grew maudlin over his nightcap – perhaps because Jude stayed up with him.

'Have you given any more thought to college?' he asked one night.

'Not really. I'll do Arts, I suppose. English and Irish probably. But I've no idea what I want to do with my life. When did you know you wanted to be a writer?'

'I never wanted to be a writer. It crept up on me. I wandered around a lot before I settled into it.'

Jude was familiar with the broad outline of how he had ended up where he had, but now she wanted details, because it had all become relevant to her own career and where she might take it. 'Go on.'

So Oliver talked about those untidy years. He told her about his trip to America and how he subsequently returned to Dublin because his friends were there. He wrote his first novel for want of anything better to do and when it was rejected, went off travelling to defer the career crisis that was heading his way. He ambled around Greece, living off a meagre allowance from his father, and there were so many

157

Irish students on the islands that summer, it was easy to pretend he was still one of them, with no objective other than to get burnt by day and drunk by night. When the students drifted back to Ireland in the autumn, Oliver followed. His parents had returned to London by then, but Dublin still felt like home to him and that's where he wanted to be. He tended bars, lived in a bedsit and, instead of looking for a proper job, wrote a thriller about two students being murdered on the island of Paros. This also earned an impressive array of rejections, yet the more time Oliver spent writing, the more implausible other career options became. He had come to appreciate the demands writing made on him – the discipline, the solitude even – but most of all, he discovered he had the neck for it. With one rejected novel behind him, he still had the courage to write another and stay on his feet when that too was turned down, and he would have gone on with the next one had his financial situation not required an alternative course of action. When his father told him about a job writing features for a travel magazine in London, Oliver applied and got it. He said his farewells to Dublin, after living there for ten years, and moved back to England.

The job didn't last two months. Oliver had always been reticent about why he was fired, and he didn't enlighten Jude now either. He said only, 'It was personal, and it was worth it. I fled to Cairo.'

She didn't ask why he used the word 'fled' but it struck her as odd. The rest she knew. He taught English by day and wrote by night, and his third novel, about the disappearance of an English academic at the American University in Cairo, found a publisher. The American book was never resurrected, but the Greek murder mystery, assiduously rewritten, soon made its way on to the shelves, and Oliver's wandering days were vindicated. After he married, his research was restricted to shorter trips.

'That's where I went wrong,' he told Jude. 'My first two published books were good. They were leading somewhere. But I wrote them when I had no responsibilities, no ties. Then we took out a mortgage and had Tim and . . . I stopped taking chances. A foreign location, a few murders, a little sex – and they sold. But that's not good enough any more, which is why coming here was important. I needed a fresh perspective.'

'Has it worked?'

'I don't know yet. You could read it, if you like. Fancy a glass of wine?'

'I hate wine!'

'Exactly. I should teach you to appreciate it.'

'You're not going to make me chew it and spit it out, are you?'

He smiled. It was a very sudden thing, Oliver's smile, and Jude never got used to the flash of warmth that came with it. It could light up black holes, she thought.

Oliver started packing for London a week before they were due to leave. It helped ease the agitation, the excitement. He had never been away from Tim for so long. Folding his shirts, he decided he never would be again. The gate squeaked. Jude coming back from the river.

'Oliver?'

'Up here.' She didn't come running. Oliver stopped packing. There had been something in her voice. She appeared in the doorway, her hair wet, her T-shirt damp – and her face grey. 'What's wrong?'

Her hand went to her mouth. 'I got such a fright,' she whispered.

Oliver went to her. She was shaking. He sat her down on the bed. 'What on earth happened?'

Her eyes filled. 'I'm OK. I just got a fright.'

'Tell me.'

'I was standing in the river – you know, thinking about going over the rapids – when someone yelled and I turned around and there was a kayak coming straight at me. One of those big yellow plastic things. They couldn't stop, they were right in the flow, so they knocked me over and I grabbed on to it – I didn't want to go under – and I managed to hold on to the nose and we went over the rapids like that, with me under it.'

'Christ.'

'I let go as soon as I could and swam out. They pulled in to see if I was all right – they were German.'

Oliver put his arm around her.

'Ow!'

'What?' He looked over her shoulder. Blood was seeping through her T-shirt. 'Jesus.' He lifted it. '*Jesus.*' Her back was torn to shreds.

'From the shallow bit. The stones are really sharp. Remember – where you gashed your knee? Is it bad?'

'It isn't good.'

She lay down. 'It's starting to sting.'

'No, wait. I need to shower you down.'

He helped her into his bath and showered her back, but some of the grime was embedded in the cuts. He tried to sponge it off and unhooked her bikini top without thinking. She grabbed it and held it against her, still shaking from head to foot. 'Sorry,' he said. Her calves were grazed and one of her heels had a gash in it, but nothing, he thought, needed stitches. By the time he got her back to bed, the pain had started and the scrapes wouldn't stop bleeding.

Oliver sat beside the bed, staring at her back. There was a bad cut on one shoulder-blade, a horrible graze along her spine, and bits of skin hanging off everywhere else.

'Don't start scratching your lip,' said Jude, 'do something!'

He was horrified, on several counts. It looked as if she'd been dragged for miles across gravel, like a prisoner being tortured, and being pinned between a kayak and a riverbed was the stuff of nightmares, but that wasn't the worst of it. He set to with disinfectant and cotton wool. Jude kicked her feet in pain every time he touched her and was worn out by the time he had finished.

'I'll get you some brandy,' he said. Her face in her forearms, her back bruising already, she nodded. 'Don't be so brave, love. A good cry would sort out the shock.'

When he came back up, she wasn't there. 'Jude?'

'I'm in here,' she called from the bathroom.

'Be careful, would you? Hold on to something. Don't faint on me.' He waited by the door and felt himself despairing. It was so awkward with Jude. It was like trying to nurse your mother. If Sinéad had been there – or even *Stephen* – she wouldn't have had to hug her arms against her chest or struggle to the bathroom on her own, but it was as well she did, because there were certain boundaries Oliver couldn't afford to cross.

When she came out, holding a towel against her, every step made her back throb, so she fell straight into his bed, refused supper, and eventually fell asleep.

She woke after midnight. Oliver was still there; she could hear him breathing in the dark. She gave him a shove. He woke with a jump and turned on the light. Jude lay staring at him with a half-dead expression.

161

'My head's pounding. Everything's pounding. Even my heel.'

'Right. I'll get you something.'

She wasn't as spaced out as she looked. 'I hope you're decent under that sheet.'

He kicked it off. He was still dressed. 'I was afraid I wouldn't hear you if I went into the other room.'

'That's OK. Dad always let me sleep in his bed when I was sick.'

Oliver had to smile. She didn't even see the difference.

'My back's on fire.'

He gave her painkillers, then made up an ice-pack and pressed it against her back. 'And only a few days ago,' he said, 'I was throwing ice at you.'

'That was a lot more fun.'

Oliver smiled at the head tucked under his pillow. 'Missing him?' he ventured.

'S'pose so.'

'That's a bit tepid.'

'It's the way I feel.'

'You're obviously not in love with him then. Thank God.'

'I am so. I think.'

'Could it be,' Oliver asked gently, 'that you're confusing lust with love?'

She turned her head. 'How do you tell the difference?'

'Easy. All you have to do is think about someone you really love—'

'You?'

'OK.' He pressed the ice against her shoulder-blade. 'Me and Stephen are hanging off a cliff. You have time to save only one of us – who's it going to be?'

Jude's eyes narrowed. 'Do you promise to teach me to drive?'

162

'Get me off this bloody cliff and I'll teach you anything!'

She smiled. 'All right. Me and Patti are hanging off a cliff. Who are you going to save?'

'No question. I'd save you, then jump after Patti.'

'Really? After what she's done to you?'

''Fraid so.'

'But that doesn't make any sense.'

'It's called love, Jude. It doesn't usually make sense.'

For a while, neither spoke. The only sounds were the crickets outside and the ice slushing about in the plastic bag. *One knock,* Oliver was thinking. One knock on the back of her head and she would have sunk to the bottom of the deep stretch. He knew the scrunch of those kayaks, the hollow sound of the plastic scraping across the gravel in shallow waters, and the thought of Jude being trapped in between, the thought of her seeing it coming, was enough to give *him* nightmares.

She looked over her shoulder. 'Stop it.'

'Hmm?'

'Stop thinking about Dad.'

'There are . . . similarities.'

'Except I'm still here and he isn't.'

Oliver rubbed his eyes. 'Madness. Fucking madness letting tourists take those kayaks out. They haven't a clue how to manoeuvre them.'

'At least I didn't go under.'

But you could have, he thought. *You could have.*

She held his wrist. 'Stop. I'm all right.'

He dried her back. 'Is the pain easing?'

'No.'

They had a horrible night. Oliver despaired of trying to relieve the discomfort; the grazes burned, the cuts stung, and, unable to toss or turn, Jude ached with stiffness

163

because she couldn't move off her stomach. Even lying on her side was painful to the hip that had taken a whack. When the pain wasn't keeping her awake, her head was. 'It keeps replaying in my mind,' she complained. Oliver tried to distract her, but suspected that, for all his ministrations, Jude was probably yearning for Stephen.

He was wrong about that. She was actually thinking about him. Oliver was always so caring and affectionate, and even, she supposed, loving, but there were times – and this was one of them – when she would have liked to be told that he loved her, because if he didn't, nobody did. She had often tried to press him into saying 'I love you,' but he had never yet done so. It occurred to her that maybe he didn't.

The following morning, more damage revealed itself. Jude had clearly strained neck and shoulder muscles in her attempt to hang on to the kayak, and was more immobilized than ever. Her only options were to lie face down or walk around, although she wasn't really fit to get up. She nibbled a croissant for breakfast, and then, with difficulty, finally got herself out of her bikini and into pyjama bottoms. Unable to bear anything near her back, she held a towel against her for modesty when necessary. She spent the day snoozing and reading Oliver's manuscript, and a long sleep in the afternoon dealt with the remnants of shock. Oliver made her get up regularly to walk around, as a result of which, by evening, she was able to lie on her good hip.

Her spirits were improving. After supper, she told him his novel was a bit flat. 'It needs jizzing up.'

'Just like your father,' Oliver grumbled, sitting cross-legged on the bed. 'There's no pleasing you Feehans.' But he was delighted. Not only was Jude better, *they* were better. Her accident had done him a favour: the gap had been closed, affection reinstated. Jude was warm and cheeky again, and there was no equivocation in her eyes.

'This bit's rubbish,' she said, scrunching up a page and throwing it at him. 'So's this.' Another paper ball hit him. He threw it back. 'And this is too long,' she said, tearing a page in half. She made pellets out of it and flicked them at him, while he made paper planes which soared around the room. The remaining script was used for swotting mosquitoes. Later, he dressed her back and read to her.

When he woke the following morning, his mouth ran dry. He leaped from the bed, horrified. He had slept with his protégée again – and this time without good reason. Worse, he had clearly fallen asleep first, because the light was out and Jude had covered him with the sheet. Expecting some demon to jump out and wallop him for a truly unwarranted abuse of his position, Oliver made for the kitchen feeling like a reprobate, but as the morning wore on, he became more bullish. Falling asleep with Jude was unorthodox and certainly reprehensible, but it could not be undone. Besides, every time he made a decision which affected her, he saw her parents peering over her shoulder, along with the nuns and his own parents and her friends' parents – a huge crowd judging his every move – and these accusing faces often obscured the teenager he had to live with. Jude's accident had banished the gorgeous young woman who had entranced his brother and returned the parentless girl, and if that young girl derived comfort from curling up beside him, then he wasn't going to feel guilty if he fell asleep there too. He was damned if he was going to torment himself for failing to abide by some kind of acceptable norm when their very situation flew in the face of every acceptable norm anyway.

14

The first term of the school year at St Malachy's was always the longest. September, with its maverick summer days and retrenching autumn evenings, didn't seem to know which season it belonged to, which made the girls feel they should be somewhere else. For the sixth-years in particular, this new term was spiked with wistfulness, because this was their last time around and they felt compelled to inject significance and melancholy into every event. Each day, they relived their own past and missed it, even while it remained the present, so that mundane habits, like hugging inadequate radiators between classes, became significant rituals which had to be mourned before they even ended. Their one-time gripes about the school became affectionate forbearance, and every time a bus brought them back to the convent after a camogie match, they sang more boisterously than anyone else, as if attempting to project their singing into the future so that they might still hear it when they got there. Like throwing a voice into a cave, Jude thought, in the hope it would echo forever.

She settled in quickly, for she had always found that

boarding school had a pleasantly numbing effect on the senses. Its routines were like the minutes of the day, one following the other without fail, leaving no gap through which the outside world might intrude, and so she found it easy to move from Geography to French without thinking about Stephen. Since he had no place on the camogie pitch or in the refectory, it wasn't difficult to get through the weeks without missing him. Only at night, when her mind was her own, could she return to Landor and imagine herself floating down the river on Stephen's back, but she usually fell asleep before they got down to serious necking on the beach. She always dropped off when they were bobbing over those waves.

She could, and did, miss Oliver, however. Unlike Stephen, he was there to be missed, regularly intruding on her school life with e-mails and phone calls, and whenever they spoke, he managed to slip Stephen into the conversation so that Jude knew what his brother was up to. It was a kindness, a generosity, she appreciated.

In mid-November, he rang from London with news. 'About that home I promised you,' he said. 'I can finally deliver.'

'Great! Where is it?'

She knew he was smiling when he said, 'I've bought the house in Landor.'

'*What?*'

'It's been on the cards all along,' he explained. 'Anthony offered it to me for a song when I left home – he wanted to get rid of it – but I had to see how it suited us.'

'That's fantastic!'

After a moment he said, 'You don't know how great it is to hear you say that.'

'What did you think I'd say?'

'"*Nga, nga, nga,*" or words to that effect. You're a hard case, Jude. I don't often get it right with you.'

'Well, you have this time. I *love* that house.'

'Yeah, me too. Besides, I couldn't afford anything like it in London.'

'It's a long way from Tim, though.'

'I know, but he has his own thing going without me, you know. Whenever I'm here, I'm only ever in the wings, so when he *is* living with me, I want it to be good, and that goes for you too.'

'Thanks.'

'How's your back? Healed up nicely?'

'*I* don't know. I can't see it. Fiona says I'll be scarred for life, but I won't, will I?'

'*I* don't know. I can't see it either. You aren't dreaming about it, are you?'

'Oliver, I went over some rapids on the wrong side of a kayak, I wasn't hit by a speedboat, so stop fretting.'

After he rang off, Jude went to the sixth-form common room to have her nightly hot chocolate. Fiona and Emer were standing by the drinks machine sipping at paper cups.

'Guess what. Oliver's bought the house in Landor.'

'Deadly!' said Fiona.

'Excellent.'

Jude took her drink from the machine. 'There's only one drawback. With him living in France, I'll hardly ever see him once I turn eighteen.'

'Course you will,' said Emer.

'Are you going over there for Christmas?'

'No. We're taking Tim to Scotland. And guess who'll be there too?'

'*Stephen*,' said Fiona. 'You lucky brat.'

'But he might bring Meredith. They're still together – can you believe it? Just when I have the hots for him, he goes on a bloody marathon!'

Christmas hurried forward. Within weeks, Jude and her classmates found themselves singing carols in the streets of Clifden for the last time, performing their last ever Christmas review, and eating their last Christmas pudding with school custard. Before Jude could take stock, Oliver was parked outside the convent, waiting to take her away.

'You didn't have to come,' she said, when they set off. 'I could have flown to Glasgow.'

'I had stuff to do in Dublin.'

'Guardian-type stuff?'

'I had to see the solicitor, yeah.'

Preparing for the hand-over, Jude thought. *The wind-up.*

'Anyway, you know I don't need much of an excuse to come to Ireland.'

'I wonder why. You looked wrecked. A hard night with the lads, I suppose?'

'Very, *very* hard.'

'So, how's your new home? And what's Landor like in the winter?'

'Cold. Wet. Lovely. The house is like a cave – there's no heating – but it's *my* cave and I like it. I was never cut out for suburbia.'

'Don't you get lonely?'

'You know I do, but I've got a telly now, and I've met some of the other foreigners in the area. The locals keep to themselves pretty much.'

In the sleety darkness of a wet December evening, it took

them four hours to reach Dublin, but the journey passed quickly. Jude was brimming with giddy excitement; it was Christmas, it was holidays, and although she wouldn't admit it, she was thrilled to see her substitute kin after fifteen long weeks. As for meeting Oliver's brother, and the lovely girlfriend, that was bound to be a prickly pear, but there was nothing she could do about it.

They reached Sinéad's tiny two-bedroom town house, where they were to spend the night before flying to London, after nine. As Sinéad hugged them on her doorstep, a figure loomed in the hallway behind her.

'Oliver, Jude,' said Sinéad, 'I'd like you to meet Peter Brocket.'

An imposing man with curly blond hair lurched forward to greet them with bone-crushing handshakes, then invited them into the sitting-room as though it were his own. Over drinks by the fire, Oliver and Jude discovered that Peter was a nice man. He was also the most boring stuffed shirt either of them had ever met and a self-proclaimed expert on everything from publishing to chamber music. Jude was amazed. She could not fathom Sinéad's taste. From her father to *this*. And how could Sinéad consider such a dreadful specimen when Oliver was sitting there, nursing his whisky and absolutely single, and wearing a gorgeous black shirt and jeans, in glaring contrast to Peter's stuffy cravat and canary-yellow sweater?

The evening was torture. Jude was giddy and Oliver hung-over, and Peter's sweeping pronouncements kept triggering attacks of giggling that were agony to suppress. They could barely look at each other.

'So you write thrillers, Oliver?' Peter asked over dinner.

'I do, yeah.'

'Always thought I should write a little thriller myself. Set

170

in the wine trade. I'm in the business, you see. I have some darned good ideas too.'

Oliver was looking at Peter with such bewildered fascination that Jude struggled to keep a straight face. 'Great titles,' she said, glancing at Oliver mischievously. ' "Killed by the Bottle." '

' "Jack the Sipper," ' said Oliver.

' "Strangled by the Vine." '

' "Vintage Most Foul." '

'Stop it,' said Sinéad.

Peter looked momentarily bemused, but went on. 'A great money-spinner, writing. Great little money-spinner.'

'Ninety-nine per cent of writers never make any money,' Jude retorted.

'Ah, but you have to go about it the right way,' Peter explained. 'Now, my pal James Duffleby –'

'Waffleby?' muttered Oliver.

Sinéad kicked him under the table.

'– he has some experience of PR. He'd tell you how to target the right market.'

'Thank you,' said Jude, 'but Oliver already has an established market.'

'With all due respect, Jude, I had never actually heard of him before I met Sinéad, so he clearly needs some good marketing advice.'

'And you clearly need to visit a bookshop more often.'

Oliver winced. Peter laughed too loudly, as at the precociousness of a child. 'Oh, I'm far too tied up with the business to be hanging around bookshops.'

'Well, that follows.'

'Oi.' The Oliver reprimand.

'Maybe you'd get the coffee, Peter?' said Sinéad.

'Of course, darling.'

He was endearingly attentive to her, but no sooner had he left the room than Oliver leaned towards Sinéad. 'You *cannot* be serious about this guy?'

'I'm deadly serious.'

'But Sinéad,' said Jude, 'he's—'

Sinéad raised her hands. 'Not another word, either of you. I know he seems a little pompous –'

'A *little*?'

'– but underneath he's a good man, and you should know . . . that we're planning to get married.'

They stared at her wide-eyed, then at each other.

'You mean you *love* him?' asked Jude, amazed that anybody might.

'Listen, Jude, I've had my big love story and it ended in disaster, literally. My needs are different now. I'd like a family, companionship, support. Peter can give me those things.'

'Yes, but—'

'And I can't spend my life waiting for Michael to come back, because he isn't going to, is he?'

'But there are lots of guys who—'

'Jude.' With the slightest shake of his head, Oliver told Jude to leave it.

After coffee, Jude made her excuses and retired to the little guest room, where a warm double bed awaited her. She was about to put out the light when Oliver knocked and put his head around the door. 'Mind if I bunk down in here? I'm supposed to sleep on the living-room couch but they're settling in for the late movie, so if it's all the same to you . . . ?'

'Sure. What's that?'

'Peter's old sleeping bag.'

'Eugh, poor you. And here's me with this huge big bed to myself.'

'Don't rub it in.' He threw the sleeping bag on the ground. 'He is one seriously bombastic individual, isn't he?'

'You were wicked. I nearly cracked up when you asked him what a literary agent was. As for his friend in publishing—'

'The one who prints dentistry manuals?' Oliver broke into a risible imitation of Peter. '"What you need, old boy, is someone with the right connections, and my friend Fabien Brocklehurst-Templemartin-Mooncy—"'

'Shush!' Jude giggled, turning out the light.

'The sign of a true name-dropper: dropping names no one has ever heard of!'

'Maybe you should save Sinéad from him?'

'Yeah, whisk her away from a life of multiple-barrelled names.'

'She fancies you, I reckon.'

'Ah,' said Oliver, getting into the bag. 'Ten months and five days.'

'What?'

'I've often wondered how long it would take before you started match-making on my behalf. It has been ten months and five days since I left home.'

'You count the days?'

'The hours, sometimes.'

'Well, only a few more hours until you see Tim.' She sighed heavily.

'You OK up there? About Stephen?'

'Fine. It's Meredith I'm dreading. And don't say, "I told you so."'

'I wasn't going to.'

'God, what is all this heaving and grumbling?'

'I'm trying to get comfortable. I'm too old for this sleeping on floors lark.'

'I'm not swapping, you know, no matter how old you are.'

'I'll bet.'

'Oliver, do we really have to go see Nan tomorrow?'

'Yes.'

'But she's such a misery-guts. And she doesn't even know who I am.'

'You know who *she* is and that's what matters. 'Night, nitwit.'

' 'Night. Sleep well.'

'In this yoke? It's like sleeping in a condom.'

'Listen to it.'

'Would you chuck my jacket over me?'

'Why?'

'Because it would look really smart with the sleeping bag, why do you think?'

'You're cold?'

'Freezing.'

'But if I get out of bed, *I'll* get cold.'

Oliver swore and shuffled about for his jacket. 'I'm not doing this for nothing, you know. This guardian business. When I'm past my best, you can bloody well look after me for a change.'

'Look, if you're so miserable, get into bed. I don't care.'

'You might not, but plenty would.'

But Oliver's good intentions lasted only until the freezing dawn temperatures found him shivering and wide awake. When Jude woke the next morning, he was sound asleep in his sleeping bag in the bed beside her – and Sinéad was knocking at the door. Using her hands and feet, Jude pushed until Oliver fell on to the floor with a grunt.

Sinéad put her head around the door. 'Just wanted to say bye, and have a great Christmas.'

'You too. And thanks for last night.'

'Gotta dash. Bye!'

As the door closed, Oliver opened one eye. 'Talk about being kicked out of bed.'

They arrived in London late that afternoon. Stephen greeted them at the airport with enthusiastic hugs, and it was an unnecessary cruelty, Jude thought, that he was wearing a suit, because she had always been partial to men in suits. It was like a punishment for fancying him – and she did, sadly, still fancy him. He drove them home, looking as palatable as he ever had, his every gesture quietly arousing her. Here, on Meredith's turf, jealousy seared through her.

Back at his flat, Stephen handed them mugs of coffee. 'Great to see you two 'n' all, but where are we all going to sleep tonight?'

Oliver looked over the back of the couch. 'Aren't you staying with Meredith?'

'Ah. Well. Therein lies the problem. Meredith and I split up last week.'

Jude stiffened.

'Aha!' said Oliver. '*Plus ça change—*'

'I'll have you know I broke all previous records.'

'What happened?'

'It came to the end of its natural life is all.'

'Bugger,' said Oliver. 'Another night on a hard cold floor.'

'Yeah, right,' Jude muttered.

'I'll take the floor,' said Stephen, 'you take my bed. Jude can have the sofa-bed.' He smiled at her and might have pierced her lungs in the process, so shallow had become her breathing.

'Suits me.' Oliver gulped back his coffee. 'Right, I'm off to see Tim.'

'Me too,' said Jude.

Oliver hesitated. '. . . Tomorrow.'

'But I haven't seen him for even longer than you!'

Stephen got up and went to the kitchen.

'I'm going to the house,' Oliver said quietly.

Jude pulled at a button on her jacket. It was so awkward, and so bloody obvious. This wasn't about her reluctance to go to Chiswick. He wanted to be alone with his son, and there was nothing wrong with that, except it reminded her once again that, in spite of everything, she was still outside the loop. She knew exactly what the house would be like on a winter's evening like this, days before Christmas. The tree would be up. There would be decorations everywhere. Over the top, in true Patti style. Jude fiddled intently with her button. She had been foolish, perhaps, to cut herself off from it all.

Oliver put his hand over hers. 'We'll all go out tomorrow, all right?'

'Yeah, yeah. Go on.'

And he went out, just like that, leaving her alone with Stephen.

She took the mugs into the kitchen.

'Don't let it get to you,' he said.

'I'm not.'

'Maybe if you cut Patti some slack . . .'

'I can't. It isn't just what she did to me, you know. It's what she did to Oliver. I'm the one who was with him, afterwards. All summer. She really, really hurt him.'

'I know.'

176

She opened the dishwasher. 'Sorry to hear about Meredith,' she said limply.

'No you're not.' Stephen was standing right behind her. She could smell him. Her back tingled. She had spent weeks steeling herself for the ordeal of seeing him with Meredith and now, in the blink of an eye, Meredith was gone, and so too was every thought of Oliver stepping into that warm, busy hallway in Chiswick. Bending over to put the mugs into the dishwasher, she couldn't but press against Stephen, and when she straightened up, he put his arms around her waist.

'Now,' he breathed into her ear, 'where were we?'

She brushed him off. 'Stop. You can't expect me to pick up where we left off when you've been with someone else for the last five months.'

'But it didn't bother you when I *had* a girlfriend. Now I don't. All the better for us.'

Jude shook her head.

'You mean I'm no longer an attractive prospect now that I'm single?'

'It's not that.'

'What then? Come on, Judy. We're spending Christmas together. What's the deal?' He turned her around. 'No pressure? No ties?'

'No sex.'

He inhaled sharply. 'Still no sex? Ouch.' Then he flashed those dimples. 'Course, it depends on how you define sex exactly.' He lifted her on to the counter and wrapped her legs around him. 'Don't you think?'

She had no means to refuse him. When he kissed her, every nerve in her body rejoiced. It was like coming around after a five-month coma.

*

'We'd better get up,' said Stephen, switching on his bedside light, 'before the Pope catches us. He's such a prig about this.'

'He worries. He thinks I'll fall in love with you and get hurt. That doesn't appear to bother you, however.'

'Why would I assume you'd fall in love with me?'

'Young girl, older man. All that.'

'Na. You're more heavily fortified than any girl I know.'

'You make me sound like a tank! Just because I won't have sex—'

'I don't mean sex. I mean you've got your defences up. Apart from Oliver, no one gets near.'

'Are you saying I have no feelings?'

'I'm saying you won't fall in love that easily, which isn't surprising after what you've been through.'

'I was in love with Thierry.'

'Bull. You played that pretty cool when it suited you.'

'Maybe, but I'm not a bit cool about you.'

He rolled on to her and pressed his nose against hers. 'Yes you are. It should be in the eyes, but yours have nothing to say to me.'

'And that suits you?'

'Frankly, yes. Apart from anything else, I'd never survive the school term! Besides, one Sayle male is enough for any girl to put up with. Having one watch your every move and another in your bed just ain't good mathematics.'

They had dinner when Oliver returned, and afterwards, Jude sat back and considered the two men. Stephen knew her intimately. Straightforward and easy-going, he could slot her into his life without difficulty and make her comfortable there. Oliver, in contrast, could be moody and stern, yet he was predictable and reliable, where Stephen was not.

178

Oliver was better company too, because there was a depth to him which she had yet to find in his brother. In the two, she had the steady and the wild, the dark and the light, but while she opened herself to Stephen's bright vivaciousness, she kept clear of that part of Oliver which always remained in the shade. It was Stephen, she mused, who should have been the thoughtful one, what with those piercing dark eyes, but they reflected more mischief than mystery, while the light sparkle of Oliver's eyes was in sharp contrast to the grey realm behind them.

'Any chance,' he asked them, 'I can trust you two to behave yourselves if I turn in?'

There was that sudden tension again, like after the water fight in Landor.

'Not that again,' said Stephen. 'You're overstepping the mark, Oliver.'

'Stephen, stop.' Jude kissed Oliver's cheek. 'Go to bed. You may not be able to trust him, but you can trust me, and I wish you would.'

He went to bed.

A week later, in the Sayles' farmhouse in Scotland, Jude had a very good Christmas. She had Tim, she had Oliver, and she had Stephen as often as possible. Even Mrs Sayle welcomed her amongst them, although she would not have done so had she known about the groping that was going on behind her back.

Tim's grandparents gave him Scalextric, which Oliver and Stephen spent an hour setting up on Christmas morning. They were pretty keen to play with it too.

Stephen placed one of the cars on the track. 'I'll give you a head start,' he said to Tim.

'Wait a minute,' said Oliver, 'he's *my* son.'

'I got here first.'

'Oh, for God's sake,' said Jude.

Tim took the controls from Stephen. 'I want Jude to play.'

'But she's only a girl. She doesn't know how to drive, mate.'

Jude kicked his ankles.

'I'll teach her,' said Tim. 'What's your driver's name?' he asked Jude.

'Em . . . Damon.'

'Ooh, careful, Tim,' said Stephen. 'Damon Hill is one hot driver.'

'Who's Damon Hill?' asked Jude.

'He's a Formula One driver.'

'Oh. No, this guy is named after Damon Albarn, from Blur. He's a total god.'

Stephen sighed. 'Give me those controls.'

'Don't you have urgent work in the kitchen?'

'So you push this to make it go,' said Tim, 'and we start here.'

'And I'm going to beat you.'

'No you're not,' Tim laughed. 'You're only a girl!'

That night, when Stephen was warming mince pies in the kitchen and the older Sayles had retired, Jude sat by the fire with Oliver and fiddled with the bracelet he had given her. 'Will you promise me something?' she said.

'Shoot.'

'If I have my own place in Dublin next year, will you and Tim spend Christmas with me?'

'Of course.'

'Even if you have a girlfriend and want to be with her instead?'

'Even if.'

'And even though you won't be my guardian any more?'

He smiled. 'Jude,' he said. 'Where else would I be?'

15

'Bloody typical!' Jude said to Fiona, coming to their table in the bright, sun-filled refectory. 'Just when we have exams coming up, Connemara has a heatwave!' She sat down, endured the embarrassment of hearing the boarders sing 'Happy Birthday' to her, and relaxed when the ordeal ended.

'How's it feel to be eighteen?' asked Emer.

Jude was leafing through a stack of cards. 'Peculiar.'

'It's better than peculiar,' said Fiona. 'You can vote, buy a pint, see X-rated movies.'

'Yeah, but who's my next of kin? That's what I want to know, because I don't think I have one any more. I think it's me.'

'Uh-uh,' said Fiona. 'It's Lee!'

They laughed. Her classmates gathered around the table, urging her to open their gifts, but this was the day she and Oliver went their separate ways and Jude was curious to know what he had to say about it.

He had nothing to say about it. She rushed through the cards again, but there was nothing from her former guardian. He might as well have punched her. Henceforth he could forget her birthday without even feeling guilty, *but did he really have to forget this last one?*

Fiona grimaced at Emer. 'Bit rich.'

'He'll probably phone,' Emer said.

'Phoning's easy,' said Fiona. 'A prezzie would have been nice.'

Jude made an effort not to care as she ate her cereal, but she was upset, and Oliver didn't often upset her.

'Jude Feehan?' Sr Aloysius wove through the tables, all flushed and pleased. 'Happy birthday, dear.'

'Thanks, Sister.'

'There's a rather large parcel waiting for you on the front step. You can run along and get it, if you like.'

Reflecting her own expression, the faces around the table brightened as Jude got up. *So he hasn't forgotten*, she thought, hurrying out, but what had he sent that was too big to be brought to the refectory? A car? She pulled open the heavy front door and looked down. There was nothing on the step. Holding the door with one hand, she looked left and right. There was nothing outside the school, no present, but the day caught her senses. The sky was pale with morning mist, the air crisp, and twenty yards away, leaning against the wall, Oliver stood watching her.

'I feel like I've been hung upside down and spun around,' said Jude, when they drove away ten minutes later.

'My pleasure.'

'How on earth did you persuade Sr Al to let me out so near the exams?'

'Just my natural charm, I suppose.'

Jude beamed. 'Where did you come from, anyway?'

'I flew into Dublin last night. Hit the road at dawn.'

'Well, thanks. This is the *best* present. Oh, congratulations!'

It was Oliver's turn to beam. 'Great news, isn't it? And I suppose I have *you* to thank. I "jizzed up" the book like you told me to, and lo, an American publisher steps forth.'

'Will it do well?'

'Who knows? I'll be hitting the publicity trail next year, telling everyone it's the best thing I've ever written.'

'Is it?'

'It's certainly better than the last two, but it isn't The One.'

'Which one?'

'The good one. I agree with Michael. I'm convinced I must have at least one really good book in me, but I can't seem to find it.'

'But this one wouldn't have got an American publisher if it wasn't good.'

'It's commercial. There's a difference.'

'God, you're never happy.' Jude rolled up her sleeves. 'I wish Sister had let me change out of my uniform.'

'I can't believe she lets you wear those skirts so short.'

'She doesn't. We hitch them up when she isn't around.'

Oliver slowed down. 'Now listen, you. Remember the day I came to tell you about your dad?'

Jude dipped her head.

'Right. Stupid question. Well, I promised myself then I'd come back one day and we'd go to a beach and make up for what we did to this place. What do you think?'

'Great. As long as we don't go to the same beach. I'm never going back there.'

'Fair enough. Let's find ourselves another one.'

'Don't you want breakfast?'

'I had breakfast with Sr Al, and very nice it was too.'

'Whereas mine was rudely interrupted . . .'

They stopped at the crafts shop beyond Letterfrack, where Jude had scones and several cups of tea and chattered on, as she was wont to do, but Oliver silenced her momentarily when he handed her a small box. 'Happy birthday, love.'

The box held a small gold key on a chain with a tiny diamond embedded in it. 'Oh, my God.'

'Sinéad designed it.'

'It's too much.'

'No, it isn't.'

'I *love* it. But don't I have to be twenty-one to get the key to the door?'

'That's not the key to the door. That's your means of escape.'

'From what?'

'Me.' He put the chain around her neck.

'You know very well I don't want to escape.'

'Ah, but you should, you should. Come on. Let's go find that beach.'

As they came out into the sunshine, Oliver looked up at a large pink house overlooking the inlet. 'Talk about the Pink Palace. What is that place?'

'A country house hotel. I plan to go there sometime for a romantic weekend with a nice man. Preferably Stephen.'

'Romantic, my foot.'

They drove out along the winding road, past yellow sloping bogs dotted with mounds of stacked peat, through Cleggan and on towards Claddaghduff. A few miles on, they took a right, in search of their own secluded bay, and came to a narrow track. Jude jumped out of the rented car and climbed on to a stone wall to see what lay beyond the fields. 'This is it!'

Oliver parked. They climbed over the wall, walked across a hillock and came to a barbed-wire fence. Beyond it, a small bay of fine white sand sloped out below them, dipping into the Atlantic. 'Unbelievable.'

Jude looked at the barbed wire. 'How do we get over?'

He lifted her up and deposited her on the other side. 'Like so.'

She ran down to the rocks and began clambering about, while Oliver walked down to the sea, his jacket thrown over his shoulder. It was getting hot. Bird prints made patterns across the wet sand and two oystercatchers stood in the shallows. He had never seen Connemara in such spectacular weather, nor ever explored its hidden bays. It was as close to paradise as he had ever been.

'Look,' Jude called from the rocks. 'A private bath.'

He made his way up to her. She had found a sandy pool about a foot deep and several feet long. 'No crabs or seaweed! You could lie in it.'

Oliver jumped on to a large flat rock. 'Ah, but this is what I'm looking for.' He lay down and closed his eyes. 'A bed.'

'Stay that way. I'm taking off my tights. How long have you been planning this? I thought you were in France.'

'I came back last week. I'll hang on now until Sinéad's wedding, then we can all drive over in July.'

'Will Tim be OK this time?'

'Yeah. We handled it badly last year.'

'So,' said Jude, sitting down behind him. 'Can I have my money now please?'

'No.'

'But it's mine. I can blow it all in one go if I want to.'

'I wouldn't advise that – not if you want a roof over your head.'

'Can't I splash out a bit? I *had* hoped to celebrate my

independence by buying myself a *really* expensive outfit for the wedding. We don't want to be outclassed by Peter's stuffy friends, do we?'

'Heaven forbid.' Oliver smiled without looking up. 'About the money, Jude. You do know there isn't enough to buy a house outright, don't you?'

'So I'll rent somewhere.'

'That would be a waste of capital. It'd be much wiser to buy, but it'll be impossible for you to get a mortgage as long as you're a student.' He leaned on his elbows and looked over his shoulder. 'So I was thinking, I could make up the difference, if you like.'

'How? With what?'

'I'll take out a small mortgage.'

'You mean, buy a house together? In Dublin?'

'Yeah. I need somewhere nearer Tim, but I'm never in London long enough to warrant getting a place there, so instead of squeezing in with Stephen, we could spend the odd weekend and half-terms in Dublin. That's if you wouldn't mind sharing with us occasionally?'

'Of course I wouldn't. I'd love it.'

'In time, you can either buy me out or we'll sell up.'

'Are you sure?'

'Absolutely. Getting you on to the bottom rung of the housing market should be my last act as your guardian. You must have your own home.' He lay down again.

Jude rested her chin on her knees. 'You're my home,' she said, not caring what he thought. He didn't budge. 'Will you still look after my money and stuff?'

'S'pose so. I'll still look after you too, until some unfortunate bloke takes you off my hands. Speaking of which, how was half-term?'

'Fine. Your mum was great.'

'My mum was great. I see. How about my brother?'

'He was only there for three days.'

'I hope you were careful. If Mother ever finds out about you two, blood will be shed – and it won't be Stephen's.'

'We were careful. We went to a hotel.'

'Ah, Jude!' Oliver sat up. 'For crying out loud, this has got to stop.'

'Why?'

'Because it's sordid. It's unbelievably shallow. It was bad enough at Christmas, the two of you groping every chance you got, but checking into hotels for quick thrills is too bloody cheap. I wouldn't mind if I thought for a moment he'd commit to you, but you know very well that he won't.'

'Yes, I do know that, but thank you for reminding me – *again*.'

'Messing around with him every time you meet is a risky business. I wish you'd cut it out.'

'Eighteen now. Can do what I like.'

Oliver sighed. 'You don't half wear me out, you know. I don't understand how you can take this in your stride.'

'I can't help it. He only has to walk into the room and I'm putty in his hands. Then he walks out again and I don't really care. Much.'

'I should never have let it happen.'

Jude scratched the back of his shirt with her toe. 'Let's not talk about it. No point arguing when you've come all this way. Can I have your sunglasses?'

'Here.'

She went down to the sea. Translucent and blue, it had the colour of a crag of iceberg just below the surface of Antarctic waters, and was almost as cold. Swimming seemed like an attractive prospect until her toes met the water and a sharp sting ran up her calves, but as her feet adjusted, she paddled for a while, the waves hitting her legs and sometimes wetting the hem of her skirt. She couldn't believe she was there. Thanks to Oliver, she was up to her knees in the sea on a small beach on a hot May day instead of being stuck in English class discussing *Silas Marner*. This was one of those halcyon days she would never forget. After a while she climbed back to the rock and lay down, pulling at her blouse to expose her midriff, and dozed off.

They woke simultaneously, stiff and hot, an hour later. Oliver groaned and rolled on to his stomach. 'Ugh, I shouldn't have slept. I feel grotty.'

Jude rolled on to her side and looked at her little diamond. 'I love my pendant.' She sat up. 'So anyway, Mr Sayle, I'll bet you're relieved you're not responsible for me any more.'

'Relieved? Don't be daft. I don't see that anything has actually changed.'

'And yet you marked it by coming to see me.'

'Well. No harm in marking the end of our legal association, even if it doesn't actually change things, is there? I mean, let's be realistic: do you have any idea what rate of interest you're getting on your investments?'

'No.'

'And your solicitors are . . . ?'

'Those guys in Dublin . . . What're they called?'

'If I've told you once—'

'Yeah, yeah, but that stuff bores me.'

'Right. So if I were to walk off into the sunset, you'd be in deep shit, unless I give you a crash course in investment finance right here and now.'

'No, thanks.'

'Seems we're stuck with each other for a bit longer then.'

'But do you wish we weren't? Don't you feel glad this big burden has been lifted?'

'Not really. Just a bit sad, I suppose. I mean, a father never stops being a father, does he? But a guardian stops being a guardian at the stroke of midnight. Or is meant to. It isn't quite fair. I'm supposed to just switch myself off like a light.'

Jude smiled. 'Poor Cinders,' she said, but she had never loved him more.

He sat up and looked across the bay. 'You know, when I came over here to get you after Michael died, I was blind terrified. It freaked me out that you were about to burst into that office and I was the only person in the world who could make decisions for you.' He grimaced. 'As it happens, it hasn't been so bad. You've been a bloody handful, mind, but the fact that my responsibilities towards you come to an end today strikes me as yet another distancing from your parents, which is sad.'

'I'm glad you feel that way, 'cos I'm sorry too.'

'You should be rejoicing. You're *out*.'

Jude fiddled with her pendant. 'Yeah, out and on my own.'

'You're not on your own. You never will be.'

'Maybe, but I can't help worrying. I mean, what'll happen when you find yourself a serious girlfriend? She's not going to want me hanging around, especially since I don't have the same excuse for living with you today that I had yesterday.'

'You don't need an excuse.'

'And what about next summer when I have my own place – can I still go to Landor? And what about Christmas and—'

'Hey, calm down. You and me and Tim, we make up some kind of family unit and I don't want that to break up just because you've turned eighteen. It's good for Tim. It's good for all of us. Whatever happens, there'll always be a bed for you in my house, right?'

She nodded.

'But there is something you *do* have to take on board – responsibility for your grandmother. As from today, you're her next of kin.'

'Oh *gawd*. If that woman must live for ever, the least she could do is appreciate it.'

'The way you talk about her completely belies the way you behave with her.'

'The dutiful granddaughter?'

'The *loving* granddaughter, I was thinking.'

'Hardly. She scares me . . . but sometimes she looks at me in this odd way – you know, not quite so cross – and I feel almost fond of her, but then I start thinking . . . I dunno.'

'That she might have been a great grandmother, if she'd been well?'

'Yeah. That's what makes me so mad.' Jude pulled up her striped blouse to get some air under it. 'This heat is too much!'

'Let's paddle.'

They walked the length of the short beach in the water. 'So, how'd I fare?' Oliver asked. 'Has everything been to your satisfaction, Miss Feehan?'

'Yes, thanks. You've been a good financial adviser, an excellent travel agent, and you have a gorgeous brother.'

'Oh. That's . . . to the point.' He took off his shirt. 'Why do I get the feeling you're leaving something out? You haven't wanted for anything, have you?'

Jude squinted at the sky.

'I see. Seems I did fall down somewhere.'

'It's just . . . I never know where I stand with you, and

you make sure I don't. And that's hard, especially when there's no one else.'

'But that's the problem. There *is* no one else, which makes it difficult sometimes. You often hone in on me far too much.'

The tone of the conversation had changed and Jude didn't care for it. 'Oh, never mind. You've been a perfect guardian and I love you very much for everything you've done.'

'Well, now you won't have to love me quite so much.'

Jude picked up a twig. 'You make it sound like a burden,' she said, scribbling in the sand. 'Is it?'

'A bit.'

She looked up.

'You asked.'

'I suppose I can be overwhelming at times.'

Oliver took his sunglasses from her nose and put them back on his own. 'Let's just say we react differently. You gush, whereas I gave up gushing twenty years ago, you know?'

It was clear Jude didn't know.

'What I mean is, you respond to life, to me, to everything, like a teenager. I deal with it all as an adult.'

'I know that.'

'Yes, but you always want more. You want me to meet you on your level, on your terms, and I can't do that.'

Jude frowned at her drawing in the sand. 'You're saying I shouldn't expect any more than I get?'

'I'm saying you can't expect me to respond to you, or to anything else, the way you want me to. I'm thirty-seven – I've got twenty years on you.'

'Nineteen.'

By a deft sleight of tongue, Jude noted, he'd managed to have this conversation without really mentioning love,

192

which is what she thought they were talking about. It didn't seem fair that he was so evasive. Surely everyone needed to hear 'I love you' now and then? Yet Oliver seemed to be reprimanding her for expecting it. It was too hot, however, to ponder it. 'Well, thanks anyway,' she said. 'Thanks for everything the whole business entailed.'

'It's been my pleasure and my choice. Don't ever forget that.' He looked at the sea. 'Fancy a swim?'

'We'd have to skinny-dip!'

'Why not? There isn't a soul for miles.' He opened his belt.

'*Oliver*.'

'Turn around. You'll know when I'm in the water.'

Jude turned away. 'Honestly! What would Sr Al say?'

'She'd be too overcome by my powerful physique to say anything. Anyway, at least I can't be accused of corrupting you any more.'

'You? Corrupt me? That'll be the day.'

He yelled in pain when he hit the water. Assured that the private bits were concealed, Jude watched as he swam in the bitterly cold sea. She envied him. She wanted to join him, to repeat in Ireland the glorious swims they had had in France, and it was so hot. He'd be fair; he'd look away if she stripped off. Besides, they were both adults. Who'd care if they swam naked in the same waters? Who'd know? . . . *I would*, she thought.

When Oliver got out, Jude lay with her face on her arms. 'You should have joined me,' he said, drying himself with his shirt. 'It was fantastic. Unbelievable.'

'As if I would.'

'Oooh. Prudish Judish.'

'Feck off.'

He pulled on his jeans. 'Come on, I fancy a pint.'

*

193

After lunch in Clifden, they headed for the coral strand at Ballyconneely. As they drove, the Connemara hills bestowed an unfamiliar potency on the countryside and seemed to retreat from the heat in search of the shade they were accustomed to. It was impossible to look anywhere but at these humpy mammoths and, in the shimmering air, they were all the more entrancing for their coy reflection of foreign beauty. It was like having a Grecian sky above Irish hills, and Jude found it impossible to believe her time in this place was coming to an end. She thought about the convent. In every distress, its predictability had soothed her; with every upheaval, its routine had absorbed her into normality, even as normality rejected her. And these hills, which for years had embraced and healed her, were also letting her go. It seemed inconceivable that she would no longer sleep with the soft air of Connemara diluting her dreams.

The smashed coral of the beach hurt their feet as they walked barefoot across it, but it was comfortable to lie on. They lay for some time without speaking, shading their eyes occasionally to make contact, to ascertain by a glance that neither felt like moving. The long May evening lied, promising to stretch on indefinitely, leaving Jude right there in paradise, where all the elements of happiness fused together and suggested no end to the day.

When Oliver walked down to the water, dwarfed by the scintillating ocean beyond, Jude considered how deeply she loved this odd individual with whom she had been left. How easily he rejected that love. He didn't need it, of course, as she needed his, and even asked to be released from its constraints. She would oblige. She would ease up, lay off, make no further claims to his affection, and even though it saddened her that she had no right to demand his love, she would not be overwhelmed. For if she should lose him now in spite of his promises, if he should vanish from her life as he was free to do, then she would always have this exceptional day to look back on.

He came towards her. 'Next time I see you, the exams will be over.'

'If that day ever comes.'

'Course it will. It'll all go fine as long as you don't lose your head.'

'And if I do?'

Oliver grinned. 'I'll find it for you.' He leaned over and pushed back her collar with his fingers. 'Damn. You're burnt.'

Jude caught his eye, and at that moment the tie that bound them slackened its hold and left them free to slip apart.

part two

16

'Oliver?'

'Sinéad. How are you?'

'I'm big, bored, and impatient, as you'd expect. How are you?'

'Great. How long to go?'

'Three weeks. A lifetime. How are things over there?'

'Oh, you know, I'm struggling on here, sitting under my tree with cheese and fresh bread and a wonderful local wine . . .'

'Sounds lovely. You're alone then.'

'Yeah, why?'

'I thought Jude might be with you.'

'In the middle of term?'

'Oh, right. I'm hopeless at making out these university timetables.'

'If you want to speak to her, she's at home.'

'Is she?'

Oliver sat forward. 'Isn't she?'

'I . . . Have you heard from her recently?'

'Why? What's happened?'

'Nothing. I just . . . I haven't been able to make contact and . . .'

'Cough it up, Sinéad. Is something wrong?'

'Look, I hope not, but I think so. She was due here for dinner last week and she didn't show. She didn't phone either. I was a bit miffed – I presumed she'd forgotten – but when I didn't hear from her, I called to make sure she was OK, but I couldn't get through. And the thing is, I still can't.'

Oliver stood up. 'Well, is it ringing out or engaged or what?'

'It *was* ringing, but now it's engaged. Maybe it's been cut off?'

'We pay by direct debit. What about her mobile?'

'Switched off, from what I can make out, and, well, I thought she must have gone over to you.'

'Christ.'

'When did you last speak to her?'

'Saturday.'

'Oh good. So she's all right, then?'

Jude had not been all right. Oliver had been unable to get two words out of her. She had insisted she was fine, that she just needed a good night's sleep, and when he had pressed her, she hung up. Like Sinéad, he'd been miffed, but he called back two days later. There was no reply, so he sent her a text message, to which she replied, 'I'm OK! Will call next week.' He couldn't force her to speak to him, so he had left it, but now, remembering her voice as it had been that night, he wished he hadn't.

Hearing this, Sinéad said, 'I'd better go over there and see what they're up to.'

'Please. And if you could stand over her until she phones me, I'd be grateful.'

'No problem. I'll go now. They're bound to be in on a Wednesday night.'

As soon as they hung up, Oliver dialled Jude's number. Engaged. Or was it off the hook? He tried her mobile. Nothing. It had been switched off, lost, stolen, or dropped into the bath. He text-messaged her, but there was no response. He called the house again, and the lonely beeping repeating itself in far-off Dublin made him feel cold all over.

This was the first time in years Jude had given him real cause for concern. She was always there at the end of the line, cheerful and chatty, particularly since she had moved into her new home in Ranelagh, a three-bed redbrick terraced house, which Oliver bought with her when she had started college eighteen months earlier. They had brought all her parents' furniture out of storage and installed it in the house, which had been very disconcerting, particularly for Jude, who could smell her childhood again and kept waking up in her parents' bed thinking she was back in their old home. This was also the bed her mother had died in, but Oliver never mentioned that, because Jude never asked. When she got used to these belongings, they brought her comfort. Her father's desk was now her own, his books graced her shelves, and she kept her shoes at the bottom of the walnut wardrobe where her mother and grandmother had kept their shoes before her. She had, at last, a context all her own.

Fiona rented one of the rooms during term, because her home in Howth was too far from the campus to travel to and fro, and living together again patently agreed with both girls, especially since there were no nuns to scold them when they turned the place upside down. But the first year had been hard going. Jude had fretted about how much money she had and how much she was spending. She had called

Oliver frequently about rattling pipes, and damp patches, and bills with red print on them. She studied too much and socialized too little, and then arrived in Landor at the start of the summer and crashed out completely. Like any student landing home, she was delighted to be released from all responsibility, and for several weeks Oliver had indulged her. But she had never been quite so lazy around the house and when he finally took her to task, she looked up from her deck-chair, shaded her eyes, and said with a smile, 'It's about time you got narked. I was beginning to lose respect for you.' And with those words, Oliver realized that at some point in the course of that fraught year, she had grown up.

Her second year had been much easier so far. She was calmer and less studious and, as far as Oliver knew, was thoroughly enjoying the student life – so why did he now have such a sense of foreboding?

He made coffee and took it outside; it was a warm spring evening. He stared at his mobile, willing it to buzz with an incoming message. It remained mute. Oliver counted. It had been fifteen weeks since he'd seen Jude. They had spent Christmas with his parents and the New Year in Dublin with Tim. He ran over all the conversations they'd had, over lazy breakfasts and late dinners, and remembered no suggestion of unhappiness in Jude, but there was that bloke she fancied. Kevin. He was a likely source of trouble. He had informed her that they could only ever be friends because he had recently espoused celibacy, and her decision to accept this, to take the relationship on his terms, had been as incomprehensible to Oliver as her tolerance of Stephen's inconstancy.

The house phone rang. He ran inside and grabbed it. 'Jude?'

'It's me,' said Sinéad. 'There's nobody home, but Jude's

car is here, so they can't have gone far. I left a note telling them to phone one of us.'

'Where the hell are they?'

'I don't know, but they're probably grand. They are students, after all.'

Three hours later, when there had still been nothing from Dublin, Oliver phoned Sinéad again.

'Not a beep,' she said. 'But the pubs are only just closing.'

'I've got a horrible feeling about this. If she was having trouble sleeping, maybe she took something – too much of something?'

'Don't be silly. What about Fiona?'

'Good question,' said Oliver. 'Why hasn't *she* replaced the receiver?'

'Can't you get her on her mobile?'

'I've tried. She's not picking up. I'm getting a bit frantic here, Sinéad.'

'Look, I shouldn't have alarmed you. I'll go over early tomorrow and catch them before they go to college. I'm sure there's a perfectly reasonable explanation for this.'

'All the same, I think I'll try Fiona's parents. They might be able to throw some light on things.'

Fiona's parents, the Mahons, weren't at home either, and the unanswered ringing of their phone was as irritating as the engaged tone on Jude's number. There was nothing more Oliver could do, and a creeping unease kept moving in on him. He had never heard Jude so subdued as when he had last spoken to her, and he had little doubt that his inability to contact her was being orchestrated from her end. She had taken the phone off the hook to block *his* calls. He was sure of it now. The relentless beeping kept telling him so.

They still had as much contact as when he was her guardian; indeed, they had become even closer recently. Oliver found Jude easier since she had matured, and the sometimes cloying dependence she had displayed while still at school had dissipated, leaving a more balanced relationship behind it – an excellent friendship, in fact. But there was one aspect of her life which she would not discuss with him: her continuing relationship with Stephen. They only had to coincide in the same country at the same time for their sexual fumbling to resume, even if both were seeing someone else, and Oliver hated everything about this liaison. Stephen's casual attitude to sex had rubbed off on Jude, and although she hadn't slept with anyone else, as far as Oliver knew, she regularly slept with someone who neither loved her nor made any attempt to do so, and that was OK as far as she was concerned. Oliver longed for her to find something deeper, to discover the whole point of making love, but he had made these feelings so clear to her that she refused to discuss it. Now, as his mind raced, he became convinced that the evasiveness he had detected in her voice pointed directly at his brother. He picked up the phone and rang Stephen in London.

'Ol? What's up?'

'Have you seen Jude recently? Wake up, Stephen.'

'No. Why?'

'You haven't messed her up, have you? Could she be pregnant?'

There was a long pause as Stephen digested this attack through the fog of sleep. 'Pregnant? Are you kidding?'

'I warned you, Stephen. You wreck her life and I'll fucking wreck yours.'

'Would you like to tell me what's going on?'

'Jude's upset about something and she won't talk to me

about it, and since you're the only bugger she won't talk to me about, I naturally assumed you had something to do with it.'

'Well, you assumed wrong, shithead, so go do your guardian bit with someone else.' He hung up.

Oliver dialled Jude's number again. It had become a reflex action, but it was still engaged.

He spent a restless night. Early the following morning, he tried the house and Fiona's parents again, and received the same shrill rejection from both. The Mahons could be away, he thought, but it was bizarre that he couldn't make contact with them when the silence at Jude's end was becoming intolerable. The simple act of pushing a key into a door would resolve all this, but he was too far away to do it.

Sinéad rang an hour later. 'There's still no sign of life over there, and, well, the milk hasn't been brought in. They must be away.'

'In the middle of the week? Without the car?'

'Did you get hold of the Mahons?'

'No one there either.'

'Really? Maybe they've all gone away together?'

'During term?'

'Look, does anyone have a spare key so I can get into the house?'

'Yeah,' said Oliver. 'Me. And I've a bloody good mind to use it.'

'You're not thinking of coming over?'

'I don't know what I'm thinking, except that Jude has vanished off the face of the earth and there's fuck all I can do about it from here.'

'Oliver, they're well able to look after themselves, so stop fretting. I'll ring if I hear anything.'

Before sitting down to work, Oliver tried the Mahons once more and this time Fiona's father answered. With a surge of relief, Oliver explained that he was trying to get hold of Jude. 'They seem to be away. You don't know where they've gone, Bill, do you?'

'They haven't gone anywhere.'

'No? So why can't I get hold of them?'

'Fiona's spending quite a bit of time here at the moment, as you can appreciate.'

'What about Jude?'

'I've no idea. I'll ask Fiona when I see her.'

Apparently unconcerned with Oliver's plight, he hurried off the line, leaving Oliver tapping the phone against his temple.

It was, without any doubt, the slowest journey he had ever had the misfortune to endure. At such short notice, the only route the airlines could suggest was Zurich to Dusseldorf, Dusseldorf to London, and London to Dublin, with several hours spent in transit along the way. Door to door, stopping overnight in Zurich, it took the best part of twenty-four hours to get to Ireland, and during all that time he couldn't make his mind stop. It was Fiona's absence that had spurred him to travel; if anything had happened to Jude inside the house, nobody would know. She could have fallen down the stairs and still be lying there; she could be violently ill with meningitis or salmonella; she might have taken too many sleeping pills.

The facts were probably far less dramatic and he suspected he had turned over-reaction into an art form by rushing to Dublin, but even if an empty house and a car parked on the street amounted to no more than a forgetful student who was staying with a friend, he would not regret coming. He knew Jude well, and he knew with certainty that he had been right to take these flights. Something was wrong, and it was neither accident nor illness. It had been in her voice that night, in the way she had spoken to him. It was, he realized now, as if she had recoiled into her skin.

He arrived in Dublin at six that Friday evening, two days after Sinéad's call. When the taxi stopped outside the house, he experienced a mixture of relief and apprehension. His questions would soon be answered, but balanced against this deceptive sense of well-being was the fear of what those answers might be.

He glanced at Jude's little red car, the present she had bought herself with her mother's money, pulled his carry-all over his shoulder and covered the path in three steps. Crossing a threshold had never felt so good.

'Jude?' he called, coming into the hall. 'Jude?'

He ran upstairs to her bedroom and saw her pyjamas thrown across the unmade bed. She was at least on her feet. Downstairs, the kitchen was empty and cold. There was a packet of biscuits on the table, soggy teabags by the sink, and an open bottle of milk in the fridge. The milk was sour; very sour. Oliver stood back and ran his thumb along his lip. Nobody had been there for days. Panic filtered past his pores and made its way into his system.

He wandered up the three steps to the table in the hall and replaced the receiver that had been tormenting him. There was a list of phone numbers pinned to the wall. He started with the dreaded Kevin.

'Oliver who?'

'Sayle. Jude's friend.'

'Oh, Oliver! How're ye?'

'I'm fine, thanks, but I was wondering if Jude's with you?'

' 'Fraid not. She's at home, I think.'

'That's where I'm calling from. I can't track her down. Could she be up at college?'

'Could be, but she hasn't been in much recently.'

'Why not?'

Kevin hesitated. He registered a hint of desperation in Oliver's voice and he didn't want to get involved in whatever weird relationship Jude had with her former guardian. 'No idea,' he said.

Oliver made more calls – no one had seen Jude for ages – but it was his conversation with Emer, her school friend, which validated his decision to come.

'I thought you'd show up eventually,' she said.

'Why?'

'She's been in such lousy form. She's been horrible, frankly, and we were just saying the other day that you'd be able to sort her out. I almost rang you.'

'Have you any idea where she is?'

'I thought she was hanging around at home.'

Back in Jude's room, Oliver went through her things. He opened her drawers, rifled through her clothes and shuffled through papers on her desk. The knapsack she used for college was leaning against her chair, her diary inside it. He read it without compunction. For over three weeks she had made scarcely any entries. Before that there was some kind of scribble on every page: *Coffee with Kevin. See Prof. H. at three.* '*Finished essay.*' Another recent entry read, '*Oliver phoned. Patti pregnant! O. delighted for Tim.*' That had been their penultimate conversation, a month before. Then, as he leafed through the recent blank pages, Oliver came across an entry which made his heart trip. On the day before he had last spoken with her, Jude had written: *Falling apart.*

What did she mean, *'Falling apart'*? How far apart had she fallen before going out, and where was she falling apart now? He dredged through every aspect of her life and found no chink through which disaster might have slipped. So what had gone so drastically wrong to make her disappear like this? He swallowed hard. There was collapse in those words and Jude had never yet collapsed. Why would she do so now? *Why?*

He flipped through her diary, but there were no more entries.

Pregnancy kept coming to mind. If she had become pregnant, it was possible she had gone to London for an abortion, but if Stephen had nothing to do with it, who could the father be? Kevin, the celibate? In the bathroom, another shock lay in store: Jude's toiletries were all there. Where had she gone without her toothbrush? Where had she been all week?

In an attempt to shake off the pervasive gloom in the house, he lit the coal fire in the living-room and made tea. He tried to stop the questions that were coming at him like eager horses towards a high fence. There was milk on the doorstep and little food in the house, but that was his Jude, lazy and disorganized; it didn't mean she wasn't about. She could be staying with a boyfriend, only coming home to change, and since her car was outside, this boyfriend was obviously local. Oliver picked up his keys. He headed out and went into every pub within walking distance, pushing his way through the Friday evening crowds, only to emerge, each time, dejected.

He then drove out to the Coal Harbour, her special haunt, but found it dark and deserted. Coming back through the university campus, he scanned the pavements without success, and headed back to the house despondent.

There were lights on when he got there. The relief was such that Oliver stood for a moment on the pavement before letting himself in.

'Who's that?' she called from upstairs.

Oliver went to the foot of the stairs. She was in for a shock.

'Jude?' came the voice, and Fiona looked over the banister.

They stared at each other.

'What are you doing here?' she asked.

'Where's Jude?'

'I don't know.'

'What's been going on around here? I've been trying to get hold of you two for days! Where on earth has Jude got to?'

'I said I don't know.' Fiona went back into her room.

Oliver took the stairs three at a time and stood by her door. She was packing a small suitcase. 'You must have some idea? When did you last see her?'

'Days ago. I haven't been here much.'

'Is she all right?'

'Apparently not.'

'Why? What's wrong?'

'I have absolutely no idea and frankly, Oliver, I have enough on my plate at the moment without taking on Jude's angst, whatever it's about.'

Oliver watched as she zipped her case closed. 'But she's gone missing!'

'She'll turn up.'

'That's not good enough, Fiona. Can't you ring around and see if—'

'No, I can't. Excuse me.' She pushed past him.

'Where are you going?'

'Home. Mum isn't well. I only came back for clothes.'
With that, Jude's usually chirpy friend ran down the stairs
and left the house without another word.

Oliver remained on the landing. Jude had obviously hit
rock bottom over something which she couldn't discuss with
anyone. She wasn't at a friend's house, so could she be with
somebody new? Some stranger?

He walked around the house, eating biscuits and
muttering. He was so desperate to see Jude, to hear her
voice, that his mouth was dry. A long night stretched out
ahead; he knew he wouldn't hack it alone.

Sinéad arrived at ten past ten.

'You should be in bed,' said Oliver.

'I wouldn't sleep. God, you look awful.'

'I don't know what to do. There could be a hundred
logical explanations for where she might be, but I don't
believe any of them.'

'What if she's trying to contact you in Landor?'

'I can access my answering service. There's nothing from
her.'

'Then we're probably fretting unnecessarily. We've no
real proof that anything is even amiss.'

'Apart from the fact that she's completely fucking
disappeared!'

'Look, she's probably curled up in bed with some
wonderful guy, madly in love, with no interest in speaking
to anyone or going anywhere. We've all done that.'

'Why is the phone off the hook then?'

'Go and sit down. I'll make tea.'

'Thanks, but I need something stronger. Would you stay
by the phone while I go down to the off-licence?'

When he returned, they went over everything together.

They talked about every person Jude knew, every word she'd spoken when they had last seen her, and drew a blank. They couldn't but conclude that she had been perfectly happy when they had last, individually, seen her. It appeared something had taken place recently that had sent her running.

'I thought you were mad coming over like this,' said Sinéad. 'Now I'm not so sure.' She sat forward. 'My God – I hope she hasn't been raped.'

'Good Christ.'

'That would be enough to send any woman off the deep end.'

'She'd tell me. I'm sure of it. She'd tell the cops.'

'But if it was date-rape? Someone she knew?'

'Jesus, if that Kevin bastard touched her, I'll have his—'

'Don't be silly. He's a pussy cat.'

'He's a frustrated tom cat, if you ask me. But what if it was someone else? Some guy who was afraid she'd report him? What if he's abducted her?'

'Oh, let's get off this. It's bound to be far less dramatic.'

'Is it? She's gone, Sinéad, and as far as we know, the only thing she has with her is her handbag.'

'Oliver, get a grip. I know it isn't like her to go off like this, but you mustn't think the worst.'

'I'm going to call Stephen.'

'Well, hello,' said his brother. 'About time you rang to apologize.'

'I'm not ringing to apologize.'

Stephen was shocked when Oliver told him what was happening, but he could throw no light on Jude's where-abouts or state of mind. After hanging up, Oliver didn't go back into the living-room. Whisky wasn't all he had bought at the off-licence. When Sinéad opened the door, he was leaning against the wall, drawing on a cigarette as if his life depended on it.

'Oliver! You can't go back on the fags. Jude'll kill you.'

'That's fine,' he said, scratching his lip. 'If she was only here to kill me, that'd be just fine.'

'Come near the fire.'

'It's bad for the baby.'

'I'll make an exception.'

'I'll come in a minute.' He went down to the kitchen to smoke. Jude's diary was on the counter. He went through it again, meticulously, reading every entry for every day in the previous month and separating the flimsy, sticky pages with a firm rub in case he'd missed one. He had.

When he went back to the living-room, Sinéad was sitting staring at the fire. He held Jude's diary in front of her. She squinted at the one word written that Wednesday and then looked up. 'No.'

'Why not?' he asked. 'At some point this week, she walked out of here with no car and no luggage. She left here with nothing. Now, either she meant to come back and hasn't been able to or she didn't need anything where she was going.'

'She wouldn't do that.'

He pushed the diary close to her face. 'Read it! "*Enough*." It's right there!'

'I don't care. Jude wouldn't go off the deep end. She's far too strong.'

'That's the problem. She's always been too damned strong for her own good.' He turned about the room like a caged lion. 'She obviously couldn't hack it any more.'

'She can hack anything.'

'So why is her car here, Sinéad? And her clothes and her toilet bag? Where *is* she?'

213

Sinéad nibbled at her cuticles. Oliver wasn't ranting. They had found no reasonable explanation for Jude's absence; anything could have happened. She might have been mugged, or worse. Sinéad struggled to her feet. 'I'm going to call the Guards.'

It was half past one when a squad car pulled up outside and two police officers came to the door. They seemed to crowd out the living-room when they came in, but only one of them sat down.

'In a case like this,' he said, 'we wouldn't normally file a missing person report at this juncture. Students often disappear – they're usually asleep on someone's floor getting over a party – but we'll make some preliminary enquiries.' He turned to Oliver. 'And you are the girl's . . . ?'

'I was her guardian before she came of age.'

'Who is her next of kin?'

'I am.'

'She has no living relatives?'

'A grandmother and an aunt.'

'But—'

'Her grandmother is senile and her aunt is a complete waste of space.'

Sinéad intervened. 'It would be fair to say that, to all intents and purposes, Oliver is Jude's next of kin.'

'So, no one has seen her since you spoke to her last Saturday?'

'No one we know.'

'And you believe she might be in a state of distress?'

Oliver nodded.

The questions went on, and the more they went over the details of Jude's disappearance, the more desperate Oliver became. It sounded so unredeeming. Nothing he said threw even a chink of light on the situation and this was made all the more clear for him by the policemen when they honed in on certain details with grim faces. They did not appear to feel they had been called out on a wild goose chase. They flicked through her diary.

One of them said, 'Do you believe she's capable of harming herself?'

'Oh, please!' Sinéad gasped.

Oliver stood over the fire with his back to them, his hands on the mantelpiece, his head dropped between his shoulders. They waited for an answer, they prompted him, but he made no comment.

The officer stood up. 'We'll check her bank account tomorrow to see if she's made any withdrawals and we'll ask local stations to keep an eye out, but we can't throw it open yet. There's every likelihood she'll turn up soon.'

After seeing them out, Sinéad went over to Oliver and leaned against his shoulder. 'I wish I'd never met Michael Feehan,' he said. 'He's brought me nothing but grief.'

'You know that's not true.' She ran her hand across his back. 'You should get some rest and see what the morning brings.'

'You go. Go on back to Peter.'

'I'm staying until this is sorted.'

'You don't need it, Sinéad. You've already seen Michael cut to bits. You don't need this.'

'Nor do you.' She sat down on the couch.

He threw himself into an armchair. His bright uneven eyes reflected the firelight. 'You know why they wanted to know who's her next of kin? So they'll know who to call if they need someone to identify her.'

'Would you stop thinking like that?'

'I have no option. Jude wouldn't do this to me, Sinéad. In her worst moments of self-indulgence, she wouldn't consign me to hell unless she had no alternative.'

'Hell? Surely not.'

'Why not?' He stood up, took his cigarettes from the mantelpiece. 'That's where I'll be if she doesn't come back. Not that I'd expect anyone to understand that. After all, I was only doing a mate a favour. Washed my hands of her as soon as she turned eighteen. Glad to be shut of her.'

'I know it's more than that.'

'Yes, but how much more? How much more am I allowed? I'm not her father, nor her brother, nor even her guardian.'

'You're her friend.'

'That doesn't cover it. Not by half. She's been under my skin since the day she was born.' He lit a cigarette and collapsed into the chair. 'I've buried her mother and her father. If I have to . . . If I had to . . . It would be too much. Too bloody much.'

She squeezed his arm.

'Where are you, Jude? *Where the hell are you?*'

Sinéad slept for some hours on the couch. Oliver made coffee, then paced the hall, smoking his way through the early hours, his stomach churning with apprehension. *'Falling apart.'* *'Falling apart.'* She had fallen apart and he hadn't been there to put her back together again and then she'd had *'Enough.'* He cursed the wretched Feehans and cursed the wretched love they had drawn from him, one after the other. If this ended badly, it would be one Feehan blow too many. If Jude had, for some unspeakable reason, thrown herself off a cliff, such a wound would be beyond healing, Oliver knew, because Jude had been good. She had been good for him, and she had kept his head together when he'd lost Tim. Her love had steadied him; that candid love, which he had so often ducked, had given him purpose when he had no other. If he were to lose it now, and her with it, he wasn't sure he'd get through it.

He had been afraid to speak when asked if she had the potential for suicide concealed somewhere within that spirited character, but now he faced it. Tragedy had a way of absorbing people, of sucking them in and making them tragic, and there was tragedy in Jude's make-up, however well she had coped with it. She had been so battered and shred as a young girl that the damage could never have been entirely smoothed away. That was what he most feared – not that she had been mugged in an alleyway, but that the ruptures in her soul had been rent without warning, leaving her unable to support whatever it was that had come her way.

He could see her. He could see her standing on a beach, at dawn or dusk, facing the sea. He rubbed his eyelids to block it out, but she was still there, contemplating the ocean. Her feet were bare and her heart was breaking; and he was too far away to do anything about it.

Sinéad woke after six and was relieved to see Oliver stretched out in the armchair. She had feared he might go out, wildly searching for Jude in the night, but he was sitting there, still smoking. 'Did you sleep?' she asked.

'An hour. Sort of.'

They listened to the milkman dropping bottles on the doorsteps; there was nothing to say. All they could do was wait. Wait until the Gardaí got back to them; until Jude phoned; until something happened.

At five past seven, the phone rang. Oliver, who appeared

to be in a trance, was out the door before Sinéad had blinked. She held her breath and listened. It was Stephen, hoping for news.

When Oliver came back in, she said, 'If we should get a call, you need to be prepared.'

'Prepared for the worst? What do you think I've been doing all night?'

'I mean quite the opposite. If Jude should phone, you'll have to go to her, and you can't go anywhere in your present state.'

As she spoke, a key turned in the front door. They leaped up, Oliver pulling the door open with such force that it almost hit Sinéad in the face, and tumbled into the hall together.

It was Peter. 'Someone left their keys in the door.'

Oliver banged his forehead against the wall. 'No. No. No.'

'No news, then?' asked Peter. 'Nothing?' Sinéad shook her head. 'I'm sorry, Oliver, I didn't mean to—'

'Leave him,' said Sinéad, leading her husband into the living-room.

'I've been so worried, darling. Are you all right?'

'I'm fine, but he's not.' The sight of Peter made Sinéad weaken. 'And if anything's happened . . .'

'Shush.'

Oliver kicked open the door but didn't come in. 'If she does it – if she's done it or is going to do it – she'll do it on a beach. She'll swim out.'

'I told you not to talk like that!' Sinéad shouted.

Peter frowned. 'You don't mean—'

'The question is,' said Oliver, 'where? I think she'd head out west.'

*

Sr Aloysius was at Mass when Sr Paul limped in and told her there was an urgent call for her. She fled the chapel, wondering who had died on her.

She picked up the phone. 'Hello?'

'Sr Aloysius, this is Oliver Sayle.'

For a moment, she said nothing. 'Mr Sayle?'

'Sister, I need your help.'

'Gracious. It isn't Jude, is it?'

'Yes. I'm afraid I've lost her.'

Later that morning Sinéad called as many of Jude's friends as she could find and asked them to look for her, to ask around. Oliver kept to his post by the mantelpiece. When one concerned acquaintance phoned, he stormed into the hall, grabbed the receiver from Sinéad and slammed it down. 'Keep these sodding people off the phone!'

'These sodding people are trying to help!' She pulled his arm. 'You're a complete wreck. What good will you be to Jude when we find her?'

'*If* we find her. Don't tell me to sleep. There isn't a hope in hell of it.'

'Well, at least stop hanging over that mantelpiece!'

He went to his room, stretched out on the bed and rang Stephen.

'Still nothing?'

'Nope.'

'Listen, it'll be all right. That's one girl who has her head screwed on tight.'

'I'm not so sure. I've seen it, you know. I've watched her keeping it all under wraps.'

'Maybe, but whatever's happened, it isn't your fault, Oliver.'

*

At ten past eleven, Sinéad pulled her additional weight up the stairs and went in to Oliver. He was lying with his hands behind his head. She sat on the end of the bed. 'Would you eat if I made you something?'

The phone rang downstairs. Oliver threw his legs around Sinéad, leaped up and got down to the hall before she reached the door. 'Yes? Hello, yes?'

Sinéad prayed, and prayed hard, because with every hour that passed, the minutes grew longer. She felt discomfort in her belly, as if her nerves were toying with her unborn child, making it cross and agitated. As she came down, she saw Oliver slide to the ground, and the shock of his collapse made her own legs weaken. She fell back on to a step. 'Peter!'

Her husband came running from the kitchen. 'Darling!'

She pointed at Oliver.

For several moments, no one moved. Peter loomed over Oliver, trying to read his expression. He was sitting against the wall and the only perceptible movement he made was a slight repeated nod. Sinéad remained on the stairs.

'Yes,' Oliver said. 'Thank you. Yes. I'm on my way.' He dropped the phone, closed his eyes, and inhaled as if he hadn't done so for days.

Peter replaced the receiver. 'The Gardaí?'

'No. The nuns. The nuns have found her.'

Sinéad cried out.

'Is she all right?' asked Peter.

'They think so.'

Sinéad joined Oliver on the floor. 'Thank God. Where is she?'

'She's in Letterfrack. In a hotel near the convent.'

'You were right!'

'I'm leaving as soon as I can get up – if I can have your car? Jude's heap of junk would take forever.'

'You're not fit to drive to Connemara. Let Peter take you as far as Galway. He can get the train back.'

Oliver was too weary to argue.

17

Oliver had never heard of the Manor House, but the directions were simple and, after leaving Galway, he drove like a raging maniac, taking Peter's estate car around corners in such a manner that it seemed to bend like a piece of rubber. He could have driven with his eyes closed, so often had he taken Jude back this way, but who would drive such a road with their eyes closed when beyond Maam Cross, the Twelve Pins lured you forward, encouraging your foot to press harder on the accelerator and draw you more swiftly into their kingdom? Oliver knew no greater source of satisfaction than speeding west into Connemara, but now it was different. Now, the Twelve Pins stood between him and Jude and he wished they would flatten themselves like a body reclining to allow him to get straight to her, instead of forcing him to drive all the way around them. Even Derryclare had lost its beauty, for it stood like a great wall carrying a Halt! sign and refused to budge. The scenery Oliver so admired seemed dark in the mid-April afternoon and Lake Inagh looked black, deep and dangerous. As he neared Letterfrack, his heartbeat accelerated. Beyond the village, he came around the bend at Ballynakill Harbour far too quickly and slammed on the brakes.

She was there, right in front of him. At the far side of the inlet, about 400 metres across the water, she was no more than an indistinct blot on some rocks at the foot of the hill, but he knew it was her. He knew her posture, her stance; he would have known her even if she had been shrouded in black. The Manor was perched on the hill overlooking the inlet – it was the Pink Palace, the place he'd asked Jude about two years before, where she'd planned to spend an illicit weekend with Stephen. Oliver glanced across the bay at the slouched figure on the rocks and put his foot down. The car skidded forward.

He drove along the Manor's driveway, parked outside the hotel, and noticed a pathway leading off through the garden to the left. He took it, winding his way past azaleas and rhododendrons until he reached a low wooden gate which led into woodland. The path became steeper. Propelled by urgency and the inclination of the slope, he half ran through the trees, tripping on emerging roots and sliding on dried conifer twigs until, at the foot of the hill, he came out on to the stony shore. Jude was sitting hunched up 150 metres away, cool as bedamned and staring towards the hills on the other side of the bay. This was all he had wanted for several miserable days. Nothing else. Only the sight of Jude, doing anything, anywhere, but alive and well and near him.

'Jude!' His voice echoed down the inlet.

She turned, and cried out when she saw him. He walked towards her. She tried to run, stumbling occasionally on slippery stones and hopping from one flat bit of ground to another, while Oliver marched forward, never taking his eyes from her face. Her hair was pulled into a ponytail and

223

she was wearing one of his sweaters, like she always did when she was in a bad mood or had a period, and as they drew closer, both broke into a run. They threw themselves at each other with such momentum that they nearly fell over.

'What are you doing here?' Jude cried.

'Looking for you,' he said, squeezing her. 'Finding you.' He pulled back to look at her. 'What's happened? What's going on? Are you all right?'

She was shaking with the shock of seeing him. 'Yes, I . . . I'm fine.'

'So why did you take off like that?'

'Is that why you're here?'

'I'm here, Jude, because you disappeared without trace. I've been sodding frantic! I even called in the police!'

She gasped.

'Yes. *And* your friends have been scouring Dublin *and* all the nuns in bloody Connemara have been looking for you!'

She put her hand over her mouth. 'Oh, God.'

'You have some serious explaining to do, young lady. What the hell did you think—'

'Don't be cross with me.'

'Why not? Christ, Jude, I haven't slept for three days, I can't remember the last time I ate, and here you are in a four-star country-house hotel sleeping off whatever madness prompted you to send me into a tailspin!'

'Stop yelling at me!'

He pulled her close to his face. 'I thought you might be dead, do you understand? I thought you'd done yourself in!'

'*What?* How could you think that?'

He squeezed her elbows. 'Does the word "Enough" ring any bells?'

'Oh, God, no, that's not —'

224

'What was I supposed to think? Or don't you give a toss?'

Her eyes filled. She began to sink, as if the ground was vanishing beneath her feet and Oliver's clasp on her arms was the only thing holding her up. He let go and turned away.

'Oliver, please.'

He shook his head, still trying to contain an explosive mixture of fury and relief.

'Don't be angry,' Jude cried. 'I couldn't . . . I can't . . .'

Oliver swung around and pulled her against him.

'I'm so sorry.'

'I thought I'd lost another Feehan, Jude. I was out of my mind.'

'But why? I—'

He drew back. 'Because I love you, for God's sake, why do you think?'

Jude was shivering. Oliver opened his jacket and put her under his arm. 'You haven't been raped, have you?'

'Is that what you thought?'

'Are you pregnant?'

'No.'

'Is it Kevin then? Stephen?'

'No, no. It isn't that straightforward.'

'Straightforward?' Oliver sighed. 'Let's go up.'

'How did you find me?'

He opened the gate that led into the wood. 'Intuition. I figured you'd come west.'

'But how did you find me here?'

'The nuns rang every bed and breakfast in Connemara. When Sr Ignatius phoned this place, they were cagey, so she knew they had you. In the end, they owned up. How did you get here?'

'I hitched from Galway.'

'When?'

'Wednesday, I think.'

He stopped. 'So you *were* at home when we were trying to get through. Why did you leave the phone off the hook?'

'I didn't want to talk to anyone.'

'And your mobile?'

'Switched off.'

'That's not good enough, Jude. Last night was hellish.'

'I wasn't thinking clearly.' She led the way through the garden and into the hotel. Her room was on the ground floor. It was a long salmon-pink room with tall windows, a green carpet, and heavy antique furniture.

Oliver took a good look at her. Her hair was greasy, her face wan, she was lost in his big sweater, and yet he heard himself say, 'You're a sight for sore eyes.'

'*I* am? I've never been so glad to see *you* in my entire life!' She put her hand over her eyes and wept. Oliver went to her. She knocked her forehead against his shoulder. 'I'm so sorry. I didn't mean to worry you.'

He stroked her cheek with his knuckles. 'I suggest soup. You look like you need soup.'

Jude went into the bathroom to wash her face. Her skin was blotchy, her eyes puffy, and she hadn't even started yet.

Oliver took off his jacket, sat on the couch at the foot of the bed and patted the seat beside him. 'Come here, you.' She ambled over, arms hanging, and sat down. 'What's all this about?'

She pulled his handkerchief from his pocket. 'Fiona's mother is dying.'

'*What?* God, that explains it. There was never anyone home when I rang and when I did get through, Bill was really short with me.'

226

'They're always at the hospital.'

'That's really rough . . . But right now I need to know what's wrong with you.'

'That's what's wrong.'

'Eh?'

'I hope you're going to understand, Oliver, because no one else does.'

'Understand what?'

'Can we wait for the soup?'

'More waiting?'

They waited. Jude went to the window, leaving Oliver wholly perplexed. This was wide of the mark. What had Fiona's mother's illness got to do with Jude? 'Tell me, then,' he said, 'how you ended up coming to this place.'

'I hadn't slept. For ages. I spent every night tossing and it was getting worse, so I went to my GP. That's what I meant by "Enough". Enough with not sleeping. Anyway, she gave me pills and when I came out, I couldn't go back to the house. I'd been there on my own for three weeks and I couldn't face it any more. It seemed like a good idea to go away. I thought nobody would notice – I'm not exactly flavour of the month – so I went into town and caught a train to Galway.'

'But you had no clothes.'

'I didn't care about that. I got here that evening, took a pill, and I've been sleeping ever since, seems like.'

'Why didn't you tell me? You knew I was concerned. How could you leave me with that wretched phone beeping day after day?'

'Because when I left home, I didn't know I wasn't going back. I was in a daze.'

'But you've had plenty of opportunity to phone me since.'

'Look, don't go on about it. I didn't want to talk to you, all right?'

'Why not?'

She looked away. 'You're too close.'

'Will you talk to me now? I've come a long way, Jude.'

She nodded. A waitress knocked and brought in a tray which she placed on the table in the corner of the room.

'Here.' Oliver held out a bowl of soup.

'I'm not hungry.'

'I don't give a curse. You'll eat.'

She ate. When they had finished, Oliver took cigarettes from his jacket. Jude's mouth fell open. He stared straight at her as he lit up, then stretched out on the bed. 'Come on, then. Let's have it.'

Jude sat cross-legged by his feet, fiddling with the key he had given her, which she always wore around her neck. 'Fiona's mother has some kind of inoperable brain tumour. She only has a few weeks left. The night Fiona told me, she cried for hours, saying she couldn't bear to see her mother wasting away and how incredibly brave she was being. She asked if my mother accepted her death that way too, but I couldn't tell her, could I? I don't know what kind of a death my mother had. And then Fiona said I'd understand better than anyone, and I said, of course, that I'd be there for her.' Jude blew her nose. She kept opening her mouth and closing it, as if she didn't know which bit to go with. 'But I've been a lousy friend.' Tears flowed down her face and dropped on to her hands.

'You're not a lousy friend. You're a very good friend.'

'No, but you don't know what I did, and even you won't get your head around it. I can't.'

'What?'

'As soon as we went to bed that night, I started to churn. I felt sick and giddy and it took me all night to work out why: I resented Fiona,' she whispered. 'I resented her, I almost hated her, when she needed me most!'

'Why?'

'Because – it's so ridiculous – because I felt as if she'd stolen something from me. Taken away my one defining characteristic: the dead mother. That's *my* routine; *my* baggage. And I resented her because she's had her mother for fifteen years longer than I had mine. I mean, I just thought, well, she's dying, but she isn't young like my mother was, and her kids are all grown up, and she's been there for Fiona when she had her first period and did her first exams and got her Leaving Cert. She's had a mother for all those things – I haven't.'

'But she won't have her mum when she gets married or has a baby—'

'*I know*. And that breaks my heart too. I *do* feel for her. I really do, but, oh, I can't explain, it's so confusing. I couldn't bear to see her upset and yet another part of me wanted to say, "What have you got to complain about? You've had her all these years and you'll still have your family!"'

'Shush.' Oliver pulled her down beside him. 'Easy. Did Fiona pick up on this?'

'Of course she did. I couldn't bear talking about it, hearing about it, and it got to the point where I couldn't be in the same room with her. Oh, she got the message all right. I tried to explain to Emer and Kevin that something inside me was running out of control, and they said, "Yeah, tough, but Fiona needs our support right now." But I couldn't give her my support, I couldn't even look at her! She's my best friend, Oliver, she always has been, and now, when her mother's dying, we're not even speaking. I've been horrible. And I know what the others thought. They thought *I* wanted to be the tragic figure, that I couldn't cope with Fiona having all the attention, and Kevin even said, "But that happened years ago!" As if the years make any bloody difference! No matter how much time passes – I'm still alone.'

Oliver smoked and stroked her cheek with his knuckle.

'I know it sounds like jealousy, but it feels like envy gone mad. I've always envied her the relationship she had with her mum, I always thought it great they got on so well, but now I can't help feeling bitter that they had it so good and yet I can't bear for it to end for them. It's easy for the others to be sympathetic, to tell her she'll be all right, but I know exactly how rotten she'll feel for years and years. I mean, I miss my mother and I hardly knew her, so how's Fiona going to cope?'

Oliver stubbed out his cigarette. 'This has nothing to do with Fiona. She's just the spark at the end of a fuse that's been waiting for a match for a very long time.'

'My friends are all I have. I don't want to be like this.'

'I know you don't, love.'

'But they all turned against me. They thought I was being a selfish bitch. Kevin even said he was ashamed of me – as if I wasn't ashamed of myself – and then they ostracized me. After Fiona moved back home, no one came to the house. No one phoned. In college they gave me a wide berth. Not one of them was able to work out that this was bringing up old history for me.' She caught her breath. 'I stopped going to college. I couldn't bear it. It was a nightmare, wandering down corridors where no one could see me, so it was easier to stay home where nobody *could* see me, but that was awful too. It was so empty, and the silence kept reminding me that everyone was angry with me, that I'd let Fiona down. All I had to do to fix it was to contact her, but I couldn't carry it off. I was afraid if I did—'

'It would bring it all back?'

'Yes, and that she'd expect too much of me.'

'Why didn't you tell me this when we spoke?'

'Because by then something else was happening and I didn't want you to know. By leaving the phone off the hook, I could blot you out.'

'Go on.'

'At night, in a sort of half-baked sleep, I started having these dreams. Awful ones, about Catherine. In the first one, I was in my old room at home and I heard her calling. When I went to the door of her room, you were asleep in the chair and she was trying to wake you, but she couldn't reach you and she was struggling . . .'

Oliver swallowed.

'You were in another dream too, when she was being sick, and in another Dad was trying to get out the front door and he couldn't open it and you came out and the two of you fought and you hit him. It was *awful*.' She looked up at him. 'Why were you in all those dreams?'

'Because I was there. Because they're not dreams.'

Jude seemed to relax. 'That's what I thought. It got so I couldn't close my eyes without remembering something horrible.'

Oliver couldn't move, even though he was getting cold lying still. 'So that's where you've been these last weeks, my poor love.'

'I couldn't get away from her. It was like drowning in something dense, like tar, something sticky I couldn't get off. I tried, Oliver, I really tried. I thought I could pull myself out of it, but it was as if my soul was shrinking and I was afraid that if it shrank any further, there'd be nothing left of me!'

They lay for a while without speaking, Oliver staring at the green silk draped over the head of the bed, Jude fiddling with the button on his shirt pocket. When she spoke again, she was all cried out; her voice was dull and determined. 'I'm sorry I worried you, but I'm not sorry you've come. A few days ago I didn't want to know what you know, but now that I've had some sleep and the dreams have stopped, I need answers. Answers only you can give me. I want to know everything – what kind of death she had; how many pieces Dad was broken into when that boat hit him.'

'Oh, Jude. To what end? What good will it do? Your memories of your parents are happy ones. Keep it that way.'

'But now there are other memories. Unhappy ones. They've come back. I couldn't hold them down any longer and I want them straightened out. You're the only person who can do that.'

Oliver sighed. 'No.'

She leaned on her elbow. 'No? No, you won't tell me? But I have a right to know. You owe it to me.'

'I don't care. I'm not doing it.'

'You have to.'

He rolled towards her, his face near her forearm. 'Don't do this, Jude. Don't even ask.'

'It was that bad?'

'Worse.'

She pulled him by the hair to make him face her. 'You've never spoken to anyone about it? Not Patti?'

'She didn't want to know.'

'Not even Dad?'

'Above all, not him.'

'Then you must tell me, as much for your own good as for mine.'

'Why? Bad enough that one of us is carrying it around.'

'Wouldn't it be lighter for two?'

'It would be heavy for you. Very heavy.'

'But what's the point of me going through all this if it ends up unresolved? What good can I be to Fiona, to anyone, if these ghosts pop up when I least need them? Please, Oliver.'

'It's just that I don't think I can.'

'Of course you can. Do it for me.'

'It wouldn't do you any favours.'

'You're wrong. You know you're wrong.'

'I'm not wrong. Your mother died a hard death. Painful and humiliating. I was a kid. I couldn't understand how someone so beautiful could be so . . . spoiled. There's no point going into details. I never want to go back there and if you love me, you won't ask me to.' He looked at her. 'They're gone. We're left. We have to make the most of that, so don't go picking at me like a scavenger, trying to feed on the bits of me that are rotten.'

'Surely that's the purpose of scavengers? To pick away the bad bits and leave the rest clean?'

Oliver rolled on to his back. 'Good try, but the answer's still no.'

'How can you refuse to tell me about my own mother?'

'"Mummy." Say "*Mummy*!"' There was a chilliness in the way Jude referred to her mother as 'my mother' or 'Catherine', the remoteness of which had always hurt Oliver. It was as if she could keep her mother at a clinical distance by never referring to her by the name she'd used as a child, and Oliver believed that as long as that distance

233

remained, Jude would never truly grieve for her. 'Say it.'

'I can't. It won't come.'

'What we both need,' said Oliver, 'is a hit of caffeine and sugar.'

'Chocolate, even.'

He sat up with as much effort as if a roller-coaster had passed over him, and looked around the long bedroom. 'When you go walkabout, you certainly do it in style. You can afford this place, can you?'

'No, but you can.'

'I see. Just rely on good ol' Uncle Ol to pay off your credit card, eh?'

Jude put her foot against his back and pushed him affectionately.

'I'll get the bags and check in. Sinéad packed some things for you. Why don't you sink into a bath while I see if I can find some chocolate?'

'OK.' As he reached the door, she said, 'Oliver?'

'Ya?'

She hesitated. 'Don't get another room. I couldn't bear to be alone another minute.'

'You really think I'm about to let you out of my sight at this point? No chance.'

'Thanks. And thanks for coming to save me. Again.'

He winked and left the room.

Twenty minutes later, Jude emerged from the bathroom wrapped in a towel and bumped into the waitress who had come with another tray. 'You can imagine what they think,' she said when the girl withdrew. 'You're the older married man; I'm your bit of fluff who ran away in a huff because you won't leave your wife the way you said you would.'

'Less emphasis on the "older", please. And I'm not married.'

'I'll bet they think you are.' Jude inspected the tray. 'What's this? Chocolate mousse?'

'Last night's dessert. I told them my girlfriend was pregnant and craving chocolate. "Funny," I said, "with the wife it was always onions."'

Jude smiled, giving Oliver leave to relax for the first time in days. It was only a small, fleeting smile which made no impression on her underlying mood, but it made her look better. She settled on the bed and dipped her finger into the mousse. Oliver handed her a cup of tea.

'Tea and chocolate,' said Jude, flatly. 'Life itself.'

'Shouldn't you get some clothes on?'

'Oh, sorry. Where's my bag?'

Stretched out on the bed, Oliver raised his chin and blew out a lungful of smoke.

'When did that start?' Jude had dressed and was sitting at his feet, eating chocolate mousse.

'Last night, I suppose. Seems like days ago.'

'Will you stop again?'

'Hope so. Hey.' He nudged her with his foot. 'Guess how much I love you.'

He was making light of it, but Jude was used to that. Besides, he'd told her on the shore that he loved her and that would probably have to do her for another ten years. She threw her eyes heavenward. 'How much?'

'Enough to spend three hours in the car with Peter Brocket.'

'You want a reward?'

'Enough,' he went on, tipping ash into the ashtray, 'to be

235

driven wild at the thought of anything happening to you.'

Jude blushed. His timing was good. She needed to hear this now, more than ever before; to hear that someone really cared, in spite of her bitterness and failings. She sucked her spoon. 'You never said so before.'

'I shouldn't have had to. However, I now realize that if I'd spelt it out sooner, you might have behaved differently these last few days. You might even have called me.' He held her gaze. 'So from now on, you should understand: you're where it's at, as far as I'm concerned. You're right up there with Tim. I've known you since you were two days old. We've been through some shit since then and we've chalked up a lot of time together, so the next time you get churned up about something – don't leave the phone off the hook, don't go hitching cross-country alone, and above all, don't take pills of *any* description!' He swallowed the remains of his tea. 'Because at this point, Jude, I wouldn't much relish living without you. I'm going for a bath.'

He left her sitting there, astonished.

A long hot bath drained all Oliver's remaining energy. Wearing boxer shorts and a shirt, he crashed on to the bed, face into a pillow. 'I'm so tired I feel sick.'

'I don't even know what time she died at,' said Jude.

He groaned. 'I thought we'd dealt with this?'

'Don't you think she'd want me to know what she went through?'

After a long pause, Oliver said, 'I don't know.'

'And isn't it about time you dealt with it?'

'I have dealt with it. It was a long time ago and I got over it.'

'No, you didn't. If you'd got over it, you could talk about it.'

236

'I *can* talk about it. You're just the wrong person to talk to.'

'I'm the only person, surely?'

Oliver winced, his face still buried in pillows. 'Jude, leave me alone on this one. I've done everything else you've ever needed. You've had everything you wanted from me. Can't you let this one thing go?'

'If I do let it go, how do you propose to resolve the way I feel about Fiona?' He didn't answer. 'Are my memories accurate? Was she calling out and vomiting blood and did you and Dad fight?'

Oliver rolled over and put his head on her lap. 'I've slept four hours in three nights. Or is that three hours in four nights?'

'And why wasn't she in hospital when she was so ill? I want to know everything, Oliver. Everything.'

'Jude.' He put his hand to her face. 'Please. If you really must know these things, I'll tell you, but I have to sleep. Let me sleep first.'

She squeezed his hand between her chin and shoulder.

He closed his eyes and passed out.

18

Early sunshine was glowing through the long cream curtains
when Oliver woke twelve hours later, almost exactly where
he had fallen asleep. Jude had pulled the heavy counterpane
over him and was so deeply asleep beside him that he suspected she had taken another pill. Remembering his state of
mind twenty-four hours before, he reached over to her. This,
he knew, was not what Michael had expected of him. This
curious platonic intimacy which had developed between them
was not what her father would have envisaged when, years
before, they had spoken about her care. And yet Oliver
remained comfortable with it. As a child, Jude had been
much cuddled by her gran and her dad, and she had always
come to him expecting the same. He had allowed it to continue into the awkward teenage years for the simple reason
that he couldn't allow her to mature in a vacuum of physical
affection. Besides, it came naturally to them and he saw no
reason to suppress it.

The Manor was ideally situated for such an undertaking
as they began later that morning, when they took the story
to the great outdoors, to filter it with air in the hope of
diluting its impact. They walked through the woodland and

along the pebbly shore, where the sea was as still as black ice, and Oliver began, as best he could, to tell Jude what he had so often tried to forget.

'Catherine wanted to die at home. They'd done what treatment they could – I was living in London then – and Michael called to say I should come to say goodbye. So I came and I stayed. I didn't particularly want to stay, it was more that I couldn't seem to leave. The atmosphere in the house was ghastly. Two demented mothers, a man whose heart was breaking, a child who was blocking it all out, and in the midst of it all, a beautiful young woman decaying in her bed. I wanted to run, back to the safety of a numb existence in London where I wouldn't have to witness the atrocity that had befallen you, but I couldn't budge. Catherine seemed happy that I was there for Michael, but I was there for her too.'

'What was she like, really?'

'You mean aside from being brainy, beautiful and incredibly capable? She was very . . . happy. Her happiness was quite entrancing, in fact; it certainly charmed the hell out of me. I simply didn't know any women like her. I was dating girls who were planning their twenty-first birthday parties, for God's sake, whereas Catherine was in another dimension. She was five years older than me; she had qualified; she'd had a baby. I thought her amazing, but as Michael frequently pointed out, I didn't have to live with her. I didn't have to cope with her fastidiousness, her manic tidiness.'

'Tidiness? Oh dear. Not like me at all then.'

'Certainly not, and you think I'm bad. Your mother was the kind of person who wiped the table when you lifted your mug to drink!'

'Dad made her out to be a paragon of perfection.'

'Yeah, well, he never said a bad word about her from the day she died, bless him, but she had her faults.'

'Like what?'

Oliver thought about it. 'I'd say her worst failing was that she was an intellectual snob. She could be very intolerant of people who didn't match her intelligence, who didn't challenge her, and there were a lot of people like that because she could be pretty damn intimidating. She couldn't bear complacency. That's what attracted her to Michael – he was driven, even at twenty – and because his ambition was entirely intellectual, she couldn't resist it. She swept him up before he could blink. She knew what she wanted.'

The stones beneath their feet were becoming mossy, so they headed back towards the gate. 'And when it came to dying, she knew how she wanted to do that too: at home, with her family. That's where I came in. With my usual sense of timing, I arrived in time to witness the worst, so all my memories of her are tainted by those last weeks.'

They stepped back into the woodland.

'She wasn't eating by then, and her body was like a stick you'd pick up on a winter walk. Her hair was short and spiky, she had a horrible grey pallor – the colour of death, I suppose – and even her eyes were losing it, growing yellow and dim, although her hands were still lovely. Her fingers were graceful, but strong,' he took Jude's hand, 'just like this, and we could always gauge the pain she was in by looking at her hands. Michael's mother did most of the work during the day and we took over at night. Her own mum sat around moaning. It was tough on her, losing her only daughter, and she's never got over it, but God, she was a pest. She kept telling Catherine she should have stayed in hospital, that this was very bad for the child – the child who could lie with her mother and tell her stories and distract her from the dying.'

Half-way up the path, they came to a great lump of

granite, flat as a table top, opposite a fuchsia bush. Oliver sat on it, lit a cigarette and leaned over on his knees. 'In fact, her being at home made it easier on you. She didn't go off to some cancer ward and not come back; she just got sicker and weaker, and after she died, you told me you were glad she wasn't sick any more.'

'But why didn't Dad get help looking after her?'

'The usual reason: she didn't want a white uniform fussing over her. She wanted her friends, and she certainly kept us busy. I spent a lot of time looking after you. I got you up. Took you to playschool. Collected you. Read you stories and put you to bed. I don't know what I didn't do.'

'Was I nice to you?'

'No, you were a brat. You hadn't a clue what was happening, but you blamed me for most of it. We had incredible fights.'

'About what?'

'About which socks you'd wear and what you wanted in your sandwiches. You were never happy until you'd found something to reproach me for.'

'Oops.'

'Yeah. Some things never change. One day I got so fed up, I threatened to put you in a letter-box and post you away somewhere, as a result of which you insisted on crossing the street every time we came to a sodding letter-box!'

Jude smiled.

'You exhausted me. Most nights, I fell asleep as soon as you did, but it worked well that way: I slept for the first part of the night, then Michael called me for the dawn shift.' Oliver blew smoke through his teeth. 'Let's go in. This isn't the stuff of pleasant walks in the countryside.'

In their room, they stretched out on the bed, with pillows propped up behind them.

241

'Was she an easy patient?'

'On the face of it, yeah, she was brave, but I saw another Catherine. The one I still see. The one who sometimes cried in those awful early hours, who ranted and raged, and wanted to be saved. She was frightened, that was the worst of it. I could cope with just about everything, but her fear – of dying, of death, of losing you, of you losing her – that was intolerable.' He took a deep breath. 'She was furious that she was powerless to do anything about it. That was new for her: powerlessness. New for me, too.'

Jude noted, when he smoked, that his hand was shaking. She waited for him to continue, then prodded him.

'We put down long maudlin hours together. I never got the cheerful, coping Catherine when we were alone during the night. I saw the despair. And the pain. Christ, I knew about the pain. She engraved it on me. Sometimes she squeezed my wrist so hard, her nails drew blood . . .' He was pausing now every few sentences. 'And then she extracted a promise that I would never tell Michael about the darker bits. She wanted him to think that she didn't mind dying.'

Jude's throat tightened. After a moment she said, 'Did she extract the same promise with regard to me?'

She had to wait for a reply. 'No,' he said finally, 'probably because you were too small for it to be an issue, and thank God she didn't.'

'Why?'

'Because you're even harder to refuse than she was.'

'Did she talk about me?'

Oliver's eyes were locked in the middle distance.

'Oliver? Did she say much about me?'

He swallowed. 'When she could.'

Jude had to push for every word now. 'Go on.'

'What upset her most was knowing you'd forget her. She

hated that you would never come to know her as a person other than "Mummy". She hated . . . that you'd forget what she looked like and sounded like; smelt like even.'

'And I did.'

'Yes . . . Sometimes,' he said quietly, 'when you're close to me, I find myself wondering why I've got everything that she wanted so much.'

Jude lost him. He rolled over to stub out his cigarette and remained with his back to her. She wanted to urge him on, but thought better of it. Instead, she thought about what he had said so far. A new woman was emerging in her mother. The competent young solicitor was a bit obsessive and an intellectual snob, and when she had to die she was terrified – no Joan of Arc as her bereaved husband had always depicted. Jude thought about this other, flawed woman. She had always loved the fragments of Catherine's memory, but now she was beginning to like her as well, because she was no longer so intimidating, and she had Oliver to thank for that. She rested her chin on his arm. 'Come on. You've earned yourself a pint.'

He continued when they reconvened in their bedroom that afternoon. 'It got worse as it dragged on. When she couldn't get out of bed any more, things really began to slip. We kept expecting her to fall into a coma – in fact, we longed for it – but she was too strong for her own good. Her mouth was dry and her eyes were dry and everything was horrible for her. Her skin itched. Her breathing rasped. She vomited, often, this awful dark stuff, choking her as it came up. It even made us sick. On separate occasions, Michael and I actually threw up. It seemed such a betrayal of her.'

Jude covered her eyes.

He turned to her. 'I warned you. Will I sugar-coat it?'

'No.'

'That's the way she died, your mum. I wish I could tell you otherwise, but she was so sick that it was nauseating; so sick that her mother-in-law knelt on the cold flagstones in the kitchen every day and prayed for her to be taken; so sick that in fifteen years I haven't forgotten one detail of what she went through.'

'You must forget. You must let it go.'

'No. I owe it to her to remember. It's the very least I should do.' He swallowed some water. 'We shouldn't have been minding her, I know that now, but no one expected her to go on for so long. She was expected to slip away in the night, elegantly, quietly, but she didn't. She fought the bastard . . . Michael was in tatters. His mother begged him to get help, but he was resolute: he would look after Catherine to the bitter end – and bitter it certainly was. He only cracked once. That's the night you remember. He got himself into such a state that he tried to run out of the house, shouting that if he couldn't take any more, how on earth could she endure it? I lost my temper because my nerves were frayed too and I thought he was letting her down. I whacked him one and then turned to see you sitting on the stairs. It was getting to you by then. You kept waking up, and that's what's coming back to you now: all your little nightmare excursions through the house of horrors. Grown men fighting; mothers weeping and saying their prayers; your own mother, hanging on as if everyone depended on it.'

'How did you cope?'

'I didn't cope. I was twenty-three, Jude. I'd never seen anything like this. I didn't know about death without dignity. I didn't know beautiful young women could be destroyed like that. I got through every day in a daze. We all did. We did the necessary and stood around afterwards, wondering how we carried it out. When Michael finally conceded that we needed help, a rota of nurses came along. In practical terms it was a huge relief, but it didn't stop her dying. And dying smells, you know. It hangs in the air, like a poisonous brew fermenting, so we burnt incense to cover it.'

'God, this is cruel.'

'It *was* cruel what went on in those weeks. It was the mind of the cancer that got me. The way it remained oblivious to the collective will of those around it. The way it defied the treatments and painkillers, and sucked her in with appetite, wiping its mouth with a flourish, while we stood around, pleading for mercy. Even when Catherine couldn't battle it any more, when she went blank, even then it didn't stop. It stayed for as long as it wanted to, hanging around like a boy on a street corner stomping on insects with the heel of his boot. Sometimes she'd look at us, not wanting to beg but begging all the same to make it leave her alone, to let her die, if she must, with some particle of control, some whit of dignity. It paid no attention. It was on a spree, ingesting everything that was good in her, digesting it and spewing it out, putrid and ugly, and she saw her own ugliness and *hated* it.' His eyes filled. 'So did I.'

Jude shuffled across the bed and held him.

'I thought about killing her, you know. So did Michael. We even talked about it. It was pretty chilling. Talk about male bonding.'

Again, he paused. Jude gave him time, then said, 'Let's finish this.'

Oliver took more water. 'I woke one night and went to her room. Michael was asleep in the chair and Catherine was lying on her side watching him. She didn't see me, so I stood there, watching her watching him. I often think about

245

it, about the drift in her eyes, and Michael snoozing, completely unaware that she was slipping away. I said, "Catherine," not because I thought she'd hear me but because it needed to be said. Someone had to speak her name, one last time, before she left. Then I went back to bed.

'I've often regretted that I didn't go over to her then and tell her how much I loved her or, you know, something worthy and significant. The next morning, it was too late. Michael called me at six in a panic, saying he thought her breathing had changed. I called the doctor, the mothers and Meg, her best friend, and we gathered around, waiting for the off, the mothers racing through the rosary as if they were praying against time.'

'What about Daddy?'

'He lay with her.' Oliver knocked his head against the bedstead. 'It was horrible. Love turned abject, passion turned sour. A man made so very small. At twenty-one minutes to eight, the doctor said it was over and all hell broke loose. The mothers keened, Michael sobbed, Meg wept. It was hideous.'

'You?'

'I felt very, very tired. And relieved. God, so relieved. She was out of the pain, we were only coming into it. Then I started worrying that all this ghastly noise would wake you and I did not want you to wake. Not to that. So I went to your room to see if you were stirring and that's when it hit me. You were lying with a teddy over your face, and you had no idea that in the next room all that love had been taken away from you. It seemed so spectacularly unfair, even to a kid like me. I broke down, completely broke down, and you didn't even stir.'

19

'I can see six different hills,' said Jude, standing by the window.

Oliver came and stood beside her. 'Have I been too rough on you?'

'On yourself maybe. Not me. It's like being introduced to my mother for the first time. I wish Dad had told me this stuff.'

'You were too young.'

'Who told me she'd died?'

Oliver glanced out. 'That's another day's work. Let's get cleaned up and check out the restaurant. A change of scene will do us good.'

'I don't want a change of scene.'

'I do.'

'I'll have something here.'

Oliver tilted his head. 'Always about you, is it, Jude?'

'Look at the state of me. I feel like I've been skinned.'

'And I need some sustenance.'

'So go and have it.'

His eyes narrowed. 'I don't particularly want to be alone

tonight – can't imagine why – but hey, don't let that bother you, *pal*.'

She caught his arm. 'All right. I'll come.'

During dinner, Oliver distracted Jude by regaling her with the fabricated life-stories of other guests in the elegant dining-room. Afterwards, they went to bed and lay in the dark, and Jude talked about the endless days she had spent alone in her house, despair creeping over her like a rash.

'You should have told me,' said Oliver.

'I was trying to cope. I have to learn to manage without you.'

'Why?'

The following morning, when Jude woke, a waitress was leaving a tray on the table and Oliver was leaning against the sash window. He winked. 'I ordered for you.'

Jude stretched. 'What about you?'

'I had kippers in the dining-room.'

'Yuk. I never heard you get up. Those pills really knock me out.'

'You should stop taking them.'

'No. I might start seeing things again.'

'If you do, I'll send them away.'

Jude sat up. 'Wow. What a day.'

'I really love this part of the world. Look at the reflection on the water. You can even pick out individual trees.' He took the tray and placed it across her lap.

'I don't know why you look after me so ridiculously well,' she said.

'Nor do I.'

'What do you get out of it?'

'You, I suppose.'

She buttered some toast. 'Are you fit to carry on?'

'I've told you everything. What else is there?'

'The aftermath. Who told me. What I said.'

Oliver lay across her feet.

'I suppose you told me. Dad left all the dirty work to you.'

'That's not fair. *He* told you your mother had died, of course he did. Then he brought you in to see her.' Oliver grinned. 'And you said, "But she's still here! I thought you said she'd gone to heaven?"'

Jude smiled.

'I stayed on after all the fuss died down. I'd lost my job, of course—'

'So *that's* why you were fired from the magazine! Because of us?'

'Because I didn't show up for weeks, and compassionate leave doesn't extend to non-family members. Anyway, being jobless allowed me to stay and help out. I did the cooking and cleaning and tried to get the air of death out of the house. I thought I was doing everyone an enormous favour, but I was actually letting Michael wallow. As long as I was there to look after you, he didn't have to do it. He couldn't cope, and I couldn't blame him.'

Jude was eating her fried breakfast with an improved appetite.

'But he had a daughter who needed him and he was losing touch with her, so Mum told me in no uncertain terms that I had to get out of there. For you, that meant losing both your mother and your nanny in the space of two months, but I did it anyway. I walked.'

'Was I upset?'

'You sulked for three days, apparently. That brought

Michael back to earth quick enough. He became devoted then, so you mustn't blame him. You can't blame a man who'd been eviscerated.'

'What did you do?'

'I tried to pick things up in England. Beforehand, life had been a breeze. I knew people got cancer and died, but not the Catherines of the world and not that way. It was shocking to me. It disturbed something in me. It was the first time I'd known real pain and, frankly, I believed I deserved a longer spell of innocence. I found this gulf between me and my London friends. They were still on the other side of the divide, where life is one long hedonistic adventure, and I resented them and God, or whoever was in charge, for making me cross over alone. I'd lost all my optimism, all my aspirations. Within two months, I found myself in Cairo, as far from the whole miserable episode as I could get, and middle-aged before my time.'

When Jude had dressed, they walked down the road to the short pier on the bend, where two old fishing boats lay dying, and sat back to back, supporting each other in the sunshine.

'Some people assumed I was in love with her,' said Oliver, unprompted. 'Even my mother thought so, but it was more than that. Watching someone die is more intimate than any love affair. No one has ever been as close to me as Catherine was in those weeks.'

'Not even Patti?'

'Not even you.'

'You're not in the least bit over it, are you?'

'I don't know about getting over it, I only know that the hardest part about losing someone isn't that you can't survive without them, but that you *can*.'

'I know.'

He looked over his shoulder. 'Yeah, course you do. Anyway, I met Patti two years later and it was great. Falling in love restored me. It turned on the lights, reignited the future. She worked hard at putting me back together again, but then Michael died and she couldn't face dragging me out of the pits a second time. And that wasn't selfishness. It was her way of coping, because she loved him too.'

'But that means your marriage broke up because of Daddy dying?'

'Let's just say, it didn't help. Life seemed very grey after he died. He and I had never spoken about those grim weeks when we nursed Catherine, but it held us together. It gave us something beyond ordinary friendship, this intimate knowledge of the grossness of dying, and when he was killed, I hated him for leaving me with it all – for leaving me with you, dammit. Truth is, I didn't want you, Jude. I wanted to give you back.'

Jude looked across Barnaderg Bay. There was no view of the open sea; instead, peninsulas on either side interlocked, woodland and bare hill meeting at one end of the inlet, closing it in.

'You were simply too much like both of them for me to want you around. That's why Patti left everything to me. She knew that if she took you on, I never would. And now the joke's on me. You're the fulcrum. My prop.'

'When did you stop wanting to give me back?'

'Never. I still want to put you in a parcel and return you to the people who should have had you all along.'

'I'd better keep clear of letter-boxes then.'

He stood up suddenly. Jude fell over. 'Come on. Time for my Guinness.'

'There must be something better for you,' she said, linking

arms with him as they walked the quay, 'something beyond the Feehans. I mean, talk about the Curse of the Feehans.'

'Hey.'

'Maybe I should give you a break? Maybe we should disengage?'

'Is that possible?'

'It must be. It isn't very appealing, but it might be what you need, and certainly what you deserve.'

'An enforced break wouldn't untie the knots, love. We've been swallowed by the same shark, you and I, and we're sitting in his belly nursing the same wounds. No disengagement is possible – and even if it was, I wouldn't want it.'

'We've brought you nothing but unhappiness.'

'It'll pay off in the end. Somewhere, somehow, I'll get my dues. Besides,' he added quickly, 'you don't make me unhappy.'

Jude rattled his arm. 'Close,' she teased. 'Very close!'

In a pub in Cleggan called 'Oliver's', Oliver dipped his moustache into a creamy pint of Guinness.

'Now I know what's wrong with your books,' said Jude primly.

'Eh? What?'

'This is. We are. The Feehans. All this stuff that's happened – everything you know about living and dying – you won't write about it. Your characters know nothing about it. They're always over there, at the far side of the room. There's no soul in your books.'

Oliver drew a line through the moisture on the side of his glass.

'Oh. You know this already,' she said.

'Jude, if I were to sit down every day and torment myself with all the shit in life, I'd never get up again.'

'But you can't write like that!'

'Excuse me, but when you have written *and sold* five novels, you can tell me about the creative process, right?'

'Wrong. You're not proud of any of those novels. You can do better. What's the point of going through all that if you don't benefit?'

'I don't wish to benefit, or profit, from your parents' deaths.'

'It wouldn't be about them, it'd be about you. And it's out now. You've talked about it, cried about it. You can use it.'

'Drop it, Jude.'

'Would Catherine be impressed with this bland stuff you churn out?'

'Oh, it's bland now?'

'Isn't it?'

'My editor doesn't think so.'

'Editors play safe. You're the one who has to take chances.'

Oliver put down his pint and stared at it.

'Am I right or am I right?' Jude said.

'You're a pain in the butt is what you are.'

'I can't believe you're prepared to settle for less than you're capable of.'

'Listen, those events permeate my life, right down to losing Patti and Tim. At least when I'm working I can escape all that stuff. Writing *with* it would mean dwelling on it and I'm not prepared to do that. I don't have to play the tortured artist. I simply do it for a living.'

'But you *are* tortured.'

'The last few days have been torture, granted, but whose fault is that? Besides, if I'm such an abject failure, how can we afford to stay in a place like the Manor?'

253

Jude nibbled on a crisp. 'I still dream about that villa in Beverly Hills.'

'Earn it yourself then.'

'I can't. I'm going to be in college for years doing my doctorate.'

He looked at her in amazement. 'You've decided to go on? Jude, that's fantastic!'

'Right, so if I'm going to be a poor academic, *you've* got to bring in the cash.'

Oliver smiled, relieved to see the girl, and her humour, come back to him. This was the Jude he knew, resurfacing in spite of the weights on her heart, her sheer buoyancy outweighing all else. 'It's so nice to know you love me for my art and not my wallet,' he said.

The tension in Oliver's neck had eased; he no longer felt so taut and tired. The worst was over. He had always known that one day Jude would ask these questions, and now she had and it was done. As they sat at the foot of the lawn in the evening sun, listening to pheasants tiptoeing about in the bushes behind them, he enjoyed a sense of release greater than he could have anticipated.

Jude, also, claimed to be refreshed. 'It's so liberating to know what she was like. You've really brought her alive for me.'

He wasn't convinced. She spoke these words as though she were reading them on an autocue. Could this truly be her reaction to hearing for the first time how her mother had died? Or was she still holding to the scaffold, gripping the cold steel, instead of letting herself fall into the mud of grieving? If so, then this rare opportunity to deal with the past had been missed, and Oliver suddenly recognized something in Jude that he had never been able to put his finger on: a

254

certain protective shallowness. There was a lack of depth in her dealings with people, himself and Tim excluded, which, he now saw, allowed her relationship with Stephen. She had loved Thierry, in a teenage sort of way, but had dumped him without a blink, and now she declared herself in love with a self-acclaimed poet who espoused celibacy. *How safe,* Oliver thought. *How very neat.* Even her friendship with Fiona, when put to the test, had failed; Jude had been unable to respond to the demands of deep affection. It worried him, especially now that she had dragged his most unpalatable memories from him, with all the effort of pressing a sponge through a sieve, and had emerged seemingly unmoved. It had cost him so much and her so little. And she had yet more to ask of him.

'Is it true that parts of Daddy were never found?'

'Who told you that?'

'I heard it. At the funeral.'

Oliver sighed. 'He lost an arm and shoulder on impact, but divers, well, they retrieved them.'

'I wish the guys who killed him had hit a wall in their rotten speedboat.'

'They were just lads having a lark. They were in the wrong place when the steering snapped.'

'I want to go there.'

Oliver gaped.

'I want to see the place where he died.'

'I don't.'

'Take me there.'

'Oh, Jude, *please*.'

When they ambled back into the Manor, the receptionist waved the phone at Oliver. 'There's a call for you. Will you take it here?'

'Thanks.'

A few minutes later, he followed Jude into the bedroom. She was leaning against the shutters by the sash windows, her arms crossed, her hair still in that unflattering ponytail, her face a little brighter than it had been two days before. She turned. 'What is it?'

Oliver hesitated. 'That was Sinéad. Fiona's mother died yesterday.'

He might have struck her. 'Oh!' Her hands went to her face. She stared at him open-mouthed, then slowly slid to her knees. She made no sound at first, but when at length she breathed in again, her throat gurgled with guilt and grief. Oliver went to his jacket, rifled through its pockets for cigarettes, lit one, and then went over to where she was sobbing by the window. This he was ready for. He had been for years.

'Up,' he said. 'Come on. Up.' On the bed, she curled up like a foetus. Oliver lay behind her, took one long drag on his cigarette, stubbed it out, then held her. 'Go for it, Jude.'

She cried as she had never done; loudly, quietly, uncontrollably. At first, her sorrow swayed between her own desolation and Fiona's, but it soon abandoned her friend and became entirely selfish as she withered beneath the weight of what Oliver had told her. Years of restraint and control, inherited from her mother, were washed away as by an overdue monsoon, and while she lay sobbing, Oliver breathed easily, thankful that she would not go through life hardened by a determination to be unmoved by her own story.

She seemed to be shrinking in his arms, and as she slid further into the trough which she had carefully straddled for years, he knew that if she didn't hit the bottom by her own momentum, she would have no way of pushing herself back up again. She muttered questions he didn't bother to answer

256

– the imponderables, the whys of it all – and she raged at her mother's suffering, but she kept jamming on that too vulnerable word. He pulled his arms tightly around her. 'Say it, Jude. Let me hear you say it.'

She shook her head and curled more tightly into a ball, but moments later it came out of its own accord. 'Mummy,' she whispered, and Oliver was moved. He hadn't heard her say it in fifteen years, and as she kept on saying it, her crying became easier.

The shuddering of her body had eased. She was lying with her back to him and seemed to be asleep. With his arm trapped under her, Oliver's hand had gone numb, so he flexed it to restore the blood flow. But Jude was not asleep. She slipped her hand across his palm and squeezed his fingers.

Their hands clasped on the pillow, neither of them moved.

20

A week later, on a low brick pier at Puerto Pollensa in Majorca, they lay in the evening sunshine. It had taken Jude two days of sleuthing, using the landmarks that Sinéad could remember, to find the small supermarket where her father had bought their groceries, and this stretch of beach, cradled between two keyhole-shaped piers, was probably the spot where he had brought in his boat when he had come to get the carton of milk.

Oliver took pleasure in looking at Jude. There was something new in her, a lightness that had never been there before, and although the vast blue Mediterranean was for her a panorama of death, she derived strength from it. She walked along the shaded promenade and looked out; she stood on her hotel balcony and looked out; she sat in cafés sucking on spoons of ice-cream and looked out. It seemed to bring her peace.

Oliver, by contrast, felt haunted. He could not escape the sound of the collision and, although he had not been there to hear it, he heard it now, whenever Jude stopped talking. He heard it especially at night – a great whack, the thud of fibreglass, the crackle of splintering wood, a hollow splash.

Cries, too. Sinéad's cry. The Spaniards' screams. The wail of sirens. Here, where it had happened, it was too easy to visualize, too easy to hear what must have been heard when his friend had died, and the sounds banging inside his skull didn't let up until this, their last evening, when he noticed his eardrums no longer reverberated around unheard sounds. Perhaps he too was finding a cure here.

Jude looked about at the sharp sandstone hills, spotted with scrub, and at the multitude of yachts bobbing about on their moorings. The sea was calm and unthreatening. 'If only he'd jumped.'

'Yes.'

'I wonder what happened to Sinéad, stranded out on the yacht.'

'*She* jumped.'

'What?'

'Into the water. She tried to save him.'

'Oh God. Of course she did.'

'So did one of the lads on the boat.'

'Bit late to be a hero.' Jude scanned the bay. 'I suppose you could die in worse places.'

'That's for sure.'

'But you could die in Ireland. He would have wanted to die in Ireland.' She slipped her sunglasses down her nose. 'Were you never going to come?'

'Dunno. Maybe I was waiting for you to ask.'

'I'm glad we're here. It's like spending time with him. Looking at what he looked at. Eating what he ate. Sitting in cafés where he sat.'

'At least we know he was having a good time.'

'Yeah, with me tucked away in boarding school!'

Oliver smiled. Jude was on the rise. She was like a person recovering from a bad flu. She had lost weight, sleep, appetite;

she had been through a wringer three times over – in Dublin, in Letterfrack, and finally at Mrs Mahon's funeral, an ordeal even Oliver had found trying. But afterwards Fiona had reminded Jude that when her father had died, her friends had spent more time avoiding her than helping her, so they were quits, apparently, and they made their peace. This, more than anything, had restored Jude, and even coming to Majorca had not set her back. Oliver sat up. The next day, she was returning to Dublin and he was going to England, and although the timing was lousy, there was still one thing left for him to do. 'Jude? There's something I need to tell you.'

She swung around. 'Bloody hell, Oliver Sayle! If I counted the times you've said that to me! What now? You said you told me everything in Letterfrack.'

'This isn't about your parents.'

'What then?'

'It's . . . Stephen.'

'My God. What?'

'He's, um, getting married.'

Her mouth fell open. Her hand went to her chest.

'He only told me the other day. They were about to let me know when you went AWOL.'

'Vanessa?'

'Yeah. I had no idea they were so serious. Had you?'

Her nose wrinkled. 'Sort of.'

'Sorry to land it on you now. You all right about it?'

'Of course.' She glanced at him. 'There was never anything—'

'Oh, spare me the protestations! You slept with him on and off for two years, so don't try telling me this doesn't mean anything, *please*.'

'All right, so it *is* a bit of a shock. Satisfied?'

He looked away. 'Is it still going on?'

260

Jude drew shapes on the concrete with her finger. 'No. He came over to Dublin last November brandishing a condom in one hand and an ultimatum in the other. And that was it, really.'

Oliver turned in amazement. 'What are you saying? You never had sex with him?'

She smirked. 'Ah. That's shocked you.'

'You mean *Stephen*—'

'Even Stephen can be held off.'

'I don't understand. I really don't.'

'I didn't want to be another conquest, that's all. And I sort of had something on him because I wouldn't do it. It gave me a sort of . . .'

'Power?'

'Yeah. Anyway, it wouldn't have meant anything to him. He swore it would – because he'd had to wait so long! – but he didn't care enough for him to be the one. Nor did I, actually.'

'And I was so sure you'd be left heartbroken,' said Oliver ruefully.

'Don't get me wrong, I love him to bits. I just couldn't fall *in* love with him. Not for want of trying, I should add.'

'Why not? He's one of the nicest people I know – when he isn't screwing around.'

'Too nice, maybe. I mean, he's so light. He's not shallow, but he's not very serious either. About anything.'

'That's what I love about him. He isn't carrying around any of my miserable baggage. Still, I take your point.'

'Pity. He's still the most unbelievably attractive man I—'

'All right. Stop panting. I get the picture.'

'When's the wedding?'

'August. In Scotland. She's from Oban. They met when he was up with the parents.'

'I suppose I'll be invited?'

'Absolutely.'

'Ugh. Will you take me? I couldn't bear to go on my own.'

'I'll take you.'

'Even if you fall passionately in love in the meantime and want her to come instead?'

'Even if.'

'Promise?'

'I promise, but be warned. He's asked me to be best man.'

'That's OK. I just couldn't bear to stick out like an abandoned spinster.'

'You won't.'

Jude lifted her face to the sun. She was slightly tanned and her hair was tied up in a tight bun. 'It should be *you* getting married.'

'I've had my turn. It's Stephen's go. Hope he makes a better job of it.'

'You could marry Chantal. You've been with her four months now. She sounds lovely.'

'Yeah, and her English is about as good as my French. We're actually coming unstuck over the language problem.'

'So find someone else and get married and have babies and live happily ever after.'

He laughed. 'You don't ask for much!'

'It's all over now,' said Jude seriously, 'all this stuff that's been hanging over us. It's been dealt with. For the past five years I've felt as if there was a blade stuck into my ankle, but every time I tried to take it out, I couldn't reach it. Now you've pulled it out. We both have to move on.'

Oliver sighed and nodded.

'Do you feel any different?'

He raised his chin towards the sea. 'I still don't feel great looking out there.'

'Me neither, but I'm going to deal with that right now.'
She stood up and slipped off her dress; she was wearing a
bathing suit underneath.

'What are you up to? The water's freezing.'

'Not for a girl brought up in the cold waters of the Irish
Sea.' She eased herself into the water and was instantly
immobilized with cold. '*Jeeeezus.*'

'Brought up in the Irish Sea, were you? France, more like.'

'Feck off. This is what I came here to do and I'm doing it.
Look in the pocket of my dress, would you?'

He pulled some green weed from her pocket. 'Whasis?'

'Moss. From the West.'

'Very dead moss.'

'Give us.' She stored the bundle of dried plant in her
cleavage. 'Bye.'

'Wait a minute. How far out are you planning to go?'

'I'll know when I get there.' She began swimming. Oliver
stood on the short pier cursing. She was a good swimmer,
but not a very fit one. What did she think she was doing?

Jude swam through the waters where her father had died.
It was clear and green and not very deep. She could still see
the sand and occasional notches of seaweed on the sea bed,
and she swam slowly and evenly so as not to tire, her arms
coming over and down as if in some religious ritual of
invocation. Up and over. Up and over. The sea grew darker.
She twisted around to rest, closing her eyes against the sun.
Then she turned again and tried to find her bearings in
relation to the supermarket, the beach and the spot where
the yacht had been moored. The accident would have happened still farther out. She swam on until she came through
a patch of warm water. It was as warm as a bath, for no
reason, several hundred yards from the beach, so she chose
this as the place, and lay floating. The sea lapped about,

her hands paddled gently beneath her. With her ears underwater, she called out, 'Daddy?' and the word echoed through the sea. He must have thought of her as he went under. As he went down. He *must* have. 'Daddy?' It sounded loud enough to travel for thousands of miles, like a dolphin's cry, and yet no one but herself could hear it. 'I love you, Daddy. Come back soon.'

Sinéad flashed through her mind. Jude jolted into an upright position. Sinéad had thrown herself into this very water, this deep water, and had swum towards the wreckage of her lover's boat, screaming probably, and swallowing sea, and maybe even swimming through blood . . . It was too hard to imagine, but Jude trod water frantically, suddenly terrified she wouldn't be able to swim all the way back in. It was so deep here, so far out. *Jesus, I'm sinking*, she thought, then saw with relief that Oliver was swimming towards her. When he reached her, she grabbed his neck. 'I thought I was drowning!'

'What kind of stunt is this? Have you completely lost it?'

'I had to!'

'Like hell! Of all the stupid, bloody irresponsible—'

'It isn't stupid.'

'Do you realize how far you've come?' Jude let go of him. 'For crying out loud. Swimming out here in an emotional state . . .'

'I wanted to say goodbye properly.'

'By risking your own life?'

'I'm not risking it!'

'You could have!'

'Stop yelling at me!'

'You promised not to pull any more stunts like this.'

Jude sniggered suddenly, then laughed. Putting her head

back in the water, she laughed hugely, and it was a lovely sight.

'Christ,' said Oliver. 'You *have* lost it.'

'Look at us. Way out of our depths in freezing water, and we still manage to argue.'

Her resilience, her recovery, her very cheerfulness moved Oliver to speak in plainer terms than he had ever allowed himself. 'Jude, I may not be Michael, but I do love you very much.'

'I know you do. I've finally worked that out.'

'Where's the weed from the West?'

She reached into her bathing suit. 'It's a bit crass, isn't it? Throwing weeds after him. He'd hate such sentimentality.'

'You can bring flowers next time.'

'No.' Jude raised her arm and threw the small, soggy, clump of Ireland. It landed nearby and floated. 'I'm never coming back here. Nor is Dad. He's coming home with me.'

21

Oliver could have taken Shelley right there, up against his car, but since it was their first date, he did the decent thing and led her to his room instead. They fell on to the bed. He nose-dived into her cleavage, she reached for his zipper. He moaned; she simpered. Then she raised her arm above her head – and screamed.

'Holy shit!' She threw Oliver off and leaped from the bed. 'What the hell's that?'

'What?'

'There's something in the bed!'

He switched on the light. At the far side of his bed, Jude turned stiffly, squinted, and said, 'Oh. Sorry.'

Oliver closed his eyes.

'Who the hell is that?' Shelley yelled, adjusting her clothes.

'It's only Jude.' With a flick of his head, Oliver told Jude to leave.

She slid out from under the sheet.

Shelley stood askance, as though she had leapt from a bed full of spiders. 'Man, what is this? Some kind of threesome?'

Jude slunk out of the room.

'God, no. Jude is my, er, niece.'

'You sleep with your niece?'

'No! Of course not. She was probably watching telly and—'

Jude poked her head back into the room. 'I was. I fell asleep—'

'Out!' said Oliver.

'Don't worry,' said Shelley. 'I'm outta here all right!'

'I meant her, not you!' Shelley stormed down the corridor. He hurried after her. 'Shelley, I can explain. She's just a kid.'

'That's no kid.'

'I look after her.'

'I'm sure you do!'

Jude heard further remonstrations out on the street, followed by the sound of Shelley's car pulling away. She stood in the corridor, trembling from such a rude awakening.

Oliver stormed back up to his room and slammed his shirt on to a chair. 'Fuck and double fuck!'

Jude hovered in the doorway. 'You said you probably wouldn't be home tonight.'

'Go to bed, Jude. Your *own* bed!'

She went to her room, but could not sleep. She had no doubt been an odd sort of encumbrance for Oliver over the years, but she had never before so drastically interfered with his love-life and the whole laughable incident left her with a sense of foreboding which caused her to toss for most of the night.

She had been in Landor for ten days and, so far, it had been exceptional. Much had changed since their time in Letterfrack, herself most of all, and she was beginning to reap the benefits. It was as if she had been balancing a plate on her head all her life, afraid to move lest it should fall and shatter, but now that it had been taken away, she could look up and all around her. She looked at herself most of all, and saw that her character had roots, her behaviour reasons, her moods and contradictions all emanated from the same source. She was no longer enervated by the fact that she had lost both parents by the age of fifteen; instead, she saw what it had made of her.

She had also acquired new confidence. In Letterfrack she had unintentionally driven Oliver to admit that he loved her, and this declaration had given her worth. Discovering that she could draw as much love as the next person was like escaping a net. She moved more swiftly; she looked taller; her laughter was deeper and far more frequent.

Oliver also felt different. Talking about Catherine had been like watching an old home movie he had been afraid to see because everyone in it was dead. He had sat through it now and, although the images were still clear, they were no longer sharp. But it was in relation to Jude that he felt most changed. He had always been a little afraid of her, afraid of a backlash, of a dreadful eruption of suppressed emotions, and now that it had happened he no longer had to avoid it, as he always had, by keeping a tight rein on his feelings for her. Consequently, there was a new clarity in every word spoken between them and in every gesture made. When she jumped on him at the airport with unrestrained affection, he knew she no longer needed him and this, above all else, eased his load.

Her visit started well. They quickly slipped into old habits: lazy breakfasts under the catalpa, reading news-papers over French bread and coffee, and the early-evening swim, which had long since become a ritual in their daily routine, when they went gushing down the river or dawdled in the backwater chatting. Oliver always stayed in longer, to

268

exercise on the far side by swimming against the current, while Jude strolled along the bank. In the pink glow of evening, his crawl was so steady that it gave her pleasure to walk as she watched him, and at such times she experienced both rhythm and stillness, companionship and solitude. She had acquired an inner balance and it proved as satisfying as she had expected it to be.

All this was before Shelley. As she lay awake after that ludicrous, and literal, slap in the face, when Shelley's arm had hit her, Jude wondered why that one event made her so very uneasy.

Oliver had met the American in a *boulangerie* in Mouchard, when she had become flustered by the currency and he had stepped forward to help. The attraction had been mutual and immediate. Shelley had wavy black hair, bright green eyes and legs like a gazelle, and when they went to a café afterwards, Oliver learned that she was divorced, had two teenage kids back home, and was spending the summer with her cousin in a villa outside the town.

Following the contretemps in the bedroom, it took him two days to persuade Shelley that he was not into kinky sex, but when he did, the pleasant pace of Jude's life abruptly changed. Oliver essentially vanished. His work was the first casualty of the affair, the evening dip the second, and everything else followed. He woke late, had a coffee standing in the kitchen, then spent the day with Shelley. In the late afternoon he returned to shower and change before going out again. If he came home at all, it was near dawn.

Jude tried not to mind. She read, cycled, swam as usual, but without Oliver's regular breaks dividing the day, the hours dragged. This was very different to those long summer days when she had kept herself company while he worked, perhaps because the emptiness of the house made her own company much heavier. Worse, there were no croissants when she got up every morning, and there was something miserable about cycling to the *boulangerie* to buy only two. She attempted to make breakfast the glorious endless repast they had made it, reading under the catalpa while sipping coffee, but she invariably looked up at the still, tense garden and felt a dragging loneliness, which was accentuated by the voices that drifted over the wall from the family next door.

She had no friends in Landor – she usually brought her own. Most summers a string of visitors came to stay, but this was to be their quietest season yet, with only Tim expected, and it was fast becoming a ghastly prospect. The locals were either elderly or commuters, the people at the river transitory, and passing conversations with tourists were no compensation for the empty house she had to live in.

The house had certainly changed. Oliver had even become messy. Jude would go to his room to open the curtains and find socks and shirts on the floor, thrown off before a shower and stepped over afterwards. With some affection she picked up his dirty clothes, wryly amused that Oliver Sayle could ever become untidy, but the hard bit was that he had become untidy towards her also. Barely aware of what she was doing or where she was, he stepped over her like over a pair of underpants every time he went out. Sometimes he came home to sleep during the day, but still all Jude could hear was the drone of bees in the Virginia creeper.

To make matters worse, a heat-wave set in, bringing additional stillness and quiet. Everyone slowed down, stayed in. Only the river gurgled on energetically, cheeky and cheerful and cool. Jude loved its clear water, the stony,

270

sepia-coloured bed, and she often sat on the plinth of the old bridge, thinking. Downstream, the Loue was green, reflecting its thickly wooded banks, and she liked to remember the day she and Stephen had taken a rubber boat around the bend, through more rapids and past their island, to the next village.

One day she sat on the shore and watched a little tot, knee-deep in the river in a green top and wet knickers, peer into the water in search of pretty stones. 'M'man,' she called, finding one, ' 'garde comme c'est beau!'

Further along, a father was pushing his child around in an inflatable swimming aid. He said to his wife, 'C'est trop grand.' She was paddling some feet away with another child – a thin woman in a bikini, with a saggy bit of tummy where her babies had been. 'Ah, oui,' she replied, and Jude wondered if her own parents had spoken to each other like this, casually, intimately, about her and her little needs when they had taken her swimming in the cold waves off the Kerry coast before the monster came.

With families all around her, Jude thought a lot about her parents, and since she was no longer closed to such thoughts, she let them run and saw played out before her the family life she might have had. It was like watching someone else's holiday videos, only far more moving and beguiling.

She wondered that Oliver didn't wonder. It had been only two months since she had crumbled beneath the weight of another loneliness. It seemed odd that he didn't worry – he had always been so good at it – but it didn't appear to concern him that this solitude might get to her, might make her fray at the edges. Instead, *she* worried. She feared the demons would come back: her mother, with her horrible death; her father, thrown into the air, splashing into the sea in two pieces.

271

But the only demon that came to spook her was Stephen. It was impossible to be in Landor and not be pursued by memories of their time together. She counted the summers they had courted there – her seventeenth, eighteenth, and even nineteenth year, always with the scowling Oliver disapproving. The last year had been the least cordial. The sex question. Stephen grumbling, saying she had come of age. Jude not knowing, exactly, what held her back, except that she had only her own self-regard to guide her and felt instinctively that launching herself with Stephen was the wrong way to go. Besides, her reluctance had made him hungrier, and he never lost interest.

Now she suspected she had made a dreadful mistake. She could have been his lover, might even have had his love, if she had asked for it, and so every which way she turned she was tormented by visions of what she had lost. He was everywhere. She saw him waiting for her as she tumbled through the rapids; imagined him lying with her on the stones; and late at night, she was sure she could hear the squeak of his door as he tiptoed across the hall to her room. Torture, it was, and all Oliver's fault, too, for not being there to distract her.

It was hard to sleep. The heat and solitude kept her tossing, and the scratching of the crickets seemed louder than usual. She damned her ears for all the sounds they gathered. Even during the day she heard too much. The church clock chiming on the hour. The housemartins calling to one another high over the house. The whistle of a bicycle free-wheeling past the gate. These were the sounds that kept her company, and irked her.

Her time there had become like the weather – dense, stiff, close – as if the silence would have to break like a storm before all could be clear and companionable again.

272

When a fireworks display was due to take place in the town, she thought Oliver might bring Shelley home for the evening. Instead he said, 'There are fireworks on at the bridge tonight. You should go.' How, she wondered, had such a sensitive individual become so careless? She walked over to the bridge, found a place by the railing and waited for the show to begin. A lady walked past with a toddler on one leash and a white shaggy dog on another, and called out to a friend that it was the baby's first time. And the dog's too, she added. 'Ah, baptême de feu!' her friend laughed.

Beside Jude, a spindly, wrinkled granny told her grandchildren about the first time she had seen fireworks. The Catherine Wheel had fallen over, she told them, and set all the other fireworks alight. It was all over in two minutes, she chortled.

Jude gave up. She wanted to take part in a conversation, not eavesdrop, so she walked home. The house was dark. Horrible. She cursed Oliver for spoiling it. From her bedroom window, she watched what she could see of the fireworks and thought things couldn't really get much worse.

They could. The following day, the old lady in the blue frock, who had become a fixture in Jude's vista over the years, sitting outside her kitchen door across the road, was taken away in an ambulance. Her daughter put a suitcase into their car and followed.

That evening, Jude was sitting on the old bridge when Oliver drove past. Seeing her there, he drew to a halt and got out. 'You look terrible,' he called.

'Gee, thanks.'

'Actually, you look lovely,' he said, coming over, 'but you cut a bit of a sad figure sitting here.'

She took off her sunglasses and looked at him.

He pressed a pebble into the ground with his toe. 'I know. *Mea culpa.*'

'We need shopping.'

'Christ, I forgot. You haven't gone hungry, have you?'

'I will do if we don't do a food shop in Mouchard – that is, if you can spare the time?'

'Listen, love, I'm sorry I haven't been around much, but Shelley thought her cousin might be peeved if she stayed out a lot, so —'

'Dear me. Couldn't have that.'

He put his hands in his pockets and one foot on the wall. 'Jude, have you any idea how long it's been since I . . . since someone really *did* it for me?'

'Do I care?'

'I thought you might.'

'And I thought you might care about leaving me alone for nigh on ten days.'

Oliver looked so shamefaced, she wished she hadn't spoken. She didn't really want to spoil his party, and he *had* twice asked her to join them for dinner but she had declined, insisting that she was perfectly happy left to her own devices. It had been hard to say otherwise. She had never seen Oliver so smitten. His good humour never faltered, and when he emerged from the shower every evening, his hair wet and his beard trim, Jude swore he had never looked so well. Since she desperately wanted him to find love again, this should have pleased her.

It didn't.

Her second meeting with Shelley Rilette was not much better than their inauspicious introduction. Shelley simply appeared at the breakfast table one morning and somehow brought that whole bedroom scene with her. Jude had no

274

idea she had stayed over; Oliver's women friends rarely did. Out of deference to Tim, he had never brought strange faces to the breakfast table, but here was Shelley, wearing one of his shirts and sunglasses too big for her face, and Jude couldn't help feeling undressed. Her summer pyjamas – shorts and a string top – were not exactly adequate attire for entertaining strangers, and when Oliver put his hand on her bare shoulder to reach over with the coffee pot, she saw the gesture register with Shelley.

But at least breakfast had come home again – croissants, *pains au chocolat*, figs, nectarines and multiple cheeses. Jude tucked in, and so failed to greet the American as effusively as she might have, but she need not have worried on that score, because Shelley had enough effusiveness to power a space shuttle. She *gushed*. Her voice a little too loud, she raced through so many diverse subjects, one tumbling over the other, that Jude found it hard to follow the line of conversation. Shelley zapped sentences the way some people changed television channels.

She *loved* the Jura – *so French* – but she missed the sea; she was Californian – California was by the ocean, she explained to Jude – and to be away from the sea was *death* to a Californian. Chocolate made her come out in hives. Had Oliver ever seen the *Letterman Show*? Trouble with France was the language. You'd think in these days of MTV and CNN, the whole world would speak English. In America, you could travel for thousands of miles and still be understood.

Jude made an attempt to contribute. 'Except that many migrants in the States have a poor grasp of English, don't they? Which makes them even more marginalized.'

'Pardon me?'

'They—'

But Shelley was *oohing* the apricot jam. 'Did your brother really make this? Man, he's gifted.'

You don't know the half of it, Jude thought wistfully.

'*You* speak good English,' said Shelley.

'Sorry?'

'For an Irish person.'

Jude didn't follow.

'You speak Gaelic in Ireland, right?'

'Oh. No, not generally. English is our first language.'

'Although as it happens,' said Oliver, 'Jude is an Irish scholar.'

'I know she's Irish,' said Shelley.

'I mean Irish as in Gaelic. She's studying Irish at college.'

'Oh, sure. Like anyone actually *studies* at college. Right, Jude? I partied my way through Loyola!'

Jude turned away, whistling silently.

Such was the nature of their every encounter. Shelley prattled and Jude tried to hang on, like someone grasping the flaps at the back of a moving truck; every time she got a foothold, she was kicked off by another flux of inanity. It became a challenge to stick with Shelley, to follow her through to a pause and still know what she was talking about, but this proved a feat too difficult in those hot July days, and although Jude remained fascinated by Shelley's sheer verbal energy, the entertainment value quickly wore thin when Oliver's conscience caught up with him. Having spent too much time away, he now spent too much time at home. The increased presence of the enamoured couple was of little benefit to Jude, however. She was no longer alone, but she had no company. It was a double-edged sword. She had a choice between having Shelley and Oliver there together, or nobody there at all.

Shelley also resented Oliver's insistence that they

regularly slept at his place. 'How can I really go for it with her just next door?' she whined one morning. 'I mean, hell, hon, what's the point of a quiet orgasm?'

'I suppose it is something of a contradiction in terms.'

'Pardon me?'

Jude tried to relate to Shelley, but there was a vacancy about her which was difficult to penetrate. She had the attention span of a gnat, her world view extended no further than the Californian border, and she had no conspicuous opinions about anything. Jude soon worked out why she talked so much. It was because she had so little to say. Like bubbles bursting on top of the coffee, her words amounted to nothing.

Even Oliver seemed little engaged in Shelley's chatter – but then, he had the means to block it and did so *ad nauseam*. In the garden, by the river, they never let up with their snogging, and in the early-afternoon lull, when Jude lay reading in the hammock, she could even hear them making love upstairs. There was no escaping the heat of their affair, and apart from the awkwardness of being caught in its glow, she was also jealous – not of Shelley, but of Oliver, and all the sex he was getting.

Shelley soon became like his watch – wrapped around his wrist at all times. Every time he moved into any space occupied by Jude, the American quickly followed, so that when he joined Jude one afternoon on the plinth, his lady friend immediately threw herself into the river, for the first time, only to find herself sucked through the chute and momentarily dragged underwater. She emerged spluttering and gasping, and as she struggled to swim into the backwater, Jude jumped in and pulled her out of the flow. Catching her breath, her voluminous hair stuck to her face, Shelley

277

laughed, and Jude laughed with her. For a moment she liked her – the bright open face, the vivaciousness even – but when they clambered on to the plinth, and Jude realized that her short conversation with Oliver had already ended, the feeling quickly passed.

'Man, there's some pull right there,' said Shelley. 'You know, on one of the beaches back home, there's a rip tide that drags people out every year. It's *horrible*. They swim out and they're never seen again.'

'Shel—' said Oliver.

'Must be weird to drown, don't you think? To feel the sea swallow—'

'My father died in the sea,' said Jude, for Oliver's sake.

'Gee, that's right. Ollie said something about that.'

If Jude needed one good reason to seriously dislike Shelley, 'Ollie' had to be it.

'You have to come to LA to see our ocean, Ollie. France has nothing like it.'

'Not this far inland anyway,' said Jude.

'I'd love to,' said Oliver, 'but I'd hate that flight.'

'Oh, there are ways of avoiding jet-lag.' Shelley adjusted her gold lamé bikini. 'Drink lots of water on the flight – no alcohol – and the real trick, my cousin says, is to keep in rhythm with your Circadian rhymes.'

Jude couldn't help it. She sniggered.

Oliver shot her a piercing look, then said gently, 'I think you mean *rhythms*, Shelley. Circadian rhythms.'

'Rhythms, rhymes, what's the difference?' Shelley wrinkled her nose. 'But I guess you're hung up on words, being a writer and all.'

Jude sighed. How did Oliver endure it? The attraction had to be entirely physical, and yet even Shelley's good looks were thwarted, in Jude's harsh view, because she was utterly lacking in style. No matter what she wore, it failed her, and she pranced around like a supermodel turned bag lady, while Oliver – the best-dressed man Jude had ever known – didn't appear to notice. He went out every night looking like he'd walked out of Armani's, with a woman on his arm who seemed to have been dressed from a car boot sale. It gave Jude a great lift, because the Californian was getting right up her nose.

But Shelley was not quite as dense as Jude liked to believe. Oliver found her warm and entertaining. She was easy, affable company and she understood how he felt about Tim. She was exceptionally loving also, and he had missed that. It was good to wake up every morning and hear her say, with genuine affection, 'How you doing, honey?' He could see, however, that her sincerity did not extend to Jude. Threatened by the presence in his home of an attractive young woman who had no clear reason for being there, Shelley went into over-drive around Jude; hence the hurried, nervous disgorging of her every passing thought.

This fulsomeness took its toll on Jude's patience; her every comment became barbed. While Oliver remained immune to Shelley's vacuous babble, he sat up sharp when Jude began turning into her mother. Openly disdainful of Shelley's lack of intellect, she took every opportunity to demonstrate it by engaging Oliver in conversations about Irish politics, Chaucer, Dadaism, and any other topic bound to silence his girlfriend. He blamed himself; Jude was clearly bored out of her mind, but when he decided to give her more time, it was already too late. She had been living in an isolation pod for so long that she had made up her mind to get out of it.

One morning, Oliver called her from the dining-room when he heard her coming into the kitchen. 'Sweetheart? Pet? My only true love?'

She came to the door. 'My God. You're working.'

'Darling, dear one—'

'What do you want? You look completely hung-over.'

'I am, but if you could find it in your heart to make me a strong coffee while I look around for my brains, I'd be eternally grateful.'

He was sitting with his head in his hands when she brought him the coffee. 'Found your brains yet?'

'Nope.'

'I think I know where they are.'

He took off his glasses. 'None of your cheek, young lady.'

Jude glanced at the screen. 'Been a while since you did any work.'

'Go away.'

'Why won't you let me read this one?'

'You can, when I've got it right.'

'Has Shelley seen it?'

'No.'

Relieved, Jude went to the open doors. 'You seem to have quite a weakness for beautiful women, Mr Sayle.'

'Don't most men?'

'Mmm. I suppose the male physique is ugly enough to allow women to use their heads when selecting their mates.'

'Speaking of which, how's it going with that nice Dutch lad from the campsite?'

'"Nice Dutch lad?" Don't patronize me.'

'I'm not, I just—'

'You just want me kept busy while you're off romancing *Mastermind*.'

He looked over. 'No need to get bitchy.'

'I'm sorry, but I just don't get it. What do you two talk about?'

'That's classified.' He slurped at his coffee. 'Look, I know Shelley gets a little giddy, but she feels threatened by you.'

'That's her problem.'

'No, that's *my* problem. I wish you'd make her feel more comfortable around here.'

'I would if I could get a word in edgeways.'

'You intimidate her. She thinks you're incredibly bright.'

Jude snorted. 'Well, I am, by comparison.'

Oliver slammed down his mug. 'Don't be so fucking condescending!'

After a lengthy impasse, during which Jude stared at the garden and Oliver stared at his screen, she came over and eased herself on to the table to face him. 'I withdraw my unseemly comments about Shelley. By the same token, you cannot expect me to like the same people as you do.'

'But we usually do like the same people.'

'Shouldn't that tell you something?'

He moaned, and pressed his fingers against his temples.

Jude ran her fingers slowly through his hair. It made him look up. 'I'm going to ship out,' she said.

'Ship out?'

'Go home.'

'*What?* No way.'

'Come on, Oliver, be realistic. Shelley finds me intimidating, apparently, and I find her, well, boring, which makes it impossible for you.'

'No. I won't let my love-life drive you out of here. This is your home.'

'It doesn't feel like home at the moment. Not when I'm clearly *de trop*.'

'You aren't *de trop*, and I won't have you leaving. Christ, how can you land this on me when I feel like my head's been through a blender? This is the only time of year I get to see you properly.'

Jude got off the table to massage his neck. 'But you're not seeing me.'

'Ah, magic. And what the hell would you do in Dublin all summer?'

'I'll work for Sinéad. I could use the cash.'

'No. You need a break, especially after what's happened recently.'

'Well, I'm not having much of a break here.'

'Lower.'

She pressed her thumbs into his shoulders. 'I don't understand why you're arguing. It'd make everything easier for you.'

'Look, I want to spend time with you, it's just—'

'Fine, so stay an extra week in Cleigh after the wedding and we'll see each other then.'

'But what about Tim? He'll be so disappointed if you're not here.'

'If it weren't for Tim, I'd have left a week ago, but I can't hold out any longer. I'm lonely and in the way, and I've always promised myself I would never come between you and your lady friends.'

'I don't care about that. I won't have you leaving.'

'Why not?'

'I'd feel I'd let you down.'

'You're not letting me down.' She sat up on the table again. 'Look, it's like we said in Letterfrack: you need to get on with your life without having me strapped on to your back.'

'It so happens I find it very comfortable with you strapped to my back. I'd probably fall over if you weren't there.'

A breeze came through the open doors. Jude shivered. Oliver's reluctance to let her go, when he had everything to gain by it, alarmed her. She wondered if something more final than she intended was occurring. Was the disengagement he thought impossible actually taking place? She had always believed there could be no end to this relationship – it was her food, her drink, her root – and yet it was probably as vulnerable to external forces as any other. It might even have outgrown itself, just when she thought it had reached its apex. 'Look at me,' she said.

The large sloping eyes locked on to hers with unexpected intensity.

'I have to go. It's the only thing to do.'

He shook his head. 'Sod you, Jude. Sod you, anyway.'

22

The silence woke her. The silence of her house, of her street, of the city. There was no hum of traffic, nor the muffled slam of a car door, nor even the lilt of a voice carried on the air. Was there anybody home, Jude wondered, in all of Dublin?

She had slept and re-slept and double-slept. There was no avoiding it any longer: she had to get up. She had to face the empty house and her empty life; she had to fill them. Fiona was still living with her family, and the rest of their friends were in America and around the Continent. Jude dragged herself down to the kitchen, turned on the radio and turned it off again. The summer schedule. She hated the summer schedule. 'Well,' she told herself, 'now we'll find out what you're made of.'

She wasn't made of much that first week. She read a lot of magazines and ate a lot of toast. The weather was dull, the evenings long. There was something stirring about summer evenings, about days that refused to end and nights that refused to begin, and Jude had always loved and hated the summer stretch in equal measure. It demanded an audience; it insisted you be out enjoying the light and it waggled its finger if you stayed indoors watching television. Not that she cared. She was in a television frame of mind and, with its numbing influence, managed to blot out the horror of finding herself alone in Dublin in the middle of summer, so very far from Oliver and Tim, and her gushing river.

'I've been home for a week,' she admitted to Fiona when she finally rang her.

'A week? But why? What brings you back so early?'

'It's a bit of a saga.'

'A saga? Excellent! I'm on my way!'

Later that afternoon, stretched out on a rug in the back garden, Jude told Fiona about Oliver's new romance. 'You won't believe how we met. The first night they went out, I fell asleep after watching telly in Oliver's room. I've done it before – I switch off and pass out, and he kicks me out when he gets home. But this time, when I woke up, they were hard at it right beside me and Shelley sort of hit me. She went ballistic.'

'Jesus, you must have died! What did Oliver do?'

'Oh, I got the quiet, restrained, "I can't believe this is happening" look.'

As Fiona pressed her for details, events in France acquired a comic dimension, hitherto unseen, which soon had them rolling about the lawn. 'And whenever Oliver uses a word with more than two syllables in it, she goes, "Pardon me?"'

Fiona doubled over.

'And the clothes! She thought nothing of wearing a light cotton dress which was so see-through you could see the labels on her underwear! You could even *read* the labels!'

'Ugh,' groaned Fiona. 'How does Oliver stick it?'

'By keeping his nose pressed against those boobs. I'll bet she's had a job done. You know, she actually had me thinking, "Come back, Lee, all is forgiven!" At least I knew where I stood with *her*. Shelley hates me being around Oliver, but she won't admit it.'

'Is he serious about her?'

'Na. He's fairly infatuated, but he knows he needs someone smart. Mind you, she was smart enough to get rid of me PDQ!'

Fiona pushed her hair behind one ear. 'What about Stephen's wedding? Is Oliver still taking you?'

'God, yes. He knows I'd rather die than go alone.'

Fiona frowned. 'You're going to need a serious outfit for this affair.'

'Yeah, and I've already found it. It's a red linen dress, calf-length, fitted, with a very low back. And I've seen this incredible black hat, completely flat, which you wear perched on the side of your head like a satellite dish.'

'Hmm. That should make the groom regret his nuptials.'

Three weeks later, at Glasgow airport, Jude knew something was wrong as soon as her eyes hit Oliver's. She chose to ignore it. Seeing her beloved Stephen commit himself to someone else for evermore wasn't going to be easy, and she needed to keep on top of things if she was to carry it off with flair. Whatever Oliver's problem, she hoped he'd keep it to himself.

She hoped in vain. Five miles from Cleigh, he pulled in on a quiet stretch of road, turned off the engine and ran his thumb along his lower lip.

'What is it?'

He looked out over the steering-wheel. 'Shelley's here.'

'*What*?'

'I brought her with me, all right?'

Jude got out of the car and threw her hands in the air. 'Rrrrrggggghhh!'

'I couldn't very well *not* bring her, could I?' asked Oliver, getting out.

'You bastard! You frigging bastard! You promised me!'

'I know I did. I'm sorry.'

Jude stormed up and down. 'How could you do this? You know what this wedding is going to be like for me! You promised you'd take me. Why didn't you tell me?'

'It was a last-minute thing.'

'Oh, and you don't know how to use a phone?' Intense irritation gurgled in Jude's throat. Oliver was relieved the car stood between them; she might have hit him otherwise. 'You could have warned me.'

'I knew if I did, you'd blow a fuse and might not come.'

'I wish I'd had that option! Now I'm here for a bloody week because *you* wanted to spend time with me.'

'You can still spend time with me.'

'Yeah, you and Shelley. Whoopee! Like she really enjoys my company! And what about the wedding? If I'd known, I could have brought someone else.'

He slid his glasses up his nose. His eyes seemed bigger than usual, closer, as if she could take them off his face and put them in her pocket.

'Is this what I get for leaving you and Shelley in glorious isolation in France? Didn't I deserve this one little day?'

'I wanted her to meet everyone.'

'That couldn't have waited? Fuck you, Oliver!'

He watched her over the roof, his chin resting on his wrist.

'This is just great! I'll be sitting there like a bloody eejit.'

'You can still be with me, with us.'

She put her hands on the bonnet of the car and shook her head. 'What am I doing here?'

The sight of Mrs Sayle restored Jude somewhat, but seeing Shelley set her back again. She was wearing a pale floral affair, which had lost its purpose somewhere along the way. Spurred on by anger, Jude managed a spirited performance.

'Shelley, wonderful to see you. And what a simply gorgeous dress!'

As they went into the kitchen, Oliver threw Jude a filthy look. He was on to her.

Mrs Sayle turned her full attention to Jude when they sat down for tea and, gossiping like two schoolgirls, they soon managed to bore Oliver and Shelley out of the room.

'We're going for a walk,' said Oliver, getting up.

'Excellent, dear,' said his mother. She pulled at the neck of her sweater as the door closed behind them. 'Ach, that's better.'

Jude grimaced. 'She's fairly full on, isn't she?'

'I didn't mean Shelley. I meant you. You and Oliver. Och, what a cold wind you brought in with you.'

'We had a fight on the way home.'

'A fight? What's new about that? It usually warms things up. No, this is something else.'

'Is it?'

'Isn't it?'

Jude didn't know where to look. 'He broke a promise. It was important to me, but I'll get over it.'

Mrs Sayle crossed her arms on the table, her beady eyes twinkling. 'You're co-dependent, that's what I've always said.'

'Sorry?'

288

'You and Oliver. I know it sounds like so much psycho-babble, but in your case it's true and it's no good thing.'

'How do you mean, "co-dependent"?'

'Can't live with. Can't live without. You've too much history, the both of you.'

'But that's what makes it work – *when* it works.'

'No, Jude. It isn't right for a young girl like you to spend so much time with a troubled man like Oliver.'

'Troubled?'

'Your parents and his divorce – it sits on him all the time.'

'No, he's over all that. We talked everything out in April. It isn't hanging over him the way it used to.'

His mother sighed. 'He does seem more cheerful right enough. Or rather, he did, before you arrived.'

'I'm sorry, Anna. I wish I could let it pass, but I'm fairly furious with him.'

'A promise is a promise, I understand that, dear. But if I were you, Jude, I'd say now is the time to start letting go. I don't see that you and Oliver can do much more for each other.'

This was so unexpected that Jude stopped breathing; her diaphragm halted as suddenly as if a cog had jammed its wheels. A second blow in less than an hour! This weekend had never looked like an easy proposition, but it was turning into a sandstorm: painful grit whichever way she turned. Mrs Sayle's tone had been chummy but firm, and it forced Jude to wonder if she had outstayed her welcome in the bosom of this family. She had arrived seeking comfort from Oliver's mother; she found instead a shivery isolation and a finger pointing towards the door.

At lunch, Shelley talked almost without taking breath. She loved Scotland; it was *really something*, the scenery was *wild*, and the weather was *something else*. Jude picked at her food.

'In the pub last night,' Shelley chirped, 'I had a whole half pint of stout.'

'A whole half?' echoed Mr Sayle.

'But how come nobody's wearing kilts around here?'

'It's mostly ceremonial dress now,' Mrs Sayle explained. 'You know, Highland *ceilidhs* and weddings and the like.'

'Weddings! So you'll be wearing kilts tomorrow?'

Oliver laughed. 'That'll be the day!'

'We wouldn't get Stephen into a kilt for love nor money,' said Mr Sayle.

Shelley beamed. 'Gee, that's disappointing, isn't it, Jude? I'll bet you'd love to see Steve in a kilt, huh?'

A piece of brown bread jammed in Jude's throat. Mrs Sayle's eyes shot on to her; she was a past master at deciphering innuendo.

'Wouldn't we all,' said Oliver hastily. Jude scowled at him. He'd told Shelley about her fling with Stephen, the weasel.

But Oliver's girlfriend had only just begun. When Mrs Sayle expressed concern that Jude wasn't eating, Shelley came on like a chainsaw running amok in a quiet forest. She wrinkled her nose at the older woman and said chummily, 'I guess it's the wedding.'

'Whatever do you mean?'

'Yes,' said Jude. 'What do you mean, Shelley?'

'Well, it can't be easy, what with you and Steve and all.'

Even Mr Sayle looked up. His wife, her knife raised mid-air, looked from Oliver to Jude to Shelley.

The American blinked at the slice of bread she was buttering. 'It's always tough when an ex gets married.'

Jude could hear Oliver breathing.

'An ex?' said his mother. 'Jude?'

Unable to look at Oliver, Jude didn't know which way to turn.

'Oliver?' said Mrs Sayle. 'What does this mean?'

Shelley popped a crumb into her mouth, eyebrows arched high.

'I think what Shelley means,' Jude stammered, 'is that I've, em, a bit of a crush on Stephen. I mean, I did have. Once. Nothing . . . you know, just a silly . . . Excuse me.' She got up and left the room.

'She's lying,' said Mrs Sayle.

'She isn't,' said Oliver. 'You must have misunderstood, Shelley. It was an infatuation. She got over it long ago.'

'But you said—'

'If something happened between Stephen and Jude,' said Mrs Sayle, 'I want to know right now.'

'Nothing happened, Mum. And even if it had, they are consenting adults, you know.'

'But that's just the point! Jude has stayed under my roof many times when she was *not* an adult and if Stephen . . . well, I would hold you entirely responsible!'

'Me? How do you manage that?'

'Your primary responsibility as her guardian was to protect her and to teach her to behave in a decent and respectable manner.'

'Oh, right. And where's Stephen in all this? The blessed innocent incarnate, is he?'

'You know very well Stephen is completely guileless with women.'

Oliver laughed. 'Your partiality is truly astounding, Mother!'

'This is exactly why this whole arrangement was a mistake from the start. Jude should never have spent her formative years with a single man.'

'It seems to me,' said her husband, 'that if Jude had a bit of a thing for our Stephen, Anna, you can hardly blame Oliver. I believe he's done a marvellous job with her. She's turned into a splendid young woman and I'm sure a very sensible one. Now, we have a wedding in this family tomorrow and this bickering is hardly the way to start proceedings.'

'That child has been in our family these last five years, Dan. I'd die if I thought—'

'No need to die, Mother.'

'Give me your word that nothing happened.'

'Mum, you're edgy because of the wedding.'

'Gee, I'm sorry,' said Shelley. 'I didn't mean to start a quarrel.'

Jude was speed-walking along the lane behind the house when she heard footsteps behind her. Predictably, he had come after her. Unpredictably, she would send him right back where he came from.

'Oi! Jude!'

'Fuck off.'

'Eh? What have I done?'

She turned. It was Stephen. Another shock. She hadn't expected to speak to the groom alone during the entire weekend.

'I drove up and saw you taking off,' he said. 'Whasup?'

Jude strode on. 'You might as well know that over lunch the lovely Shelley told your mother about us. Good one, eh? Don't you just love her? Isn't her timing *just neat*?'

Stephen stopped. 'Ouch. I'd say Mummy's not dead pleased with me.'

'Oh, don't worry. She'll blame Oliver. She always does!'

'Did all hell break loose?'

'I don't know. I left before I killed that bitch.'

'Oi, easy does it. My mother may be difficult but—'

'I don't mean your mother. I mean Shelley. She's trying to come between me and Oliver and she's bloody well succeeding.'

'So don't let her.'

'I wouldn't if he was worth the effort, but I'm beginning to wonder.'

She climbed over a fence and headed up the low hill behind the house. Stephen followed. 'Hey, slow down, would you? I have to talk to you.'

'Jesus! What is it with you Sayles?'

'I wanted to apologize for not telling you I was getting hitched. I meant to, but then you went on that downer and I thought it might be better coming from Ol.'

He was standing just below her. She wanted to touch his face, his lips. 'I didn't mind.'

'All the same, I'm sorry you heard it from someone else.'

They walked on. Half-way up the hill, they sat on a familiar rock. It brought back memories of the times they had come up there for a snog.

'So I take it you don't like Shelley much?'

'What's there to like? *Air*?'

Stephen winced.

'You?'

'I think she's nice,' he said. 'Really bubbly. Great body too.'

He grinned when Jude thumped him. The dimples she loved pierced his cheeks, the dark eyes that had once wanted her glittered in the afternoon sun, and the waistband of his jeans was as inviting as ever. Jude could only ponder. She had been more comfortable, more intimate, with this man than with anyone. No one else had bathed with her, washed her, taught her to walk across a room with no clothes and no embarrassment. She had learnt passion, had even cried out, with him. Whatever sexuality she carried into other relationships, it had been sparked by Stephen, who lay on the rock in a T-shirt and jeans looking like a dark-haired Adonis. It was a tragedy that he was soon to be a bridegroom and it was impossible, at that moment, not to be wholly in love with him.

'Oh God!' she said suddenly. 'If your mother finds out we're alone together – the day before your wedding – she'll kill someone!'

'Yeah, and it'll probably be my best man. I'd better get back.' Stephen stood up, hesitated, then kissed her lightly on the lips.

She watched him go. There was nothing for it: as long as he lived and breathed, she would fancy him, ache for him. How could she not, when he was sexuality itself, walking, talking – and getting married?

There were several cars parked outside the house when Jude went back an hour later. Stephen's friends were arriving from London, and when she sneaked in, the place was buzzing with rattling cups, telephone calls and laughter. Jude usually slept in a large room at the front of the house, but this had now been allocated to Oliver and Shelley, leaving her in a poky room at the back. As wide again as the single bed, but not much longer, it was a depressing little place to ruminate on all the wrongs being done to her, as she was doing when Oliver let himself in.

Jude jumped to her feet and pointed towards the dining-room. 'What was all that about? And what did I do to deserve it?'

'She didn't mean to land you in it. She thought it was common knowledge about you and Stephen.'

'Bullshit. That little slip was as deliberately placed as a land-mine.'

His eyes hardened. 'To what end?'

'To cause trouble between us. And it has.'

'Why should it come between us?'

'Because you've betrayed a confidence. I'm not public property, Oliver. You had no right to discuss my private life with that woman.'

'That woman is my partner and partners share things – as you'd know if you could only hold down a decent relationship!'

He thought her eyes were going to go on fire. 'That is so low,' she said.

'Sorry.'

'I suppose you even told her I didn't want to come to this wedding alone?'

He shifted uncomfortably. 'I had to explain why I hadn't asked her sooner.'

'Jesus, this has become humiliating before I even get to the church.'

'What was I supposed to say to her – and to Stephen, who invited her? That *you* didn't want her here?'

'You could have told the truth – that you were committed to me. Or am I that easily dispensable? I mean, talk about cursory dismissal!'

'So I fouled up. I'm sorry. But can we please drop it and concentrate on giving Stephen a good send-off?'

'Easy for you to say. You weren't made to look like a love-sick loser.'

'What Shelley said was unfortunate, Jude, but it was not deliberate.'

'No? The concept of discretion must be beyond the realm of her limited understanding then.'

'Ah. There's the crux of it. She doesn't meet your exacting intellectual requirements, does she?'

'It's *your* intellectual requirements I'm concerned about. What's happened to them? You've hardly done any work since June and you're spending your time with someone whose grey matter is mostly lodged in her chest.'

Oliver came at her. 'You mind your tongue,' he growled. 'And may I remind you that what I do or don't do is none of your sodding business.'

She raised her chin. 'It is my business. *You're* my business, and you're going out with an airhead.'

'Ach, I'm not hung up on people's brains like you and your mother. I take people as they come.'

'Yeah, and I'll bet she comes often.'

Oliver thumped the wardrobe beside him. 'Jesus, but you drive me to the limit sometimes!'

'And I reached my limit when my love-life was blurted out to your entire family. Have you any idea how humiliating it was?'

'Yes! But I warned you about getting involved with Stephen and I told you this would happen if you did. There are always repercussions to shoddy behaviour, Jude.'

Had blisters appeared on her skin, Jude wouldn't have been surprised. '*You* can talk. You were busy shagging my aunt at the time!'

'Keep your voice down!'

'No!'

Oliver paced the tiny room. 'This is insane. I was looking forward to this weekend. To seeing you. So tell me what it'll take to clear the air, because I won't have this going on around my parents.'

'You could muzzle your blasted girlfriend for a start.'

'And you could stop behaving like a spoilt brat!' He

296

pulled his hands around his neck to contain his temper. 'Listen to me. Come Sunday morning, we'll find some isolated hill, you and I, where you can shout your brains out if that's what you need, but in the meantime I suggest you get your ass downstairs and give Mum a hand, because if you don't, she'll think you really do have something to hide.'

Mrs Sayle was in the kitchen, making tea. Jude sidled up and offered to help.

'Oh, there you are, dear. Run out to the pantry, would you, and get the fruit cake.'

Jude breathed a sigh of relief. The morning's rebuttal and the lunchtime lie had either been smothered by events or dismissed by Oliver's mother, which was lucky because the only way Jude could get through the wedding now was with Mrs Sayle propping her up. She worked hard in the kitchen, clearing all around her, and ran in and out of the living-room, bringing tea to family friends. Shelley mingled in both rooms, drawing appreciative attention from Stephen's mates, while Oliver stood by the Aga with the lads, scowling. Jude kept as far from him as she could and concentrated on making herself so useful that her behaviour would be considered above reproach.

But when it transpired that everyone was going out to dinner, she knew she couldn't do it. She told Mrs Sayle she had a pounding headache and cried off, praying that Oliver would be in the restaurant before he noticed her absence, but when she tried to escape to her room before they left, he cornered her in the hall.

'Mum says you're not coming. I say you are.'

Jude kept moving. 'I am not.'

'I thought we agreed to put a hold on all this?'

'I didn't agree to anything.'

He grabbed her wrist. 'My brother is getting married tomorrow and you'd better not bloody ruin it for me.'

'Why not? You've ruined it for me.'

'He isn't your brother!'

'Let go. You're hurting.'

His eyes narrowed. 'So are you.'

Jude pulled away and ran up to her room.

The following morning, while she was fixing Tim's bow-tie in the living-room, it seemed to Jude he was the only Sayle who still loved her. 'I'm sorry I wasn't in France, Tim.'

'That's OK.'

'Did you miss me?'

'Yeah.'

'But I'll bet you had great fun with Shelley?'

'Yeah.'

A mine of information. 'Go on. You're done.'

Oliver came into the room as Tim ran off. Jude tried to follow, but Oliver put his arm out and caught her around the waist. 'What have I done to make you so mad? I brought my girlfriend to my brother's wedding. What's the big deal?'

'You broke a promise, and gave me no warning. You allowed me to take a week off work for no good reason whatsoever, and you shared my private feelings with some-body who is incredibly indiscreet. All that adds up to a very big deal.'

Oliver turned away, his hands on the small of his back, then looked wearily over his shoulder. 'Tell me what I can do to make up for it then. We can't go on like this.'

'Come to Dublin before you go back. Spend a few days.'

'I can't. I'm going to the States with Shelley.'

Jude shook her head. 'Better mind those Circadian rhymes.'

'I thought this was what you wanted? You've been haranguing me for years to settle down with someone.'

'Someone with a bit of substance would be nice.'

'You're really pushing it, Jude.'

The groom burst in, dressed in all his finery, and stopped in his tracks. 'Wow. You look stunning, Judy . . . But what's that dinner plate doing on the side of your head?'

Neither Jude nor Oliver could raise a smile.

Stephen's face dropped. 'Whasup?'

Oliver looked at Jude. She looked away.

'Hey.' Stephen pulled them both against him. 'Whatever's going on here, I suggest you kiss and make up right now. I don't want long faces at my wedding, especially on my bloody best man. So go on. Make up.'

Jude's guilt was overwhelming; she couldn't allow this fracas to ruin the day for either brother. 'Sorry,' she mumbled.

'Clear off a minute, would you, Steve?'

'Certainly. But make it good!'

Oliver lifted Jude's hands and looked over her red dress and long black gloves. 'It's my loss not having you on my arm today. You're going to blow the town away.'

She slipped her hands out of his.

'I'm sorry for breaking my promise,' he said, 'and for hurting you to get what I wanted, but as for the rest, your petulance provoked it.'

A veritable dictionary had to be stopped in Jude's throat. 'Fine.'

Oliver bent his knees to try to catch her eye. 'Are you OK in there? About Stephen?'

She picked up her bag. 'You've forfeited any right to know how I feel.'

*

299

Jude spent most of the day smiling. Her facial muscles almost seized up in the process, but it got her through the ordeal. She was no longer sure what the ordeal actually was – spending the day in Oliver's company or seeing Stephen get married – but she was marginally warmed by Mrs Sayle's exhilaration. In a smart suit and sky-blue hat, the groom's mother sat in the front pew of the church gazing proudly at her spruced-up boys.

Jude also watched Mrs Sayle's sons as they stood fidgeting by the altar, waiting for the bride, but unlike their mother, she was in torment, body and soul. Her body yearned for Stephen, her soul for his brother. Stephen had added colour to his formal get-up by wearing a luminous orange waistcoat, and he looked spectacular. Jude couldn't take her eyes from the shoulders, clad in black, that had once heaved over her. It was agony to remember, and because she had no one to lean on, she stood as stiff as a stalagmite and sore all over. As for Oliver, she was trying hard to forgive him the possibly small sin of bringing his lady friend to his brother's wedding, but the sense of betrayal remained like an unshiftable block inside her.

When a swell of excitement heralded Vanessa's arrival, Jude hoped to see a collapsed pavlova coming down the aisle, but the bride's dress was understated, she wore scarcely any make-up, nothing in her short brown hair, and white rubber flip-flops on her feet. Simplicity itself. Stephen greeted her at the altar with an expression Jude had never before seen on his face. *Love*, she thought. The rat.

After the ceremony, she stood outside the church with Tim, watching the photographer pushing people about, and when the Sayle family were called, she gave him a gentle shove. 'That's you, Tim. Go stand with your dad.'

'Oi!' called Stephen. 'Judy. Get over here.'

'Yes, yes,' said his mother. 'Come along, Jude.'

'You're an honorary Sayle today,' said Stephen.

Tears pricked Jude's eyes. She walked self-consciously towards the group and when she joined them, Oliver took her arm and held her in front of him. For a moment, their quarrel was forgotten, for he alone knew what it meant to her to be included in a family photograph. It had simply never happened before.

Later, as guests made their way to their tables in the large marquee which had been erected in Vanessa's garden, she found she had been seated beside Tim. When Oliver came past, she stopped him. 'Is this your bright idea? I get to babysit?'

'Where else would I put him?'

'With you, maybe? Or couldn't you be bothered?'

He inhaled sharply. 'If I won the Nobel Prize for Parenting, Ms Feehan, it wouldn't be good enough for you.'

She sat down.

Oliver leaned over her. 'My patience is wearing pretty damn thin, Jude.'

He walked off. She tried to swallow, but her mouth was dry. She was pushing him and pushing him and if she didn't stop soon, he'd fall away altogether. And yet she couldn't stop herself and she no longer knew why.

Her seat was facing the main table. During the meal, Oliver caught her eye only twice, and didn't wink. Jude tried to smile, knowing it would make all the difference, but couldn't. '*Sod you, Jude,*' she kept hearing him say. '*Sod you.*'

The meal over, Vanessa's father made a predictably moving speech, Stephen's was sweet and to the point, and

Jude shuddered when Oliver stood up. She knew he was nervous and, seeing the shake in his hands and the repeated scratching of the lower lip, she couldn't but empathize. Even at his own book launches, he loathed making speeches. Instead of portraying Stephen as a hapless clod, he spoke of him with unmitigated affection, although he did say that the shock of losing Only Child status at the age of eleven was like being knocked off the road by an articulated lorry. He sat down to an appreciative round of applause. As he gulped back some wine, Jude breathed more easily.

She longed for the day to be over, which made it drag all the more, and she couldn't help remembering the last wedding they had attended – Sinéad's – a far happier day, much of which they had spent in hysterics. In the church, when Peter's voice had suddenly boomed out his vows, it was so startling that many in the congregation had jumped, which made Oliver and Jude crack up. Tim, wanting to join in, had roared loudly, 'Ha, ha, ha!' They had stood side by side in the pew, heads bowed, shaking like jellies, trying to contain themselves. After the meal, Peter's pompous speech, again too loud, created the same effect, so that all Jude could remember was painfully suppressed laughter, and a great night spent dancing.

How things had changed. Now as the music got under way, Jude chatted to another girl at her table, but her eyes kept wandering to the dance-floor. There was one happy man to be seen there, dancing in his bright orange waistcoat with his lovely wife, and even Jude couldn't begrudge them such delight as they had found together. Stephen deserved nothing less. Not far away, Oliver and Shelley were moving quite differently, pressed together like a baked bean sandwich, obviously not far off escaping for a bonk in the bushes.

'I'd love another glass of wine,' said the young woman beside her, 'but I shouldn't. I have to drive to Glasgow first thing tomorrow.'

Jude's ears pricked up. 'Glasgow? Any chance of a lift?'

'Yeah, sure. If you get up early enough.'

A finger ran down Jude's back. She grinned; Stephen was irrepressible. 'That's a bit cheeky at your own wedd—'

It was Oliver. He extended his hand; she joined him ungraciously on the floor. With several drinks on board, he was more relaxed now. 'Come on,' he grinned. 'Lighten up. There must be some unattached males around here somewhere.'

'What makes you think I want one?'

He squeezed her. 'You can be unbelievably maddening sometimes! I'm only trying to make conversation.'

She looked away. The music – Annie Lennox singing '*Why?*' – sliced into her.

Oliver drew her closer, but it was like dancing with an ironing board. 'Can't we give this antagonism a rest, Jude?'

'You make it sound so easy.'

He sighed. 'You know I love your lovely long fingers, but you're going to pierce holes in my arm if you dig them in any deeper.'

'You can talk. You're holding me so tight I can hardly breathe.'

'Maybe we're clinging on because we're losing our grip?'

Jude turned her face away, but moments later allowed her cheek to rest on his shoulder because that must not happen. They must not lose their hold.

As the song ended and another began, Jude heard that awful 'Ollie?' and turned to see Shelley, her hands clasped, her woolly purple top clashing with her mud-brown suit. 'May I?' she cooed.

Oliver looked helplessly at Jude. She lifted her hands from him. They danced off, leaving her standing amongst the smooching couples. Finding her feet, Jude turned to flee and barged into Stephen.

He slipped his arm around her. 'May I?'

'God bless your timing, Stephen Sayle!'

'Whasup?'

'I was dumped in the middle of the dance-floor by your brother.'

'Oh dear. So things still aren't right?' He spun her around, brought her back against his hip. 'You're being too possessive, Jude.'

'Hmm?'

'Of Oliver. You'll have to ease up. The more you push, the more he'll dig in.' He twirled her again. 'At last. I've been waiting all night to dance with the only lover with whom I never actually made love.'

'It's my greatest regret,' Jude whimpered.

'*Now* she tells me.'

For a full ten minutes, Jude enjoyed herself. There was mute familiarity in the way they held each other and their hands were clasped without a shred of awkwardness. Jude could feel Stephen's fingers on her back, his sweaty skin through his shirt, and she longed to step in, to press against him.

'Mind if I cut in?'

Jude dragged her eyes from Stephen's chin. It was Oliver. She did mind.

Stephen grasped her to his chest. 'Are you going to dump her again?'

'Sod off,' said Oliver, taking Jude. 'Go find your wife.'

'*Wife*,' said Jude. 'When did he ever grow up enough to have a wife?'

'When we weren't looking, dear.'

She leaned into him, primarily to annoy Shelley, but it was a relief, also, to escape the heat generated by Stephen for the cool comfort of being with Oliver.

'I should take one myself,' he said.

'Hmm?'

'A wife.'

Stephen whirled past with Vanessa, his shirt open, waist-coat flapping. 'Sorry?'

'I'm thinking of getting married again.'

'*What?*' Now he had her full attention. 'You can't be serious!'

'Why not? I'm in love with her.'

'Oh, really? And what was that you once said about mistaking lust for love?'

'I'm not making that mistake.'

'How can you possibly tell when you've spent most of the summer in bed?'

'Don't start, Jude.'

'Oliver, you met her two months ago. You'd be jumping in blindfolded! Don't you remember how hard it was to jump out?'

'When you know, you *know*.'

'Except you didn't know last time, did you?'

His jaw tensed. 'Don't make this any worse than it already is.'

He looked so stern, so serious, that Jude sniggered. 'I can't believe I'm hearing this. For God's sake, be in love by all means, but don't be thick about it! Why on earth would you want to marry that creature?'

305

His arms dropped; his big eyes stood still. 'That's it. You're all out of chances.'

He walked away, out of the marquee and into the darkness.

23

Christmas was awkward. Jude had plenty of invitations, but nowhere to go. Sitting on the outskirts of a Sayle family Christmas was one thing, but playing umpire to any other family would emphasize her situation too harshly. Instead, she opted to stay at home and invite similarly kinless types to join her, but when Fiona shipped out two days before Christmas and everyone else scurried to their homes like lizards to their rocks, Jude struggled to keep even a sliver of Yuletide spirit alive in her own heart. Every time the phone rang, she jumped, pointlessly; there would be no seasonal reconciliation. There would never be a reconciliation, not after the way she had behaved, swatting at him relentlessly like a woman at a fly, and then vanishing without a word. Wherever he was, she could feel his anger. It would take years to dilute the fury that must have built up with her words and deeds and her rejection of his happiness.

'You're being too hard on yourself,' said Sinéad, when she called in on Christmas Eve. 'I mean, he effectively turned up on a date with another bird in tow. You were entitled to be angry.'

'You don't think I overdid it a bit?'

'I think you shouldn't have taken off. That was a mistake.'

'There was no point staying. We were getting absolutely nowhere.'

'Yes, but look at you now. Alone at Christmas.' Sinéad sipped at her wine. 'Is he still paying his share of the mortgage?'

'Course. He wouldn't pull the plug on that.'

'Did any of them send Christmas cards?'

'Nope.'

'I suppose *he* cooked your Christmas dinner last year?'

'Sinéad, get off it, will you? I'm trying to forget about Oliver, not sink into my mulled wine in despair.'

'I'm sorry, but I sat here only eight months ago and saw the anguish that man went through when you were missing. How could you end up on a one-way collision course four months later? How did everything get so bad so quickly?'

'Don't you think I ask myself that every other day?'

'They're the only family you have.'

'They're not my family – surely that's the point?'

'Phone him. Apologize for taking off. Blame Stephen.'

'There's no point. We'd come to the end of . . . whatever it was.'

'But friendships don't go up in smoke in the space of one weekend.'

'Oh, yes they do.'

They stared into the fire, sipping their wine.

'"No disengagement is possible,"' Jude said quietly.

'Hmm?'

'Oliver said that once, about us. Warts on the same thumb, thorns on the same rose, that kind of thing. And I believed him. You know, I love Tim, I miss him, but Oliver

. . . he's like another side of me. He's the part of me that makes sense.'

'Oh, Jude. You should never have let this happen.'

After surviving Christmas alone, Jude knew Easter could never be as bad, especially as her final-year thesis absorbed her every waking hour, but three weeks after Easter, Oliver insinuated himself into her life just when she was growing accustomed to living without him.

One evening in April she came in from college and found Fiona and her boyfriend, Theo, sitting at the kitchen table looking glum. Convinced she had walked into a row, Jude resolved to leave them to it as soon as she had made tea. 'Don't mind me,' she said cheerfully. 'I'll be quick. However, you should know that I had coffee with Bob the Ag Student today.'

Fiona glanced at Theo. 'You did?'

'Please don't over-excite yourselves on my account.' Jude stood with her back against the counter. 'He may be enthralled by pigs, but he does have *very* wide shoulders and –'

'Jude—'

'– I can't reject him on the basis of wavy hair, can I?'

'Have you seen today's paper?'

So it was about her, this atmosphere, and it didn't take much to work out which aspect of her life it concerned. 'No.' The kettle clicked off.

Fiona picked up *The Irish Times,* shook it at the appropriate page and held it up. Oliver Sayle, in grainy black and white, stared back at Jude.

'Profiled in the Arts section,' said Fiona. 'It's his new book.'

Jude scarcely moved. 'He's plugging a book?'

'Yeah. It's an interview.'

'An interview? Where? When?'

Fiona read through the article, her eyes shooting back and forth. 'Er, seems to have taken place in the Shelbourne.'

'The Shelbourne? You mean . . .' Jude kicked the fridge. 'Fuck him, anyway! He comes to Dublin and doesn't even phone. He knew I'd see this!'

Fiona bit her lip.

'The nerve. He comes plugging his rotten book without even . . . It's that bitch-face of a girlfriend. Stupid bloody brain-dead Yank! . . . Does it say if they're married yet?'

Fiona held out the paper. 'Why don't you read it?'

Jude snatched it and went upstairs with a mug of tea. When she closed her bedroom door, the tears came. He'd really done it this time. There was no going back now; he clearly didn't want to.

It made her weep just to think that he had been in town, that he had sat in the Shelbourne Hotel having tea with a journalist while she sat in a lecture a few miles away, completely unaware . . . How could he? How could he *do that*? She glanced at the newspaper. One of Oliver's eyes, warped by a fold in the paper, looked at her crossways, as if he still didn't understand. She straightened it out. It was his usual inexpressive, dour self. His face was unreadable, his eyes bright even in newspaper print. A profile in *The Irish Times* – quite a coup. Jude cursed. Where did he stay? In a city in which he owned a house, he had apparently stayed in a hotel. Such was their alienation.

She read the article. It mentioned her briefly, in relation to Oliver's long-standing links with Dublin, but something else drew her attention. According to the journalist conducting the interview, this new book was being acknowledged by critics as a departure for Sayle. A dark tale of guilt and

310

vengeance, *The Subtle Kill* was sure to bring him a whole new readership, but the author was evasive about what prompted such a change of direction, saying only that it had been a challenge. *A challenge from whom?* Jude wondered.

The book puzzled her. Oliver hadn't let her read it the previous summer and now she knew why – he had been planning to surprise her with his new style. Momentarily, pride got the better of her. 'I knew you could do it. I *knew* it!'

That weekend, she scoured the papers for reviews of *The Subtle Kill*. Most were good. There were dissenters, such as the reviewer who expressed surprise at finding a somewhat talented writer hiding behind such loathsome thrillers, but the critics generally admired Sayle for breaking out of the safe niche he had made for himself.

Jude waited. She had received all his other books by special delivery, but when this one didn't come, she was forced to buy it. 'This man owns half my house,' she felt like saying to the bookshop assistant. 'This man brought me up, and here I am buying his bloody book!' She went home, settled into bed with tea, toast and chocolate, and began reading *The Subtle Kill*, which she believed was the legacy of Letterfrack. Any doubts she might have had about this vanished when she saw that it was dedicated to her mother. She was moved, and she understood. If this was his first intelligent book, it could be for no one else. Jude turned to the Acknowledgements. Her name was thrown in with half a dozen other people, whom he warmly thanked for their support, and he finished off with special thanks to Shelley. Jude slammed the covers closed. Shelley had no claim to this! She had no idea where it had come from! . . . But it still had to be read.

'So, what's the verdict?' asked Fiona, when they went out walking the next day. 'Is it better than his other stuff?'

'That wouldn't be difficult.'

'Oh, come on. I enjoy his books. They're a good read.'

'Yeah, a good *light* read.'

'Ooh, snotty. So what about this one?'

'It's heavy-going. Comic in places, but very dark.'

'Tell me all. I haven't time to read at the moment and even if I did, I wouldn't spend it reading a gloomy book.'

'Well, I'll try. It's about a young woman and her very manipulative, but gorgeous, widowed mother. Mother suggests to daughter that her husband is having an affair – sowing seeds of doubt into what was a perfectly happy marriage – and even provides proof, and she puts enormous pressure on her daughter to leave the two-timing shit. Instead, the daughter kills herself. She leaves a note saying she did it because she's heartbroken, but also as an act of vengeance – she was six months pregnant, see, and her husband had been desperate to have this baby, so she killed it to get back at him.'

'So far, so much like any other book. Adultery, suicide. The vengeance bit with the baby is a bit grim, though. Go on.'

'Well, Mother is riddled with guilt, because it never occurred to her that the girl would actually *kill* herself, and the husband goes into abject depression because he adored the wife and was mad for the child, and he wasn't even having an affair in the first place. Mummy-in-law comforts him and eventually – you'll really have to read it – seduces him.'

'Seduces him?'

'Mmm. Don't forget, she's very sexy and beguiling. Imagine, say, Susan Sarandon with Tom Cruise. Anyway, this goes on until the strain of sleeping with his mother-in-law finally gets yer man thinking. He begins wondering why his wife was so certain he had a lover and how her mother can entertain the thought of having an affair with her dead daughter's husband, when her dead daughter killed herself because she thought he was having an affair.'

'Yeah. How can she?'

'Because Mother set it all up in the first place. She set them both up.'

'Why?'

''Cos she was obsessed with her son-in-law and couldn't bear the daughter to have him.'

'Except she didn't expect her daughter to kill herself?'

'No. That wasn't part of the plan, but she gets over that unfortunate detail.'

'I can't believe Oliver wrote this stuff. He's such a nice man.'

'Anyway, husband persuades mother-in-law to tell him everything by swearing that he loves her more than he ever loved the daughter, and once he knows—'

'He goes to the police?'

'No, he decides to destroy her, to wear her down until she has no dignity left, and she, of course, has to destroy him too, because he drove her to effectively murdering her own daughter. He uses humiliating sex, really awful graphic stuff, and she uses subtlety, undermining him gradually with this killer charm, until finally—'

'Don't tell me!'

'Why not? You said you didn't want to read it.'

'I've changed my mind.'

'But I'm longing to tell you the climax! And it isn't your type of book. You'll hate it.'

'*You* didn't hate it,' said Fiona primly. 'In fact, I'd even say you're impressed.'

'I wouldn't go that far. It's clever, but it isn't going to walk off the shelves. It's too twisted.'

313

'You can't give him credit for anything, can you? Aren't you just a tad proud of him?'

'Nope.'

'Oh, I get it. "Shithead, prickhead, bastard: but come back please, all is forgiven?"'

'Nothing is forgiven.'

'Poor Ol. Six years trying to keep *you* happy!'

Another landmark in Jude's life – her twenty-first birthday – came and went in May, unmarked by any Sayle. Her friends rallied around, but Jude caught herself hoping that Oliver would turn up and sweep her off the way he had when she was eighteen. He didn't, of course. If he could come to Dublin and not even phone, he wasn't about to acknowledge her birthday.

Bob the Ag student, however, did acknowledge it. He came to the bar to buy her a drink and, even though he was a bit gauche, he had the burly good looks of a rugby player and was more of a gentleman than any of the lads Jude knew. And yet, every time she lay on her bed and tried to imagine him in it, Stephen arrived unannounced and elbowed Bob aside. The trouble with her fantasies about Stephen was that so few of them were fantasies, and so reliving their curious, unconsummated affair always ended badly, because Jude was finding it increasingly difficult to accept that she had let Stephen get away.

With her final exams marching towards her, however, she had little time for Bob or fantasies as she and Fiona fell into a pattern of study, study and more study. When the early-summer light faded late in the evenings, they often walked the quiet streets of Ranelagh, longing for the day when they could stay up all night without books pressed against their noses. During the day, they studied in the library, and one afternoon when Jude was deep into a play by Congreve someone tapped her shoulder.

'Fancy a coffee?' asked Bob.

Is the sky blue?

He was a walking example of everything she hated in men, Jude realized when he sat down opposite her in the coffee shop, yet he remained attractive. 'What brings you over to the Arts Block?' she asked.

'You.'

Her insides turned over, but her expression remained composed. 'Oh?'

'I was wondering if you'd like to go out sometime?'

'Thanks, that'd be lovely – when my finals are over, obviously.'

He grimaced. 'I was afraid you'd say that. The thing is, the day after I finish my exams, I'm heading off to Germany to work for the summer.'

Jude didn't know whether to laugh or cry. Was she thwarted in love or what?

'But when I get back in September, we could take it from there maybe?'

He took her hand. He didn't have dimples, but his green eyes were actually quite lovely. Her elbows slid fractionally towards him. He leaned across the table and kissed her, which made her giddy, and desperate for more.

'Let's spend the day together.'

'No.' Jude drew back. 'I've got Middle English tomorrow.'

'September then?'

'I'm going to America in September. With Fiona and Emer.'

'October?'

Jude grinned. 'October.'

*

The night Jude's results were posted up, Bob telephoned from Stuttgart. They had to shout at each other to be heard, because the house was full of rowdy revellers, but Bob had passed his fourth-year exams, Fiona had sailed through final Law, Theo had scraped second Law, and Jude, also, had got what she wanted: a Two One. A second-class honours Arts degree. After screeching her delight to Bob, she jived around with friends, but in a closed-off section of her soul a dull loneliness throbbed like a fresh bruise. Oliver would have been so proud of her, had he still cared.

'You're the only person I know,' said Fiona, sitting in the garden at four the next morning, 'who has started going out with someone who isn't even here.'

'It isn't much fun,' said Jude, lying on the damp grass. Overhead, dawn was diluting the starlight. 'Especially tonight. Going to bed alone when I've passed my exams! Honestly!'

'Yeah, but before you know it, you'll be rushing into his arms with a *soooper* tan.'

'Yeah, and I plan to be ready. I'm not putting it off any longer. I'm going on the pill.'

'The pill? Ugh. It made me puke. Why don't you use condoms?'

'I don't want my first lover to be clad in rubber, thank you very much.'

'Suit yourself. I just hope Bob won't know what he's up against.'

'What?'

'Stephen Sayle.'

'Bob the Ag student, I'll have you know, is going to be the cure to Stephen bleedin' Sayle.'

*

316

For the first time in years, Jude had nowhere to go for the summer, and it was then, in those longed-for study-free days, that she noticed the emptiness that had come to inhabit her. Every morning, when she made her way to work in Sinéad's shop, she struggled against this inner hollow. She could not accept that Oliver was still an issue almost a year after Stephen's wedding, nor could she admit that Bob and her BA (Hons) degree were failing to compensate for the Sayle family, but Oliver had guided her so astutely towards academic success that gaining her degree was a bit like having a party that nobody came to. She didn't even attend her conferring ceremony; it seemed pointless without anyone there to applaud her achievement. The day the results came out had been bad enough, with everyone reaching for their mobile phones to call their families. There had been no one hanging by the phone impatient for Jude's news, so she had been forced to stand around, waiting for everyone to finish their calls, while the joy of doing well sank inside her like a dead weight.

None the less, she was determined to fill the ditch Oliver had left behind him. He had brought her through adolescence perhaps. He had pushed her forward with his fingers pressed into the back of her neck, had established her home and eased her way through college, but here was an end to his role in her life. Her trip to America would be the watershed. It would broaden her horizons, test her independence, and set her on course for a new, Sayle-free lifestyle.

She should have known better. Even in absence, Oliver interrupted her life with such regularity that she should have known it would not be so easy to rotate her feelings. One wet evening at the beginning of August, she came in from work just as the phone rang.

317

'Hello?'

'Jude? It's Stephen.'

Three words, and he made her feel as if she had run a marathon. 'Stephen.'

'Hope I'm not calling at a bad time, but I'm trying to get my head around the fact that you haven't been in touch.' His voice was cool and sharp, like sugar passing over a tooth cavity. She had never experienced this end of him.

'In touch?' She tried to conceal her breathlessness.

'With Oliver.'

'Oh, that. I doubt he's noticed.'

'That's hardly the point. He soon will.'

'Listen, he hasn't been in touch with me either, Stephen.'

'No, well. It's a bit difficult with all those tubes stuffed up his nose.'

Jude's legs gave way; she sat on the stairs. 'What?'

'Jude, you ought to be here. He was flat out when it happened and he's got a bit of a battle ahead. And Mum's losing it.'

The words hardly left her throat. 'What are you . . . ?'

'If you were here, she might ease up.'

'Stephen! What are you talking about?'

There was a very long pause. Then: 'You don't know?'

She shook her head.

'He's had appendicitis.'

Jude exhaled. 'Appendicitis! I thought something really serious—'

'It *is* serious. His appendix burst on a flight from LA four days ago. He has peritonitis. How much more serious do you want?'

'Jesus.'

'He was lucky. It didn't get critical until they hit the ground at Heathrow.'

'My God. Where is he?'

'He's just been brought out of intensive care. Where are *you*, Jude?'

'Stephen, I had no idea. Why did no one tell me?'

'I was under the impression you had been told.'

'How is he?'

'Lousy.'

'But is he going to be all right?'

Stephen sighed. 'He's pulling out of it. But if his appendix had burst any sooner, like out over the Pole, he'd be dead right now.' Jude didn't speak. His exasperation loosened out. 'I wish you'd come over. If money's a problem, I'll take care of it.'

'Is that what he wants? Is he asking for me?'

'No, but he must be wondering where you are.'

Jude felt her heart tighten. For a moment, she had seen a way out of this, but Stephen had inadvertently closed the door only seconds after he'd opened it. 'Listen, Stephen, if Oliver wanted me to be told about this, you can be damn sure I would have been, and since he hasn't, he hardly wants to see me arrive at his bedside.'

'Of course he does.'

'How do you know? Is he conscious?'

'Yes.'

'Right. So all he has to do is ask. When he asks, I'll come.'

'What the hell's got into you? This is Oliver we're talking about. Remember him? The guy who made just a few small sacrifices for you?'

'Yes, and this is Jude. Remember her? The honorary member of the family who got dumped as soon as the honour was bestowed.'

'Listen, I don't know about that, nor do I care much at

the moment. All I know is that you took off after the wedding, leaving Oliver in a blue fit—'

'And you didn't bother to find out why, did you? Which is fine by me, Stephen, but don't think you can click your fingers and make me jump. Your entire family has blotted me out. Why should I come running now?'

'If you want to be part of a family, Jude, you have to take the good with the bad. But I'm not going to argue. All I care about is getting Oliver well. I thought that would be your priority too.'

'You said he isn't critical.'

'He isn't, but he's seriously ill, and you're one of the closest people to him!'

'Shelley's there, isn't she?'

'Yes, but . . . God, is that it? Even in a crisis you don't want to be around Shelley?'

'Stephen, *nothing* would stop me going over if I thought Oliver wanted me there, but as things stand, I don't think he does.'

There was a long pause. 'He said you had a fucking deadly edge when it suited you. I see what he means.'

Jude heard herself say, 'Call me if he dies.'

They hung up simultaneously.

Her stomach rolled around like a tumble-dryer. Her eyes poured. Her feet took her from the front door down to the kitchen sink so many times that Fiona fancied she could see a groove running through the floor.

'He nearly died and they don't even tell me. That gives some measure of where I fit in these days: exactly nowhere, and if that's where they want me, then that's where I'll bloody well stay!'

'I know you're hurt, Jude, but this isn't the time to be

proud. I mean, let's not forget who walked out on whom. And what if he—'

'Dies? I'll have to live with it, won't I?'

'Don't be so ungrateful! You should go over to him. Patch all this up.'

'I *can't*. I want to, Fiona, of course I do. I'm desperate to see him! But I can't go if he doesn't want me there, and he obviously doesn't. We haven't spoken for a year. The stress of seeing me now would probably finish him off!'

After speaking to Stephen the way she did, Jude had no recourse whatsoever to the Sayles, and while the one person who had cared for her through every hardship lay ill, she had no access, no news. Her guts churned with concern, with disbelief that she had brought things to this deadlock. She toyed with the idea of using Tim as a source of information, but struggled against it until she realized there was another door that must be forced open.

A week after Stephen's call, Fiona came in from work and found Jude sitting on the stairs, crying.

'Oh God. Not bad news?'

'No, he's OK. He's going to be fine.'

'So what's wrong?'

'Relief, I suppose.'

'You spoke to him?'

'No. To Patti.'

'You rang *Patti*?'

'I had to find out somehow, didn't I?'

'But – didn't she mind after all this time?'

Jude smiled. 'She was thrilled. We've both been so stupid. She apologized for throwing me out and I apologized for being so stubborn. I should have called ages ago.'

'So how's Oliver?'

'Better. He'll probably be discharged soon, and Patti thinks he'll head to Landor as soon as he's fit. His mother's driving him around the bend. Sounds like he's in rotten form.'

'He's bound to be, after a trauma like that.'

'I have to see him, Fiona.'

Fiona sat on the step beside her. 'It's about time you realized that.'

'But it means I won't be coming to America.'

'Jude! We've been planning this trip all year!'

'I know, and I'm sorry, but I have to sort things out. There's unfinished business hanging over me and I can't go on living in a permanent state of indignation. Patti gave me a right rollicking. Told me this is about Oliver, not me, and she's right. I'm in his debt, whether I like it or not, and I've behaved like an ungrateful child. I owe him an apology.'

'No argument there.'

'And with him being ill, well, I may have brazened it out, but if anything had happened to him, I'd have an awful lot on my conscience now.'

'So go and see him. You'll be back in plenty of time for America.'

'I can't go to London. I can't go grovelling in front of Shelley and Stephen and the whole darn family.'

'They'll be fine. They'll be glad to have you back.'

'I'm not talking about a reconciliation. Quite the opposite. I'm going to wipe the slate clean. I want Oliver out of this house.'

'Out of the house?'

'I'm going to buy him out. I can't go on living in a house that's part-owned by someone who won't have anything to do with me, can I? I mean, you and I could come home one day and find Shelley ensconced here.'

'Heaven forbid.'

'And I want to be the one to say thanks, sorry and goodbye.'

Fiona frowned. 'Jude, are you sure about this? Sort things out by all means, but be careful how you go about it or you'll end up on your own.'

'I always have been on my own.'

'That's just not true. You've always had the Sayles.'

'And now I have Bob.'

'Bob is romance! It might not last a month. At least Oliver has staying power.'

'Where's his staying power now?'

'You threw it back in his face, remember?'

'Right, so I'll go to France, say I'm sorry about everything and agree to, well, some kind of split. A clear break instead of this lingering row. And somehow I'll buy this house from him.'

'Is this what you really want?'

'Yes.'

'All right. Do it. But be careful, Jude, because we all need someone.'

24

He looked like Stephen, she thought, when she stepped off the train in Mouchard and saw him leaning against the glass shelter with his hands in his pockets. She had been in the last carriage and had to walk the length of the long, curved platform. He made no move to come to her. She had called the shot, but he scored the point.

Oliver didn't see Jude amongst the disembarking commuters. His eyes had latched on to a woman with a short dark bob, pale shoulders, and sunglasses perched on the end of her nose. When he looked away from her, he saw Jude, clad in jeans and a T-shirt, her long hair over her face, loping along from the back of the train. He glanced again at the woman in the flowing orange dress coming through the crowds and, with the discretion afforded by his sunglasses, took in the neat waist, the long arms, the slow stride. When she got too close, he looked back towards Jude.

'Oliver?'

The voice startled him. Jude was actually standing six feet away, her pale shoulders catching the evening sun, her new bob making her the woman he had been watching.

He pushed himself off the shelter. 'I thought that was

you,' he said, nodding towards the backpacker. Shocked that he had been giving Jude the once-over, he led her to the car without another word.

It was a new car, low and sporty and, Jude noted as she got in, smelling of leather. It was a tight fit inside.

'So.' Oliver turned in his seat. Jude expected him to say, 'Shelley's here,' as he had that day in Scotland when he broke up their little world with those two words. But he said, 'A guilty conscience is a great motivator.'

She took off her sunglasses, and sighed.

'I've no food in. I wasn't expecting visitors, so if you think you can control the histrionics, I'll take you to dinner in Dôle.' He pulled his jacket from under him. 'And you can take those daggers out of your eyes, thanks.'

She raised her chin and put her sunglasses back on. Fiona was right. There was power in clothes. She had insisted that if Jude looked good, she'd feel good, so she had changed out of jeans into a halter-neck dress and high heels on the train, mostly for Shelley's benefit, but also to dispel any notion that she was a child needing a good telling off. It had worked. Oliver would not undermine her. He was wearing a grey suit and a white shirt, and he smelt like he'd just got out of the shower. He and Shelley were probably going out later. He was probably in a hurry. Jude wanted to look out, away from him, but her eyes were drawn back. He looked different. He'd lost weight since the operation, but it was more than that. His glasses probably. They were darker than usual; to reflect his mood, no doubt.

'Are you better?' Her voice rattled.

He chuckled. 'You ask this *now*?' He drove some way before speaking again. 'How were the exams?'

She cleared her throat. 'I passed.'

He turned, alarmed. 'Passed?'

'I got a Two One.'

'Oh. Right. For a moment there, I thought you'd flunked out on the honours.'

Jude waited.

'Well done.'

She looked out. In vast fields on either side of the road, sunflowers stood like an immense crowd of people gathered at a peace rally, holding hands and swaying. Majestic, worthy, delightful. But the sight was spoiled by the thought of the tubs of margarine they could end up in. 'How's Shelley?'

'Fine.'

Another pause.

'Your grandmother?' he asked.

'Dead.'

'*What?*'

Got him! 'To all intents and purposes. Don't know why she bothers staying alive, seeing as she hates it so much. She's such a waste of living.'

An even longer pause.

'How's Tim?'

'Great.'

'Your parents?'

'Good.'

Silence again.

They were halfway to Dôle when Jude swung around. 'Your beard! It's gone!'

'Good Lord, has it?' Oliver put his hand to his shaven cheek. 'So it has.'

'When did you do that?'

'Two weeks ago.'

'I thought you'd cut your hair or changed your glasses!'

'It takes people that way.'

Jude removed her sunglasses and took a good look at the

face she'd never seen. That was the soapy smell she got off him – aftershave. 'You look so different.'

'So different you didn't even notice.'

'I like it. It's very . . .' Jude stopped. She was getting carried away. For an unguarded moment, they'd almost been having a conversation and if that happened, if they started getting chummy, everything would backfire. Oliver also went quiet. The sudden shift in tone had taken them both unawares and was welcomed by neither.

In Dôle, he parked by the Canal du Rhône and they walked across the bridge into the medieval part of the town. Oliver led her to a restaurant on a quiet offshoot of the canal. They took a table by the railing, which was decked with geraniums and petunias. It was a warm, clammy evening. As Jude glanced around, the temptation to take Fiona's advice and salvage something of this relationship almost overwhelmed her. Oliver put on his glasses to read the menu. Jude sneaked a look over the top of her own menu. She scarcely recognized the thin face and hollowed cheeks. He didn't have his brother's dimples, only a few subtle lines around his mouth. Smile lines.

'What'll you have?'

'Steak and a salad.' On the water below her, red geranium petals floated with green leaves in the shape of a question mark.

A waiter with a thick moustache, and wearing the smile of a man who was having an excellent day, came over. While Oliver ordered, Jude became intimately acquainted with every inch of their table, inspecting the salt-cellar and pepper dispenser, the small vase of flowers and the creases on the tablecloth.

Oliver took off his glasses and sat with his arms crossed on the table. 'Well?'

'Hmm?'

'What's this about? I get a call from Paris saying you're on your way. No notice. No question of whether it suits me or not.'

Jude bristled.

'You said there was something you wanted to sort out.'

She swallowed. 'A few things, yes.' Nothing came. A dozen times she had made this speech in her head, witty and forthright, and now it wouldn't come at all – which gave Oliver the advantage.

'A few things? A list of recriminations as long as my leg, no doubt. Whereas I have only one question, so why don't I start?'

Feck. She had dropped out of the sky and he was still ready for her, sharp as a blade.

He leaned forward, his voice low and coarse. 'Leaving aside Stephen's wedding, all I really want to know is why you didn't come to London last month.'

Jude sat back, stunned.

'I rushed across Europe to bail you out last year, but you couldn't even cross the Irish Sea on my account.'

'The way things were, I decided not to go over unless you asked me to.'

'You needed an invitation? I'm sorry, they don't hand out gilt-edged cards in the intensive care ward.'

Right back where they started – the quips, the digs, the getting nowhere – but Jude steeled herself. 'Yes, I *did* need an invitation. How could I presume you wanted to see me when you didn't even come near me when you were in Dublin?'

'No, no,' said Oliver firmly. 'We're not turning this around. Dublin's another story and it doesn't even compare to what happened subsequently. I was seriously ill, Jude, but you didn't even bother to send a Get Well card. I know things were far from sweet with us, but would a phone call have been too much to expect?'

'Was a phone call too much *for me* to expect? I got zilch, Oliver. Not a beep out of anyone. I didn't even know it had happened!'

'You got plenty of calls.'

'You mean Stephen? That was days after the event and it didn't even come from you.'

'Shelley had already called for me!'

He was shouting – quietly, as one does in public – but he was the one who shouted first. *He lost his cool first*, thought Jude. Then she heard what he'd said. 'Pardon?'

'She called you and Patti as soon as I came out of surgery. Patti and Tim turned up immediately. You never turned up at all.'

'I never spoke to Shelley.'

'She called three times, Jude. Three times.'

'No. No, I didn't speak to her once.'

'She left messages – not on your mobile, I hasten to add, because you've clearly changed your number. I wonder why.'

'It wasn't deliberate. My phone was nicked.'

'Right, so I gave Shelley the house number. She left messages on the machine.'

Jude leaned forward, her heart racing. 'Oliver, I don't *have* an answering machine!'

He scowled. His eyes darted about as he remembered this salient fact.

'If I'd known you'd sent for me, I would have come. I told Stephen that as soon as you asked, I'd be there.'

His eyes stopped shifting about and settled on her.

'I'm not that ungrateful. Shelley must have been dialling

the wrong number, because I never heard a word from that hospital.' *And it's just the kind of stupid thing she'd do.*

The waiter poured a little wine into Oliver's glass. He tasted it and nodded.

'Look,' Jude went on, 'I'm sorry about everything. That's why I'm here. I apologize for the wedding and everything else, but the only reason I didn't go to see you in hospital was because I thought you didn't want me there.'

He shifted about.

'Don't you believe me?'

'Yes,' he said quietly. 'Yes.'

'I don't understand why Stephen didn't tell you what I said.'

'He didn't even tell me he'd spoken to you.'

'Well, you can take my word for it. Someone else got Shelley's messages. She must have assumed she'd got through to the right number. In fact, whoever got those calls must have wondered what to do, especially if she said it was an emergency.'

Oliver inhaled, screwed up his eyes and fiddled with the pepper. Jude realized she was losing the run of herself – behaving as if they had only met to iron out some unfortunate creases on the tablecloth between them, not pull the whole thing off – but it was hard to contain the relief that Oliver had sent for her. 'My conscience is clear. If I'd got those messages, nothing could have stopped me going over . . . But I do want to apologize for Stephen's wedding. I'm not sure what got into me, but I'm sorry anyway, and the other reason I wanted to see you, well, the main reason, is that we need to sort out the house. You obviously don't need it any more and, well, this seems a good time for me to buy you out.'

'Buy me out?'

'Yes. You don't even stay there when you're in Dublin, so—'

'Ah. Back to that, are we?'

Their steaks were brought, with side salads and a bottle of water. Jude wondered what hope she had of swallowing even the slightest morsel, but she nibbled on a piece of celery to keep herself busy.

'Do you have any idea how long I was in Dublin in April?'

She shrugged.

'I was there for seven hours. Out of Manchester by seven, in Dublin by nine, Belfast by six. The itinerary had nothing to do with me – the publicists do that and their job is to get me as much exposure as possible in as little time as possible. Their brief doesn't include sorting out my private life.'

'You could have phoned.'

He threw up his hands. 'To what end? With all the shit that had gone down, how on earth could you and I have had a civilized conversation in the time I had available? Certainly I could have phoned you. I chose not to. It would have resolved nothing.'

'You knew I'd see that article. You knew I'd find out you'd been over.'

'It was out of my hands.'

'You could have warned me.'

'Frankly, Jude, I had other things on my mind.'

Bastard. She fiddled with her food. Oliver didn't even look at his. 'So how do you propose to buy me out?'

'I'll get a mortgage.'

'And how do you plan to fund it?'

'I'll work.'

'What about your MA?'

'I've finished college. I'm not going back.'

331

'But you were dead set on an academic career and you're good enough for it!'

'Don't care. Don't want to do it any more.'

'What'll you do instead?'

'I'll do a secretarial course and work in an office.'

'So why bother with college in the first place?'

'Listen, I didn't come here to discuss my career. I—'

'And you clearly haven't discussed it with anyone else, have you?'

She stuck her fork into the steak and carved it up, not because she wanted to eat it but because she needed to carve up *something*.

'I didn't think so.'

Jesus! He was right back where he most liked to be, playing the Sensible Grown-up telling her what to do. 'I've made up my mind,' she said, chewing. 'All I want to know is, can I buy the house?'

She couldn't get used to that bare face. He had a cleft in his chin she had never known about. He wasn't smoking but he might have been; he scratched his lip with his thumb, the way he used to do with a cigarette between his fingers, and when he sat back with his hands resting on his lap, it might just as well have been with nicotine-induced patience.

'You can't afford to put yourself through a Master's, is that it?'

'Of course I can. I could work part-time in the shop and I'd get teaching hours, but I'm not interested.'

'I can put you through another year of college without even noticing.'

'Thank you, but I didn't come here for your money. I just want to buy the house.'

'Why?'

'Because I'd like to have the freedom to come home any

time and know that I won't find Shelley cooking you an omelette in my kitchen!'

'That'll be the day.'

'I *know*.' Jude's teeth grated. 'I know you don't want to come back – surely that's the point? It doesn't make sense that you own half the house I live in when we don't have anything to do with each other any more!'

'Oh, look. Take it. Keep it. Have it as a twenty-first birthday present.'

Jude looked up. 'I don't need charity.'

Oliver put his hands behind his neck and growled in exasperation. Then he smiled. 'D'you know, you haven't lost it, Jude. Not an ounce of it. You still have the capacity to make me want to howl with frustration!'

Blood oozed from the steak as she pierced it with her fork and sliced it.

'I'm not offering you charity – I wouldn't dare – but I won't have you wrecking your career just to get me out of your life.'

Jude chewed.

He leaned forward. 'And do let me reassure you: there's as much chance of Shelley cooking a fucking omelette in your kitchen as there is of me doing so!' He threw down his napkin.

It hurt, but Jude steadied herself. She popped more meat into her mouth, swallowed it dry, and said, 'I have no interest in arguing about this.' She glanced at Oliver's plate. 'Why aren't you eating? You need to fatten up.'

It was no good. No matter how hard she tried to stamp it out, their old banter kept insinuating itself into the conversation like a true dinner-party bore, making itself right at home, wholly unaware of the domestic tension it straddled.

Oliver didn't move. 'What are you doing here, Jude?'

333

She put down her knife and fork. 'I told you. I want to clear things up.' A wave of nausea passed over her. 'Look,' she fiddled with her napkin, turning back the corners and running her nail along them, 'I know I behaved deplorably at Stephen's wedding—'.

'The less said about that wedding, the better.'

'I ruined it for you.'

'We both ruined something far more important.'

Jude glanced up; his expression had softened and it disarmed her. 'I hate all this,' she said, speaking at last without strategy. 'I hate the way everything turned out. This year has been very, well, bewildering, and I'm trying to make of it what I can, but as long as you own the house I live in, I feel tied. To you *and* to Shelley. And I don't know what you want any more. If you want to cut all contact, I'll understand. Honestly. You've done more for me than even friendship could expect, and I can cope financially, one way or another, but what I can't cope with is . . .'

'Is?'

'You coming to Dublin without telling me, and your brother bawling me out on the phone, and reading articles about you when I don't even know you've had a book published. I won't sit on the perimeter any longer. I'm either in or out, and since it's pretty clear that I'm out, I want to make a proper break. Let's pull the plug instead of dribbling out of one another's lives like water from an over-flowing bath. I don't want to go on wondering if I've anywhere to go or not, or if I have any claim to anyone.'

Oliver scarcely moved.

'I tried to let it go, but when you were ill, it became too fuzzy. I didn't know what you wanted me to do or what I should have done, and I won't go through that again. I need to know, clearly and simply, if you want me in your life or not.'

334

This was far from what she had planned to say, but it was much closer to the truth. She hadn't intended to give him an ultimatum, but seeing him across the table, hearing them argue again, left a familiar sound echoing in her ears which she wanted to amplify. She acknowledged, finally, that she would have him back, if he would come; that she would even endure his awful wife if necessary, because there were still moments, days even, when she needed to wallow in unconditional love.

She had to wait a long time for Oliver's reply. She rolled the stem of her wine glass between her fingers. He watched her.

'Tout va bien, Monsieur?' The waiter with the perma-smile looked at Oliver's plate.

'J'ai fini, merci.' The waiter cheerfully swept away the untouched meal. 'He must have got laid this afternoon,' said Oliver, pouring another glass of wine.

'That's not a good idea on an empty stomach.'

He took a piece of bread roll. 'I don't know where to start,' he said. 'We had a row and that's it as far as you're concerned. Buy me out, cut all contact, end of story. No attempt to set things right. I have to say, I didn't think it could be that simple. However, if that's what you want, I won't stand in your way, but for what it's worth, my interpretation of events is a little different. You did behave badly at Stephen's wedding. So did I. But when I woke up the next morning and discovered you'd taken off, I was,' he inhaled sharply, 'I turned inside out. I couldn't believe you'd run away like that.'

'I wasn't running away. I was "letting go", like your mother told me to.'

'Mum? What's she got to do with this?'

'The day I arrived, she told me you and I were no longer

any use to each other. She suggested I should "let go". Sunday morning seemed a good time to do it.'

'Bloody hell. I told her to keep out of it.'

'She had your best interests at heart.'

'That's when she's at her most dangerous.' He dipped his chin. 'I see. So Stephen got married, we quarrelled, and Mum threw you out – quite a raw deal in one weekend.'

Jude shrugged.

'Look, I didn't contact you at Christmas because I was over here, up to my neck in work. Even Tim didn't come. I presumed you'd spend Christmas with Sinéad.'

'You didn't even phone!'

'Nor did you.' He raised his eyebrows. 'After Christmas, the PR stuff got rolling, I had to go to America, and work didn't ease up until just before I collapsed.'

The waiter brought the dessert trolley. They shook their heads. As Oliver went on, Jude began to feel as if she were caught in a draught of warm air. 'It's not that I haven't thought about you – I have – but it was like knowing the car needs a good wash when you don't have the time to do it and you're too ashamed to drive it around, so you leave it in the garage, waiting for a proper polish instead of a quick bucket of water.'

'I'm a car now?'

His grin came at her like an arrow. 'Yeah. A Ferrari Dino. A classic.'

'What does that make Shelley?'

He thought about it. 'A Corvette Stingray. Listen, Jude. I was planning to organize something after your exams and my book tour – a holiday or whatever – but then I collapsed and you didn't bother to pick up the phone and things looked very different.'

336

Big baby-blue eyes. Baby-blue indeed. More like being targeted by ice missiles.

'Very bloody different. I deserved better from you.'

'Of course you did.'

It was the warmest thing she had said all evening.

'I asked Shelley to call you after the operation because it seemed like an ideal opportunity to be reconciled.'

'Is that what you wanted?'

'Of course. Didn't you? Don't you?'

The cool stare didn't seem so chilly any more. Jude sucked in her lips.

'Surely our ridiculous relationship can endure a break without suffering permanent damage?' Oliver asked. 'I don't deny we had a comprehensive brawl, but we were due a major crash. In fact, it's amazing it didn't happen sooner, when we're both so headstrong and petulant and miffed with the world. We held out for years, but we ended up with a degree of closeness that could only self-destruct as soon as one of us became involved elsewhere. And that's what happened – only it shouldn't matter. It shouldn't mean any more than a redrawing of the contours. Going back a bit. The way I see it, my job isn't done yet. I promised Michael I'd look out for you and I'm still doing that.'

'Not this year, you weren't.'

'It had been six years, Jude. I was due a sabbatical.'

She nodded.

'But it never crossed my mind there was anything final in it. Buy me out of the house? Why? As far as I'm concerned, it's yours.'

'But what if you'd died? I'd have been out in the road. I'd have had to sell it to pay off the mortgage.'

'No, you wouldn't. That's all dealt with, but if it makes

you feel better, we'll take my name off the deeds, because you're not leaving college to pay me off. That would be madness. And I don't understand how you can say we have nothing to do with each other any more. We both know that's impossible.'

Jude didn't know whether to be relieved or sorry. There was a mild sense of disappointment that her anticipated swipe – when she would whisk him out of her life with a sweep of self-contained argument – was not going to plan, and yet she could feel the loneliness she had lived with all year shrinking inside her. She jumped when Oliver took her hand, but familiarity rushed back with a simple squeeze.

'As for wanting you in my life, it isn't a question of having you in my life or out of it, you're simply on it. On me. Like a fingerprint. A defining characteristic. A crease in my lifeline.'

Jude was welling up.

And still he went on. 'You're the only constant I have, Jude. You're the one I don't care about; don't have to care about. I shouldn't have to prove anything to you, or defend anything, because no matter what happens I should be able to rely on you. I've earned your love, dammit.'

'What about Tim? Stephen? They're constants too.'

'Tim has Patti. Stephen has Vanessa. I have you. It may be circumstance, it may be chance, but it's by choice, also, that I trust you and love you without mitigation. No conditions, no concessions. No question of whether you are in my life or out of it.'

Jude covered her eyes. 'Stop.'

'Hey.' Oliver moved to the seat beside her, put his arm on the back of her chair and produced the inevitable handkerchief.

'I thought you were done with the Feehans. You ought to be.'

He kissed her hand. 'Never, my love. Never.'

They strolled along the narrow path, with limestone town-houses on one side, water on the other, until the canal came to a dead end. Oliver stuck out his elbow; when Jude passed her arm through, he welcomed it by pressing it against him. She had steeled herself so very hard against something so very different that her limbs wobbled without the support of the courage she no longer needed.

'Have you grown dramatically?'

'No, it's these heels.' At the end of the watery cul-de-sac, they stepped on to a wooden footbridge. Jude went to the railing and looked down at the canal. Oliver came up behind her and pulled her against him. She yielded, exhausted from pushing hard against a wall which had no intention of moving. 'I thought I'd catch you on the hop,' she said wearily. 'How were you so ready for me?'

'I wasn't going to let you get away that easily.'

'Why not? I'm nothing but a pain in the ass, you always say.'

'My saddle sores have cleared up.'

She smiled at the face next to hers and noticed the shadow where a beard used to be. 'Can I touch it?'

'What?'

'The face. I never knew you had one.'

He took her hand and ran her fingers along his cheek. 'I wasn't born bearded, you know.'

'Could have fooled me.' She took her hand away.

'Is it an improvement?'

'Might be. You're a bit thin still. I hope Shelley's fattening you up.'

339

'Shelley can't cook, Jude. Not to save her life.'

'Are you serious?'

'That's why she won't be cooking any darn omelettes in your kitchen!'

'*Our* kitchen.'

On the other side of the bridge, a tunnel led up to the gardens beside the main canal, where rows of cruisers, locked up for the winter, were lying side by side like children in a dormitory.

'Tell me what happened when you collapsed.'

'There isn't much to tell. I felt grotty in LA, started getting sick over the Pole, and thought I'd die of pain long before we even banked towards Heathrow. The flight was given landing priority, but I'd passed out before we reached the terminal. Not a high point in my life.'

'You poor thing.'

'It wasn't fun. Vomiting relentlessly in an aircraft loo with a dagger in my side – not much fun at all. Actually, it was a nightmare.'

'I'm sorry for being a heel about it.'

He didn't say anything; he had not quite forgiven her.

'I was afraid you'd die,' she said quietly.

Oliver stopped, took a deep breath and shook his head. 'That's so bloody obvious. Why didn't I think of it?'

'You were a bit busy staying alive.'

'Even so. Anyone could have worked that out, but none of us did.'

'Let's just forget about it.'

'Let's do that. Let's go home.'

Jude was reluctant. The thought of hearing that 'Ollie!' shatter the gentle evening was too much to contemplate. 'Can we leave it a bit? I promise to try much harder with Shelley, but we're just getting back on track and —'

'Shelley's in the States. So come on, there've been a few changes at the house I want to show you.'

'Such as?'

'I've put in a pool.'

'No way!'

'I promised Tim I'd do it as soon as I had the cash.'

'And now you have, because the book's done so well?'

He wobbled his head, tipped back on his heels, and said coyly, 'Mostly because I've sold the film rights.'

Jude gasped. 'Seriously?'

She had never seen him look so sheepishly delighted. 'Ya.'

'Fantastic!' She threw her arms around his neck and jumped up and down. 'You did it! I knew you could do it.' He hugged her, and there was a moment, an odd, orphaned moment, which belonged somewhere else. She let go. 'That's so great.'

Oliver squeezed the back of her neck and directed her towards the bridge. 'Let's go home.'

'Listen . . . I don't even know if you're married or not.'

He held up his hand. 'No ring.'

'Have you set a date?' The prospect of such a wedding was too dreadful to contemplate.

He was walking backwards, just ahead of her. 'Speed it up, you.'

'I can't speed it up in these heels.'

'So take them off.'

She took the hand he offered and pulled off her sandals, and there was awkwardness again, fleeting but certain, as they released their hands a fraction too late. Jude read the signals with the accuracy of long association: Oliver was bothered. 'A redrawing of the contours,' he had said, and this was what he meant. They would have to establish some distance. The casual intimacy of old would have to be sacrificed for Shelley. And Bob. And yet she took his arm again, and again he pressed hers to his side.

At the car, he pushed her gently on to the bonnet.

'What is it now?' she asked ruefully.

'Time we sorted out that bloody wedding,' he said, pacing. 'I know I blew it. It was boorish of me to turn up with someone else after promising to take you, but every time I tried to make my peace with you, I got whipped for it.'

'I was hurt. You'd never hurt me like that before. You left me out on a limb.'

'For which I apologize, but you were like an only child who couldn't have her own way.'

'I know. It was unforgivable of me to laugh when you said you were getting married.'

Oliver put one foot on the bumper. 'Yeah, well. Truth is, Jude, I never had much intention of asking Shelley to marry me and, for what it's worth, we split up last month.'

'What? So why did you say it?'

'Because you had driven me to such extremes of exasperation that I took one wide swipe to knock you off the moral high ground you were standing on – and I even failed at that. I'd had a bit to drink also.'

'But that means you walked off because of the way I responded to something that wasn't even true.'

'I walked out on you that night because of your presumption and intellectual smugness.' He took his foot down.

Jude sat awkwardly on the bonnet, her hands in her lap. What was this worth? More indignation? There was no accounting for what had happened that weekend. The lie probably matched her assumption that she could tell him whom he could love. She sniggered, suddenly. It came on her unexpectedly, the need to giggle, to laugh at herself and her outrage, at her ranting back in Dublin, when she poured

342

scorn on Oliver's pitiful choice of women. Whooping with delight at the fool she had been, she felt bright and dazzling, like a fresh coat of paint on a tired wall.

'I know you didn't like her,' said Oliver, 'but this is a bit excessive, isn't it? What's so hysterical?'

'Me! My righteous indignation! My conviction that I knew what was good for you. I set myself up for it, I really did.'

Oliver watched her, the long orange dress draped over the bonnet of his car like fabric in a display, her shoulders shaking lightly, her bobbed hair bouncing. The way she did this sometimes, the way she melted into laughter when he least expected it, made him want to pull her up and hold her. 'Crazy, you are.'

'Oh!' she guffawed. 'What did you say? You've split up?'

'Ah, it finally got through.'

'God, that's great. I mean, that's awful. Is it?'

'What do you think?'

Jude stood up and kissed his cheek, stifling the mutinous giggles that had her in their grasp. 'I'm sorry, my love. You must be devastated?'

'Do you know,' said Oliver, letting her into the car, 'that that's the first time in twenty-one years you have ever called me anything other than "Oliver"?'

25

On the swinging garden seat beside the new kidney-shaped swimming-pool, they sat without speaking, one with a cold beer, the other with a tub of double chocolate chip ice-cream, listening to the quiet gurgle of the pool's filter and the soothing rattle of crickets. Swinging lightly, weary but calm, they were like two canoeists who had survived white waters and emerged at last into a still pool, but even as it became obvious that they were being dragged into yet more turbulence, they chose, independently, not to paddle away from the brim. Instead, they allowed the drift to catch them, knowing it would carry them wherever it chose to go.

'It certainly gets my vote,' said Jude. 'This big long garden has been begging for a pool. And the terrace is lovely.' She tucked her legs up beside her, careful not to put them on Oliver's lap as she once might have, in view of his uneasiness with their contact on the quay. 'So what happened with Shelley?'

'Aside from the fact that I wasn't prepared to live in the States and she had no intention of coming here, we got bored. My collapse brought it to a head. I was still in hospital when we called it a day.'

344

'So you came back here alone? But that's plain stupid after an illness like that.'

'I had no option.'

'You could have gone home to Mummy.' Oliver grunted. 'You still need looking after – you're like a rake.'

'Get to it then.'

'I will. You can start with this.' She reached over with a spoonful of ice-cream. Oliver hesitated, caught her eye in the dim light, then held her wrist and ate. The spoon was warm from her mouth. As she chattered on, he wondered if she could truly be that naïve.

'I'm sorry for not getting on with Shelley,' she said. 'For not even trying to.'

'It was fairly mutual, wasn't it?'

She sucked on her spoon. 'Mmm. I think it would be fair to say that, on balance, she didn't like me much.'

'It was distrust, not dislike. She never got over the shock of finding you in my bed.'

Jude caught the whites of his eyes and saw him blink at her. Disconcerted, she reached over with more ice-cream.

'Truth is,' he said, 'I'm not sure she *did* call you from the hospital. Things were so bad between us by then, you were probably the last person she wanted to see turning up.'

'Well, she didn't get in the way of that book, that's all I care about. I knew you were on to something last summer and I thought you'd blown it because of her.'

'You've read it?'

'I had to buy it!'

'Oh dear.' He put his hand on her foot. 'Do you want a refund?'

'Absolutely.' She prodded his leg with her toe. 'Na, it was worth every penny. But where did it come from, so suddenly like that?'

His thumb ran along the sole of her foot. 'I'd had it in my head for years, but couldn't face writing it. And you know what happened then.'

'Letterfrack?'

'Mmm. It wasn't only your lecture about my lousy books, it was all that talking. Getting air into those closed spaces.'

His hand had not left her ankle, but rested on her foot as it often had when they sat like this, yet Jude was unusually aware of the contact. Like a branch weighed down by a light bird, it seemed as if his fingers were making an imprint on her skin – his thumb beneath her heel, his palm on her ankle, the tips of his fingers moving over the bridge of her foot as they shouldn't have been; as she knew they shouldn't have been.

'Don't suppose you want tea after all that ice-cream?'

'Course I do,' said Jude. 'And toast.'

'Christ, I'll never understand your stomach.'

They went into the kitchen. While Oliver made tea, Jude busied herself with the toaster, but they coincided at the fridge when they both leaned in and momentarily forgot what they were looking for. Confusion slipped across Jude's face; her eyebrows dipped. She grabbed the butter, Oliver took the milk. As they straightened up, he put the jug over her shoulder and gave her a hug. 'I missed you something rotten.'

'Me too.' Jude pulled back, but her eyes took their own route and hooked on to his. She dragged them away. 'Feck. Toast's burning.'

They ate on the newly laid terrace, a Louis Armstrong CD playing in the background, and discussed Jude's exams. After spending such a vital year starved of one-on-one attention, Oliver's interest made her light-headed.

'And now I really must swim,' she said, soon after midnight. She went upstairs to change, then came out to the pool and slid into the water, propelling herself with a gentle kick towards the deep end.

Oliver gathered their plates and took them to the kitchen, where he leaned against the counter for several moments, arms crossed and eyes closed, until the sound of her swimming drew him out again. 'Here, Flipper,' he said, standing at the edge of the pool. 'Have a kipper.'

'What is it?'

'Chocolate.'

'Yes, please.' Jude swam over. 'Give us.'

He held it over the water. 'Jump for it.'

'I'm not a bleedin' dolphin, am I?' She tried, nonetheless, to propel herself upwards to his outstretched arm, but the more she leaped, the more she laughed. 'Give it to me, you rotter!' He leaned over. Jude took the chocolate between her teeth, her lips brushing against his fingers. 'Tease,' she mumbled, swimming away.

'You can talk.'

She didn't hear him, wasn't meant to hear him. He followed her to the shallow end, where she stretched out by the steps. 'Just look at that sky.'

Oliver didn't look up.

'What's wrong with you? You haven't gone all morose on me, have you?'

He crouched down. 'Jude?'

She swished the water about as if she were in an enormous bath. 'What?'

'Look at me.'

She didn't want to. 'What is it?'

'There's something going on here that has never happened before.'

347

Her heart dipped. 'I don't know what you mean,' she lied, swimming away. She did several lengths then, but had to get out eventually, and when Oliver met her at the steps with a towel, she let his arms come around her, as they had done countless times before. He looked baffled and rubbed her back ineffectually; Jude's gaze settled on his loosened tie.

'I'll get dressed.'

'Fancy a bit of Clapton's *Unplugged*?' he called after her.

'Yes, but just skip that "Tears in Heaven" song.'

Under the warm flow of the shower, Jude found that she was shaking uncontrollably.

She got back into the dress which she had worn to better Shelley. Fitted to the hips, it pulled her in and pushed her out in all the wrong places, giving her too small a waist and too much cleavage, and it was quite unsuitable for an evening spent hanging around the pool with Oliver. And yet, for some unfathomable reason, she put it on again.

He handed her a glass of wine when she came on to the terrace, where the mood had already been dictated by a slow piece of Clapton on acoustic guitar, his raspy voice drawing attention to his blues. Conversation seemed inappropriate, impolite even, and though tempted to dance, Jude sat by the table and listened, unable to compete with the volume. As it moved on to a livelier track, Oliver rocked about in his chair.

'Isn't this something else? You can't beat it.'

'Oh, absolutely,' she said drily. 'Excellent.'

'You were reared on Clapton, you know. Your mother played him constantly when you were in the womb.'

'I wonder who told her to do that?'

He grinned. 'I wanted to make sure you had a proper start in life.'

348

Momentarily irritated, Jude said, 'Jesus. Is there no corner of my life you haven't got into?' And even that sounded all wrong and made them both look in opposite directions.

She wanted to dance. The jazzy blues made it impossible to sit still, but she couldn't let Oliver misunderstand, not with this new edginess between them.

But he couldn't stay still either. 'Come on. We can't sit through this. Up.'

They took off, stepping across the terrace to Clapton's unplugged 'Layla', grooving along as only close friends can. Oliver spun her around, brought her in, stepped between her feet and walked her backwards, mouthing words about giving her consolation when her old man had let her down . . . 'Oi,' he said. 'Stop trying to lead.'

'I'm not.'

'You are. You always do.' He grimaced as he mouthed more lyrics.

'You're nothing but an ageing hippie.'

The tension between them had eased. Jude laughed at his antics, but when 'Layla' ended and a slower song ensued, the air filled again, as swiftly as if a gust had rushed out from the house. Oliver didn't hesitate; he brought her closer. She conceded, easily, resting her cheek on his shoulder, her face turned away. Their habitual banter was nowhere to be found as they stepped about the terrace, but Jude wasn't looking for it. Clapton was saying it all, in 'Running on Faith'.

His audience clapped. Jude returned to the table.

'What did you do for Christmas?' Oliver asked, pouring more wine.

'I had friends in. Muslims, mostly.'

'Fun?'

'Yeah. Was yours?'

'Not really. Patti had Tim, so it was pretty bleak.'

'You had Shelley.'

'She was in the States with her kids.'

'Oh God, and I thought the two of you were having a wild Christmas together.'

'Well, we weren't, but that's history. How about you? Found anyone better-looking than our Steve yet?'

Jude was determined not to tell Oliver about Bob. The relationship was too new to withstand his scrutiny, but her hesitation gave him answer enough.

'I see. Anyone I know?'

'I'd rather not talk about it.'

'That's unusual. It must be pretty special.'

She tried to say, 'Very special,' but she looked at him and nothing came out, nothing at all, and Oliver wouldn't look away or make anything easier. He simply held her eye and drank his wine, and something very hot bubbled inside her chest.

'Hang on, hang on, hang on,' chuckled Clapton, after mucking up an introduction. His audience laughed. He started again. Jude breathed.

She kept promising herself she would go to bed after the next song, but couldn't. She was enjoying the music too much, she told herself, so she stared ahead, nodding gently to the beat, and when it slowed again, Oliver hauled her to her feet. They danced, or rather leaned against each other and rocked a bit, scarcely stopping between tracks. A weight rose from Jude's stomach and settled in her throat, making her breathing shallow. Oliver would know that her hands were shaking, that all of her was shaking, because the respectable distance with which they usually danced had been squeezed out. Her breasts pressed against him, her waist harnessed by his arm, and her face turned in this time towards his chin, they swayed, taking an occasional step in deference to the beat. Oliver laced his fingers through hers, brought their hands against his shoulder. Jude tried to think about something else, something mundane, like laundry and shopping lists, but the song, 'Old Love,' wrapped itself around them, ever more seductive, pushing them closer and warning them all at once.

Oliver ran his knuckles across her cheek, but the gesture failed to restore fondness. Instead, their eyes held steady. He put her arms around his neck to bring her closer. Her heart or stomach, or whatever it was that responded to such stimuli, lurched sideways. Clapton picked off a solo.

Oliver's hand moved across her back. He rubbed his chin along her face. Kissed her cheek. Hesitated. Breathed against her ear. Moments passed before he kissed her cheek again, and again. Then he kissed the side of her mouth and stayed that way, loitering on the edge of her lips. They moved minimally, in some pretence of dancing, as they waited, in their half-kiss, for courage to bring him around. He could still go back, they were thinking. He could still abort. No, he couldn't, they agreed. And so he kissed her, fully.

Clapton finished with a light flourish; his audience roared appreciation. The kissing went on.

Oliver broke away suddenly, took her hands from his neck and put them by her side. 'Bed. You must get to bed.'

She tried to speak, but he put his finger to her lips. 'Not now.'

Jude stood in her room, arms hanging, jaw limp. Events had raced so far ahead that she couldn't keep up, let alone make sense of them, so she stood without moving, unable to formulate any thought. Then she slapped herself across the face. 'Get a grip.'

She brushed her teeth, climbed under the mosquito netting over her bed and lay back, rigid. 'Like a frightened bunny,' she said quietly. 'Got a fright and ran. Just after he'd found a carrot too.'

She could hear *Unplugged* replaying itself. Or was Oliver replaying it? He was probably having a stiff drink, she thought, for how could either of them sleep on such a night? Surely they were never meant to? Surely they should be seeing the night out together, tossing and turning, rolling over and around each other? Barricading themselves into separate rooms in a pathetic attempt to cool things down could only serve to heat things up. She sympathized with the moral contortions Oliver was no doubt struggling with, and knew she should slip away before he became any more embroiled. He had had enough trouble on her account; this kind of torment he didn't need. She should take the plate away, but she couldn't move. Couldn't move from him.

She got up and cautiously parted the curtain. Oliver was sitting on the garden seat at the far side of the pool. She thought about going down, but he was better left in whatever place he had gone to the moment he'd stopped kissing her, where regret had been immediate and damning. Jude lay down again, like a penitent in her cell, put away in the nunnery for the unseemly desire she aroused. The soft bed was as uncompromising as a steel bench, the dark walls of her spacious room were closing in, and the cool night air seemed stifling and thick. Her thoughts spun, not around the seduction, unlikely though that was, but around the rejection. It was akin to being forgiven and then punished, loved and then scorned.

The hand that had steadied her since before her mother's death had knocked her off balance, so that she hung upside-

352

down as from a bar in a playground, her world inverted, her horizon upended, and all things the wrong way about. And yet this new perspective didn't bother her. It didn't bother her because she was riddled with longing. It was in her hair and under her fingernails. It made her organs swell, making them grow out of size and pulsate against the restrictions of her rib-cage and pelvis. Her neck was stiff, her calves seemed to sweat, and her ankle – that treacherous bone that had been so partial to his fingertips – tingled still, and asked for more. And even though she had never experienced such want, she knew she was not as troubled as the man out by the pool.

She knew he was suffering but, being the cause of it, could see no way of alleviating it. She peeked out again. He had switched off the pool lights, but she could see him, like a black hole wandering in space, invisible but solid, dark but moving, sucking in the light of her eyes. 'Old Love', the song that had drawn them into kissing, was playing again. She went back to bed and listened to lyrics about loss and confusion. *But I am not confused*, she thought. *I am a lot of things, but I am not confused.*

She slept somehow, sometime. Waking often, turning often, getting up to pee often, she woke again at nine and knew she couldn't sleep any more. On her way to the kitchen, she passed Oliver's room. The door was ajar. She stepped in. He was asleep, stretched out, face down and fully dressed. Seeing that face, as familiar to her in sleep as awake, she covered her mouth. 'Oh hell.'

She brought breakfast back to her room. The house was silent, still. The pool gurgled outside her window. They were in a bubble, a mad, insane little bubble floating

353

without reason in the wrong direction, but she wouldn't be the one to prick it. She couldn't bring herself to get up, so she went on reading magazines, waiting for Oliver to stir.

After eleven, she heard him showering, then going to the kitchen. Her hands began to shake. She wondered if she would have to confront him. A knock on the door came as her answer.

He came in, grim-faced, holding two mugs. 'Oh. You've had already.'

'I'll have more. Thanks.'

He handed her a mug and went to the window, where he stood in his dressing-gown, looking awful. This was the last thing he needed, Jude thought, on top of the book tour and Shelley and his collapse. *Get up then, and leave him alone.*

'What can I say?' he asked, looking out, his elbow against the wall, his chin on his wrist. ' "I'm sorry"? "It won't happen again"?' He turned. 'I can be as contrite as the next man, Jude, but I can't turn back time.'

'There's no need to be contrite.'

'You think not?' He stared out. 'I don't know what happened. I mean, Christ. How do we get over this one?' He looked to her for an answer.

'You can stop hitting yourself over the head for a start.'

'You think this is what Michael expected when he asked me to look after you? You think he expected me to seduce you?'

'Oh, for God's sake!'

'He left me in a position of trust and I've abused that trust – his and yours.'

'If Dad were alive, he would have no say in what happened last night, so why should it matter when he's dead?'

'Alive or dead, he deserves better from me.'

'Don't be so hard on yourself.'

354

'You have to understand something.' His voice was unsteady. 'I swear to you that I have never lusted after you, Jude. Never. There were no ulterior motives in anything I did and there was no hidden agenda. Until last night nothing like that had ever crossed my mind. Not once. You *have* to believe that.'

'I do. It never crossed my mind either. Well, not since I had that crush on you when I was twelve.'

'How can you joke about it? Don't you understand what's at issue here?'

'Of course I do.'

'You don't seem to.'

Jude fiddled with her sheet; Oliver looked out.

'I'm so sorry,' he said eventually. 'I don't know what else I can say.' He rubbed his eyes. 'Somehow we've got to get back to where we were yesterday, before all this.'

'You mean, pretend it never happened?'

'That would be impossible, but at least we can make sure it never happens again.' He looked at her hard, then made his way to the door.

'Why?'

Oliver stopped, and said without turning, 'I can't believe you said that.'

The day dragged, went nowhere, did nothing. Jude wanted to leave, but as long as Oliver wanted her there, she couldn't move. She thought it unlikely they would ever be able to return to what their normality had been, but they could at least try, because if they could overcome this latest demon, they might well retrieve the easy companionship that had always been theirs. And for that, they needed Bob. He would save the day by sweeping her into a relationship which would cancel any lingering tension with Oliver. She

sat by the pool with her feet in the water and tried to draw
excitement from her forthcoming reunion with Bob, but
instead found herself wondering when it had happened. Was
it when she had leaned against him by the canal and felt his
cleared chin against her face? Or when he had held her hand
so that she could take off her shoes? The sun was hot on her
back. She wriggled her toes on the step beneath the water.
When did this happen?

There was a long, celebratory meal going on in the garden
next door. Their neighbours' extended family had gathered
for some occasion and frequent bursts of laughter rippled
through the early afternoon.

Oliver called Jude to lunch. As she sat down, he said,
'The next time I'm home, I'll speak to Mum about what she
said to you at Stephen's wedding.'

'Why bother? She was right. Can't live with, can't live
without.'

'I'd like to prove her wrong.'

'Keep trying then.'

There was an unpleasant stillness in the hot afternoon. It
was all heat, water, and Jude was lonely. Oliver was everywhere, except where she was. He didn't really want her
there, and yet couldn't let her go, so they remained in limbo,
Jude lying by the pool, Oliver wandering at a distance, and
the neighbours shouting over the din of their own gathering.

Just after four, Jude woke from a snooze. Sitting up to
rub sunblock on to her shins, she caught a glimpse of Oliver
leaning against the living-room door, watching her. There
was no disguising his expression and no smothering its
effect. Everything raced. She threw down the lotion and
stormed towards him. He went inside and sank into the
couch.

'This is ridiculous,' she said. 'I'm leaving. Why should I hang around here when you're moping about like a boy who's crashed his first car?'

'Moping? I'm not moping, Jude, I'm in fucking shock!'

'I couldn't care less. I'm going home.'

'Running back to Dublin won't solve anything.'

'And this is?'

'What do you suggest?'

'I suggest you stop tormenting yourself about what happened and ask yourself *why* it happened.'

'I know why, but that doesn't allow for it. Why do I have to explain this to you? I've broken the oldest rule in the book. It's like a doctor and a patient, a lecturer and a student. I came at you with an unfair advantage. I may not be your guardian now, but I have been and I should have remained someone you could trust. Now I've muddied the waters, nothing will ever be clear between us again.'

'Why is it all *your* fault? What about me?'

'You're a woman of your own mind, I know that, but it's where we've come from that matters. I've been in a position of authority all your life and that will have influenced your reaction last night. You couldn't come into this any other way.'

'I thought we came into it as friends.'

'Perhaps, but it's been a very unequal friendship, and on that basis I shouldn't have allowed things to get out of hand.'

'I know what I want, Oliver!'

That startled him. 'Well,' he said, 'you'd be ill advised to want me.'

'How can you let formalities get in the way?'

'They are not *formalities*. It's a question of ethics, and the ethics in this case are pretty damn shifty. I'm standing on quicksand here, and I have your parents looking over my shoulder, saying, "Bloody hell, Oliver, she's half your age and she's our baby!"'

Jude turned on her heel, went out to collect her sarong, and came back in fuming. 'If you don't want me – fine. Take me to the station.'

'Sit down.'

'Why?'

'Because I'm asking.'

She tied her sarong, sat on the arm of the chair and accidentally slid into it.

Oliver wouldn't look at her. 'It isn't that I don't want you,' he said quietly, 'it's that I *do*. I only wish I didn't, because I'm way out of line. This is a betrayal of everything I've ever done for you, of everything I aspired to as your guardian. Of the very word "guardian"! I was meant to protect you from the likes of what I've become.'

'Oliver,' she said severely, 'you're *wallowing*!'

'I am not. I'm trying to do the right thing and you're not helping. Running away isn't the answer. Whatever it takes, we have to get all this into perspective.'

'Into whose perspective? Yours? You're the one who's running away. You want to rub it out like a spelling mistake and I don't happen to think it was a mistake in the first place!'

'Yeah, you've made that pretty clear. Frankly, I find your attitude unbelievable.'

'I'm only following my instincts.'

He stood up, exasperated. 'That's very nice for you, I'm sure, but my instincts are in chaos! You're like my own daughter – have you thought about that one? Have you?' She recoiled into the seat. 'I held you when you were two days old. I watched your mother nurse you and I carried you around when she died – what am I supposed to do with all that? *What?*' He slapped back into the couch and scraped his fingers through his hair. 'I feel like I've defiled you. Michael would beat me to a pulp.'

'He wouldn't have to. You're doing it yourself.' She came over to sit with him. 'I wish you'd leave my parents out of it.'

'It isn't only them,' he said, picking at the wax gathered around a candle on the table. 'I don't want to risk this. We've too much to lose. *I* have too much to lose.'

'Why always the bleak view?'

'Because it's the only view there is. Jude, if we were to start a physical relationship . . .' He glanced at her. 'I'd be in at the deep end. You're carrying layers of my love as it is – if I were to fall in love with you, you'd crumble under the weight of it all.'

'Who ever said love was heavy?'

'I say so. And I can't afford to get that badly hurt this far down the line.'

'Why would you get hurt?'

'You wouldn't stick it out.'

'How can you say that? You're the only person that matters to me.'

'Exactly. The only person. You're twenty-one. I'm forty. The last thing you need is to tie yourself down to a middle-aged goon who wants nothing better than to be tied down. You need to dabble in life, to toy with the world. No matter how much you think you want me now, it wouldn't last.'

'How can you be so sure?'

'Because I've earned my pessimism. You, on the other hand, deserve your optimism. So go and enjoy it. This would be all wrong. As wrong as anything could be.' He broke a piece of wax off the candlestick. 'But I'll always be there for you. If we can just get around what happened last night—'

Jude stood up. 'Maybe I don't want to.'

The lovely orange dress looked treacherous in daylight as she stuffed it into her bag, holding her heart tightly in place. He had no faith in her; he saw her as a flippant child who would toss him over when she tired of him, as if she ever could. How could he so underestimate the depth of a lifetime's feelings, crossed, now, with the momentum of this new attraction? He wanted normality after this, the comfort of old slippers. He wanted her to obliterate a longing so powerful that she could barely move. 'Well, I won't,' she told the mirror. 'I'd rather live without him than live without wanting him.'

The man she would never see again was still sitting on the couch, his shoulders curved, his blue shirt hanging off him. Jude stood beside him. 'I'm off. I'll hitch to Mouchard.'

He grabbed her wrist and held it without looking at her. 'Don't.'

'We'd never get back to where we were. Even if I wanted to, which I don't.'

'You've turned me inside out. Let me get my bearings before you go.'

'I've got to get out of here before I lose my own bearings.' She pulled away and made for the hall.

'Jude!' Oliver dashed after her, overtook her in the hall, and stood with his back to the front door. 'You can't walk out on me now.'

'I bloody well can. I wish I'd never come—'

Oliver grabbed her and kissed her with a desperation that knocked against her teeth and gave gratification such as she had never known. It was as if warm water was being flushed through her, washing away everything that had gone before. She dropped her bag, and thought she might weep. Oliver fell against the door, pulling her with him. Her lips caught on his stubble. Her mind declutched, her thinking stopped; every notion – confusion, apprehension, affection – became physical, sexual, hot.

When they relaxed their hold, Oliver picked up her bag. 'I'll take this upstairs.'

Jude sailed past the catalpa, kicked off her sandals, and walked down the steps into the pool. Her long skirt floated, spreading out around her, a yellow sphere in a transparent sky. She took long steps through the water and stopped, her arms raised so as not to sink her skirt.

'You look like a water-lily,' said Oliver, coming in behind her.

'I feel like a Venus Fly-trap.'

'That makes me a fly.'

Her chin came over her shoulder. 'I'm not trying to ensnare you.'

'I know.'

She fell gracefully into the water and floated away, her skirt billowing around her legs. Oliver threw off his shirt and swam over to her, spinning her around like a log to kiss her. This was even more difficult than the night before. With no shadows to dim their faces, they could see the light reflected in each other's eyes, and there was no loud music to camouflage the sound of their tongues clicking. Jude was conscious that her top would be transparent when she got out and the bareness of Oliver's back against her inner arm embarrassed her. They had frolicked in water before, but the contact then had been without recourse.

They paddled back to the shallow end and stretched out by the steps to continue necking.

361

In time, Oliver rolled away with a resigned sigh. 'I knew I wouldn't hold out,' he said. 'I didn't really want to.'

'You should have let me leave.'

'I'd never have seen you again.' He kissed her fingers. 'And we couldn't have that, could we, Jude? I've too much of myself invested in you.' He pulled her on to him, resting her shoulders on his chest, their faces to the sun. 'Have you any idea how this started?'

'Nope. You?'

'I've lost the plot entirely.'

'Something happened by the canal,' she said.

'And you went with it.'

'It seemed right.'

'Not to me. And what about the age thing? I'm damn near twenty—'

Jude squinted at him. 'Haven't you done enough soul-bashing for one day?'

Oliver had never noticed before that she was beautiful. Beyond recognizing that she was attractive and had more style than any woman he knew, he had only once before actively appraised her – during that first summer when he had tried to appreciate Stephen's attraction to a girl of seventeen. He had seen it too, but the eight-year age difference had bothered him and it horrified him that with an added eleven years on his brother, he was the one lusting for her now. But back then she had scarcely escaped the clutches of adolescence; now she was a young woman. And such a young woman. As she chattered her way through dinner under the catalpa, he saw at last the beauty that had previously been blitzed from his sight by her personality. She was unusually pale, having worked all summer, but she radiated well-being and her eyes picked up the light of the candles. Her nose was neat and unpretentious. Her eyebrows had a bend, a quirk, that suited the turn of her mind. Quite deaf to her chatter, Oliver made his way around her. He took in the narrow frame, the odd freckle, her mother's hands. Her loose cotton shirt had been left open a button lower than usual, allowing flashes of cleavage and bra strap which, as intended, made him ache to take steps he feared to take.

Jude hadn't expected this reserve in him; she became aware of it later when he kissed her at length, as they swung gently on the seat, but kept his hands strategically removed from strategic places. She was mildly relieved – it was still disconcerting to see those large friendly eyes only a nose away – and yet she longed for more.

Oliver sensed her restlessness. 'Let's turn in,' he said, getting up.

They locked up and went upstairs. Outside her bedroom door, Oliver pecked Jude on the cheek. 'Night.'

'Isn't this a bit silly?'

'Girls do it all the time, don't they? "Sorry, but I'm not ready yet." '

'But we've slept together before. Not to do so now doesn't make sense.'

'It makes more sense than ever.' He kissed the back of her hand. 'I can't take this any further, Jude. Not yet. I need time.'

'Time?'

'To dispense with the child.'

Jude sighed. 'Any other woman would strip off and seduce you.'

'But you're not any other woman. That's why this is happening.'

'Oliver—'

He raised his finger to her mouth. 'No.'

'Stop.' She put his hand down. 'Quit being the guardian. Calling the shots.'

'Be fair then. We've been close for a long time in a very different way. It's hard to shake all that off.'

'Not for me.'

Her candour was titillating. Oliver couldn't account for the honesty with which she admitted to wanting him and wondered if it was frightening him off as much as their history was. 'We're not ready for intimacy,' he said. 'At least, I'm not.'

26

The river had never been warmer in Jude's experience, or so low; it had absorbed the heat of a long, hot summer and needed a refill, a sharp, cold refill of mountain rain. There was nobody on the beach, apart from two bikers sitting in their leathers, smoking, so the rapids were Jude's alone. She bobbed over them, enjoying this communion with the Loue, this unexpected return, and when Oliver came across the bridge, she got out and hobbled across the stones to him. 'Nice day at the office, dear?'

'No.' He kissed her, and something caught in her throat. 'I wanted to be here with you.'

He threw down his towel and handed her his watch to put in her bag. Jude knew his gestures, his habits, so well. He took off his sunglasses and pulled his shirt over his head. She watched in horror. What had she been thinking? This was *Oliver*, for crying out loud!

'Let's go.' He took her hand and headed towards the water. Jude hated it. Like a little girl being led into a party that she didn't want to go to, she felt self-conscious – sick, even. 'I don't think I'll get in again,' she said, retreating to the towels, where she sat with her knees against her chest.

The air was muggy. Even the insects seemed lethargic, subdued by the density of the atmosphere. Everything was waiting for that first rumble in the distance, the first raindrop.

Jude watched Oliver swim. He was happy. She had made him happy, and the day before she too had been happy. And yet when he had kissed her just then, the elation vanished. She sat on her towel in turmoil. Oliver swam near the wall, where the current was weaker. She'd been so clear all weekend. So certain. *Why?* Had she been so desperate to have him back that she made herself fancy him? Or had it been sheer randiness that suddenly made him attractive to her? As she watched him swimming, she was assaulted by unwelcome reminders of what they'd been doing. Blood rushed from where it had lodged all weekend and flooded her face, as embarrassment coursed through her so loudly she was sure the bikers could hear it banging against the sky. She had kissed *Oliver*. And had he not been so restrained, she would have done a lot more besides. The sensation of his wet skin under her arm came at her, like a snake slithering across her flesh, and made her shiver with revulsion. The turbulence of her mind raced to her stomach, making her queasy. Oliver had been right all along; it was an unspeakable error of judgement. Where had she *been* all weekend?

He got out of the water. Jude didn't look right. Her hand over her mouth and her knees pulled against her chest, she was staring hard at her feet. He crouched down. 'What is it?'

'I'd better go home. I'm having a panic attack.'

'About us?'

She nodded.

'Fair enough. I've had mine.'

As they hurried back to the house, great purple storm clouds were coming in over the hills, darkening the day. Jude ran upstairs as soon as they got home.

'Jude?'

'I'm going to be sick!' She ran for the toilet, fell to her knees and hung over the bowl, gasping. Nothing happened. She sat back on her heels.

Oliver hovered by the door. 'Are you OK?'

'It's passing.' A flash of sheet lightning; distant thunder.

'I'll get you some water.'

Another flash of lightning, followed by a low rumble of thunder which built itself up to a satisfying *whack*. *It's going to be a big one,* Jude thought, crawling on to her bed. She liked these massive French storms, when the skies cracked and flushed away weeks of intense heat with a display more violent than anything an island like Ireland could produce. The thunder was louder, the rain more torrential, the lightning more terrifying than at home, but none of these could now excite her more than her own recent behaviour.

When Oliver brought her a glass of water, she was lying with her head under her pillow. 'Come out of there,' he said.

'No. I don't ever want to see the light of day or anything ever again.'

'You mean you don't want to see me.'

'Just leave me alone for a bit.'

She pulled the pillow off her face as soon as he left the room. After more sheet lightning, thunder came over like a fighter jet. 'What have I done?'

She reached for her phone to text Fiona. But what to say? How to explain *this* in a text? So she teased it out with herself instead. 'It's not as if I slept with him,' she reasoned.

The pillow went over her face again. 'But I would have given half the chance! Oh God, what was I thinking?'

'So I kissed him,' replied the other voice – her *id*, perhaps.

'Big deal. Friends of mine kiss foul-looking strangers in nightclubs all the time. At least Oliver's cute.'

Jude threw down the pillow. 'He's not *cute*,' she said out loud. 'He's *forty*!'

'He's older than me, sure, but—'

She sprang into a sitting position. 'Older? *Older*? He lost his virginity before I was born! He's a whole different generation. He's . . . he's got these grey bits in his side-burns and wrinkles around his eyes and—'

'Sounds good to me.'

The cushion was hurled across the room at her invisible, argumentative self. 'What about Bob? I've been unfaithful to him.' She got up to pace, but a flash of lightning made her jump back from the window. She peeked out at her lemon tree as she pulled over the shutters. The air was cooler already, while her own outbursts had relieved nothing. Her thoughts remained hot and bothered and sticky.

A gentle tap on the door. 'Talk to me, Jude.'

Another ferocious bang overhead, as two masses of hot air crashed together like sumo wrestlers in the sky. 'Tomorrow.'

'I can't hold out that long.'

'You'll have to.'

At last: the rain, in torrents, slashing on to the leaves of the catalpa and splashing off again. A soothing sound, refreshing and steady.

Jude managed to sleep by blocking out every thought, every memory. She struggled away from both, knowing that if she could reach sleep, if she could only cross its borders, she would be calm – and she was, until she woke at five the following morning and it all pounced on her again. She held her arm over her eyes to shut out what was already within, then conceded defeat and faced it. Yes, she and Oliver had kissed. Often. At length. Repeatedly. And enjoyed it. She sought out that pleasure, brought his arms around her and tried it out, but her stomach withered. Mortification had made their contact gross in her mind.

It had been a blip. An aberration. A dreadful misinterpretation of relief. They had misread delight for desire. But how to wash away their mistake without losing each other? She could not countenance losing him again; he was her soulmate, her parents, her motivation, her one true friend. Why should she do without him, when already she did without siblings and relatives? Why should she do without Oliver because she kissed him? The embarrassment would surely retreat with time and one day they might even laugh about the silly turn they once took together.

It was a sunny, fresh day. Downstairs, at nine, she found a note from Oliver. He would be out for the day, it said; he had things to do in Besançon. Silently Jude thanked him, knowing what it must have cost him to give her this space. She spent the morning cleaning the house and chastising herself for toying with him. Later, she went down to the river. Only the day before it had been like a natural Jacuzzi bubbling with her own goodwill; now it flowed furiously, as if to reproach her.

At four, Oliver joined her. She was sitting on the stones, staring at the grey-brick wall that fronted the Loue. He tried not to trespass upon her, but rejection had made him raw with desperation and she saw that he was stretched, taut, that the tendons in his face were flexing with apprehension. He handed her his watch.

'You can't swim,' she said, 'it's too high after last night.'

'I'll be fine.' But the river took him downstream so swiftly that Jude stood up, alarmed. Some way down, he managed to pull himself out of the turbulent middle channel and began swimming against the current.

Jude walked in the shallows, allowing the familiar to restore her. The yellow evening light, like a watercolour wash on canvas, paled the beach; the pebbles beneath her feet and the gush of the cool waters were like a multi-layered lullaby. The clutch that had held her stomach began to ease. They would get back; like two people who had taken the wrong train, they would get back to the inter-section and continue their journey as they were meant to. They *would*. Her consternation began to fade. Facing the fence and knowing she could clear it brought an extraordi-nary euphoria. Peace was sneaking over her again.

Oliver's swimming was erratic. She would tell him, short and sharp, that he had been right, that they must go back or go nowhere. She would apologize for behaving like a hungry spider, for contributing to the waves of disappointment that made up his life, and he would forgive her. Generous as he was, he would even be pleased to hear she was involved with someone else. Jude smiled at him with old love. 'I know you,' she said aloud to the man in the river. 'I know you.'

Then she heard a voice say, 'You'll never meet a better man, Jude.'

It was her father. One day when Oliver was leaving for London, they stood in the street waving him off and her dad had said, 'You'll never meet a better man, Jude. Remember that.' He had never seen Oliver again.

Her father's best friend was coming out. Jude picked up his towel and walked towards him, into the river. She smiled. He didn't. The grey around his temples was louder in his wet hair and the lines about his eyes profuse as he squinted against the sun. He knew what was coming; he saw it on her face. Her expression was easy now. Her battle was over and he'd lost. The storm water pressed against her calves as she stepped towards him, holding the towel, but when he took it, she didn't stop. She put her arms around his neck and kissed him.

He dropped the towel and held her, and so they remained until Jude lost her footing on the slippery stones and the river knocked her over. 'Bloody hell!'

Oliver helped her up. 'What happened to that panic attack?'

'I don't know.' She frowned, looking around as if she had lost something in the water. 'It was here a minute ago.'

He kissed her lightly. No revulsion crossed her face. 'Why the sudden change of heart?'

'There was a tunnel on the road, that's all. I've just come through it.'

'But yesterday I was making you ill.'

'I'm on the pill,' she said, struggling out of the water. 'It makes me nauseous sometimes.'

They made their way over to the remaining towel. 'We'd want to be mad,' said Oliver, 'to get involved. It'd be like holding hands and jumping off a cliff.'

'I'm game.'

He nodded. 'Me too.'

'But you said you'd get hurt.'

'I probably will, but my guess is it'll be worth it.'

'I'm soaked,' said Jude, squeezing out her shirt. 'Again.'

'So you're on the pill?' said Oliver, drying his wrists. 'Who's the lucky bloke?'

'No one's got lucky yet. Least of all me.'

'You mean . . .'

'Yes, yes. That's exactly what I mean.'

371

'Good Lord.'

'Should've had your brother.' She handed him his watch.

He looked bemused. 'You've never made love?'

'Nothing like labouring the point, Oliver. I tried it once, all right? It didn't work.'

'Need I ask with whom?'

'You need not.'

'I thought you didn't want to be one of Stephen's conquests?'

'I didn't, but we got carried away once. Or maybe twice. But it seems my virginity has a mind of its own. Just as well. We weren't using anything.'

'Christ. I thought I taught you to be sensible.'

'Oh, and you've never taken a chance, I suppose?'

Oliver gathered their things. 'But there is someone? You said so the other night.'

'It would seem that's over before it even began.'

'I really thought you were backing out.'

'I was, but then I heard Dad.'

'Sorry?'

'Did it ever occur to you that he might be pleased about this?'

Oliver shook his head. 'I knew Michael better than you did, my love, and believe me, he wouldn't be patting me on the back right now.'

'But I heard him. He said it's all right.'

After they had showered, they sat by the pool sipping wine, and Oliver began the seduction Jude was longing for. He pushed her over on the grass and spread his weight along her. *At last,* she thought. She braced herself when his hand ran along her rib-cage – but he went no further. Instead, he rolled off and lay with his arm over his eyes.

372

'What's wrong? Oliver?'

'Sorry. Can't.'

'Why not? What is it?'

'Complicated is what it is.'

'You're not . . . I'm not making you . . .'

'Course not.' He tapped his forehead. 'The problem's up here. They won't go away.'

'Who won't?'

'The dead.'

'That's your bloody conscience working overtime.'

'Why wouldn't it? Michael has been looking over my shoulder since I was thirteen and it isn't easy to dispense with him when I'm trying to make love to his daughter – whom he *left in my care*.'

'My parents have no right to interfere with my sex-life, alive or dead.' She leaned over him. 'They're gone, Oliver, and I'm here. Alive and kicking. Flesh and bones.'

'Yeah, and it's the flesh I want.' He grinned.

'Do you? Really?'

His great eyes swept across her face like a beam from a torch. 'You have no idea. But this would be unlike anything else.'

'I know that, but I don't see the point in putting it off.'

'Nor do I, but everything gets in the way.'

'We need an exorcist then.'

'More than that.' He covered his face again. 'Oh, Jude. It isn't only your parents who haunt me every time I touch you. You do too.'

'Me?'

'Every time I close my eyes, I see you there, aged sixteen, and fourteen, and . . .'

'Oh God.'

'I don't know how to stop it. It's like a ghastly slide show

I don't want to see. Every time I kiss you, you're there in your Rupert Bear pyjamas or your school uniform . . .'

'*Oh God.*'

'You think I'm not impatient to get down to some serious love-making here? But that wretched child keeps coming back at me. A horrible little spook. *Why?* What's my sub-conscious trying to tell me? That I'm some kind of closeted paedophile? A Humbert Humbert lusting after my pubescent charge?'

'Stop it!' Jude sat up. 'Just cool it. This is to be expected. You've seen me through every stage of growing up, but that doesn't mean you harboured lewd thoughts about me, so stop freaking out because if you don't, we'll never get over this. And we *have* to get over it.'

'Let's go away. This house is riddled with all that guardianship stuff. A change of scene might be just what I need.'

'*I'm* just what you need.'

He smiled. 'Yeah, I know that.'

'You should let those spectres come. Let them through. If you do, they might just run on past and go away.' She kissed his neck and opened one of his shirt buttons. 'Have you tried keeping your eyes open?'

'They're still there.'

She opened another button. 'Let them come. I'm bigger than all those little Judes. I'll blow your ghosts away.'

'You don't know what you're dealing with.'

'I know better than anyone.' Her mouth made tracks across his chest.

'Stop.'

They found a place called Cavalière on the Mediterranean coast two days later. It was a long drive, but they wanted distance from Landor. They needed a new vista, and Jude wanted the sea. The main street ran alongside a curved stretch of beach, flanked by pine trees, where a few end-of-season stragglers were lying on the white sand. In the village square, the old men played *pétanque,* their steel balls making a muffled *toc* in the sand when they knocked together. After checking into a smart hotel by the beach, Oliver and Jude had a drink on a terrace overlooking the sea, and Jude was moved by a depth of contentment which she had never even aspired to.

Dressing for dinner proved awkward. Sharing a room as friends in Letterfrack had actually been easier than sharing as a couple who had not yet been intimate, but Jude welcomed the discomfort of changing in a steamed-up bathroom, because it could only encourage Oliver to hurry things up. She pulled on the red linen dress she had worn to Stephen's wedding and thought wryly that she could never have imagined, when packing it, that she would end up wearing it with the sole intention of seducing her former guardian, but that was exactly what she hoped to do. She could not, she knew, endure another evening of harmless necking, because Oliver had become so attractive to her that it pained her to look at him. Although she had long taken for granted the style, the charm and the sideways grin, she now became ensnared on everything he did. It was the way he changed gears when driving, the way he took his credit cards from an inner pocket, the way he held his wine glass and wore expensive shirts – all this drew her attention and made her halt momentarily, so that she was constantly being distracted by mini-attacks of arousal. Even the simple act of putting on his glasses seduced her, and it wasn't like Stephen or any other man she'd known, because the attraction lived in a place she had never been to before. She wanted intimacy not simply because of physical craving, but because she needed absolute access to the person beyond.

They had dinner on the terrace. Glancing around at the other diners, Jude said, 'I think we make quite a smart couple, even if you are old enough to be my father.'

Oliver ran his hand over his tie.

'I love the way you move,' she added.

'So. The famous dress you wore to the famous wedding.'

'Yeah. It's a bitch to iron.'

'You looked amazing that day. You were making me wild.'

She looked up from her chocolate roulade. 'Sorry?'

'This hasn't been as sudden as we like to believe. It goes back a bit.'

Jude could see her seduction evaporating. 'Don't start that again. You didn't fancy me before.'

'No, but this couldn't have happened just like that.'

'Of course it could. Especially with us. All other issues were dealt with.'

'Maybe, but think about that wedding, Jude. There was more going on than broken promises. There was tension between us from the moment I picked you up at the airport.'

'Because of Shelley.'

'No. It was sexual tension, pure and simple.'

Jude blushed.

'Don't you wonder what might have happened if I hadn't brought Shelley along?'

'*No.*'

'Well, I do, and the more I look back on it, the more convinced I am that that's exactly why I brought her.' He leaned forward. 'Think about last summer, before I met Shelley. We were moving on to something else even then, don't you think?'

376

Jude was appalled. How far back was he going to go? 'Don't be ridiculous. You were besotted with that woman. Every time I looked at you at the wedding, you were looking at her.'

'And every time I looked at you, you were looking at Stephen. So the question is – why were we watching each other so much when we were both supposedly involved with someone else?' Oliver pulled back his shoulders. 'Things changed, Jude, and it wasn't last Friday. Don't you see? Don't you see *when* they changed?'

'I suppose you're going to say Letterfrack.'

'Am I wrong?'

She looked away.

'We were both in a high state of distress when I found you, and then we spent two days digging up coffins, sorting out the bones from the flesh. It wasn't possible, after all that, to re-establish the status quo. We'd gone too far along a different line. It was a bit like making love – tearing away layers, exposing yourself – no friendship could ever be the same again.'

Jude threw down her napkin, and her challenge. 'Speaking of making love, let's go up.'

They made their way upstairs with ambivalence. Oliver still feared the child who haunted him, Jude the repercussions of continued frustration. As they walked into the room, he switched on the light and stood fiddling with the key. Jude took the key, turned off the light and kissed him, willing his demons away, willing herself, in school uniform and pyjamas, far from his mind. She pushed his jacket off his shoulders. His hands were clammy on her back; his fingers slipped inside her dress, but without conviction. He didn't stop her when she loosened his tie, so she opened his collar, while he hesitated around the zip of her dress. He was faltering. Determined to exorcize his doubts and expel his self-control, she pressed against him. That helped. He opened her zip and ran his hand around the small of her back, then nudged the dress away, and Jude prayed there would be no turning back.

There wasn't. Oliver took over. He shoved her towards the bed, where they shared no history and had no past. In spite of the darkness, Jude knew his eyes were open and she never left off them, holding his blackened gaze to hers, that he should see no one else. She still worried that he might pull back, spooked by the child who travelled with her, but when he moved across her rib-cage to nuzzle the dip between her ribs, she knew they were finally alone. She pulled out his shirt, opened his belt, then lifted her hips to be taken from her clothes, and ran her hand down his back when he pulled off his own. They lay quietly, taking pleasure in bare contact, in the touch of toes and the tickle of hair and the digging of elbows. Breathing together. Fingertips seeing in the dark. Jude relaxed, as one restored after exile. She felt like a monarch butterfly arriving in Mexico after a long migration. Instinct had led her here, had propelled her across the unlikely. She had found the tree she would nest in, and the means of survival.

Oliver had never wanted anyone as much as he wanted Jude at that moment, but he had to keep repeating to himself that the woman lying with him was nobody's daughter, nobody's ward. He took it slowly, surely, and the depth of pleasure was so raw that Jude could hardly bear it. Oliver lay over her. They didn't speak. He asked. She said yes.

When it was done, beams of smug satisfaction crossed between them. 'Of all things,' said Jude. 'Of all ridiculous things, that we should end up like this.'

'Indeed. Not quite what one would have expected.'

'So this began in Connemara, you think?'

He put his fingers through hers. 'I could tell you the exact moment.'

She squeezed his fingers.

'That's when I crossed over,' he said. 'That's when I started to fall in the wrong direction. Not in Dôle. Not last week.'

'Fall?'

'In love.'

Jude turned to him.

'You don't think I'd let this happen for anything less, do you? After Letterfrack, everything else became untenable.'

A bright shaft of sunlight, streaming across the bed, woke them too early the following morning. When Oliver came out of the bathroom, Jude turned away.

He laughed. 'Typical! She spends days trying to seduce me and then goes all coy.' He lay down and pulled on her shoulder. 'Turn around. Look at me.'

When she did, her face filled with horror. 'Oh, yuk!'

'That's a great start.'

'Your scar. It's horrible!'

'Well, it was pretty messy in there. They had to open me up and hoover me out.'

'Ugh, revolting! Honestly, you shouldn't be having sex – you'll burst.'

'Right-oh.' He made to get up. Jude pulled him back, laughing. He yanked the sheet away. 'Hello, lover.'

Jude touched the scar. 'Hello, you.'

Jude slid into their new relationship as easily as a seal on to ice, but it was not as easy for Oliver as he pretended. The little girl ghost no longer haunted him, but his conscience did. He had always loved Jude from the inside out, but now he loved her also from the outside in, and this bothered and disappointed him. Their love-making felt like adultery. Adultery against their own peculiar but pure relationship as it had been.

His feelings for her were a paradox he could not escape. To love her like this would have been impossible without their history; to love her like this should have been impossible in view of their history. Their affair sullied the brief he had been given, the honourable duty bestowed on him, and yet he sought no escape from it. Adultery, after all, is sweeter for its forbidden nature, and having made the union, sundering it seemed pointless and too painful to consider. And yet, he continued to feel like someone who had for years worked painstakingly on a piece of intricate knitting, only to pull it apart with one yank, leaving the wool all scrunched and used up.

Other issues soon peeped over the parapet. One afternoon when they were having tea on the terrace, they talked about Tim.

'He'll have to be told,' said Oliver.

'I wonder what he'll make of it. I wonder what I make of it myself. It's peculiar having an affair with someone I've loved all my life.'

'Sorry to disillusion you, but there was a time when you couldn't stand the sight of me, and the feeling was entirely mutual.'

'Really? When was that?'

'Oh, when you were seven, eight. At one point, I even put off seeing Michael to avoid being subjected to his brat of a daughter.'

'I was that bad?'

'Wicked is the word that comes to mind.'

They picked up their respective books and read for a while. Jude had her foot on Oliver's knee; his thumb turned around her ankle. *Time to drag him upstairs,* she thought, but instead she said, 'Oliver, are you sure that by having an affair with me you're not living out some unconsummated thing with my mother?'

He looked up. 'Take that back.'

'Well, I have to wonder, don't I? You admit to being mad about her.'

'Take it back, Jude, or I'm out of here.'

'Sorry.'

'She was five years older than me and my best friend's wife!'

'Yeah, all right. Calm down.'

'And I never said I fancied her.'

Jude picked up her book. *You didn't have to say it.*

On their last night, they strolled along the beach. Jude looked up. The sky was in cahoots with her delight and sparkled like an effervescent drink. Charmed by the warm September evening and by her life as it now was, she soared. There had never been anything like this; nothing at all. Every restitution she had ever needed, she found in Oliver's love, and for the first time that she could remember, nothing was missing. Not family, nor siblings, nor even her parents.

She slipped her arm through his. 'Are you really very rich now?'

'Do you care?'

'Of course. Why do you think I'm sleeping with you?'

'I'm pretty comfortable, yeah.'

'So you can support me if I stay here?'

'Jude—'

'I'm not leaving you again. I can't.'

'You can and you will. You have to do your Master's.'

'Don't speak to me in that guardian's tone. I could get a job teaching English.'

'Jude, use that considerable brain of yours. Do the Master's, as planned, and if you want to go on with a doctorate afterwards, I'll move back to Ireland.'

'If you're going to move, move now. Let's not be apart any longer. Enough is enough.'

'My love, I can't. I'm thick into a book. I can't just up and move to Dublin on a whim.'

'I'm not a whim!'

He grinned. 'I wish you were. Look, I'm going to the States next month to see people about the screenplay and I'll be dropping in on Tim on the way back. I'll call in on you too – if you go back to college.'

'Blackmail?'

'Your career is not going down the drain because of me. Go and get stuck into that thesis, and we'll see how things stand – with work *and* with Tim – after Christmas.'

'You think he'd object to us living together?'

'He'll need time to get a handle on this. Besides, we've lived apart before. We can do it again.'

'The thought makes my stomach lurch. You might meet someone else.'

'That isn't even possible.'

Jude slipped off her sandals; the sand was cool. She walked down to the sea in the dim glow of night light. The moon shone like a low-wattage bulb, throwing a beam across the water which unfurled to their feet. 'It's like an aisle, leading us to our own private altar.'

'Ah, but will we ever get there?'

'I'll make sure we do. I'm going to make up for all the

times I've behaved as if your only purpose in life was to be at my beck and call.'

'You already have. This is my pay-back; the return on my investment.'

She walked backwards along the shore. 'You've never been loved the way I can love you. Inside, outside. Upside, downside. Every which way about. I'm like one of those old-fashioned bar heaters – you know, the ones that glow bright orange? You've plugged me in and I'm glowing hot and bright, and if anyone tries to interfere, I'll burn their fingers off.'

'I wish I could spirit you away to a desert island where no one *could* interfere.'

'Couldn't do my MA on a desert island.'

'You couldn't leave me either.'

Jude stopped; Oliver walked into her. 'I'm not going to leave you. I love you.'

'Marry me, then.'

She put her arms around his neck. 'No.'

27

Living without Oliver was no longer the inconvenience it had once been. It was no longer like living with a dull sense of something missing, but with a sharp awareness of an absent necessity. Living without Oliver, Jude decided, was like being in one of those nightmares in which she couldn't breathe and woke up gasping. The only escape was study. The only comfort was sitting by the fire, drowning out the dawdling minutes by listening to Eric Clapton. When her friends complained that she shouldn't have broken up with Bob if it was going to make her miserable, Jude merely sighed and silently counted the days.

She was counting the hours by the time Oliver arrived in early November. They held each other for a long time at the airport, but in the car soon forgot about the finer aspects of being together; they lost sight of everything but sex. After a heated journey from the airport, they finally got inside the house and fell against the front door, wrestling with their clothes.

'Is anyone here?'

'No. Fiona's in town.'

Oliver pulled Jude's sweater and blouse over her head. 'God, I missed you.'

'Ah! Your hands are freezing!'

He manoeuvred her towards the staircase. She stumbled, but he caught her as they fell back on to the steps. They clambered some way up, nuzzling and groping, then stopped to kiss. Oliver's cool, fresh eyes consulted her. She smiled; he reached for his belt.

Later, they were lying in bed chatting when the front door banged shut.

Jude bolted upright. 'Jesus. There's Fiona!'

'So?'

'Look at us!'

'What about it?'

'I haven't told her yet. I haven't told anyone!'

'*Jude!* Why the hell not?'

'How could I? They see you as my surrogate father!'

'But now they're going to find out in the worst possible way.'

'I'll go down. You zip into your room.'

But just as Jude jumped out of bed, Fiona knocked on the door. 'Jude?'

Oliver whispered, 'You've asked for this!'

She pulled on her dressing-gown and stuck her nose out the door.

'Sorry to disturb,' said Fiona, 'but have you forgotten you were supposed to pick Oliver up two hours ago? Sinéad's downstairs waiting to see him. He isn't stuck out at the airport, is he,' she tried to look into the room, 'while you've been having fun back here?'

'Of course not. Tell her I'm coming.'

*

'Hello, love,' said Sinéad, when Jude came into the kitchen. 'Hope you don't mind me dropping in, but I just *had* to see Mr Sayle! It's been two years, you know.'

'Really? That long.'

'Where is he?'

Fiona poked her in the ribs. 'So what's going on upstairs, Jude? Who, pray tell, are you entertaining up there?'

Jude emptied out the water that Fiona had just put in the kettle, refilled it and plugged it in again. Sinéad watched. 'It must be love, whoever he is.'

Jude faced them. Two birds with one stone. 'There's something I need to tell you.'

The women exchanged glances and quickly sat down, their faces eager with anticipation.

'When I was in France—'

'You met someone!' said Fiona. 'I knew it.'

'And he came over with Oliver,' exclaimed Sinéad. The two women nodded at each other.

'So *that's* why you dumped Bob,' said Fiona.

'And that's why you've been so miserable since you got back.'

'But why all the secrecy?'

'And may we now meet him, *please*?' asked Sinéad.

'Tell him to come down. I'll bet he's a smooth, suave *Français*.'

'He's probably called Claude.'

'Whatever he's called, he's pretty hot, judging by the debris in the hall,' Fiona giggled.

'Cut it out, you two. You're on the wrong track.'

'Oliver!' Sinéad stood up to embrace him as he came in behind her.

He grinned at Jude's sulky demeanour by the sink.

Sinéad considered his face. 'I don't know. I liked the beard myself, and you've lost that writery look.'

'Writery? Now, there's a word.' He came to stand with Jude.

'Come on, Ol,' said Fiona. 'Tell all. Who's her secret lover?'

'It isn't for me to tell.'

'What's his name? I'll call him down.'

'You can't,' said Jude. 'The point is, I mean, the thing is . . .' She looked pleadingly at Oliver. He shook his head. 'Look, an awful lot happened in Landor, unexpected stuff that might seem strange to everyone, which is why I find it hard to talk about —'

'Get to the point,' said Fiona. 'You had some big love affair, right? So why don't you bring the guy down so we can all meet him?'

'I don't have to bring him down. You're looking at him.'

'Quit the messing,' said Fiona, 'and that's in bad taste, if you don't mind my saying so.'

Jude could only leave the room. Oliver followed, but he stopped at the door. 'I understand now why she was reluctant to tell you.'

'*Ohhhh Jayzuz!*' Fiona banged her head on the table. 'What did I say?'

Sinéad sat still. 'He's old enough to be her father.'

'He *is* her father! He has been for years! I'm going to puke!'

'No, wait. There's eighteen – nineteen? – years between them? That happens.'

'He was her guardian, for God's sake! He's *in loco parentis*! He isn't supposed to . . . to . . .'

'But they've always been close, maybe—'

'They were in bed together! I mean, *please*!'

Sinéad nodded. 'Do you know something, Fiona? I think this is right.'

'And I think I want to die. Me and my fat mouth.' Her eyes widened. 'How long do you think it's been going on?'

'Not long. You know Oliver.' Sinéad raised her chin. 'My guess is this goes back to when she disappeared. That must have flipped things over.'

'But they didn't see each other for over a year.'

'Exactly. All that stuff at Stephen's wedding – this is what she was running away from.'

Jude was standing by her bedroom window when Oliver came in. He put his arms around her waist. 'Bad taste,' she said flatly.

'Listen, when Fiona comes to apologize, accept it graciously, will you, because we caught her on the hop. More than anyone else, she saw me in guardian mode, and then she suddenly finds we've become lovers. It's a big leap for anyone to make. Give her space.'

'Is anyone going to give us space? Funny, isn't it, how you can wander into a woodland as lush as this one, after spending years lost on the steppes, and find people slinging arrows because they have their own ideas about where you should find happiness?'

'If you'd told them sooner, they could have got used to it before I turned up.'

Jude smirked. 'I can't wait to see how easily *you* tell people. People like Stephen, for example.'

'I'll tell him outright. Soon as we get to London.'

The knock came on the door.

*

They went to Jude's Graduation Ball a few nights later. Oliver felt very old, and very sober, and extraordinarily uncomfortable, surrounded by twenty-somethings, many of whom didn't feel particularly comfortable, either, with a recently lauded author at their table. It clearly made them think that they had to sound intelligent, but the more they drank, the harder they tried to be clever, and the harder they tried, the more spectacularly they failed.

Oliver was relieved to escape to the dance-floor. He took Jude's hands and held them behind her back, pressing her against him.

'Not so close. It makes Fiona and Emer uncomfortable.'

'What does? Seeing an old thing like me dance with a gorgeous young thing like you?'

'It's the background, not just the age. People see you as family.'

'Good. With a bit of luck, I will be one day. In fact, the sooner we arrange another legally binding contract, the happier I'll be.'

'This is beginning to feel like pressure, Oliver. I saw your first marriage break up and it wasn't entertaining. Besides, you swore you'd never marry again in the midst of passion.'

He grinned. 'But I like you and know you, as well as passionately adore you.'

'Yeah, well,' she pressed her nose against his face, 'it's all just passion for me, I'm afraid.'

'At least tell me if you mean never, or just no.'

'I mean no. Right now, marriage is like an island on the horizon. One day I might take the ferry across the sound to check it out, but not yet.'

Later, Oliver watched Jude as he had never done before. He watched her moving about in her own world and wondered how he might fit into it. He noticed that while she was at ease with Fiona and Emer, and even Theo, she seemed marginally adrift from her wider group of friends, and that was not his fault. The circumstances of her life had distanced her. She had grown up surrounded by adults, and that was why two people so far apart in age could have such an intense relationship as theirs. That was why she didn't bore him but most of her friends did, why she could match him intellectually and had been able to do so for years. Maturity had come in one swift blow on a Connemara beach when he told her there was nobody left to her, and ever since she had lived with a different perspective to those of lighter experience. And that was good, Oliver thought, as he watched her move amongst her friends in her slinky white dress. Good for their future.

The following week, they went to London to see Tim. Jude was nervous about meeting Patti for the first time in five years, but she wasn't prepared for the emotional throwback she experienced when they pulled up outside the house.

'How do you do it?' she asked Oliver. 'How do you come here, like a visitor, when it used to be your home?'

'With difficulty.'

'The last time I walked down that path, I had no idea I wasn't going back.'

'I can go in alone if you like.'

'No. If you can do it, I can.'

Patti greeted them with warm hugs. Jude was rattled. Everything was so familiar, so apparently unchanged, that she almost had to check she wasn't wearing her school uniform. Even fourteen-month-old Lisa, gurgling in her mother's arms, reminded her of Tim at the same age. Oliver immediately took Lisa from Patti. 'And how's the little lady?' he cooed, but he handed her straight back again when Tim came down the stairs.

And then he was gone, dragged upstairs to play with Tim's new PlayStation, and Jude was left alone with Patti. They went to the kitchen, Stephen's former domain, and she heard herself say, 'You must have missed Stephen.'

'How so? Oh, you mean after the separation?' Patti smiled conspiratorially. 'Actually, I missed him *terribly*. I had to learn my way around my own kitchen again!'

They laughed, and the intervening years vanished. Patti had reverted to form, as if there had been no estrangement. She looked good, cheerful, absolutely unchanged, but Jude would have to spoil it all. Patti had to be told what Tim would soon know.

Patti put the baby in her high chair and made tea. 'Oliver's looking great,' she said, 'as great as he's been sounding recently. In fact, he has that suspect glow about him. Love, is it?'

'Mmm. Think so.'

'And about time too. Who is she? Please say she's an improvement on his last girlfriend.'

'That wouldn't be difficult.'

'Good. I don't mean to be bitchy, but I have Tim to think about.'

Jude was squirming.

'Will he like her? Do *you* like her?'

Biting her lip so hard she almost drew blood, Jude said, 'Patti, it's me.'

Patti stared at her, long and hard. Then she sat down. 'Oh God, Jude. No.'

'There was nothing else I could do.'

Patti rubbed her eyes and sighed.

Conversation was stilted and awkward over tea, but when Patti thought she heard Oliver coming down the stairs, she grabbed Jude's wrist. 'Jude, listen to me. You need a family. Your own family. You need to hook up with some young lad, someone who has nothing to do with any of us, who'll never really understand what you've been through. Someone fresh. It would be disastrous for you to hitch yourself to the Sayles like a third shoe. You've got to go and find that lad, and get a mortgage and buy a house and work your butts off together, like any young couple, and then one day, please God, you'll have a child. And I promise you that on that day, when you hold your own baby for the first time, everything will be restored to you. *Everything*. That's what you must go after, Jude. Staying with Oliver would be like staying alone. No matter how much you love him, or he you, staying with him will mean chaining yourself to your childhood and no one should do that.'

Upstairs, Tim received the news with a nonchalant shrug and, 'Ten points! Wow!'

They stayed with Stephen and Vanessa in their home in Ealing and, as they sat chatting in their cosy living-room later that evening, Jude couldn't take her eyes off Stephen. Oliver took note.

'It isn't what you think,' she whispered, when the Sayles went to get dinner. 'He's still gorgeous, mind – fabulous hips – but his wondrous beauty is going no further than my eyes.'

'Thank goodness for that.'

'Honestly. I pour my love all over you and you can still doubt me.'

He smiled, but seemed distracted.

'All right, old man. What's up?'

'Eh? Nothing.'

392

'Spare me. Let's have it.'

'You won't like it.'

'You're not seriously jealous, are you?'

'Yeah, I am, but not the way you think.' He turned his wine around the glass. 'I wish it was us, that's all. Seeing Vanessa like this makes me broody.'

'Oh *gawd*.'

'I'd love it if you were expecting.'

'I'm only twenty-one!'

'Michael was twenty-two when he had you.'

'Yes, but you wouldn't really wish it on me, would you?'

'Maybe not, but I wish it on myself. I'd love another kid.'

'Nonsense. You're just having a mid-life crisis.'

The great eyes settled on her. 'Jude, sometime soon you're going to have to acknowledge the implications of being involved with someone who is twenty years older than you.'

'Nineteen. And what about my PhD?'

'You must do your PhD, of course you must. I'm only asking that you might at least *consider* having a family before I'm a drooping geriatric.'

'But that only gives me another two years!'

Oliver tweaked her side.

'Isn't it odd to think,' she said seriously, 'that our child would be your parents' grandchild, Tim's half-brother or sister, Stephen's nephew or niece . . . It'd all be a bit smothering, wouldn't it? Like in-breeding.'

'Where the hell is this coming from? *In-breeding*?'

'I dunno. Something Patti said, probably. Anyway,' she fluttered her eyelids, 'planning to tell them soon, are you?'

'That's for sure. We're not sleeping in separate rooms.'

But dinner came and went, and coffee came and went, and still Oliver said nothing.

393

When they climbed the stairs to the two small rooms on the top floor, Jude smiled. 'Congratulations, Ol. That's the way to do it. No beating around the bush.'

'I didn't know where to start. There was so much to catch up on.'

'Excuses, excuses.'

'At least give me credit for telling Tim. That was the hardest part.'

'Telling Patti was the hardest part. You've no idea how hard.'

'Hmm. Don't you just love the way everyone's so happy for us?'

'I can live with it. Night. And do sleep soundly, won't you?'

'Hey. You're coming with me.'

'No. We are *not* sleeping together without telling them.'

'Yes, we are. He's only my kid brother.' Oliver bundled her into his room. 'Anyway, we'll be up before them. It's Sunday – they'll sleep late.'

Jude woke the following morning with a shiver. Oliver's finger was sliding down her spine. She looked at the clock. Nine. She should go back to the other room. Oliver moved closer and lay against her back. He was warm, and hot. His hand crept along her inner thigh. *I should get up,* she thought, *before the others do*. Oliver edged her knee over his legs. The house was quiet. Stephen and Vanessa were probably asleep, or similarly occupied. Jude turned to kiss Oliver. The clandestine nature of their love-making – the impression that they were doing it on his parents' couch and had to be quiet – heightened the excitement and made Jude giggle. She rolled on to her back; Oliver kissed her eyelids, whispered his love and slid into her.

The door opened. Stephen stood staring at them. He put

the phone to his ear, said, 'He'll call you back later, Mum,' and closed the door.

He was hacking at mushrooms on a chopping board when Oliver came into the kitchen. With one glance, Stephen hurled the full force of his anger at his brother. 'Frightfully sorry for interrupting,' he quipped, the attempt at levity quivering beneath the weight of fury, 'but I didn't knock because I thought you might be asleep.'

'You didn't interrupt. You know how I hate to leave a job unfinished.'

The knife sliced through several mushrooms at once. 'This is the best yet is all I can say.'

'Stephen—'

'You deserve a frigging award this time, mate!'

Oliver looked at him.

'How long's it been going on, that's what I'd like to know? In fact, that's what most people will want to know.'

'Not long.'

'I hope for your sake that's true. I mean, Jesus, Oliver. *Jesus.*'

Oliver wandered around the room, barefoot and in a dressing-gown, scratching the back of his neck.

'You're such a fucking hypocrite. You warned me off because I was too old for her – but a twenty-year gap, that's no problem apparently!'

'This is different.'

'Oh, please. That sounds like a line from a very bad novel, but then most of your novels *are* pretty bad.'

'Thanks.'

'I worry about you, you know. I mean, what is this – some kind of family conference? First the dead friend's sister, now his daughter. Don't suppose you'd like to have the granny while you're at it?'

Oliver eyed his brother, his voice low. 'You're sailing too bloody close to the wind.'

'You're the one who's close to the edge, pal.'

'What the hell is eating you, anyway?'

Stephen swung around. 'I trusted you, that's what's eating me.' He waved the knife towards the door. 'I trusted you with her!'

'Well, I'm sorry I didn't live up to your expectations, but can't you stop dancing around like a whirling dervish?'

'I always admired the way you coped with Jude. No matter what else was going on, you did your best for her, but this brings you down, brother. Way down.'

'That's quite damning in view of the fact you haven't a fuck what you're talking about, and it's a bit rich coming from you.'

'There is no comparison and you know it! Jude wasn't entrusted to me for safe-keeping.'

Oliver sat down. 'She is safe, in my keeping.'

'Not any more, she isn't.'

'Fuck you!'

'Is that what you'd say to Michael?'

'Leave him out of this.'

'Yeah, you'd like that, wouldn't you? After all, this is just what he expected, I'll bet! And what about her, Oliver? She's relied on you all her life. She *needs* you. How *can you* take advantage of that when you're damn near twice her age and you've been screwing around since before she was born?'

Oliver had no answer.

Stephen started stabbing sausages. 'You must have had some bloody brainstorm is all I can say. This is Jude you're shagging. Remember Jude? Your so-called *protégée*?'

'Not any longer! And I'm sick of being reminded of it.'

'If you're going to sleep with her, you can expect to be reminded of it. You're selling her short, Oliver, and it stinks. It bloody stinks!' He took eggs from the fridge with such ferocity that Oliver wondered how they didn't end up on the floor.

'Ease up, would you, Steve? Because I could use your back-up here. I'm in the mire.'

His brother's eyes narrowed. 'Which is exactly where you should be if you're going to muck around with a girl in Jude's position. You're all she has. What happens to her when this goes belly-up?'

'What happens to me? Eh? I've got as much to lose as she has. And all this righteous indignation is a bit much, Stephen. I have neither sold her short, nor taken advantage, nor abused my position. She's a woman of her own mind. It was a mutual decision and one not taken lightly by either of us.'

'Well, guess what, Oliver? It was the *wrong fucking decision*!'

Oliver kicked the foot of the table.

'This'll do her no good at all. You should have had the cop to fight it, you stupid git.'

'Oh, right, like you're an expert on self-restraint!'

Stephen leaned over the table, an egg in one fist. 'I wouldn't fuck my protégée,' he said quietly, 'that's for sure.'

Oliver stood up and thumped the table. 'I didn't, you bastard!'

'Ah! Sod you!' Oliver's fist had inadvertently landed on Stephen's hand. Egg yolk and broken shell dribbled from his fingers.

'You had it coming, you trussed-up, self-righteous ass.'

'Of all the women, Ol. Of all the women fluttering around you, what possessed you to try out this one?'

'Love, I suppose.'

'Oh, spare me.'

'Here.' Stephen put a coffee in front of his brother and sat down. 'Sorry for blowing off, but you've lost your bleeding marbles. She's still a kid and, thanks to me, her experience doesn't go much further than the Sayle brothers. Hell, if I'd known I was clearing the way for you, I'd never have touched her.'

'If I'd known this was on the cards, I'd never have let you.'

'You're not just larking about?'

Oliver looked up.

Stephen sighed. 'How *do* you do it? You keep leaving yourself wide open for that family to strip you raw.'

'The Curse of the Feehans, Jude calls it.'

'I've seen you go through the grinder once too often. I don't fancy your chances if you lose out this time.'

'Me neither, but I'm bracing myself.'

'Why?'

'Sixty when she's forty. Pushing fifty maybe, by the time she wants kids. She doesn't need it.'

'So why don't you do the decent thing and walk away?'

'Because it'd be like severing my own lifeline.'

'Shit.' Stephen slurped at his coffee. 'What about Tim?'

'I told him yesterday. He seemed OK, but we'll have to see how he handles it at Christmas. He'll probably shrug it off as a minor change in our sleeping arrangements, but we'll have to tread carefully.'

'You'll have to be damn careful with the parents too, if you're planning to tell them.'

'Of course we are. That's why we're going up to see them.'

'You're going to tell them *together*? Don't be insane,

Oliver! Do Jude a favour. Mum's going to blow like she never has before and even Dad . . .'

Oliver took his brother's advice. Two days later, he found himself in Scotland, without Jude or Tim, eating porter cake at his mother's kitchen table.

'I'm delighted you're coming for Christmas,' she was saying. 'It was so odd last year, without Timmy.'

Oliver's father, the silent presence at the end of every table, ran his hand over his thick white hair, his head deep in a book.

'And Stephen and Vanessa are coming too, and your Uncle Bill, so we'll have a lovely family reunion.'

'And, eh, there'll be Jude, of course,' said Oliver.

'Oh dear. I'm not at all sure how I feel about that.'

'Mother. I thought you liked her.'

'I do, but I'm still angry about Stephen's wedding.'

'You're the one who told her to get out of my life. She did.'

'That's as may be, but what about when you were ill? After all you'd done for her, she didn't even come over. Besides, I simply won't have room for her at Christmas, not with Bill coming.'

Oliver stirred his tea. 'If you have room for me, you have room for Jude.'

'You mean you won't come unless she does? Really, Oliver, you do carry your loyalties too far sometimes.'

'That's not what I mean. The point is, Mum, things have changed with Jude.'

She put down her cup. 'What's changed? What's happened to her?'

'Nothing. I mean, things have changed . . . between us.'

Her eyes twinkled darkly. 'What things? Dan, are you listening?'

Mr Sayle looked over his spectacles.

'Go on.' The colour was draining from Mrs Sayle's face.

Oliver took a very deep breath. 'You won't need an extra room for Jude,' he said, 'because we come in a package these days.' His parents looked at him aghast. He cleared his throat. 'We've become, you know . . . very close. Lovers.'

'Oh, my Lord!' His mother went to the Aga and stood with her back to them. 'Oh, my Lord.'

Dan Sayle stared at his son. 'You don't mean this, Oliver?'

His wife spun around. 'How could you? How *could* you?'

'I'm in love with her.'

'*Love?* I'll tell you something about love: Michael Feehan loved you – and this is how you repay him! It's worse than sleeping with his wife. It's worse than adultery. It's abuse!'

Oliver pushed himself out of his seat. 'How dare you?'

'How dare *you*, Oliver? How could you even contemplate such a thing? She's a child.'

'She's no more a child than I am.'

'She is to us and she should be to you! Above all to you! Have you forgotten what you've been to her?' Her eyes were wet with anger. 'It's disgusting. Oh, I'm ashamed of you. Truly ashamed!'

'There, there, dear.' Her husband made her sit down. 'Don't get into a state.'

'I always knew this was madness. She should never have been left with you. God knows what you've exposed her to.'

'Well, since I'm the villain of the piece, perhaps *she* could come for Christmas and I'll stay away?'

'You're in no position to make wisecracks,' his father growled.

'What do you want, Dad?' Oliver shoved his chair hard against the table. 'You've been on at me to settle down for ages, so why shouldn't I settle with the one person with whom I've lived happily for the last seven years?'

'Oh!'

'How long has this been going on?' His father's eyes were colder than Oliver had ever seen them.

'Two months.'

'Is that the truth?'

'Sod this.' Oliver hit his forehead with his hand and made for the door.

'Is that the truth?' his father called after him.

'Of course it's the bloody truth! And if you don't trust me, if you can't believe I wouldn't touch a girl who'd been left in my charge before she was old enough to consent to it, then I don't see what else we can possibly say to each other.'

'You're not bringing her here at Christmas,' cried his mother.

'Damn right I'm not.'

'I won't have you here, living as lovers under my roof.'

'Well, that doesn't surprise me, although a bit of support around here would have been nice for a change.' He turned to go.

His mother caught him by the elbow and pulled him around to face her. 'Don't you take the high ground with me! We only want to see you happy. It isn't so difficult to find someone to love, Oliver, without honing in on the most unlikely people. That American and now this! It's no good for Tim. Why can't you find someone like Vanessa instead of embroiling yourself with a girl half your age? Why can't you emulate your brother and settle down in a sensible manner?'

'But I am emulating him, Mum. Jude must have been, oh, all of seventeen when Stephen first seduced her.'

His mother whacked him across the face. 'How dare you?'

401

He put his hand to his cheek, one eye winking with the sting. 'You've wanted to do that for a long time, haven't you, Mrs Sayle?' He opened the door.

'Oliver, I forbid you to leave when your mother is distressed. We'll discuss this tomorrow when we're all calmer.'

Oliver turned and said quietly, 'There is nothing to discuss. I appreciate that this is difficult, that it isn't what you expected or wanted, but it isn't what I expected either, and accusing me of abuse and disloyalty, not to mention making Jude unwelcome here, is no way to deal with it. You're disappointed?' He shook his head. 'Well, so am I. You owe me an apology. Both of you. And I'm not crossing this threshold again until I get one.'

28

Oliver didn't tell Jude that he'd had enough, that he couldn't hack it any more, he simply turned up on her doorstep in December, only two weeks after returning to France, and told her he could no longer live so far from the two people he most loved. Moving back to Dublin was like returning from exile, like coming home after a long spell abroad. He had far greater access to Tim, and when Fiona moved in with Theo the following January, Oliver and Jude could at last enjoy unbridled cohabitation.

They spent most of their time working. Oliver was under pressure to turn out another novel of the same calibre as *The Subtle Kill*, while Jude researched her thesis and did some teaching. They enjoyed working quietly in their adjacent studies – the distance that had separated them for years reduced to a mere wall – and found deep contentment in their daily routine. Unlike most couples, the minor irritations of intimate living had long since been addressed. It was the outer world that clawed into their happiness.

Their new living arrangement had further alienated Oliver's parents. Mrs Sayle remained convinced she owed her son no apology for expressing her legitimate concerns, so the rift between them remained firmly in place. When Jude reminded Oliver that he was lucky to have parents and urged him to apologize, he said, 'For what? For loving you?'

What bothered him more was his relationship with Tim. It was straining. Tim felt he'd been usurped. He and Jude had always shared Oliver, but now she was living with his dad full-time and he was just a visitor. He didn't like it, and this aggravated a drift that had already been there. Spending holidays together had never really worked. It was false. Patti and Jeremy dealt with the day-to-day highs and lows of Tim's life, knew his friends, his favourite television programmes, while Oliver had become a peripheral pal. He had fought this ardently, with some success, but his relationship with Jude had made things trickier.

Jude's friends, also, seemed uncomfortable with the union. Jude was never sure whether it was Oliver's age or success, or even his increasing wealth, but he simply wasn't integrated into the fold the way other boyfriends were, and since he had little inclination to squeeze into sweaty nightclubs where no one could hear themselves speak, Jude soon fell away from her college gang. A new social life evolved. They now mixed with writers and artists and journalists; they went to plays and private views, attended dinner parties where pointless but engaging arguments took place. Jude loved to see Oliver's eyes twinkling with mischief as he held down a point with absolutely no foundation; she loved, simply, to have him there, at the other side of anybody's table, and to take him home afterwards to gobble up his mind with love-making. And yet she often wondered what party she was missing and which pub wall her pals were pressed against.

In mid-May, when she discovered those same friends were hiring a mini-bus to drive down to Greece in July, there could be no more pretence that she still belonged in the gang.

Oliver was digging a hole in the back garden when she came home after finding out about the trip. He took one look at her. 'Uh-oh. What's up?'

'They're all off on a jaunt across the Continent. Never even asked me. Honestly, just because you're a bit older and richer, they think you wouldn't want to slum it on a beach in Greece.'

'Nor would I. Been there, done that.'

'Well, I haven't been there and I haven't done that and I wish I had.'

'You've done lots of other stuff instead.'

'Yes, but I've never bummed around Europe, have I? I've never sat on a beach in Greece or been a waitress in America or done a million other things I should have done.'

'You could have gone to America last year. You chose not to.'

'Because of you. Always because of you.'

'Ouch.'

'Sorry.'

'So go with them. I don't mind.'

'I haven't been invited, remember?'

'You could ask.'

'No. I'm not going to beg. Besides, I can live with it. You've fallen out with your parents, I've fallen out with my friends. Love costs.'

'It does, but it shouldn't. Anyway, you can't afford to lose touch with people like Emer and Theo, and Fiona's been your best friend for years.'

'You're my best friend. I don't need anyone else.'

'No one can live in a vacuum, Jude.'

'I can. I don't need much love to survive.' She sighed. 'I could live in a desert, if you'd only rain on me occasionally.'

He laughed. 'If that's the case, it isn't healthy. You should do that trip if only to get back in with them,' he said, wiping his arm across his forehead and smearing mud on his face.

Jude wiped it away. 'No. I'm spending the summer in France with my family. That crowd can take a running jump.'

The doorbell rang.

'I'll go,' said Jude. She went through the kitchen, up to the hall and opened the front door to find Lee Feehan standing on their doorstep.

Jude stepped back, as if to avoid a collision, but the shock was cushioned by prescience. The notion that this would happen one day had been well buried, but never killed off.

Her aunt hadn't changed. Like an old couch nobody wanted, she was as tatty as ever and wearing that same expression which implied that Civilization itself owed her. How *had* she transformed herself into the Mediterranean-style beauty that had seduced Oliver five years before?

She said, 'I understand Oliver is here. I need to see him.'

Jude's every instinct told her not to let her in. 'Why?'

'Look, if you don't let me in, I'll wait until he comes out.'

Oliver was planting a small tree when Jude went back to him. 'You'll love this,' he said. 'It's a katsura tree.'

'And you'll love this: Lee's here.'

His arms dropped.

'Seems your bestseller has finally brought her out of the woodwork.'

He stood up. 'Fine. I'll just go and tell her to fuck off, shall I?'

'It's never that easy with Lee.'

They went up to the living-room and sat side by side on the couch. Lee was agitated. She fiddled with her hair and seemed momentarily overcome in Oliver's presence. 'I couldn't believe it when Stephen told me you were in Dublin,' she gushed. 'I thought I'd have to go all the way to France.'

'What do you want?'

'We have something to discuss. Privately.' She glanced at Jude.

'Jude stays.'

'Well. Nothing ever changes.'

'That's right,' said Oliver. 'And you, above all, never change.'

Lee didn't blink. 'We have a daughter.'

Oliver's heart jammed in his chest, as if he'd been thrown against a wall, and his breath caught in his throat. Beside him, Jude slumped, as if she'd been punched.

'What?' he croaked.

'A daughter. You know, a child.'

'But . . . Why didn't you tell me?'

'You'd made it clear you didn't want to know.'

Jude turned to him slowly, incredulous. 'This is *possible*?'

He closed his eyes. The two women waited for him to say something, but he sat with his hand over his eyes, as if to block out the consequence of his earlier, and now inescapable, insanity.

'You weren't using anything?' Jude whispered, her voice gone.

'We were. I *thought* we were.'

Lee shuffled uneasily in her seat. 'The thing is, it's been great, really. She's a good little thing, but I need to get away. I haven't been anywhere in four years and if I don't get a break, I'll positively explode.'

Oliver's eyes opened; he leaned slowly towards her, as though he were looking at a very peculiar animal.

407

'Which would be very bad for our daughter, wouldn't it? And the thing is, I've been asked to join a jaunt around India. Can you believe it? I'm longing to go back, but it really wouldn't be easy with a small child and if you could take her for a few weeks, well, a month, I'd be dead grateful and it'd be so good for you to get to know her. I'd ask my neighbours, but six weeks is a bit long for people who aren't family and anyway, she's so excited about spending time with her dad—'

Jude heard little of this. Something cold and very small pierced her abdomen and made itself at home near the heart that was beating fiercely against her rib-cage.

'Hold it right there,' said Oliver. 'I'm not spending time with any child until I have proof that she's mine.'

'You won't need proof. One look'll do it. She's the spit of you.'

Oliver's shoulders slumped. Every part of him was shaking. Jude sat stupefied beside him.

'It's such a stroke of luck you're here,' Lee prattled on. 'The money I'd set aside for our fares to France will come in handy in India. Now she can travel back with you. You can put her on to your passport, no bother. Your name is on her birth certificate.'

Oliver looked at Lee with such weariness that Jude pitied him. To have a conversation with this woman was bad enough, but to have had a child with her! 'You can't go away and leave her with complete strangers,' he said.

'I'm leaving her with her father, darling. I've been in the exclusive company of a child for the last four years and if I don't get away, I'll go mad. I need a break.'

'This isn't the way to get one.'

'It's the only way I know.'

'Running away? Yeah, that's your style all right.'

'I'm not running away; I'm taking a holiday. How many holidays have *you* had in the last four years?'

'I'm not a single parent.'

'You are now.'

'That's not fair,' Jude snapped. 'He didn't know about this child. He didn't even want her! He still doesn't!'

Lee's gaze followed Oliver as he stood up and leaned over the mantelpiece. 'Oh, but I think he does.'

'If I have a daughter,' he said, 'I'll play my part, but not this way. Not on your terms. Let her get to know me in her own time and if she's happy with me, then you can take your wretched holiday.'

'I can't wait that long. My boyfriend, Hans, is taking me to India and he's leaving next week. I can't keep him waiting.'

'I couldn't give a toss if you keep God Himself waiting. You can't abscond like this!'

'All I'm asking for is a couple of months' babysitting.'

'This holiday is getting longer by the breath! A couple of months now?'

'Something like that. You know me.'

Oliver was reeling. Shock, anger and bewilderment at the sheer depth of Lee's audacity combined to give the impression that he was standing on a rolling cylinder. He placed both hands on either side of her armchair and leaned into her face. 'I'm warning you, Lee, if she is my daughter and you walk out on her, you'll never see her again.'

'You forget that I know you too well. You saw what it was like for Jude having no mummy from the age of four; you wouldn't do that to your own daughter.'

'Try me.' He straightened up.

'I am trying you. You haven't done one weekend with her. I've done four years. I've chalked up some time off.'

'Parenting isn't a job, Lee! There's no such thing as holiday leave or flexitime. That's not the deal with kids. You hang around until they no longer need you, not the other way around!'

'But you didn't stay around for Tim, did you? Or is it one rule for mothers and another for fathers?' She stood up. 'I'll bring her around tomorrow to meet you. At eleven. Her name is Cara.'

Oliver stood in her way. 'Not so fast. I won't let you do this. All your life you've wrought havoc on the people who loved you and I won't let you do it to your own daughter, whether she's mine or not. She deserves better, damn you.'

Lee faced him with contempt. 'You're in no position to moralize with me, Sayle. You used me and scorned me and I've come for my pay-back.' She stepped towards the door.

'I'll have you for desertion.'

'Desertion? *You* can talk.'

He lurched towards her, but Jude put her arms around his neck and held him back.

Lee stared. Her mouth twitched. Her eyes darkened. 'I see now how some things have changed. Cute, Oliver. How very cute. I wonder what Michael would say if he knew you'd shacked up with his daughter?'

Oliver broke away from Jude, pushed past Lee and stormed out of the house to stop himself from hitting her.

Lee stepped towards Jude with such a malevolent grin that her niece stood back. 'Good, isn't he, the old lech? Taught you everything you know, did he? Since when? Your thirteenth birthday? Earlier?'

Taking up where Oliver had left off, Jude hit her across the face, but Lee slapped her right back. 'You've had it all, haven't you, Jude? You've had everyone I ever wanted from

410

the day you were born. Michael, and Mummy, and now Oliver.' She shoved her; the back of Jude's head hit the wall. 'But you won't be keeping him, Jude Feehan. Not you, of all people. You've already had everyone else.' At the door, she delivered her final assault. 'By the way,' she said, 'what's it like sleeping with your own mother's lover?'

The hall door slammed. Jude slid down the wall to the floor.

She was still there, still shaking, when Oliver came in ten minutes later.

He knelt down. 'Jesus. What happened?'

'Is it true?'

'Is what true?'

'Did you sleep with my mother?'

'Did I *what*?'

She grabbed his shirt with both fists. 'You heard me!'

'What's been going on here? Did Lee do this?'

'Answer me!'

'That question doesn't warrant an answer. What in hell's got into you?'

Weakened, she leaned back against the wall. 'Your ex-lover had a go at me.'

'She knocked you about?' He went out to the hall. 'That's it. I'll nail her for assault before she can spell India!'

'You can't.'

Oliver pulled out the phone book. 'Just watch me.'

Jude went after him. 'Leave it!' She pulled the directory from his hands and hurled it across the hall. 'I hit her first.'

'She should be locked up.'

'I couldn't give a shit! I just want an answer!' She shoved him backwards. 'Did you sleep with Mummy? And you'd better fucking tell me, Oliver, or you'll never see me again!'

411

'You believe Lee? How could you fall for such a cheap trick?'

Jude grabbed his shirt again, her voice hoarse and horrible. 'Tell me the truth.'

'And you use your head. For Chrissake, what do you take me for?'

'I have a right to know!'

'So work it out for yourself, brickhead. You think she would have wanted an eighteen-year-old teenager? I was a kid when they got married!'

'What about *after* they got married?' Jude thumped him. 'If you slept with her even once, I could be your daughter!'

Oliver pulled her close to his face. 'You think there's a chance in hell I'd be sleeping with you if that could be the case? Do you?' He shook her. 'You want an answer? I'll give you your bloody answer. I never slept with your mother, *but by Christ I wanted to*.'

They sat on the hall floor in shock, sipping at a glass of whisky.

'Why have you always denied it?'

'It was a crush.'

'No. You were twenty-three when she died. You were in love with her. Say it.'

Oliver knocked his head against the wall. 'Yes. I was in love with her. For years and years. I betrayed them both with my love for her.'

'Did Dad know?'

'Probably.'

'Did you love him?'

'Why do you think I never made a move on Catherine?'

'But – that suggests she'd have had you . . . Would she?'

After a long pause he said, 'Possibly.'

'Oh God. So that's why you stayed when she was dying. Not for him. Not for me.'

'I couldn't leave her. Couldn't leave her, Jude.'

'So you transferred your affections to me.'

He turned to her, his expression doleful and tired. 'I transferred my affections to Patti. That's why it didn't work.'

They sat in silence against the wall, shoulder to shoulder.

'I have a daughter. Is that what she said? I have a daughter?'

Jude nodded.

'Good Christ. And her mother is unhinged. Like a wild angry cat no one ever loved.'

'How very swiftly everything can collapse,' said Jude flatly.

'Nothing has collapsed. It's only for a few months.'

'God, you're so naïve. What makes you think she has any intention of ever coming back from India?'

'The girl. The girl will bring her back.'

'Don't kid yourself, Oliver.'

Neither of them slept that night. In the morning, Jude wouldn't get up, even though Oliver was buzzing around like an agitated bird from eight o'clock, moving his work into Jude's study so that his study could be turned back into a bedroom when his daughter came to stay. As ten-thirty came, and then eleven, his agitation increased at the same pace as Jude's lethargy. She lay in bed listening to the radio, but when the doorbell rang, Oliver hesitated.

'I know it's a lot to ask, but please come down with me.'

She got up, in spite of herself, because love, in its bullying way, gave her no option.

They opened the door. The child looked up, blinked at her father and smiled. *How could something so small*, Jude wondered, *be so dangerous?*

'Well, hello,' said Oliver, crouching down to the child's level.

'Are you Daddy?'

He bit his lip. She had the most beautiful eyes. He wanted to say yes, *yes*, but couldn't answer for fear of lying.

Lee came up the path with a box which she deposited beside two suitcases at Oliver's feet. 'Toys.'

'Wait a minute . . .'

'Ha!' said Jude. 'What did I tell you?' She marched back to the kitchen.

Cara followed her. 'Where's my room? Do you have any cats? We have three.'

'What's going on?' asked Oliver, when Lee came back with more things.

'It's better this way. Better for her. Short and sharp. Better for me, too.'

'But I don't know anything about her. We need time!'

'You'll have plenty of time.'

He grabbed her arm. 'Wait a minute. There's something you need to know.' He shoved her into the living-room. 'If you insist on going away indefinitely, I'm going to apply for custody – and if it comes to court, I don't fancy your chances.'

'I have to get away, Oliver.'

He kicked the couch. 'Bugger you then for having the gall to become pregnant in the first place! How dare you have *my* child if you didn't want her.'

'I did! I desperately wanted her. That's why I went to France. You're the most decent man I know and the only one I'd loved, so . . .'

'So you decided to help yourself.' He sat down. 'You should have told me. I have rights.'

'Yeah, well you forfeited them when you told me to think

twice about ever crossing your threshold again, pregnant or otherwise. I did think twice. I was able to support her, and I knew I had the only part of you I was ever going to get.'

'And now you want to give it back. Five years on. Why?'

'Because she deserves a dad. She deserves you. She's a wonderful kid.'

'Stay with her then. *Please*. She needs her mother, Lee.'

The honest despair in his voice disarmed her; Lee gave up the fight. She sat down. 'Not this one, she doesn't. She'll be much better off with you.'

Oliver was unmoved. 'I see. This has been the plan all along, has it? This isn't about a holiday – you're giving up on her altogether.'

'I'm giving up on me, not her.' Lee looked at him. 'Don't you see? I can't do it. Staying in one place for so long has sucked me dry, but now that Cara's starting school, she needs stability, and I can't give her that any more.'

'Why not? It isn't difficult.'

'Oh, but it is. I thought having my own child would kill off the restlessness in me, but it's like malaria. It keeps coming back and there's no cure. I can't give her what you'll give her, especially with all this money you've made recently.'

'What makes you so sure I want her?'

'You could have thrown me out yesterday, but the thought never crossed your mind.'

Oliver stood up, his head moving from side to side, his arms hanging. 'You can't do this. She isn't a bag of used clothes.'

'I know, but there's a trace of chaos in me, Oliver. It does me no good and it will do her no good.'

'I want full custody then. I won't have you dropping by to take her away the next time your maternal urge kicks in.'

415

'You won't stop me seeing her, will you?'

Oliver felt himself shrinking. To have known Lee most of his life and to have made no impact on her sensibility made him a very small man indeed. 'How can you give up on her so easily?'

'It isn't easy. It's the hardest thing I've ever done. But I know you well, Oliver Sayle, and I know you'll be good to her.' Crying, she stood up. 'She stays up late, but she's a good eater. She sleepwalks a bit. Other than that, she's a normal four-year-old.' Lee stopped by the door. 'I love Cara more than I thought it possible to love. Why can't you see this is the least selfish thing I've ever done?'

'Because there are people who weep to have children.'

That afternoon, Oliver and Jude sat despondently in the garden watching Cara explore.

'I suppose she is mine,' said Oliver. 'But I'll do blood tests anyway.'

Jude said nothing. Lee was right. Cara looked more like Oliver than even Tim did, but it wasn't the straight black hair or cute face that laid claim to him, it was the large bright eyes.

'You're paying a high price for my folly,' he said.

She shrugged. 'What about Tim? How will he take it?'

'He was happy when Patti had the baby.'

'That was a lot different.'

'I know.'

'You reap what you sow.'

'But you're reaping it too. You seem so completely shattered.'

'I am shattered. Aren't you?' In reply, his eyes darted towards his daughter. 'Silly question. You've been broody since you bedded me. Now the child you wanted so badly has dropped out of the sky into your lap and you never even thought to ask me how I would feel about this child – *my cousin* – coming to live with us.'

For a moment, Oliver's eyes were like his brother's, a white angry rim cupping the iris. 'She won't affect our relationship any more than Tim does.'

Jude stood up, pulling her dressing-gown around her. 'But this is Lee's child. What makes you think I want *her* child in *my* house?'

'Don't be a bloody fool about this, Jude. We've too much to lose. I love you, all right? Like nobody else before or after, so don't kick me in the face when I've just been tripped over!'

'You tripped yourself, Oliver.'

'Hi, Dad.'

'Hi, Tim. You OK?'

'Yeah. You?'

'I've had better weeks. Listen, pal, there's stuff going on over here you need to know about. I'd love to come over to see you, but I can't get away at the moment, so . . .'

'What?'

'It seems . . . well, the thing is, you have a little sister.'

The condescending tone of the eleven-year-old: 'I know that, Dad.'

'I don't mean Lisa, I mean you have another one over here.'

Silence.

'See, an old girlfriend of mine came along the other day and told me she'd had a baby a few years back and that I'm her dad.'

'Are you?'

'Er, yeah. Yeah, I am, Tim.'

Another pause. 'What's her name?'

'Cara. She's four. I'm sorry to drop this on you, but I didn't know about her myself until recently.'

'Oh.'

'And look, her mum's going through a bit of a crisis, so Cara's going to be living here for a while.'

'With you? All the time?'

Oliver could hear a sulk creeping into Tim's voice. 'Yeah.'

'What about France?'

'She'll come with us.'

'But you promised we'd do stuff together.'

'We will. Lotsa stuff. Meanwhile, would you like to come over to meet her?'

'No, thanks.'

'Tim—'

'I've got to go. Bye, Dad.' He handed the phone back to his mother.

'That went down like a lead balloon,' said Patti. 'Really, Oliver, this is a bit much on top of losing his big sister to his father's bed.'

'Don't make it sound sordid.'

'Why not? It *is* sordid, and so is this.'

'Seems I've managed to upset just about everyone.'

Suddenly Patti giggled. 'What a joke. You and Lee! I should have seen *that* coming!'

Oliver was living in a strange world. His daughter was a delight, Jude as prickly as a sea urchin. He soared between pleasure and despair. He liked Cara. He had liked her the moment he'd seen her standing on his doorstep, and that moment had been branded into his being as a high point in his life, while the same moment, to Jude, seemed dark and thunderous and riveted with risk. She felt as if a weight had landed on her shoulders and she was struggling to keep on her feet.

Three days after Cara's arrival, Oliver came to her in the kitchen. 'Please, love. Shake this off.'

'I can't. This isn't what I want, Oliver. I've been on the periphery of families all my life and I can't do it any more. First it was you and Patti, then you and your parents, now it's you and her. What about you and me? Where have we gone to?'

'We're right here.'

'No. The last five months have been the best I've ever known. I've belonged somewhere. I've felt grounded. And for the first time in eight years, I didn't have to spend my days missing you.'

'You don't have to miss me now either.'

'I'm missing you already.'

Cara's excitement at her new life lived on into the fourth day, and when Jude came in from college that evening, she found Sinéad and her two-year-old son, Declan, sitting outside with Oliver, who had collapsed into a garden seat.

'We're the rearguard,' Sinéad explained. 'We came to give back-up when the first battalion crashed.'

'I'd forgotten what it's like,' Oliver moaned. 'Your mind can't even go blank for a moment, especially with a chatter-box like this one.' Jude stroked his hand. 'I'll get you tea,' he said, getting up.

'She's such a live wire,' said Sinéad.

'Oh, yes. Little Miss Personality, that's our Cara.'

'A bit on the wild side, though. I gather Lee let her run all over the place. Are you OK? You look fairly washed out.'

'Motherhood came rather suddenly to me.'

'You'll be all right. Oliver's fantastic with her.'

Jude heard Oliver speaking to Cara in the kitchen. She recognized the tone. She hadn't heard it for years, but she remembered it. He used to speak to her that way, with affection and humour, never ever talking down to her, making no concession to her smallness. 'He's had plenty of practice.'

'Well, he missed out on a lot with Tim.'

'I didn't mean Tim. I meant me.'

'Oh, yes. I see.'

When Cara came running out with Declan, Jude went in and caught Oliver by the fridge. 'Tough day in the nursery, Daddy?'

He hugged her. 'I love you to death, you know that, don't you? I couldn't do this without you.'

This encounter cheered him; he seemed livelier in the garden, especially when Peter joined them and presented a bottle of champagne to the proud father.

'This isn't a christening,' Jude grumbled.

'All the same,' said Peter, his pink face clashing with his yellow-blond hair, 'it's not every day you discover you have a daughter.'

To compound Jude's discomfort, the party atmosphere was amplified when Theo, Fiona and Emer arrived, unable to still their curiosity any longer. All agreed that Cara was a pet, if somewhat precocious, and she was obviously well used to adult company, because she moved from one to the other chatting happily. Delighted to turn the evening into a welcome party, Oliver raced down to the off-licence for a crate of wine and insisted everyone stayed for dinner.

Jude spent the evening watching the man she loved fall in love with someone else. Too often she caught him gazing at the little girl, and it made her sad, not for herself, but for the child she had been, whose only favour in life had been the steady devotion of her father's friend. That child was being blotted out, carried off, usurped now, by his love for his own daughter.

The following morning, she shook Oliver awake. 'I'm off. Get the study sorted out, will you? I can hardly find my desk with all your stuff piled on top of it.'

'Aw, Jude. Did you have to wake me? I didn't get Cara to bed until after one.'

'I need my study back.'

He pulled her back to kiss her. 'I'm mad you woke me, but when people stop being affectionate it makes way for a bloody dangerous gap, and I'm not prepared to let that happen to us.'

Jude returned that afternoon to find he had done what he could with the small room that had been her study, pushing his own things into one corner to give her minimal space in which to work. She tried to study, but was too preoccupied. With everything she felt for him, it should have been easy to stick with him, to bring up his child, and yet the ice-cold particle that had taken residence within her grew in spite of her love. To acknowledge it made her hands shake with terror. She had to control it. Surely she was strong enough to control it?

The phone rang. Oliver answered; it was Mrs Sayle. He stood wearily in the hall and endured a long tirade from his distraught mother, who had heard about Cara from Stephen, and hung up as Jude came down the stairs. In mock imitation of his mother's voice, he screeched, '"What an unpleasant little ménage you've made for yourself, Oliver Sayle!"'

'She wouldn't mind if you weren't living with me.'

'Jude, the woman is delighted. I have finally lived up to all her worst expectations. Oh, it was tough there for a while, what with me being successful and all, but she's dead happy now. Hell, I'm sleeping with a minor and impregnating women all over the place, which is just what she's expected from me all along.'

'She loves you.'

'I know. But only on *her* terms. Come on, dinner's ready.'

Dinner was trying. They couldn't speak, such was Cara's prolixity, and at the end of the meal, she announced, 'I want to go home now.'

Jude and Oliver exchanged glances. The real fun had begun.

It was a difficult week. Cara cried for her mother some of the time, sulked with remarkable efficacy at other times, and refused point blank to do anything for Oliver until he took her back to her cottage in West Cork. She was particularly uncooperative with regard to noise and frequently drew Jude out of her study screaming in irritation. Only once, when Oliver was completely flattened, did Jude agree to mind her cousin while he got some rest. Other than that, she made no attempt to help.

'I have to get on with my thesis,' she told him.

'What about my book? I haven't had time to sniff at it since Cara turned up.'

'You should have thought of that before you took her on.'

'What was I supposed to do? Leave her on the street?'

'There were options; you just didn't consider them. You welcomed her without a blink.'

'Sometimes you sound remarkably like a jealous wife.'

'I am jealous. Why wouldn't I be?'

'Because love for a child and the love between a man and a woman don't compete, Jude. They live side by side. How else do you think the world goes around? Besides, you never had any problem with Tim.'

'I don't have to compete with Tim.'

'You're not competing with Cara either!'

'Of course I am. She has your affection. Your attention. Your every waking hour. That doesn't leave much for me.'

'It's temporary. It'll settle down.'

'I've watched your heart divide this last week.'

'It could divide tenfold if I had ten children, but I wouldn't love you any less.'

'And if they were my children, you would love me even more.'

As they spoke, Cara was in Jude's study wreaking vengeance on her captors by throwing about the neat pile of papers stacked on the desk. When Jude found her, she came close to hitting her. 'You little B!' she screamed. 'That's my thesis!' Cara was so alarmed she bolted downstairs, screaming, 'Daddy, Daddy!'

Jude fell into her seat and wept. Until then, Cara had not referred to Oliver in any capacity, but Jude's outburst had driven the child to recognize him as her father, her protector, as the one she loved, or would soon love. Jude felt herself sliding further down the spiral that Lee had so deftly placed her on. She looked about to see if there was anything to grab on to, but it was like a water slide with high rims – nowhere to go except down. She spluttered quietly, willing Oliver to come and find her, to care for her feelings, for her thesis, but when he did come, he brought Cara with him. They quickly picked up the pages and took them away to sort them out, and the ice particle grew a little more as Jude was left weeping on her own. She looked at the picture of her parents on the shelf. 'Why did you leave me with no one in the world except *him*?'

*

Over succeeding weeks, during daily conversations with his
father, Tim became grudgingly resigned to sharing the
summer with his half-sister and began looking forward to
going to Landor. Cara, also, calmed down and accepted her
fate, but in practical terms Oliver continued to struggle with
the child's body clock, failing to get her to bed earlier than
she was accustomed, as she followed him about until after
midnight. The days weren't much better. Used to going
wherever she wanted, she wandered into the street so often
that Oliver became nervous of taking his eyes off her. She
never watched television, being unaccustomed to it, and
since she was used to a solitary existence in the country, she
didn't like playing with other kids either. When Oliver tried
to leave her in a local playschool one day so that he could
work, she screamed blue murder and wouldn't let him go.
Abandoned by one parent, she wasn't letting go of the other,
so he set up his computer in the dining-room and went back
to his novel with Cara playing behind him, interrupting him
with a dig in the ribs every five minutes. He came to breaking point a month after her arrival, when Jude came home
one day to find him shaking with frustration and
exhaustion.

She shrugged. 'What can I do?'

They hadn't made love for weeks. Oliver came to bed too
late and was always asleep in the morning, and the gap to
which he had alluded began to wedge itself between them.
They kissed less. Touched less. They existed in the same
house without particular affection, because the child was
never away from him. He apologized, he begged for time, he
went through several comical attempts to keep Cara
distracted long enough for him to make love to Jude, but it
never worked. She was like an oblong cushion jammed
between them and no matter how far they reached out or

the strength of their desire, they failed to make contact. Oliver was constantly tired; Jude in a state of immobilizing panic.

One afternoon, Jude shuddered when she looked out and saw father and daughter frolicking on the lawn together. She watched from the window for a long time, like a stalker spying on a man she desired but could not have. She wanted to strip Oliver of his black shirt and neat black cords; to feel the hands that grasped his daughter's waist all over her own body; to press the head of straight black hair that lay in the grass against her breast. Oliver whooped with laughter. It had been obvious from the outset that he had clicked with Cara, that in spite of his antipathy towards her mother, there was something unseen between him and his daughter which no one would ever breach. No one.

Cara had been with them for five weeks when Jude woke one morning in June and felt small toes on her back. She turned. The child was asleep in the bed between them.

'Right,' she said quietly. 'That's it.'

She got up and packed some things. In the kitchen, she wrote on a paper bag, '*You know where I've gone to,*' and left.

29

It was drizzling lightly when Jude stopped the car and looked across the lake at St Malachy's. The pupils had gone home for the summer, but she fancied she could smell the air in those rooms, hear the echo of teachers' voices and the shuffle of books around desks. She might have been sitting at the back of a classroom, so vividly could she imagine it. She released the brake and drove on towards the hotel.

Sr Aloysius burst into the parlour some hours later. 'Jude Feehan! What a wonderful surprise!'

Jude stood up as the nun embraced her. Sr Aloysius looked older, but her cheeks were as rosy, her nose as sharp and her face as warm as ever. Jude wondered why she had left it so long to visit the woman who had mothered her with such subtlety through her school years and why it always took a crisis to bring her back.

They talked about the school until tea and scones were brought by a young nun. Sr Aloysius poured. 'And how is Mr Sayle? I was most impressed with his latest book, weren't you?'

'Em . . .' *Oh God – she's read all those graphic sex scenes!*

I hope she doesn't think Oliver . . . 'Yes. Yes, it was very imaginative.'

'So glad he proved himself after all that rubbish he used to churn out.'

Jude smiled. 'Goodness, you were certainly on to him!'

'The man who sat with me here was not the person writing those books,' said Sr Aloysius. 'There was so much more to him.'

She's on to her favourite subject, Jude thought.

'Is he well? You *are* still in touch?'

'Oh, yes. He's fine.' Jude nibbled on a scone.

Sr Aloysius watched her. 'Why is it, Jude, that I feel you're on the run again? Is everything quite well with you?'

She put down her plate. 'Not really, Sister.'

'Oh dear. I had hoped all your trials were behind you.'

'So had I.'

'Is there anything I can do? You need guidance with your career options, perhaps?'

'No. Nothing like that.'

'Ah. A question of love, then?'

'Yes. It's that boring, I'm afraid.'

'Oliver?'

Jude almost toppled her tea.

The nun smiled. 'No need to be so surprised, dear. I may live in a community of sisters, but I am not blindfolded.'

'Sister?'

'I've never seen two people so comfortable in each other's company.'

'You . . . You *what*?'

'You love each other very much, I would have thought.'

'Yes, but I don't think you understand. You see, we're, we, that is, we live together now. You know, as . . . as —'

'Lovers? Yes, that's exactly what I mean. Do you know what I like most about being celibate, Jude? It helps me to see things. It gives me great clarity because I am not embroiled by the complications of my own sexuality.'

Jude was so stunned, she didn't even blush. 'But when did you work it out? Not when I was at school?'

'It crossed my mind, yes.'

Jude gasped. 'There was nothing going on then, Sister!'

'I should hope not. But there was an easiness between you which I thought might one day come to something.' She smiled. 'You still enjoy such graceful companionship?'

'Oh, yes.'

'So what are you doing here?'

'Trying to think. With your help.' Jude sat back. 'Oliver wants to get married, but I keep resisting and I don't know why, because I can't imagine existing without him. After all, I have never had to.'

'Have you any idea where this reluctance springs from?'

'I'm too young to get married.'

'Ah. And Oliver must be . . . ?'

'Forty-one next month. He says he can wait, but now there's another complication: he has a daughter.'

The nun's eyes dipped sideways. 'A son, I thought?'

'That's Tim, but he has a daughter as well. We've only just found out about her. And her mother . . . is my aunt.' It occurred to Jude that if Sr Aloysius had refused, five years before, to give Lee their address in France, Cara would never have been conceived.

'Oh dear.' Jude had finally managed to wipe the all-knowing placidity from the nun's face, but not for long. 'But how exactly does this affect you, and your decision to marry?'

'My aunt has taken off and left us with the girl. Just like that.'

428

'Gracious. How very difficult for Oliver.'

'Very difficult, but I couldn't care less. I want our lives back, Sister. I feel like I've walked into a glass door. I can see where I was going, but I can't get any closer. And my face aches.'

'Jude. Dear. You and Oliver have come through a spectacularly unusual obstacle course to find each other as you have. This child is surely just another obstacle, beyond which you will continue as you were.'

Jude shook her head. 'It isn't just the girl. When Dad was hit by that boat, I was the one who was shipwrecked. I was marooned and Oliver was my life raft. We've been bobbing along together all this time, into the troughs and over the waves, taking a soaking every now and then, but unable ever to separate. And the thing is, I can't spend my life in a raft, can I?'

'Why not? Is it sinking?'

'No, but he's taken another waif aboard and there isn't room for both of us. I should jump and swim for shore. Get my feet on to solid ground for once.'

'Oh, Jude. Such talk. Love is not so easy to find, you know, that you can be so careless with it.'

'You think I should stay with him? With them?'

'I think you should not spurn love. Where God has the grace to give it, it should be humbly received.'

An hour later, driving up the tree-shaded avenue of the Pink Palace, as Oliver called it, Jude saw the tail end of his car in the car park. *How did he get here so quickly?* Her heartbeat accelerated. When she parked, she saw him sitting by the table at the foot of the lawn. The day had cleared into a fine evening. She walked apprehensively towards him.

He folded his newspaper. 'So,' he said sharply. 'You've

run away. For the third time. It must be in the Feehan blood.'

Jude sat down and put her hands between her knees. 'I left a note.'

'You promised you'd never do this again.'

'You needn't have come.'

'I have, nonetheless.' Oliver stretched out his legs, rested his hands on his belly. 'But I hope I haven't come all this way to talk you out of anything foolish.'

She looked around. 'Where's Cara?'

'With Sinéad.'

'Good old Sinéad.'

He squinted. 'What makes you so bitter?'

'Losing you.'

He sighed. 'So I do have my work cut out. Where's all this coming from, Jude? And why now? Of all times, why now?'

'Because Cara left the door open when she arrived and lots of other stuff came marching in behind her.'

'Doubts?'

'Terrors.'

He looked away, his jaw flexing with tension.

'How long can you stay?' she asked.

'How long will it take?'

'For ever, I wish.'

'We can't dump on Sinéad for too long. Cara was less than impressed at being left there –'

And she comes first, of course.

'– but we've earned some time off.'

Jude looked up. Oliver winked, which made her smile at him for the first time in weeks. He reached across the table for her hand. Their fingers fiddled like indecisive knitting needles, engaging and disengaging. His thumb stroked her wrist. He hadn't shaved, his shirt was unironed, and he looked weary and worn. *He would benefit from a few days' rest*, Jude thought, *if I could only let him be.*

'We have the same room as last time,' she said. 'I asked for it.'

'Let's go in.'

The long salmon-pink room with the green carpet and tall windows hadn't changed, but it was dim, and loaded. Jude threw her handbag on the couch and turned to speak but, seeing Oliver standing by the alcove, forgot what she had meant to say. They stared at each other. Oliver's unkempt appearance made him look bearded in the dim light and his posture was as weary as it had been when he had come for her two years before. In his eyes also, Jude was the same dishevelled student he had rescued from herself in this same place. He twisted slightly on his feet and Jude stood, stunned, as though a seduction was about to take place for the first time. After a moment they moved simultaneously, clashing together like misdirected waves, and took on the eroticism which flew at them from every corner of the room.

Jude was nineteen again and Oliver had never touched her before. She felt embarrassed when he pulled off her blouse and her palms registered his skin with such unfamiliarity that excitement thumped against her veins as though it would never have its fill. Recent deprivation made them gluttonous, but it was the past, too, which made them tear at each other like hungry cats, and although it startled them, they responded without circumspection. Oliver slid down her abdomen to his knees, pulling off her jeans, kissing her navel; she lowered herself to him. He pushed her on to the couch, his mouth travelling so fast about her that it didn't seem to know what it was looking for, and there, on the short hard couch, they consummated the unacknowledged, unacceptable, inclination of another time.

'You were right,' said Jude, when they had climbed on to the bed. 'It all comes back to here. Do you think I've been in love with you since then?'

'No. We set off from here, that's all.'

'Oh, help. I hope it wasn't desperation that made it so good.' She stretched herself along him, relishing the bareness she had missed for weeks. 'It isn't just Cara, you know.'

'I know.'

'How do you know?'

'Because loving me should carry you over the shock of a child coming into our lives.'

'But I do love you and it isn't carrying me anywhere.'

'I can see that.' He turned to her. 'Listen, Jude. I know we've got stuff to sort out, but we haven't had time together for five weeks and we're in the most beautiful part of the country on the longest day of the year. Let's celebrate the solstice, instead of dragging through all this undergrowth.'

It was easy to relent. Jude didn't wish to spoil what had been so hard to come by and could so easily be lost.

They bathed together in the peaty water of the West and had an early dinner by a tall window in the dining-room. Oliver's eyes widened as their starters were placed before them. He hadn't been eating properly; Cara had interrupted almost every meal since she'd arrived and in those weeks, Jude realized, she had not even made him a cup of coffee. To punish him, of course. She had been punishing him since the day Cara turned up. *My God*, she thought, *how I have chastised you*.

She watched him eat, and it made her ache with love. She

wanted to mother him, mind him, feed him, fuck him, and yet she would probably throw him on the slag heap.

After dinner, Oliver looked out at the pink mist shading the mountains beyond the inlet. 'We can't stay surrounded by hills on the longest day of the year. Let's get to the coast, see the latest sunset.'

They took the road to Tullycross and carried on straight, heading west, towards a particular beach Jude hoped to find.

'What's it called?' asked Oliver.

'Carricknatrawbaunia.'

'Come again?'

They bumped along a boreen until they found themselves perched above a spread of the Atlantic that seemed as deep and expansive as all Jude's fears. As he parked by the beach, Oliver reached over to select a particular CD, and then a particular track, and he winked at Jude when B. B. King started singing 'Help the Poor'.

She laughed at the pitiful request for love in the lyrics and got out of the car. Oliver turned up the music. They danced. Twirling, exaggerating, laughing, they skidded across the gravel, Oliver aping the blues.

Behind them, night was moving in, banishing its greatest foe: the longest day. Ahead, the sun, a dim orange ball, slid thoughtlessly towards the sharp edge of the sea after an extended day's work. A curlew overhead joined in with the music, chirping its curious call, and swallows dipped about in the gloaming like bats searching for a barn. A donkey brayed behind a hill. As the sun slipped out of sight, they jived around beside the car, the Atlantic before them, Tully Mountain behind.

*

433

Oliver cried out. Jude woke with a start. 'What's wrong?' She reached out in the darkness. He was sitting up.

'Nightmare,' he gasped. Jude knelt up behind him. 'I knew it was a dream but I couldn't get out of it.'

'Tell me.'

'It'll sound ridiculous.'

'Dreams *are* ridiculous. What was it about?'

'Your mum and dad.'

'Oh, great.'

'They were taking Cara away from me. Dragging her away, and she was screaming and screaming and I couldn't get her back. I couldn't move.'

Jude leaned back, pulling him against her.

'They can haunt me until I'm white with terror, Jude, but I've done you no harm and I'll do you no harm. They've nothing to reproach me for.'

'You're talking about the dead, Oliver.'

'Whenever I dream about your parents, they're pissed with me.'

'That's your conscience working overtime. Like you said, they have nothing to reproach you for. You've made me very happy.'

'Why are you thinking of leaving me then?'

He knew; as always, he knew. She meant to deny it, but said instead, 'Because happiness isn't the only thing worth aspiring to.'

Oliver dropped on to the pillow. 'I thought we'd have longer.'

'We would have, if Cara hadn't chanced along.'

'You can't leave me,' he said, rolling over and pinning her down. You've had twenty-two years of my life. You can't do it after all this time!'

'You're probably right. I probably can't.'

434

'I couldn't live without you, you must know that?'

And the ice particle that had been growing inside her shattered, piercing her with shards because it wasn't true what he said. He *could* now live without her. Cara would insist upon it.

'I got Cara to bed at ten o'clock last night,' Sinéad said, when Oliver rang the following morning before Jude woke. 'I think she's winding her daddy around her little finger.'

'That's fantastic. Any chance you could hold out a bit longer?'

'Sure. Take as long as you like. You and Jude need a holiday.'

'A holiday?' He laughed bitterly. 'Is that what you call it? I'm in the manure here.'

'Oliver, no! She isn't backing out, is she?'

'Looks like it.'

'But why? Not because of Cara?'

'Cara's only the spur. We're up against it every other way. You didn't really believe it had a hope in hell, did you?'

'Yes, I did. I did, yes. Why not?'

'The girl hasn't lived, Sinéad, and I've lived too much. Look, thanks for minding Cara. And remember, she wanders. She's—'

'Oliver, forget about Cara. Just concentrate on your own happiness – and get it right this time.'

When Jude woke, they enjoyed a long breakfast at the table in their room. It seemed that while they ate, passing the butter and marmalade, slicing bacon and skewering grilled tomato with their forks, they were able to forget what was happening. Their last sojourn there had been so traumatic they wanted to wipe out the memories with better ones. Oliver cleared his plate and went to the window.

435

It was a dull, grey morning. 'What do you want to do today?'

'I want to pretend I'm nineteen again, and that this is all ahead of me.'

'And not behind you?'

She shrugged. 'How's Cara?'

'Do you care?'

'Yes. What did Sinéad say?'

'That you should stay with me at all costs.'

'Sinéad's right.'

He came over and stroked her hair absent-mindedly. 'I should have left you alone, free to love someone your own age.'

'Don't talk rot.'

'And I should leave you alone now, if that's what you want.'

'I want *you*. I just don't want a child as well.' She gritted her teeth. 'And something else is nipping at me, Oliver. It's like a cloud of mosquitoes following me around, filling me with dread no matter which way I turn.' She looked up. 'You have to save me from this. You've saved me from everything else.'

'I can't. I won't. I don't want you turning around when I'm fifty wishing you had a young man of thirty to make your head spin, so I won't stand in your way if you want to have a shot at something else. Someone else.' He kissed her fingers. 'But don't expect me to make it easy.'

Later, they walked through the woodland until they came to a felled tree. Oliver sat on it. 'Explain this to me, would you?'

'I'll try.' Jude sat close to him. 'I hate what Cara's done to me,' she said quietly. 'I hate what she's done to my house and my life, but above all, I hate what she's done to you. These last few weeks have been very lonely, but it's been a different kind of loneliness, and the terrible thing is I'm getting used to it. Part of me even likes it.'

He flinched, but kept his eyes firmly on the slim beech trees that gave a striped view of the inlet at the foot of the hill. 'How can you be lonely when you have me?'

'I don't know. I just . . . It's as if I can't quite see you any more, and maybe that's because you no longer exist without Cara and I no longer have the luxury of contemplating life with you, or marriage to you, or children by you, without considering her part in it. I mean, let's face it – you're not the man I fell in love with, you're a full-time father with different needs and altered plans, which comprehensively damage my own plans. Why should I settle down at twenty-two because your daughter has to start school?'

Oliver was about to speak, but Jude rushed on. 'This has opened my eyes, Oliver, and just look at the way I've been living – so *settled*, so *sensible*, so much like my parents with my eye on the ball all the time. Well, I *won't* be like them. I want more than love and work. I want space, scope, experience.'

'Listen to me,' he urged her. 'Lee has put a frigging unexploded grenade between us – are you going to give her the satisfaction of seeing it go off? We can deal with this!'

'How?'

'By giving it time. You can't expect either of us to adjust in the space of a few weeks. A couple of months' restitution in France will throw some light on things.'

'But I don't want to go to France any more. I won't spend the summer sitting around the pool making sure Cara doesn't fall into it. I won't be your unpaid nanny.'

'You do it for Tim.'

437

'I *love* Tim.'

'You could love her too! She's your cousin. The family you've never had has finally arrived, Jude!' He stood up, seething. 'I haven't asked you for one darned thing since Cara turned up. She came like a bolt out of the blue. It's been difficult, trying, and you've behaved like a spoilt brat, a jealous wife, a real horse's ass – and I've allowed it, God knows why.'

'Hey, you haven't been so lily-white either. You took Cara in without any regard for my feelings.'

'I had no choice! And why can't you understand that my feelings for her make no dint on my love for you?'

'Because she's taken so much from me. She's taken your time, your attention. Even that wink. And she's taken my childhood away. Everything you did with me, for me, every way you fleshed out my life when there was no one else to do it, you're doing now with her. What was unique to me is being duplicated for somebody else. And it was my heritage, Oliver, my only heritage.'

'This isn't worthy of you, Jude, and it isn't a legitimate reason for leaving me. You closed your heart to Cara the moment you saw her.'

'Of course I did. She has the potential to destroy us.'

'No. You're doing that all by yourself.' He walked about. 'I need your support right now. Is that so much to ask?'

'Of course not, but the thing is, I'm all out of support. Because you've become pretty costly, you know. I've shared my house, my space, my time with your child; I've lost my peace of mind and I've fallen behind with work, but I'd give up a lot more if I weren't running out of funds. I need something to live on *for me*.' She went to him. 'This is hurting me now, Oliver. You expect me to stand by while the pivot of your existence shifts to someone else, to support you while all your priorities change at my expense. Well, I can't do it. I won't let Cara dictate how I spend my life, because I've realized that my life was heading in the wrong direction. She ties us down, and that's exactly what you want.'

'I want you. That's all I want.'

'And Cara.'

'She has no one else.'

Jude stood with her back to him.

He sat down again. 'Has it occurred to you that you're treating Cara the way Lee treated you? That you're blaming a child for coming between you and her father?' He chuckled bitterly. 'And the huge irony is that you're doing it to Lee's own daughter.'

Jude bit her lip. The analogy was too horrible.

'Perhaps now you have a better understanding of your aunt?'

She turned. 'Stop. It's more complicated than that. Cara is only part of it.'

'So you said. What's the other part?'

'It bothers me that you were so irretrievably in love with Mummy. It was unresolved, unconsummated, and then she died. That's a potent combination, and it marked you for life. We both know I look like her. I behave like her. And I find myself wondering sometimes, if you're in love with me or with her reflection?'

'You can't mean this?'

She sat down with him. 'There's more. Do you realize I have no memories that don't include you? There's no part of me that doesn't have your stamp on it – not my childhood, nor my adolescence, nor my adulthood. I loved who you loved; my bereavements were your bereavements. I couldn't even lose my virginity without you.'

'You had every opportunity.'

439

'I'll ignore that.'

He nodded.

'The point is, this whole thing is overwhelming me. *You* overwhelm me. You're where I've come from and where I'm going and, I don't know, I'm beginning to feel smothered. This relationship leaves nothing to chance, gives me nothing to dream about. I feel like a bloated sponge and if I don't squeeze myself out, I'll rot.'

'But what we have – this love that goes backwards and forwards – gives us more than most people can even aspire to.'

'We can't aspire to it either. We already have it.'

'And I've bloody earned it!'

'While I've earned nothing at all. I've always been sitting passively in your nest.'

'Listen,' said Oliver, 'I understand that you need a new perspective, that you might grow better with a fresh outlook, so do it. Take a leap. Do all that spreading your wings business. I don't mind. I'll wait.'

'But I don't know where such a leap would take me. I don't *want* to know. I can't go on in this three-legged race. I have to stop living your life and start living mine.'

'You can live it *with* me.'

'How? How can I live with you and be separate from you? We've become symbiotic, for God's sake.'

Oliver picked up a twig and snapped it.

'It's my head doing this, you know, not my heart.' The more she spoke, the smaller Oliver seemed to become. 'Sr Al said, don't be careless with love, but what about being careless with life? Wouldn't it be careless to live in someone else's shadow?'

'You're not in my shadow.'

'I am. I was caught in your slipstream the day I was born.'

'And all this time, I thought you were the one pulling

me along.' Oliver stood up. 'Have you made a decision yet? Am I hanging around here just waiting to have my face kicked in?'

'Of course not. I keep hoping I'll wake up one morning and all these doubts will have vanished. Maybe, when they wear themselves out, we'll still be together.'

'But you can't be sure?'

She shook her head; they walked on through the wood.

As the day cleared, the hotel provided them with a picnic and a rug, and directed them to a spot at the foot of Diamond Hill, where they settled by a stream.

Oliver handed Jude a glass of wine. 'This is more like a first date than a last. This is where I'm supposed to pull out the ring and tell you I can't live without you.'

'Except that you can.'

'Don't be so sure.'

'Cara needs you.'

'And I need you.'

'I know. But if we were to separate '

'Can't we eat without using dirty words like that?'

And so they romanced as they ate, sharing cherries, nibbling lettuce leaves and drinking stream water from each other's palms. Afterwards, Oliver lay with his head on Jude's lap, a glass of wine in hand. 'What was the worst day you spent with me?'

'What is this, a post-mortem?'

'Come on, worst day?'

They both said, 'Stephen's wedding!' and laughed.

'Best?' Jude asked.

'Any day in Cavalière. You?'

She ran her fingers through his hair. 'The best might yet be to come.'

441

'Christ, Jude. Don't toy with me.'

'I'm not.' She looked down at him. 'Frankly, I'd rather see you with another woman than never see you again. So maybe we should go back – back to where it was just right?'

'This is just right.'

'Back to, say, my eighteenth birthday? Love in the right dimension.'

Oliver sat up. 'You can't be serious? I *fancy* you, all right? So if you don't want what I have to offer, fine, get the hell out of my life, but don't expect your good old guardian to come bailing you out any time you need someone, because he disappeared the moment he kissed you and he's not coming back!' He stood up. 'I mean, fuck, I'd never get past it if we had to play happy families!'

'That's the coward's way out. We've known each other for twenty-two years and we've been lovers for less than ten months. Why can't we retrieve—'

'Because I've fallen in love with you!'

'You can fall out of love with me. People do it all the time.'

'Is that what you've done?'

'No. No, I haven't, but I've a good mind to give it a bloody good try. We have to salvage something, Oliver, the friendship at—'

The growl that came from Oliver's throat made her jump. 'No! There is nothing beyond this. Beyond this, I have nothing left for you, because you already have it all. So you make your choice, Jude, but you make it carefully, because if you leave me, that's it. Last page. No addendum. Covers closed.'

'But what about Stephen and Tim? They're family to me, and *you*—'

He raised his hands. 'If you leave me, then you stay away from my family and you stay away from me. Please, Jude.'

'You don't mean that.'

He dropped to his knees and took her elbows. 'Come to Landor. Give it two months.'

'That'll only make it harder!'

His eyes like a cold ocean, he let go. 'Damn you, Jude. I knew you'd do this to me.'

'You should have heeded my warning. About the Feehans. This rotten family has given you nothing but grief.'

'You seem to forget that my daughter is also a Feehan.'

At dinner, Oliver ate with less appetite than the previous night. His cheeks were hollow, his eyes rimmed, his movements sluggish. He hadn't really expected this could happen so quickly. Nor had Jude, but courage had come, uninvited, and waited like the last train for her to step aboard. If she did not, it would leave without her and she would never know anything of life beyond the Sayles and the Feehans, and the Feehans and the Sayles.

'Would you give me the house?' she asked.

'The division of the spoils already? I thought you hadn't made up your mind?'

'I may never make up my mind.'

Oliver looked out. 'Let's go for a drive.'

He drove wildly, tearing past the convent as the long bright evening grew dim along the road; the lakes shone like gun-metal and the hilltops absorbed all remaining light. As they slid around a bend and drove between the Maumturks and the Twelve Pins, Jude tried to lift herself, to soar on the scenery, but she remained heavy, stuck to the seat of the car. Oliver put his foot down on the long straight stretches; Jude turned up the music. The tourists who had swarmed over Connemara by day had vanished into hostelries, where, no doubt, they were tapping their feet to traditional bands,

443

leaving the high splendour of the Pins to the low spirits of Oliver and Jude.

Some way along Ballynahinch Lake, they pulled on to the verge. They stumbled over rough, grassy mounds to reach a short stony stretch beside the lake. 'It's so black,' said Jude, looking across the water. Overhead, the first star pricked the evening. Oliver brought the rug from the car and spread it alongside a rock. They sat, holding hands, and watched the day slide away to the west, a yellow rim chased by a deep blue night.

Diminished and hurt, Oliver kissed Jude, gently at first and then with more insistence. She slid on to her back.

It hurt. It hurt because with every thrust a small, sharp stone dug into her hip, but she welcomed the pain because it distracted her from misery. Oliver made her come three times, so banishing her modesty that, like a woman racked in labour, she wouldn't have cared if a busful of tourists had seen her trying to dispel the agony. Nor did she care that her cries echoed far beyond the nonplussed hills of Connemara, because she wanted his loving deeper than was possible, longer than was reasonable, and harder than even the ground they lay on. She wanted him so violently that she wanted to conceive.

Afterwards, she found that she was weeping. She clung to Oliver, whose weight pressed her into the ground, but the tears kept coming, faster and louder, until she might have wept the whole lake.

30

Early the following morning, from the pink rock – the beached whale at the end of Carrickduff Bay – Jude saw Oliver's car come along the road and park beside hers, half a mile from where she was sitting. She watched as he made his way down to the firm sand by the water. The tide was out; it was dull, still cool, and not yet half past nine. Jude began walking towards him and as he came more clearly into focus, she could see that he knew; it was in his stride, in the way his arms fell from his shoulders. Even when she began to run – as if she was finding him, not losing him – he continued to walk, coming like an innocent man to hear a guilty verdict. Jude threw her arms around his neck in the hope that he might save her. Save them. They held each other, afraid to speak or move, so near were they to the precipice.

'How did you know where to find me?' she said eventually. 'I didn't even know where I was going until I arrived here.'

'Coming right back to where we started. You're so predictable, my love.' He looked around at what he had never been able to forget – the flat shiny sands, the curling sea, Mweelrea Mountain magnificent behind them.

'But I told you I'd never come here again.'

'So why have you?'

'Because this isn't a place to me, it's a state of mind. Desolation, I call it.'

He put an arm around her as they walked towards the rocks. 'That's my fault. I should never have done it here. I should have told you at school, instead of dragging you out to this wilderness.'

'I'm the one who dragged you, remember? I wanted to soften the impact.'

He stopped. 'What are you talking about? You mean, you knew?'

'Yes, I knew. As soon as I saw you sitting in that office, I knew something horrible had happened. You looked so wretched.'

'You seemed cheerful.'

They walked on. 'A sham. The more certain I became that something bad was heading my way, the more I evaded it, and when you lied about Dad being OK, I tunnelled even deeper into false exhilaration.'

'I should have told you sooner, but I couldn't catch you. You kept flitting off. And the longer it took, the harder it got.'

'I made it hard. I was trying to stop you saying it.'

They'd come to the end of the bay, to Jude's pink rocks.

'I thought it was all a blank to you. I thought that's why you never wanted to come back here – so you wouldn't be reminded.'

'I don't need reminding.' She walked over to the low rock and stepped on to it. 'I stood here and you were coming at me just like you are now, and you had your hands in your pockets –'

446

'So you wouldn't see them shaking.'

'– and you looked as ghastly as you do now, and you said, "Jude," and I said something to stop you, but you said again, "Jude," and then, "Michael's been killed." There was nowhere left to go then.'

Oliver shook his head.

'You took me off the rock and held me, and you kept saying you were sorry, as if it was all your fault. Then you swore that you'd always look after me.' She looked down at him. 'And you did.'

He helped her down. 'I pulled off your wings that day; now you want them back.'

'I *need* them back.' They sat on the rock. Jude pressed his hand to her lips. 'I don't exist without you. I should and I must, but I don't and I won't, not unless I break out.'

'Break me, you mean.'

'It might break both of us, but I still have to do it. I need to know that, even without you, I'm still here.' Her eyes filled.

'I must love you very badly if you feel invisible.'

'You love me too well.'

Oliver looked down the length of beach. 'And you don't love me enough.'

'It isn't that I *don't* love you, it's that I don't know how to love anyone else!'

He squeezed her knee and nodded. 'What are you planning to do?'

'I'm going to defer my doctorate and go to Greece, if the gang will have me, and then I'll rent out the house and take off for Australia or some other bloody place I've never seen.'

'So you're really cutting loose? Not just taking some slack?'

'Taking slack would be too easy. You'd still be able to

447

reel me in as soon as something went wrong.' She wiped her face. 'Please don't blame me. I'm only trying to find my own ground.'

'I don't blame you,' he said, and she saw something shift in his eyes.

'What?'

He fiddled with her fingers. Sighed. Definitely shifty. 'When I woke up the other day in Dublin and found you gone,' he said, 'an odd feeling washed over me. I couldn't put my finger on it at the time, but when I woke up and found you gone again this morning, it came back, only stronger, and this time I recognized it.'

'What was it?'

He looked her straight in the eye and said, 'Relief.'

She stared back at him.

'It was relief, Jude. Relief that I'll no longer be torn between you and Cara, that I can now do what I singularly failed to do with Tim – be a full-on, full-time, tuned-in dad without being pulled in every other direction. I can't expect you to become any kind of parent at this point in your life, but I thought I could. I've been trying to pull two incompatibles together and getting myself ripped in the process.'

'And if you dump me, you won't tear any more. Is that what you came down here to do?'

'God, no. This is your call. If you were prepared to live with Cara, this wouldn't be happening. But if you're not, then at least I can get on with doing what I have to do.'

'You're always doing what you have to do! Aren't you tired of looking after people? Little people? Wouldn't you like time for yourself?'

'Not when I've been given another chance.'

'Ah,' said Jude. 'So that's what I see in your eyes when you look at her: redemption.'

He nodded.

Jude put her elbow on his shoulder. 'You know, my idea of heaven is sitting under the catalpa on a hot July day, with the smell of coffee in the air and the sound of bees buzzing in the creeper, and you there beside me, pouring apricot ooze on to a croissant. I wish I could sit and watch you doing that this summer, and next, and when you're fifty, and sixty, and seventy . . . But if I can't, then I'll go there in my mind whenever I need to.' She nudged him. 'Will you meet me there?'

He laughed slightly. 'You've just set up an indelible connection between yourself and jam. I'll never again be able to eat apricot jam without thinking of you.'

'Good.'

She counted the break of thirty waves before either of them spoke again.

'What do you want me to do?' he asked. 'Walk away?'

She put her hand to his face. 'Go back to the good life in Landor. To our lovely house. It made you happy before. It can do it again.'

'Can it? Without you?'

'You have Cara now. She's the prize, with love from the Feehans.'

Oliver filled his lungs. His composure was cracking. 'This is like sinking into a bog. You're there, but you won't pull me out.'

'You'll meet someone else. I know you will.'

'I've already met someone else. Lots of someone elses. None of them came within a world of you. Not even your mother.' He looked at her, more damage visible in those oft-afflicted eyes. 'So don't kid yourself that you can shove me off to the happy-ever-after because that won't happen, Jude. Being without you will be like living with my eyes closed and my bones broken.'

'It won't be any different for me.'

'So why do it? Why do this?'

'Because I'm weary with loving you, Oliver.'

They sat on the pink rock, crying.

Oliver stood up without warning, holding the tips of Jude's fingers between his knuckles. 'I won't be long in Dublin. Give me a few days to clear out. I'll lodge some money in your account for your travels and I'll have the deeds sorted . . . Take care, Jude.' He dropped her hand and walked away, but she thought she heard him say, 'See you under the catalpa.'

Jude held her head between her elbows and keened; she struggled to stay on the rock, to stop herself stopping him. Tears fell down to the sand and her body sagged like an emptied bag, as though her bones had been pulverized. She tried not to look up, but her eyes lifted of their own accord.

Two hundred yards away, Oliver was up to his knees in the sea and walking further into it. Jude screamed his name and bolted across the beach.

He didn't hear; he stumbled on into the surf. She ran faster than she ever had and tripped into the water. The sea was heavy against her legs but she struggled on, pushing the Atlantic out of her way. 'Oliver! No!'

He turned.

'Don't! You can't do that!' He opened his mouth, seeing her come, tear-stained and frantic, but before he could speak, she dived towards him, determination giving her body the weight of a baby elephant as she brought him down into the breaking waves. 'I won't let you do that,' she screamed, gripping his shirt as they came to the surface. 'I won't let you!'

'I wasn't going to!'

'I love you!' A wave washed over their faces. 'I love you, you bastard. Get up!'

'I am. I am up.'

'You drown yourself and I'll go with you!'

They fell back again. Oliver spluttered, shaking water from his face. 'I wasn't going to drown myself.'

'You what?' Jude was still gripping his shirt. 'You *what*?' A wave pushed her on to his chest. His elbows made contact with the sand.

'I wasn't going to kill myself, brickhead! I have Cara to think about. I have myself to think about.'

'Oh! Oh, thank God!' She threw herself on him, kissing him wetly as they were lifted and dropped by the sea.

Oliver held her as he caught her mouth, their kisses warm in the freezing western waters, but then he laughed. 'I thought you'd lost it. Coming at me like a rhino on the charge!'

'What the hell were you doing? You're soaked.'

'I was a lot less soaked before you mowed me down.'

'You were up to your thighs.'

'I needed a short sharp shock; I needed to clear my face.'

'Oh, my love. You mean I nearly drowned you for nothing?' Oliver rolled her over, kissing her neck and breastbone. 'The arrogance,' she laughed. 'As if you'd kill yourself over me!'

He held her still. 'I don't have to. I'll probably die over you anyway.'

She pushed wet hair from his face. 'Oh no, you won't. You're one great survivor, Oliver Sayle, and life won't try you any more. I promise you that.'

The tide had dragged them into the shallows, leaving them lying on the sand, half submerged in bubbled sea.

'Look at us,' said Jude. 'Likes pieces of flotsam and

451

jetsam, thrown up on the beach. Seems my life raft has finally sunk.'

'And here you are, on the shore at last.'

Oliver struggled to his feet, lifting the weight of his wet clothes out of the water, and pulled Jude up with one hand. They stood looking at each other, panting lightly. Then he kissed the side of her mouth, as he had that first time in Landor, and walked away from everything that had followed, water squelching out of his sneakers, his black shirt stuck to his back.

Jude stood shivering in the water and watched him go, without once turning, his steps measured but heavy, until he became no more than a blur in the distance climbing over the dunes to his car. There, he stopped as he opened the door and looked back across the beach. After a moment, he waved. As she raised her arm to wave back, a sharp pain stabbed her gut. Oliver got into the car but didn't move for some time. Then she heard the engine start.

'Oliver.'

The car pulled out, turned, drove up the winding road and out of sight.

Jude fell to her knees in the surf and let out such a cry that a donkey, behind a hill, called back to her.